A PAST THAT
BREATHES

A PAST THAT THAT BREATHES

NOEL A. OBIORA

Rare Bird
Los Angeles, Calif.

For my mother,
Violet Odiso Obiora,
who gave absolutely everything to motherhood.

PART ONE

CHAPTER ONE

Footsie

Her stage name was "Footsie." A songstress, she often left flyers at neighbors' doorsteps inviting them to performances at local nightclubs and open mics they never went to, nor ever will. She was found dead in her two-bedroom apartment on Armacost Avenue in Los Angeles on January 6, 1995. At 2:00 p.m. that day, about three hours after her body was first discovered, a rash of police activity was all over Armacost Avenue. Police blocked off the entrance from Wilshire Boulevard to the north and Texas Avenue to the south and redirected traffic that did not reside on Armacost Avenue to other streets.

In this part of the city, a few blocks east of Brentwood and southwest of Beverly Hills and Bel Air, large or persistent police presence was considered a nuisance. Residents briefly came out onto their porches and leaned out of open windows to see what could possibly have called for this show of force, as they saw it. One man asked the officers why they were there and was respectfully told that a young woman was found dead on the floor of her bathroom. "Probably a drug overdose," he passed on to his neighbors who assumed the police had told him that, but they had not. The police cordoned off the woman's apartment with yellow tape and closed the main entrance to the building, allowing only tenants into the complex. Detectives Alvarez and Fritz arrived in an unmarked vehicle to take command of the investigation. A veteran of the Los Angeles Police Department, Frank Alvarez had never held any other job in his adult life. Stephen Fritz had joined the police academy after college and made detective only recently. As they parked their car, an officer with a German shepherd on a leash came out through a drop-down iron gate on the south end of the apartment building.

"The garage is underground?" Alvarez asked the officer.

"Only part of it, just slopes down like it is going under but it's on the same level."

"You picking up something?" Alvarez asked the officer.

"She was," the officer said, "but she lost it...in the garage."

Alvarez followed the officer as the dog pulled him along to return to the garage. Fritz walked up the main entrance to the building.

"Where is her car at?" Alvarez asked.

"We don't know which one yet," the K-9 officer said.

"Who found her?"

"The apartment manager. Said she told him to go in and take a look at her sink garbage disposal, and when he went, he found her dead."

"Ask him about her car," Alvarez ordered, then rejoined Fritz and officer Tse, who was leading a team of forensic officers in the dead woman's apartment on the second floor. One look at her lifeless body, lying half-naked on the floor of the bathroom, with her face turned up toward the ceiling, and Alvarez stopped in the short passageway to the bathroom.

"Don't fucking tell me she was raped in this neighborhood?" Alvarez said to Fritz and Tse, who were behind him.

"She wasn't," Tse said.

"So, how'd she die?" Alvarez asked.

"If we rule out some kind of allergic reaction to something in the bathroom that could have killed her, then I think she was smothered."

"He definitely thinks it's a homicide," Fritz said to Alvarez.

"Unofficially..." Tse added to the conversation between the two detectives. Alvarez and Fritz looked at each other as though to say that Tse should save his technicalities for the lawyers. They left Tse and continued to the bathroom. Tse returned to the adjoining bedroom. Another officer was in the bathroom placing markers on different objects, and a photographer was still taking pictures of the corpse. Both stopped what they were doing as Alvarez and Fritz stood at the door and observed. There was a slight stench in the air that had mixed with the many scented fragrances of a lady's bathroom. She was five feet six inches tall with short hair that fell over half her forehead, a doll's round face, a prominent nose, and big eyes.

"What's her name again?" Alvarez asked.

"Footsie," Fritz said.

"That's her real name?"

"Goldie Silberberg."

"We use that name," Alvarez said and walked away impatiently. Fritz stood there briefly, looking down at the corpse. "Nice work, guys," he finally said to the two men and left them.

Goldie's bedroom was lavishly furnished but a modest space. Her bed was so disproportionate to the size of the room that for a moment the officers pondered how it was delivered through the narrow doors. Tse and an officer were busy examining items and going through them with gloved hands.

"You think she knows the person who did this to her?" Alvarez asked. Tse nodded.

"He didn't have to force himself through the doors to get to her. And there was this…" Tse pointed to the trash can by the bedside in which were used condoms, tissues, and wipes. Alvarez stepped closer and looked.

"I thought you said she wasn't…" Alvarez started to say to Tse as Fritz joined them.

"She wasn't. This is all neat and tidy, like consensual stuff."

"Don't go to the other bathroom," Tse warned Alvarez.

"Why?" Alvarez asked.

"The tile looks like it's got some prints we can lift."

Alvarez went into the living room and walked out onto the balcony overlooking Armacost Avenue. There were two chairs made of interlaced belt-sized plastics wound around a metal frame and a small rustic wooden table. Standing on the balcony, Alvarez found himself looking into the apartment directly opposite him. The curtains there were pulled back, and he could see what was on the television in their living room. He put his head around the door and looked at Fritz, who was in the kitchen examining the sink.

"You come out here yet?"

"Nope," Fritz shook his head and joined him. There was no one in sight in the other apartment directly opposite Goldie's.

"You think they saw something?" Fritz asked.

"Let's find out," Alvarez said and, coming back into the living room, pulled the curtains on Goldie's living room wide apart.

"You wanna talk to the manager first?" Fritz asked as they walked downstairs into a courtyard in the middle of the apartment building.

"He ain't going nowhere, is he?"

The man who opened the door across the street was slightly built, average height, and in his thirties. He looked surprised to see Alvarez and Fritz at his door.

"Can we take a look out across from your balcony?"

"Sure," he said and stepped aside. "I was just talking to my girlfriend on the phone about you guys."

"Yeah, what about?" Fritz asked. Alvarez walked out onto the balcony.

"Is Footsie really dead?"

"Did you know her?" Fritz asked.

"My girlfriend did. She's at work."

Fritz lead him to meet Alvarez on the balcony.

"You can see clear through, if the curtain is open," Alvarez said looking straight ahead at Goldie's apartment.

"Yes," their host said. "My girlfriend said she saw them arguing yesterday."

Alvarez and Fritz turned simultaneously to him.

"She saw who arguing?" Alvarez asked.

"Footsie and her boyfriend."

"You know her boyfriend's name?" Alvarez asked. The young man shook his head.

"But he's African American."

"What's your girlfriend's name?" Fritz asked.

"Ola, Ola Mohammed. She's Caribbean but naturalized."

Fritz brought out a notepad and pen from his pocket.

"Can you give us your girlfriend's number? We just need to ask her a couple of questions really quick," Fritz said.

Then Tse appeared on Goldie's balcony and whistled. When Alvarez and Fritz turned to him, he waved them over urgently. Alvarez left Fritz with their host, Ms. Ola's boyfriend, and hurried out of the apartment.

"Rachel, the lady in that apartment," Tse said pointing to an apartment two doors from Goldie's as they stood at the entrance overlooking the courtyard. "She was very close to the dead woman, but she was no help when we got here. She was crying, and all confused. But she just came back while you guys were over there and said Goldie's manager, not the apartment manager, but the music manager, he called and told her Goldie got a call from her ex before she started coming back last night. The manager thinks she was coming to meet her ex," Tse told Alvarez.

"The ex got a name?"

"Paul, Paul Jackson."

"We're gonna need to rush those fingerprints in that bathroom, see if there's a match to this ex."

"I've got even better prints."

"What?"

"Two beer bottles in the guest bedroom, one's not even finished. The other's in the trash can. Both got prints on them. And we've got something else you'll wanna see," Tse said and led the way back to Goldie's bedroom. Alvarez watched as the uniformed officer working with Tse raised Goldie's California King mattress at an angle to reveal an intricate web of wires funneled through a pipe from which they were connected to a device that looked like a computer modem.

"What the hell are those?" Alvarez asked.

"Looks like a sophisticated RFID that tracks shit, listens to them, and transmits them," Tse explained.

"Where do you get shit like that?"

"Not Radio Shack, that's for sure," the uniformed officer working with Tse said. "We found these, too," the officer said, holding up tiny microphones the size of almonds in a transparent evidence bag.

Alvarez grimaced and patted Tse on the back. "I'm gonna go see this Rachel. And call the manager."

•••

FRITZ RETURNED FROM ACROSS the street to find Alvarez at Rachel's, and they both left Rachel's apartment briefly to talk.

"She's a hottie, ain't she?" Fritz said.

"More like a hot mess. What you got?"

"Yeah, this Ola lady did see them arguing. It looked pretty heated until someone walked into the room and he backed off."

"You got the boyfriend's name?" Alvarez asked.

"Paul Jackson," Fritz said.

"That's her ex."

"No, that's the boyfriend."

"Same guy that owns a nightclub downtown?"

"Yes, Cool Jo's Café."

"Who walked in?" Alvarez asked.

"She thinks it was some other tenant. An older guy."

"Find him!"

CHAPTER TWO
Usual Suspects

WITH A LEAD IN the case and the weekend upon the officers, Alvarez had requested that the district attorney assign a deputy to the case before he left the crime scene. Senior Deputy DA Kate Peck was assigned, and she stopped by the crime scene at about 6:30 p.m. on her way home from court.

By 10:00 p.m. that night, Alvarez was at Kate's house discussing a warrant to search Paul Jackson's house.

"Did we find the man they said walked in on them arguing?" Kate asked.

"Not yet."

"Who is he?"

"We think his name is Monsieur Arnot. He is the only tenant we haven't talked to yet, and he's an older man. Conrad, the apartment manager, also said he was close with the deceased woman.

"What are you going on for this search?"

"The two beer bottles in her guest bedroom. Looks like they had his prints."

"Yes, someone saw him arguing with her that afternoon. So, he had a couple of beers before that argument."

"Her manager said she got a call from him before she came back to the apartment. He says she was coming to meet him."

"You're still gonna need more than that—"

"To search his house?"

Alvarez was incredulous.

"You've got traces of drugs on her bedroom floor and a couple of used condoms with some blood smears on them in her trash can—neither of which we can tie to this Jackson guy yet, right?"

"Yes, and semen in the victim."

"Excuse me? You checked that at the scene?"

"No, a nurse came to the morgue because forensics figured the autopsy might not be done quickly enough."

"So, you've got semen in the victim and semen in the condom? Are you listening to what you're saying?"

"Ma'am, the only way anyone goes to that apartment and kills that woman thinking they were going to get away with it is because they weren't thinking. That's why this son-of-a-bitch makes sense. He lost his shit," Alvarez said.

"Look, I suppose we can get a search warrant with what you've got, but it is not gonna look good at trial. Let's see what else we can get before we ask for the warrant," Kate said calmly.

"Can we see if he'll let us in without a warrant?" Alvarez asked.

"Be my guest." Kate said.

●●●

"Cool Jo's Café was crawling with the undercover pigs," the business manager told Paul over the phone on Saturday morning.

"If they come back tonight, call Kenny," Paul said.

"I tried calling him. I left him messages at home and the office. I told that nigger a hundred times to get a fucking cell phone already."

"You can't fix Kenny, you best just let him be."

"You want me to come over to the house, until we reach Kenny?"

"No, you got enough on your plate with the club."

Kenny, or rather Kenneth Brown, was having dinner with friends at a half-priced sushi bar along the old Route 66 in Pasadena when he found out the police were looking for him. His mother had sent him an urgent message on his electronic pager, requesting that he call her back, and one of his friends offered him a cell phone to make the call. Kenneth had called from their table without excusing himself, but his countenance soon changed as he appeared to listen and he got up and left the booth. They could hear him shout into the phone before he was fully outside the restaurant.

"I can't say I was at the club when I wasn't. I am not a regular."

Anthony Rayburn and his wife, Mary, Anthony's sister, Cassandra, Jed Jensen and his wife, Tiffany, had known Kenneth since he arrived in Los Angeles three years previously. They were all lawyers, except Mary, who was an elementary school teacher. Every other weekend, they met and either went to a movie or had dinner and passed the time at one of their houses afterward. Infrequently, they went to bars and nightclubs.

"Everything okay?" Cassandra asked when Kenneth returned.

"The owner of this nightclub downtown is a person of interest in the murder of his girlfriend, and the club's manager is trying to use me as one of his alibis."

"This happened recently?" Cassandra asked.

"Thursday night, I think. They told the police I was at the club that night."

"Where you?" Tiffany asked.

"Of course not."

"Wait, is this the case near UCLA?" Cassandra asked. At twenty-nine years old, Cassandra was the youngest tenured professor at the University of California Los Angeles Law School.

"I don't know," Kenneth said.

"Do you know this guy well? The owner?" Cassandra asked.

"Not that well. We're not buddies or anything, but sometimes we hang out at his club, and I have represented the club a few times. When my mother came to visit for this long stay, it turned out she had a connection with his family a long time back in Philadelphia."

"And you two became close after your mother arrived?" Anthony asked.

"No. We're not close. But they started being nicer to me at the club. I didn't have to stand in line to get in the club, and the guys that work there started to call me by my name."

"What's the name of this club, 'Cheers'?" Anthony asked, and Jed laughed.

"We heard you shouting that you were not a regular, when you left to answer the phone," Cassandra said.

Kenneth had started his career at the public defender's office about the same time as Tiffany. A year later, they were laid off. He started his own practice, with Tiffany lending him a hand periodically without compensation until she was rehired. Anthony, who had been at the public defender's office before them, had since been urging Kenneth to return, too.

"What are you going to tell the police?" Jed asked.

"Hopefully not that it's the place where everybody knows your name," Anthony said. Only Jed laughed, but it brought a smile to the others' faces, including Kenneth.

"I will tell them the truth; I wasn't there on Thursday night."

"You said that you've represented this guy or his club in the past?" Tiffany asked.

"Yes, that's the other thing. Once my mother made contact with his family, I became the go-to lawyer for the club, but try to get these guys to pay your fees and they'll actually tell you that your attitude represents what's wrong with the African American community today."

"Well, here's an idea, tell the police you can't talk to them because whatever they want to know could spill attorney-client privilege," Tiffany said.

"Or," Cassandra quickly joined, "you don't have to tell the police anything. Instead, you call this guy and take his case."

"Why?" Kenneth asked.

"You are a criminal defense attorney, aren't you?" Cassandra asked.

"Who has never tried a murder case before," Jed said. Jed was the only one among the lawyers who did not have a criminal law practice. He worked for a major law firm in downtown Los Angeles and wrote country music in his spare time.

"Is that a new California Bar standard that I don't know about?" Anthony asked.

"I go through those capital case transcripts every week, and I will pick Kenneth over half the attorneys who have tried those cases," Cassandra said.

"That's not quite a ringing endorsement—" Tiffany began to say.

"I get what she's saying," Kenneth said, smiling over at Tiffany. "But Cassandra, these guys never pay their fees."

"And your other clients do?" Cassandra asked. Tiffany laughed. "Ken, do you want this case. Use it to showcase your talent, then ride it to a law firm. It could be your big break, if it's the case I think it is," Cassandra said.

"You realize Cassandra is literally offering you her services by urging you to take the case," Anthony said.

Kenneth's face lit up for the first time since the discussion began. "Are you?" he asked Cassandra, but she blushed and looked down at the tray, then picked up a piece of sushi and ate. "Seriously, Cassandra, are you?" Kenneth asked again, but Cassandra ignored him and continued eating.

"Get the case first, then you can worry about Cassandra," Mary said. At that, Cassandra smiled at Mary.

•••

AT PAUL'S HOUSE IN the San Fernando Valley, the police found an automated teller machine receipt for a withdrawal at 12:04 a.m. in West Los Angeles and a pair of shoes matching prints found at Goldie's apartment. Alvarez wanted to arrest Paul on this evidence, but Kate wanted to wait.

"The longer he's free, the more time he has to destroy evidence we haven't seen yet," Alvarez said

"Then find something else to tie him to the case and you can pick him up."

"That's fair," Fritz said to Alvarez of Kate's compromise when they were alone. "He has been sloppy so far, leaving the receipt at the house. There'll be more from him."

CHAPTER THREE
District Attorney

Deputy District Attorney Amy Wilson arrived at 8:30 a.m. on Monday morning to start her new position at the head office in downtown Los Angeles, but it seemed they were not expecting her. She waited in the lobby while someone located the division secretary who should know about her new position.

Then she waited at the secretary's workstation and filled forms for her new identity and access cards while the secretary tracked down the office that had been assigned to her. Staff appeared rushed. Most sat behind sturdy desks, hunched over documents, or peered at computer screens with an urgency that gave the office the chaotic energy of people trying to find something amiss.

"Yippee! I found your office," the secretary said excitedly after about twenty-five minutes of making calls and searching her computer database.

Two other women sharing her workspace in a four-desk enclosure laughed, and the third just shook her head. Amy was amused. The secretary was quickly on her feet and hurrying away, waving to Amy to come along. Amy thanked the other women, and they bade her good luck in her new position.

"Sorry about this. Today is one of those Mondays when we get a ton of arrests over the weekend that must be reviewed and filed within twenty-four hours," the secretary explained. "Then you add to that the O. J. circus."

"I understand," Amy said. She had noticed the activities outside the courthouse, adjacent to the district attorney's head office, where the O. J. trial was scheduled. Large vans with satellite dishes, broadcast company logos, and one big rig truck were in the parking lot. She had wanted to reply that she had thought the circus around the case was waning but decided it would show how little she knew about the most important trial her new office has had in decades.

Amy was promoted from the West Covina branch office, about twenty miles east of downtown Los Angeles, but this iconic building at the corner of Temple and Broadway was completely foreign to her until she interviewed for the job. It was not quite what she imagined it would be every time she saw it in a motion picture or the news, though she was not sure how she had imagined it. She had joined the district attorney's office out of law school as a vehicle for landing in Los Angeles but stayed after the Los Angeles riots exploded because she felt a calling to public service. Events in her life at the time also made the collegiate environment of a small branch office ideal for her.

She had chosen a gray skirt suit with a light blue silk shirt to blend in more with her colleagues or at least not draw much attention to herself. Still all eyes turned to her, partly thanks to the division secretary being her guide. The men especially appeared to hold their attention on her long enough for her to notice or acknowledge them, before they looked away. As often as men did this to her, she never got used to it and she never liked it, unless she was looking first.

"And here you are," the secretary said as she walked into Amy's new office. "These are your boxes, right?" she asked referring to five brown boxes gathered in a small pile against the wall opposite the door.

"I suppose," Amy said, and opened a couple of the boxes to examine their contents. "Yes, they are mine. They were packed for me and delivered over the Christmas break." She followed the secretary's eyes to a solitary box on the desk to the right of the door. It was a different type of box, white, with a different labeling, but nothing written on it.

"That looks like ours, though," the secretary said looking at the box. Amy shrugged as the secretary looked at her to confirm. "You want to check it? See if it came with these, too?" the secretary asked.

Amy walked over to the box and opened it. The uppermost folder in the box had a note for her.

"I think it is for me," Amy said as she pulled out the file from the box. The secretary had approached the desk as well and could see the note clipped to the file folder.

"I guess I'm done here," the secretary said as Amy occupied herself with reading the note silently. "Melissa is your section supervisor; she was the person who took you to meet Gil after your last interview," the secretary said, referring to the Los Angeles District Attorney Gil Garcetti. "She said to tell you she'll be coming around to take you to lunch, if you haven't already made plans."

Amy nodded, then quickly added, "I haven't made any plans."

"Good, if you need anything, you know where to find me," the secretary said and started to leave.

"Wait, please," Amy called out to her, and she stopped. "This note is signed Kate, with no last name. But you just said Melissa is my section supervisor. Who is Kate?"

The secretary shook her head slowly. "There are at least four Kates in this office, if you count the Catherines, and I can't tell the way they write. I'll ask around to see who sent the box to your office."

"No, don't please. It's totally fine."

"If you go through the file and it doesn't say which Kate, I'm sure Melissa can tell you. The only way anyone assigns a case to you is if Melissa agrees to it."

Amy thanked her as she left, glad that she had not looked in the file or asked for the title of the case.

The note was in one of many folders labeled *People v. Jackson*. It read:

> Dear Amy,
>
> You are second chair in this case. It is basic. Suspect Mr. Jackson has not been arrested but there is strong evidence tying him to the murder. He was the victim's boyfriend and manager until recently. It appears the victim let him go and he could not deal with it. Victim was a lounge/jazz singer. Review the file and let me know your recommendation. Do we have enough to pick him up without waiting for DNA results, which we are certain we will get? I have

scheduled a meet with LAPD for Wednesday at 11:00 a.m. Welcome to special prosecutions. I am presently in trial in Pasadena.

[Signed] Kate.

Amy was standing by the desk when the secretary left. She placed her purse on the desk, went around, and checked the chair for dust before she sat on it and opened the folder with Kate's note.

Inside the folder was the official police report as she expected, with Officer Alvarez's statement attached to it. She leafed through the other documents in the folders and to her surprise, the murder was less than a week old. There were statements by several police officers who had been at Armacost Avenue, from the first officer to arrive at the scene to the officers who cordoned off the street and those who took scientific evidence, the K-9 Unit that brought the sniffing dogs, and officers who interviewed witnesses. The date she was killed, her age—about the same as Amy's—and the location of her apartment, all made Amy feel like she was reading about someone she knew.

Her first day in this office and she had the first murder trial of her short career as a deputy district attorney. She felt uncomfortable searching the box on her desk further, dreading the crime scene photographs she was certain were in it, particularly pictures of the deceased young woman. Her visceral response to this expectation recalled the first time she shot a gun in the woods, while hunting with her grandfather. She was ten. The bullet swooshed into oblivion, clattered into leaves and fell silent. Although she was certain that she had not hit any animals, she felt every second of that experience because it was suddenly real. The hairs on her body stood, her heart beat so fast, and her blood pressure shot up, all while she stood rooted to the spot with the gun in hand. It was different from shooting in the firing range or gallery, where certitude could be verified. In the woods, her imagination ran away from her, just as it was suddenly doing with this case.

She had left some items in her car, hoping to settle down before unloading them, but now decided to get them. Kate's note concluded that Goldie's ex-boyfriend could not deal with Goldie leaving him, but nothing in the police report seems to support that conclusion. It had a sad ring of stereotype to it, which Amy did not like. Thankfully, no one in the case was famous…or infamous, she thought.

On returning to the office with the box of items from her car, she put aside the file in *People v. Jackson* to arrange things she brought in the box. She placed some picture frames on the file cabinet. There was a picture she took with her horse when she was nine, a roan she named Barrett, which first brought her the pleasures of love and horse riding, and a picture of her dog Poca. On her desk, she placed a picture of her family at her graduation from college and a picture of a group of friends from high school on a trip abroad. Among the friends was Thomas Clay Jr., whom Amy had recently started seeing last fall. She paused, looking at the picture, at Thomas in particular. If anyone had told her when the picture was taken that she would later date Thomas, she would have told them they were crazy. Someone had actually joked that he was so unlike her type. Was she his type then? The thought had never occurred to her, perhaps because she was too sheltered or too shy to find out. Placing the diplomas on the wall pins that were already in place, she made a mental note to move them when she redecorated.

Melissa came carrying a box of business cards with Amy's new information on them and more case files with imminent preliminary hearings, each involving notorious Los Angeles gangs. She asked where Amy would like to go for lunch.

"I am not too picky about lunch. A good salad will do just fine, and I can usually find one in most restaurants."

"Are you vegetarian?"

"No, but I lean that way."

"Doesn't everyone in LA?"

They both laughed. Melissa suggested they go to a Japanese restaurant a few blocks south of their office.

"Do you know Kate Peck?" Melissa asked as they left the office.

"Kate who?"

"Peck. My colleague."

"No."

"She called me last night to loan your services to her as soon as you start this morning. That's why I thought you knew each other."

"No, we don't."

"I told her I would have to talk to you about it first, because the case might have some publicity following it."

"That Jackson case?" Amy asked.

"Yes. How did you know?"

"The file was in my office with a note from Kate when I arrived."

"That's Kate. She's a good one to have on your side, but there are other cases you can help on if you don't want to accept this assignment. It might drag you into the kind of publicity you might not be ready for."

"I'm up for it," Amy said before Melissa was done speaking.

"The LA riot gifted us about seven thousand arrests, and the charges in those cases are still going through the courts, eighteen months after the riots. I'm sure you guys had your share in West Covina."

"We did," Amy said. "But mostly the misdemeanors."

"Right, most of the serious crimes came here. Anyway, we in the various sections are helping each other out as much as we can until we get a better budgetary outlook that lets us hire from outside," Melissa said.

"I understand…" Amy said.

"But there are enough cases to go round, if you would rather not be involved in this one."

"I would…I like it," Amy said.

Amy struggled to keep up with Melissa as they walked to the restaurant. Melissa was about five feet three inches with blonde hair and a face full of emotional vulnerability. Amy recalled her well from the interviews, which were before a panel of three attorneys. One would not know it now, but Melissa spoke the least during those interviews. Now Amy's supervisor, she spoke as rapidly as she walked, and cheerfully, even when she spoke of mundane issues.

The Japanese restaurant was a small sitting space with about four bamboo booths lined against opposite walls and four tables in the middle. Amy and Melissa were standing at the front, waiting to be seated, when Amy saw a woman who was sitting alone leave her table and walk toward them.

"Professor Rayburn," Melissa said on seeing the woman approach.

"I'm almost done," Cassandra said. "So, if you don't mind sitting with me, I should be out of your hair before your meal is served."

Melissa looked at Amy, who shrugged her approval, and at the attendant, who nodded.

"Sure," Melissa said and followed Cassandra to her table, where she formally introduced Amy. "Are you attending the O. J. proceeding?" Melissa asked Cassandra.

"No, the next court proceeding on that is Wednesday. Hopefully a seat opens up and I get to attend and watch. It is fascinating."

"I read an opinion piece in the UCLA Law Magazine where you were quoted as saying that 'if the defense plays the race card, they win.' Are you encouraging it?" Melissa asked.

"I believe I said that if they succeed in turning the case into a referendum on racial justice in America, they could likely win."

"What's the difference with what I just said?"

"I guess I've always understood the 'race card' to refer to a person who is exploiting their racial identity to claim that he's being oppressed. O. J. may want to do that but it won't work for him because he is not oppressed by anything. On the other hand, if even he, with all his stature and wealth, can show as a matter of fact that he is being subjected to a different process than the average white American would get under our judicial system, then you guys are going to find it hard to convict him."

"How about the facts of the case itself, regardless of the referendum on race? Are the facts of the case not convincing?" Amy asked.

"Professor Rayburn runs a criminal justice clinic at UCLA Law, but don't expect her to give you a straight answer on criminal justice in America."

"I already said, it's too soon to tell. The trial hasn't even started," Cassandra said, amused.

There was some teriyaki left on Cassandra's plate, but after she sat down with Melissa and Amy, she did not eat again. When the attendant came to take Amy and Melissa's orders, Cassandra asked for her bill, and both Melissa and Amy asked for another minute to make their selection.

"I had an ulterior motive for inviting you to sit with me," Cassandra said to Melissa.

"Why doesn't that surprise me?"

"Very funny," Cassandra said dismissively, Melissa laughed. "Anyway, we are planning a symposium on diversity, inclusiveness, and the criminal process in LA County, post riots. I was wondering if you would be willing to speak on a panel of practitioners, mostly talking about the perspective from your office."

"Sure," Melissa said "Who else is on this panel? Anyone I know?"

"Kenneth Brown, an African American friend of mine who would bring the private practice perspective. And the federal public defender has agreed to send someone as well. So far."

Amy appeared to sigh.

"Anyway, that's my ulterior motive. It will be great to have you."

The waiter returned with Cassandra's bill, and she got up to leave.

"I'll take care of this with the cashier," she said, taking the bill from the waiter.

"Your friend, this Kenneth Brown. Is he originally from Philadelphia?" Amy asked Cassandra.

"Yes," Cassandra said.

"And went to the University of Texas undergrad?" Amy asked.

"Yes, and law school," Cassandra said. "Do you know him?"

"Sounds like someone I knew, but I haven't seen him in years," Amy said.

"Do you have your card?" Cassandra asked.

"I'm sorry," Amy said, shaking her head.

Melissa looked at Amy curiously.

"Well, here's mine," Cassandra said, giving Amy one of hers, which Amy collected and said thanks.

When Cassandra left them, Melissa got up and sat opposite Amy on the side of the table that Cassandra vacated. Amy scrunched her face, seeming puzzled.

"I want you where I can watch you," Melissa said and grinned.

"I left the cards you gave me at the office," Amy said, smiling shyly.

"Of course, you did," Melissa said with her eyes on the menu, but looked up to smile at Amy.

They ordered their food.

CHAPTER FOUR

Mothers' Intiution

WORKING TOGETHER, KENNETH AND his mother, Nancy, spent more time with each other than they had since he was a teenager. Neither had given much thought to how the arrangement would work when Nancy suggested it and both were pleasantly surprised, day by day. Nancy had taken an extended leave of absence from work to visit Kenneth after his third desperate attempt to borrow funds to run his office. A schoolteacher in Philadelphia, she was already due retirement, but still working a full schedule, active and healthy for all her sixty-three years.

When Kenneth got home on Saturday night, Nancy was already asleep, and by the time he woke up, she had gone to church. On Sundays, she spent all day at the First African Methodist Episcopal Church in Los Angeles. Two services, and whatever visits to homes, hospitals, and food centers the church had scheduled for the day, meant that some Sundays Kenneth might not see her at all.

On Monday morning, Kenneth got to his office and found his mother sitting at his desk rather than hers, which was the secretary's desk in the outer office.

"Paul's mother just left, and I received her in your office," Nancy explained.

"That's totally fine. I can sit out there if you need more time in the office," Kenneth said.

"No, no, don't be silly," Nancy said, getting up.

"Was Paul arrested?" Kenneth asked.

"No, but...I think I did something I shouldn't have..." Nancy said.

"What?"

"Sister Ramatu didn't know about Paul's situation until I called her to see how she was taking it."

"Oh, Ma, no!"

"I'm sorry."

"You can't discuss anything that happens in my office with anyone. Once an attorney is consulted, whether he is retained or not, whatever he is told becomes confidential. Now, obviously, Paul hasn't consulted us, and we don't owe him any confidentiality, but just think, if he wanted me to represent him, he might start worrying about what he tells me, that his mom might end up hearing from you because you work with me."

Nancy sat down again. Kenneth could see he was not telling her anything she had not already told herself.

"And Paul doesn't have a situation yet," Kenneth said.

"He doesn't?"

"No, he's just a person of interest, like any boyfriend or spouse is going to be if someone they are involved with is found dead. Obviously he's African American so they'll lean heavily on him."

"Oh, I told her all that, just not in those words."

"How did she take it?"

"She's not taking any of it well. I think she came all the way here to have a good cry. She's doesn't want anyone over at their compound thinking she doesn't believe him or that she thinks he did it, if she breaks down like she did here at home. But what's a mother to do?"

"If they had enough on him, they would be all over him right now."

"They searched his house with sniffing dogs and all."

"Did they find anything?"

"She doesn't know, but apparently some woman said they saw him at her house that same day."

"About the time she died?"

"They don't know, but Big John got his investigator friends trying to find out."

"I wouldn't trust Big's investigators to find a freeway in Los Angeles."

"Are you gonna represent him, if they ask you?"

"If they'll pay what it would take, why not? I'm gonna need my friend who's a professor at UCLA to come in with me, which means they're going to have to pay me enough to pay her."

"You'll do a great job. Let me talk to Sister Ramatu for you."

"No, Ma. Don't jump the gun again."

"You are destined for a case like this, Kenneth."

"And you are biased."

"If they arrest him, I'm talking to Sister Ramatu."

"Let's talk about it when that happens, Mom."

•••

AT LUNCH, AMY HAD learned that Kate would be in trial in Pasadena every day for the next couple of weeks, with occasional short breaks during which she might run to the office to address urgent matters. She decided to put her recommendation on *People v. Jackson* in writing for Kate. She would have to work late and come in early tomorrow, all before she knew her way to the restrooms, not to mention the law library. Perhaps this was why the note was silent, or rather ambiguous, on the form the recommendation should take. It also explained why Melissa offered to find someone else to take the assignment.

She sat down with her notes and began to look at the crime scene photographs. There was a large pile of photographs, many of which were pictures of Goldie lying on the floor of her bathroom, with shots of her face from every conceivable angle, close-up and medium range. There were details about each witness interviewed, the time and place of the interview, including their police records if any, a list of items found in the apartment and confiscated as evidence, with their corresponding tags.

Having mostly done preliminary hearings, in which the court determined whether there was probable cause to proceed to trial against the defendant as charged, Amy knew the defense would focus on the apartment manager, Conrad Wetstone, to argue there was no probable cause. "He found the body, he probably killed her," they would insinuate. She looked again at the police report on Conrad's interrogation.

Conrad Wetstone was a graduate physics student whose driver's license showed a pale wide forehead and thinning brown hair that stuck to his head like a toupee. He had an expression like someone stuck in the middle of solving a complex mathematics problem or perhaps puzzled that his picture was being taken at all. LAPD officers followed up and verified most of what Conrad had done between 11:00 a.m. when he discovered the body and about 2:00 p.m. when he called the police. He had said he notified the building owners of the death and thought they were going to report it before he returned to campus to meet with a couple of students and go to the grocery store—to purchase alcohol, for which he still had the receipt for the officers to see. He had told two tenants, Rachel Johnson and Monsieur Arnot, about the murder. Rachel, who was closest to Goldie, had wanted to go in and see her body, but Conrad had been adamant that she would not be allowed into the apartment until the police arrived. He had collected the keys Goldie gave Rachel as well. This added to his credibility as far as the officers were concerned.

Aside from Conrad, the other evidence supporting probable cause to arrest Paul was the ATM receipt, which purportedly placed him in West LA after 12:00 midnight, the beer bottles, his shoe prints on the tile, and the K-9 dogs picking up his scent. These were not very compelling to Amy. The defense would probably not deny that Paul Jackson had been at the apartment earlier that day when Ms. Ola Mohammed claimed to have seen him arguing with Goldie. But Goldie died more than a full twelve hours later. As improbable as it may seem, Mr. Jackson could have given someone his ATM card to withdraw money for him. The police had interrogated most of the tenants at the apartment and none saw Paul Jackson at the building, even at the time Ms. Ola claimed to have seen him. A note in the file stated that the police had not interrogated Monsieur Arnot and expected to do so by the time a complaint was filed.

Alana, Amy's mother, called to ask how she liked her new office. "It's fine," Amy answered, then proceeded to tell her about the assignment she found on her desk and the work she had to do on it. Alana was not impressed. A homemaker for most of Amy's and her brother, Edward's, childhood, Alana had become chief executive of the Wilson Family Foundation.

31

"I hope this Kate realizes that the Wilsons have a memory longer than their reach," she said to Amy's amusement.

"Well, maybe she did it just so you remember that she did me a favor, by assigning a Wilson a juicy case I never asked for. Have you thought about that?"

"She has some way of showing it," Alana said.

Amy knew Alana was not being frivolous with the remark about the Wilsons' reach. Wilson was a third generation family name that had become better known for the wealth it represented than the offspring who bore it. Wilson Pharmaceuticals, Wilson Power Train, and Wilson Engineering were a few of the family-found or majority-owned businesses, not to name the others where they chose not to attract scrutiny to their family name. Alana had hoped that after graduation from law school, Amy would take a job in investment banking or a junior executive position in a well-managed company and grow in the ranks before taking over as chief executive from her. But Amy chose the one position in which Alana's sphere of influence would be wasted on her daughter. While an unsolicited call from Alana would mean so much to the Los Angeles district attorney, there wouldn't be much in it for Amy. Besides Alana knew Amy would never forgive her if she made that call.

"Your father sends his love. He left for Germany yesterday."

"They have phones in Germany, don't they?"

"Cut him some slack, will you. He's got so much on his plate."

"I thought that was your job, not mine," Amy wanted to say, but rather said, "When did he ever not?"

"He knows you judge him harshly, you know."

"Please, Mom," Amy said dismissively and decided to change the subject.

She told Alana about the lunch she had with Melissa and the young UCLA professor they ran into, without mentioning the man the professor had brought to her attention.

CHAPTER FIVE
Kate

AMY MET KATE ON Tuesday morning. The receptionist had mentioned that Kate just asked about Amy, a moment before Amy got in at eight o'clock to continue work on the Jackson file, and Amy went immediately to see Kate.

Kate's office was bathed in natural light through large windows with an unobstructed view and was big enough to hold a small conference table in front of Kate's desk. Amy surmised that Kate was probably four years older—to have risen to such a senior staff position in special prosecutions when Amy was just starting.

"Thanks for agreeing to help on the Jackson case," Kate said after they introduced themselves.

"I should be thanking you for the opportunity. I am preparing a memo for you on my recommendation, like you asked."

"Oh, you can shelf that. They arrested him last night." To Amy's surprised expression, Kate continued. "A camera on the ATM took pictures of him withdrawing the money at 12:04 a.m."

"Is that enough?" Amy asked.

"It is more than we have on anyone else. Besides, the officers picked up activities around him that suggested he might make a run for it."

Amy started to fold her arms across her chest, but quickly put her hands down, and flexed her fingers.

"The investigation continues, I suppose," Amy said for want of what to say.

"What was your recommendation?"

"To wait for the DNA."

"We've still got that coming, right?"

"But we don't know what it says." Amy decided to be more adamant in stating her position clearly, not knowing what test Kate was putting her through.

"Do you expect it will point to somebody else that no one saw going into that apartment?"

"There was evidence of sexual activity in her apartment, and it doesn't look like he slept with her and then killed her."

"So, she slept with someone else, which reinforces the fact that he was driven by jealousy to kill her."

"But why wouldn't this other partner come forward?"

"These are all good questions, Amy. Thanks. But he has been arrested and is in custody, which means we arraign him on Thursday. Can you see to that?"

"Yes."

Amy felt Kate take her complete measurement in yards and amperes without caring that Amy had noticed. She wondered what reading Kate got.

"Goldie wasn't staying at her apartment. She hadn't stayed there since she went to London to make her first record last fall. Her friend and neighbor, Rachel, was looking after the apartment for her and using it occasionally because she lived with her sister. Goldie only came there to meet Paul Jackson that day because her agent and business manager didn't want him to know where she was staying after she returned from London."

"I'm sorry, I didn't see that in the report."

"It wasn't in the report. And when Goldie saw Mr. Jackson, she made sure there was someone there to deter them from fighting, if she could. That was why the lady across the street saw someone there in the afternoon when they were arguing. LAPD thinks he led her to come and meet him again but did not show up until whomever she had arranged to be there was gone. That person was probably the sexual partner you were talking about."

"That sounds plausible, but where did they get all that?"

"From her manager…Didi Pare. And phone records that showed they talked that evening, and she tried several times to reach him very late."

"Mr. Pare wasn't in the report either."

"That's coming. LAPD will be sending the rest of the report from subsequent interviews, and the pictures from the ATM cameras to you later today."

Amy held her hands together in front of her and nodded.

"Charge Paul Jackson with first degree murder and special circumstances," Kate said with finality in her voice.

Outside Kate's office, Amy paused to exhale, then recalled the one question she had wanted to ask Kate when they met: "Why did you choose me?"

•••

Officer Gonzalez was Alvarez and Fritz's superior on *People v. Jackson*, and he was in Amy's office before noon, looking concerned. He was a thin-lipped, bespectacled veteran with a lean physique and completely shaved head that seemed oiled.

"Can I sit?" Gonzalez asked.

Amy thought he had just come to drop off the reports Kate mentioned.

"Yes, please. I'm sorry I didn't offer you the seat to begin with." Amy sat also, as Gonzalez pulled a chair.

"Kate said I should send these to you, so I decided to drop them off on my way out. But now that I'm here, there's something I need to ask you," Gonzalez continued as Amy examined the ATM pictures. It was clearly Paul Jackson in them, and there was a date and time stamp on the bottom right corner of each picture. There was not a time stamp on the photographs that was exactly 12:04 a.m. but they were all within minutes of the time.

"I think you should meet the mother of the victim. Her name is Helen Silberberg. She's here in Los Angeles, to bury her daughter."

"Today?" Amy asked. "I'll need to check with Kate. She might want to meet the mother herself."

"No, I think you should meet her, not Kate."

"This is only my second day in this office. I can't make that call."

"This woman doesn't seem all together, you see. I think it hit her really hard."

"What do you expect me to do for her?"

"She found some documents at her daughter's house that she wants to bring to us, and some letters. She was already crying before she finished telling us. I told her I would send somebody right away. I was gonna send an officer, but I think she would feel much better if you went. Seeing you will remind her that her daughter was doing the same thing many young women come out here on their own to do. Live their dreams."

"Okay," Amy said. "There's another senior attorney here I can ask. I'll let you know if she says I can."

"Thank you," Gonzalez said and started to get up from his chair. Amy got up as well and walked Gonzalez out. "Kate said you don't think we've got enough to pick him up?"

"These ATM pictures didn't really change anything; we already had the receipt that said he was at the bank at that time."

"It supports the testimony of that woman who said she saw them arguing that afternoon. The clothes he was wearing match what she described him wearing when they were arguing."

Amy had not thought of this fact.

"Still, none of that puts him at her apartment when she died."

"There were two beer bottles in the guest bedroom with his fingerprints, and we will have his DNA at trial to back it up."

"Do we know that the beer bottles weren't there when he was seen with her in the afternoon?" Amy asked.

"No, but he doesn't know that we don't," Gonzalez said. "We know that lady, Rachel, bought beer after he left that afternoon, but we don't have the other bottles in her batch to match them."

Amy and Gonzalez parted ways at the receptionist's desk, where Amy picked up a phone slip about a missed call from Neda, the colleague she was closest to at her old branch office.

Melissa suggested they wait for Kate's trial to recess for lunch and give her a call. Then she told Amy that Kenneth had called her twice today already.

"He left a message before I got to the office wanting to know if I gave you his message yesterday. Then he called back to ask if you worked out of the downtown office, because the DA's public records appeared to show that you were still in the West Covina office."

"I am really sorry. I honestly have not seen or heard from him since college."

"I can see why you don't want to call him, because you're seeing someone now."

"That's not really it…I mean, I want to call him, but we've all changed a lot since college. I know I have."

"I told him that if you wanted to call him, you would have. And he apologized."

Amy raised her eyebrows and took a deep breath.

"Too harsh?"

"No, sounds just about right. I…suppose."

With Kate's blessing, Amy called Helen Silberberg to say Officer Gonzalez had asked her to pick up some documents from her. Helen said she was staying with a family friend in the Canyons and gave Amy the address.

After one o'clock Amy steered her car on to Third Street from Broadway, headed for the perennial freeway congestion around downtown Los Angeles. She knew these streets and the canyons well.

She arrived at the address Helen had given her just as Helen was getting out of her car in the driveway. When the two women met, the older woman's eyes were red and searching to see if the two had met before, Amy thought. No sooner had Helen's eyes studied Amy than she forced a smile and pulled down her sunglasses from her forehead to cover her eyes. Amy could see the resemblance to Goldie immediately. Helen had her daughter's features, gracefully aged, and the kind of smile that separates the star actress from her double. When she put her glasses back on and smiled at Amy, though only briefly, that image of her with dark round glasses and a youthful, transformative smile became her enduring image in Amy's mind.

"Ms. Silberberg, I'm with the District Attorney's Office. We spoke over the phone," Amy said. "I'm so sorry for your loss."

The words came to Amy without a moment's reflection, as easily as though she were talking to Alana. Helen smiled, and said thank you.

The residence in the hills between Beverly Hills and Studio City had its back to the canyons. There were two other couples visiting and they were sitting in the living room. Helen and Amy sat down with them. The living room was bare, like it had been stripped to receive mourners. Beverages, snacks, and sandwiches were on the dining table. Liza, the woman who opened the door for them, lived at the house with her husband and two young children, she told Amy. She and Goldie were close friends in high school, but they rarely saw each other in Los Angeles. After a while, Liza urged Helen to go and lie down a bit, and later told Amy that Helen wanted to see her.

Helen was sitting on a chaise chair by a vanity fireplace in a large bedroom, when Amy joined her.

"You are the DA who will try the case?" Helen asked.

"I'm one of the deputy DAs," Amy said.

"The police said they arrested the man who dated her," Helen said.

"Yes, did you know him?" Amy asked.

"No, she never mentioned him," Helen said. "I remember her saying she met someone some time ago. She went to see her friend playing at this African American nightclub, and her friend called her up on stage. She was so nervous, she said, but she was really happy with her performance that night. This man had come down just to watch her when he heard her voice from his office. But she never put a name or face to him for me."

Amy nodded, unsure how to respond.

"Her father and I wanted her to consider marrying…" Helen thrust her chin up toward the door, "Liza's brother, a childhood friend who became a Rabbi, he loved her dearly. But she moved to LA instead. 'We come from different worlds,' she told us about Eli. So, if she was dating this Black guy, I'm not surprised that she didn't mention it."

"I can understand. I would have done the same thing," Amy said with a shy smile. Helen smiled, too.

"You look younger than I expected from a DA on the case," Helen said.

"There's another senior DA on the case, I'll be assisting her."

Helen considered Amy for a while, then, reaching into her bag, she brought out a large envelope.

"Goldie invited me to spend Hanukkah in London with her while she was working on her new record. We traveled to Amsterdam and Paris and Brussels together. It was the first time we really spent some time alone together since her father passed, and we bonded. When we came back, she gave me access to her safe deposit," Helen said, and pointed to a metal box on the table by her sunglasses.

There was a recording contract, a compact disc with "Sample" written across it, and a rental agreement for Goldie's apartment in the metal safe. Amy flipped through the contracts. In the spaces for signatories on the recording contract, Paul Jackson was listed as manager, but his signature was not on it. Didi Pare signed as agent and Goldie signed as artist. The rental agreement was for a term of one year ending in August 1995 and was fully paid for the entire year. However, it was not Goldie's name but Didi's that was on it.

"Thanks," Amy said. "This is important for the case, ma'am."

"These are the originals, by the way; we did not have a chance to make copies. That's why I wanted to make sure that I delivered them to the police myself."

"Of course, I'll make copies and send them back to you," Amy said.

"It's okay. I don't need them," Helen said. "The manager at her apartment building is also keeping her mail for me, until we forward her address to Seattle." Helen handed Amy the large envelope she had taken from her bag.

"Liza thought I should let the police open the envelopes, too, in case…" Helen stopped. She was about to cry.

"You can open her mail, ma'am, if you want to," Amy said, offering the envelope back. Helen shook her head.

"Call me Helen, please. That's what Goldie called me. I don't want to open it."

Amy accepted the large envelope and shuffled through the small mail envelopes in it. The return address on one of the letters had "Cool Jo's Café" monogrammed atop it. Amy held her breath. The letter was postmarked yesterday, January 9, 1995, the day Amy began her job and three days after Goldie was murdered. Amy sat quietly for a while, wondering what the postmark meant. Liza entered the room and placed a jug of water with two glasses on the table between Amy and Helen, then sat behind them on the bed.

"It is from him isn't it?" Helen asked.

"From his establishment, yes," Amy said.

Helen nodded and wrung her hands. Liza poured some water into a glass and gave it to her.

"Do you think he did it?" Liza asked.

"The police are pretty convinced about it," Amy said.

"How about you? Are you convinced?" Helen asked.

"All the evidence points to that conclusion, but we must also accept that he is innocent until we prove his guilt," Amy said.

Helen started speaking slowly, as though to herself.

"I don't understand why anyone who has even met my daughter would want to hurt her, much less someone who was dating her. She's the sweetest thing," Helen said and started crying. Amy put the documents down on the table and took Helen's hands.

"I'm sorry, we will get to the bottom of what his problem is at trial," Amy said to Helen.

"If you met Goldie, you loved her; if you heard Goldie sing, you pretty much never forgot her. Why would someone she loved kill her?" Helen cried.

"Maybe he was on drugs…" Liza started to say.

"Goldie would never date someone who does drugs," Helen said.

Amy recalled the report had mentioned that there were traces of cocaine in the bedroom but kept quiet.

"Liza's brother was willing to move to Los Angeles for her, while she pursued her music career," Helen said.

"The Rabbi?" Amy asked.

"Yes, she was really happy when she was dating him. He thought it was their choice of careers that drove her away, but then he offered to support and never judge her, and she declined."

"Maybe she couldn't stand the kind of prejudice and probably ridicule he would face because of her in the music industry," Amy said.

Helen's eyes opened wide.

"Why do you say that?" Liza asked.

"Well…Helen said Goldie told her they were from two different worlds," Amy said.

"The manager at her apartment said the police searched her house very well; did they find a diary?" Helen said.

"No," Amy said.

Helen observed Amy for some time. "That was Goldie's explanation, when she finally talked to me about it in London."

Amy smiled shyly.

"From everything I read about her and what you have told me, she reminds me a little bit of myself."

"In what ways?" Liza asked.

"Her free spirit, a big heart that can get caught between two worlds… her rather large sense of who she is and what it means, by being close to her mother."

"You got all that from the police report?" Liza asked.

Amy shook her head slowly, smiling. "Mostly from being here with you and guessing…I am so sorry for your loss, Helen. I can actually feel the bond the two of you had just sitting here with you."

Helen wiped her eyes.

"I should leave," Amy said, getting up. "I'll send copies of the documents back to you by Friday."

"Don't bother. It's difficult for me to look at them."

Amy nodded and said she understood.

She thanked Helen and left the room. Liza followed Amy to the living room and walked out to the driveway with her. Driving home, Amy recalled Kenneth and reminded herself to call him after the arraignment.

CHAPTER SIX
The Man They Called Big

Big John Stone was at Kenneth's office first thing on Tuesday morning, but Kenneth was in court. He asked if he could wait for Kenneth anyway. Big was about three hundred pounds and six feet three. He wore jogging pants, a sweatshirt, and sneakers, which Nancy guessed were the only types of clothing he could find easily in his size.

Kenneth had anticipated Big's visit and that Big might wait for him as well. He called the office at about 9:30 a.m. and asked Big to join him at a coffee shop near the Long Beach Courthouse.

"We're having a meeting at the Mallam's house this evening. Can you come?" Big asked as soon as he settled into the booth where Kenneth was waiting for him. Paul's father was referred to as Mallam Jackson since his return from Africa on his way back from his pilgrimage in Mecca.

"About Paul's arrest?" Kenneth asked.

"Me and Jo, think you can take this case? We want the Mallam to meet you."

"Who does the Mallam want?"

"Kenny, this shit is gonna be big—give you some serious Dream Team lawyers' publicity. It'll make you famous." Big chuckled and playfully reached across the table to pat Kenneth's shoulder.

"Big, you think I can convince the Mallam to give me the case by saying I won't charge much for it. But if I take this case, it will be the only thing I do for the next six months, and that's assuming the trial only goes that long. I can't afford that; who's gonna do the cases I have now?"

"You telling me you never gonna take a big case, because you can't manage the small fish you used to if you do?"

"If the big case is gonna pay enough for me to hire the people to win it and manage my small cases, then, yeah, I can. But I can't afford to just take it for the publicity. Who is gonna pay my bills?"

"Who said we ain't planning to pay you?" Big was suddenly breathing heavily.

"My mom's been on the phone with Paul's mother nonstop since this happened. Big, there is no shame in it. How many people you think have fifty to a hundred thousand dollars waiting to pay lawyers?"

"Where you motherfuckers come up with this figure anyway? Every fucking lawyer quotes the same amount."

"It's the going rate."

"The going-where rate?"

Kenneth laughed.

"This shit ain't funny Kenny. Brothers going to jail like sardines and you folks wanna bankrupt their families to get them there."

"You do the math on how much time the lawyer's gonna put in the case, and how many experts he has to hire, apply the experts' rates to their time and the lawyer's rates to his time and you'd be in that ballpark."

"So, charge a smaller rate."

"That would be the fifty-thousand-dollar figure, and you can't get too far with that amount."

"Shit, Kenny! Paul is innocent," Big said exasperatedly.

They sat quietly for a few minutes, Kenneth watching Big and Big watching his interlocked fingers and twisting them slowly.

"Big, it's a good thing you're doing for Paul."

Big looked up and considered Kenneth for a while.

"We don't have that kinda money. We did the math and barely come close to forty grand. Even with Jo hoping to get twenty grand from her condo, that still won't get us to fifty."

"Then how about the public defender. Their guys that do murder trials have a lot of experience. Heck, I'd be working there if they didn't lay me off three years ago."

This explanation appeared to calm Big down. He looked around for the waiter and did not say another word until he had ordered coffee and two plates of huevos rancheros.

"I'm going to Jones and Jones's office after I leave you. Mallam wants Mr. Jones at the meeting tonight," Big said after the waiter left their table.

"Omar Jones?" Kenneth asked.

"Yep, Mallam got him a lot of cases with the Muslim brothers who got caught up in the LA riots, and made sure those boys all paid Mr. Jones like they were paying credit cards. A lot of them still paying on installments. The Mallam made that nigger a lot of money."

"Don't assume that's gonna sway Mr. Jones."

"You don't think attorneys gonna be lining up to take this case, just to get their faces on TV like Johnny?" Big asked.

"Not unless you're going to pay them."

"If we come up with the money for the experts, you gonna take the case?"

"Big, I haven't ever tried a murder case before. If I take the case, I'm bringing another attorney in, a friend of mine who is a professor at UCLA, and she's gonna have to be paid. If you guys can afford Mr. Jones, you can afford me and my friend."

"Can you come to the meeting anyway? Just help explain this thing to calm shit down for the family. Everybody is worried sick."

"No disrespect, Big. But I am not going to the Mallam's house for anything to do with this case unless I'm the attorney on it."

"Jo thinks you should be part of the case. Just work with whoever we can find."

"It doesn't work that way. You don't choose your attorney's team for your attorney. Tell Jo I appreciate her belief in me, but I can't do what she's asking right now."

Big's food arrived. He adjusted his sitting and bowed over his plates with hands on the table as though to ensure no one else reached for them.

"I'm gonna go pay for the food and head to my next hearing, Big," Kenneth said, gathering his things to leave the booth. Big looked up at Kenneth with a smile.

"You got this?"

"Yeah, I got this," Kenneth smiled back.

"Can you call Jo?" Big asked.

"I will," Kenneth said.

"No, now, Kenny. Just go over to that pay phone and call her, before you get busy and forget," Big said. "Show the family some heart for what they going through. I bet you haven't called Paul's mother either."

Kenneth considered Big silently, before going to the pay phone. After Nancy met Paul's mother, Sister Ramatu, in Los Angeles, Nancy insisted that Kenneth and Jo meet. Both being obedient to their mothers, they met at Universal Studios for a movie, late dinner, and a very late night, chatting. Jo was two years older than Kenneth, and they became instant friends. "I'll tell your mother that I have lots of friends I can introduce you to," Jo had said when the evening was over. "And that would be your way of saying, I'm gonna get out of the way of this train-wreck-player." Kenneth replied. They both had laughed so hard about that comment. "You wish, Kenny, but you're no player. You know exactly what you want and you don't need anyone's meddling to get her." They hardly saw each other alone again, but whenever they met at gatherings, there never seemed to be enough time for them to reacquaint.

Kenneth called Jo from the phone booth where Big could still see him, and Jo picked up the phone before Kenneth heard it ring.

"Hey, thanks for calling me. Big got to you?"

"I'm with him. How are you doing?"

"Alright, can you come tonight?" Jo asked.

"I can't and I shouldn't, Jo. I will meet you anytime and let you know what I think, but not your dad. Or your mother for that matter." Jo was quiet on the other end of the line. "Why do you want me there?"

"I want him to meet you, Kenny. You are right for the case. It is as clear as day to me."

Kenneth was quiet for a moment; it sounded like what Cassandra had said to him, only clearer.

"I have never tried a murder case before," he said slowly, as though he regretted not having that experience.

"Neither had all those other guys before they got their first murder case. Ken, I will be the first to admit that my brother has made one too many stupid mistakes in his life, but I know he is not a murderer. He is not O. J.. He hasn't lived any kind of life of privilege, with people waiting on him, hanging on his every word, doing his bidding. He has worked for everything he has, even refusing help from Pa. I know you can convince a jury that he didn't do it."

"I really appreciate what you're saying but I can't lie to you or to myself about this…it's gonna cost you just as much as you'll pay if you were getting someone with the experience."

"I wouldn't ask you to do it for less, Kenny."

"I'm sorry, I wasn't suggesting that you would. But Big was…I've worked with him before."

"I know. Can you just come and tell my dad to stop looking for celebrity lawyers to take this case? He wants a big-shot attorney to fit his image as a great Imam of Los Angeles."

"What makes you think he would listen to me if he doesn't listen to you?"

"I don't know. At least, tell him what…" Jo stopped talking and Kenneth could hear her sniffling, but before he could say anything, she completed her sentence. "to look for."

Jo was quiet again for a while.

"Jo," Kenneth called out.

"Yeah, I'm here…Ken." Jo said. After another short pause, she asked: "You think he did it?"

"I don't know much of anything about this woman or the facts of the case."

"You know as much as I do, Ken. Please tell me."

"Honestly Jo…swear you won't tell another soul," Kenneth said lowering his voice.

"I promise," Jo said.

"Jo…I'm still wondering why Big hasn't been arrested, if Paul wanted to kill anyone. Period."

Jo laughed. And Kenneth hung up the phone.

•••

KATE WAS BACK AT the office when Amy returned from visiting Helen Silberberg.

"Ms. Silberberg gave me a letter sent from the defendant's nightclub to Goldie after she died," Amy told Kate.

"What does it say?"

"She didn't open it."

"Why not?"

"It was difficult for her. She said she could not get herself to even look at it."

"Why did she give it to you? You can't do it for her."

"I wasn't suggesting I should. I thought it would be evidence in the case."

Amy felt the way Kate looked at her suggested she had made a grave mistake. She handed Kate the envelope, which Kate examined in silence and swore under her breath before she asked Amy to give it to the attorney who would arraign Paul Jackson the following day so they could present it to the court.

"Ms. Silberberg also gave me a couple of contracts, including Goldie's music contract and a CD from her safe deposit box," Amy told Kate, who was not as impressed about that information as Amy thought she would be.

"Contact the record company to let them know about it before the defendant asks for everything else we have from her."

"I'll do that," Amy said and quickly added, "the rental contract shows that her apartment was paid for the entire year, but it was in her agent Didi Pare's name."

"Let Gonzalez know about that; let's try to keep this case simple, please," Kate said again and returned to her work.

Amy called the record company, as Kate directed, to inform them about the documents Helen found. The executive Amy spoke to said their lawyer would get back to Amy.

CHAPTER SEVEN
"Not Guilty"

THE HALLWAY OUTSIDE THE courtroom on Thursday was crowded when Amy arrived at 8:20 a.m. Inside, a capacity crowd. The first two seating rows were reserved for lawyers, and even those were almost full. There were more African Americans than Amy had ever seen in a courtroom. Several men carrying big cameras wore press passes around their necks, but no one was taking pictures. Amy surmised that some press people in the building from the O. J. Simpson trial had come to take notes on another Hollywood trial.

She had wanted to check-in with the court's calendar clerk as all attorneys appearing before the court were supposed to, but she changed her mind when she saw the courtroom so full. Kate had instructed her to let the deputy district attorney, who regularly did arraignments in that court, take Paul's plea. On making eye contact with the court clerk, Amy shook her head slightly to indicate she would not be checking-in. The court reporter smiled to acknowledge that she understood.

Anna Houseman was the deputy district attorney assigned to the courtroom, and she was standing next to the calendar clerk with a woman Amy guessed was another lawyer. Amy stood away from the lawyers and waited for Anna.

Among the people sitting in the row immediately behind the lawyers were two women in hijabs. Amy assumed they were Paul's family, since they must have been among the first to arrive at the courthouse to get those seats.

"Hey, thanks for the busy morning," Anna said when she joined Amy.

"I had no idea," Amy smiled.

"Was that the public defender with you?"

"Yes, Joanna Lark. Did you speak with Mr. Ross?" Anna asked.

"Mr. Ross?"

"The record company attorney; he wanted to know if I was you. He is the younger buck sitting to the left of the second row of attorneys," Anna said looking past Amy toward Mr. Ross, but Amy did not turn.

"Thanks. He can wait. I'm afraid we have a further complication in this case."

"What do you mean?"

"On Tuesday the victim's mother delivered this to us," Amy said, giving the letter from Goldie's apartment to Anna in a clear plastic evidence bag.

"What do you want me to do with this?"

"Let the court know on the record that we received mail from the victim's house yesterday and it appears to be from the defendant."

"Why can't we just give a copy to the defendant's attorney as part of the complaint?"

"That's what we want to do, but we need the court's permission to open it. The letter is post-marked after the death of the victim."

Anna opened her eyes wide and looked at Amy as though she was wondering what audacity Amy had to impose this on her in the first place.

"And you just want to observe and not participate?" Anna asked sarcastically.

"That is what I have been told to do," Amy said with a smile.

Anna took the evidence bag and went to talk to Joanna Lark again. Amy watched Ms. Lark invite an African American lawyer Amy knew by reputation, Omar Jones, to join them.

Judge Pollazo took the bench promptly at 9:00 a.m. and informed the court that Mr. Jones had requested priority. Hearing no objections, he called the case of the *People of California vs. Paul Jackson*. Omar Jones and Joanna Lark approached one of two counsel tables of about five feet in length, placed end to end in a well in front of the judge, and separated from the rest of the courtroom by a waist-high balustrade. Ms. Houseman approached the other counsel table. They announced their names and whom they represented, while the court reporter, seated between them and the judge, transcribed verbatim.

As they introduced themselves, the sheriff brought Paul Jackson into the courtroom. Amy could not take her eyes off him as he walked, swaggering side to side, to his chair. He wore a pink prison uniform and had handcuffs that had a chain attached to a pair of cuffs on his ankles. His hair was cut to the tiniest stubs, a mere shade of darkness upon his skull. He looked more like an actor than the jock that Amy had imagined from his mug shots and his description in the complaint. *What madness drove him to kill Goldie?* Amy wondered.

He walked with his head upright, his shoulders pulled back, and took his time, like it was natural for him to be in handcuffs and have the sheriff accompany him like a bodyguard. He appeared to look directly at Amy before he turned his back to her and stood between Omar Jones and Joanna Lark. Earlier in Amy's career, the accused was only a case number on a file, whose nom de guerre was defendant, and whose face she hardly recalled. Paul's face though, she did not think she would ever forget.

"What is the nature of your special appearance, Mr. Jones, when the public defendant is also on the case?" Judge Pollazo inquired.

"With your permission, your honor, and obviously the agreement of the public defender, I would like to represent Mr. Jackson for the purpose of entering his plea of not guilty, while the public defender considers his financial eligibility for representation. I am conducting an investigation on behalf of the family into the circumstances of his arrest and the evidence that supports his case that he did not commit this crime. The outcome of what we find early in that investigation will determine whether the family would take further steps to retain my services."

"Why can't you conduct your investigation independent of the public defender's case, and if you are retained, just come in and substitute the public defender?"

"Your Honor, that was the idea when I came in this morning, until we were informed that there is a further evidence to be introduced in the record at this arraignment."

"I will not be taking any evidence at this arraignment. So, you can go back to your initial plan."

"Your Honor, we are not really asking the court to take any evidence either," Anna quickly joined. "Rather, out of the abundance of caution and the protection of due process, we need to make the court aware of a new development."

"Would this require us in any way to put off the arraignment or reconsider the arrest of this defendant at this time, counsel?"

"No."

"Yes."

"Yes."

Anna, Omar, and Joanna respectively all spoke at the same time so that it was difficult identifying who said what.

"One at a time please," the court reporter said.

"The People are ready for arraignment, your Honor, with or without the new development."

Judge Pollazo shuffled a few papers together, then paused for a moment and propped up his chin on a clinched fist.

"I will be the first to admit—" Mr. Jones began, but Judge Pollazo raised his hand with an open palm toward Mr. Jones, who stopped speaking immediately.

"Ms. Houseman, what is this new development?" Judge Pollazo asked.

Anna handed the transparent plastic bag with the letter to the sheriff and explained what Amy had told her about how they received the letter. She told Judge Pollazo that she had shown the letter to Ms. Lark and Mr. Jones. Judge Pollazo examined the letter without taking it out of the transparent evidence bag.

"And Ms. Houseman, you are requesting that we open the letter and make it a part of the case file?" Judge Pollazo asked.

"Yes, your Honor," Anna said.

"Your Honor," Mr. Jones and Ms. Lark started to say simultaneously, and Mr. Jones stopped. "We would object to that request," Joanna said.

"What is your objection?" Judge Pollazo said.

"Your Honor, the letter obviously has nothing to do with guilt or innocence in this case, since the police did not know about it at the time they arrested my client," Joanna said.

"Your Honor," Anna said. "The family of the deceased would like some closure with this case, and part of that closure would be understanding why this letter from the man who killed their daughter should arrive at this time."

"The man who allegedly killed their daughter, you mean; we can all have closure when the trial is over, Ms. Houseman. I will leave the matter of the letter to be decided by the trial judge. You may renew your motion at the preliminary hearing, Ms. Houseman," Judge Pollazo said. "How long do you expect your investigation will take, Mr. Jones?" Judge Pollazo asked.

"We should be done by the middle of next week," Mr. Jones said.

"In that case, we will go ahead and take the defendant's plea, with a longer schedule for the preliminary hearing, which should be the next court appearance on this matter unless one of you files a motion for whatever purpose before the court. Is that agreeable?" Judge Pollazo asked.

All counsel agreed.

"Very well then. You may read the charges against the defendant, Ms. Houseman," Judge Pollazo said.

"Yes, your Honor," Anna said, and read the pleading charging Paul with two counts of violation of Penal Code Section 187(a), a felony for the murder of Goldie Silberberg, and Section 459, unauthorized entry of the premises belonging to Ms. Silberberg.

After the reading of the charges, Anna looked up at the judge, who asked Paul several questions as to how he was pleading.

"Not guilty," Paul said.

Anna requested that Paul be remanded to custody without bail pending trial.

Judge Pollazo agreed over Joanna Lark's arguments to the contrary and adjourned the proceeding.

"You may call the next case," Judge Pollazo said to the calendar clerk.

Anna turned toward Amy again and raised her hand to indicate that Amy should wait for her. Omar put one hand around Paul's shoulder and patted him on the chest with the other hand. They spoke briefly before Paul shook hands with Joanna and was led away by the sheriff, while Omar and Joanna left the well. Much of the courtroom started to get up, shuffling noisy.

Amy observed Mr. Ross walking toward her. He bent over, apparently to introduce himself, but Amy spoke first. "Mr. Ross?" The man nodded. He was about thirty-five years old, his cologne as ostentatious as his suit. Amy looked at him like she was inspecting a mannequin. Reaching into her handbag, she handed him a large envelope. Mr. Ross asked if Amy could meet with him outside the courtroom for a minute, but Amy shook her head and pointed toward Anna.

"I have to wait for her."

"It will only take a minute."

"Not even that, Mr. Ross; I am still waiting for Ms. Houseman."

"I will wait outside, then."

Amy shrugged, her attention still focused on the proceeding in front of her.

She sat through two more arraignments in which Anna was counsel before she stood up to leave, and let the Sheriff know that she would be back for Anna. She wanted to tell Anna that she did a good job with very little information to go on and invite her to lunch, if Anna were not busy.

"I'm sorry we got off on the wrong foot yesterday," Mr. Ross said as soon as Amy came out of the courtroom.

"It's part of the job," Amy said.

"I left your boss messages to call us back, but we have not heard from her."

"She got your messages, that's why I gave you the documents."

"I wanted to let her know why we didn't want the defendant to get the Silberberg music contract from your office."

"I can let her know, if you wish."

"The man accused of killing her cowrote most of the songs on her new record, so we had covered him with an insurance policy that would pay for his attorneys fees if he is sued for plagiarism or copyright infringement on the songs he cowrote. Unfortunately, in addition to coverage for copyright infringement, the general liability insurance policy also pays for attorneys' fees if he is charged with a criminal offense while he is Goldie's manager. We imagined a situation where he got into a scuffle with a paparazzi or something; no one envisioned paying for his attorneys fees in a case like this."

"Where he is using it to pay for his legal defense for murder," Amy said.

"Yes, up to a quarter of a million dollars per case," the lawyer answered.

"And you are seriously telling me that his access to legal fees for the defense has nothing to do with the ultimate outcome of his criminal case?" Amy asked.

"We are saying that he is not entitled to it, and if you guys hand it over to him, you will be playing judge and jury in the civil case that would decide whether he is entitled to it."

"So noted. I'll let Kate know," Amy said and walked away.

•••

AMY HAD SPOKEN WITH Mr. Ross when she returned from the courthouse the previous afternoon. The conversation had left Amy so flustered that she could not remember his name after it was over. He had asked the district attorney to return the documents to the recording company without disclosing it to Paul.

"Seriously?" Amy had asked, astounded that a lawyer she had never met would ask such a thing of her, a deputy district attorney.

"This has nothing to do with the criminal case, is what I'm saying."

"We are not the judge of that…You understand how keeping it from him when his name is on it would pose an ethical dilemma for our office, don't you?" Amy asked.

"No, I don't I'm afraid."

"Okay, I will let Kate know. She is the senior attorney on the case—"

"Don't worry. I will be calling her directly," the lawyer had said and hung up before Amy could respond.

Amy could tell Mr. Ross was the lawyer who was so rude to her yesterday. She was still irritated by the ethical compromise he had forced on her because Kate insisted that the contract be returned to the record company. After the phone call with the recording company attorney, Amy had become very curious about the lawyer's rude behavior and made copies of both the recording contract and the rental agreement, which she took with her to read at home.

•••

Nothing else was scheduled for *People v. Jackson*, Amy told herself when she got back to her office and sat down to contemplate next steps. An idle business card by her telephone caught her attention and she picked it up. It was Cassandra Rayburn's card, on which Amy had written the number Melissa gave her for Kenneth. She had still not called him. What would she say to him, after so long? What was he expecting from trying so hard to reach her? She wondered how he had changed. It made her anxious to think it had taken her this long to call him. She picked up the phone and began to dial his number.

CHAPTER EIGHT

A Feminine Elan

W HEN AMY RETURNED FROM work, Thomas's vehicle was idling quietly in front of her apartment building. She had not wanted him to visit, but seeing him standing there, five feet eleven inches of an arrow straight frame, in a dark blue suit and dark sunglasses, she was glad he had come. Partly the dutiful girlfriend and partly desirous of the escape he offered from *People v. Jackson*, she put her arms around him and felt every inch of her body alight as they kissed. He was about to pull away, but she strapped her arms around his neck and opened her mouth. The expression on his face, when she finally stopped and leaned back to look at him, pleased her. Without saying a word, she held his hand and started walking toward her apartment. She asked him about his trip, when he had left New York, and where he was staying.

He was staying at the Ritz Hotel in Pasadena, he said and asked her to come and stay with him. She agreed and on getting to her apartment, grabbed a ready-packed travel bag into which she threw a couple of dresses and shoes. She checked her voicemail again. Her brother Edward was coming to Los Angeles the following week. There was someone he wanted her to meet. It made her smile. Thomas watched her, as though he was trying to understand what was going on. As they were leaving her apartment, just as she was about to open the door, she closed it again, and threw her arms around his neck. This time, he led their slow dance to the inaudible beats of their racing hearts and the soft rhythm of her panting breaths. She had to stop him. Pausing for the applause that was her heartbeat to subside, she turned around, opened the door, and walked out. Thomas took a deep breath, exhaled, straightened his suit, and smiled to himself. Then he followed her out, letting the door shut on its own.

It was, after all, her decision to keep him at arms' length while he courted her. Even then, mostly at Alana's urging, did she overcome her cold feet on the first few dates. He had proposed to her over the three weeks' vacation she took before starting her new position, but she had turned him down because she could not be sure that he would have proposed had she not told him about the compromise she made with her Catholic faith. Earlier in their courtship when he expressed his frustrations with the pace of their relationship, she told him she had made herself a promise not to engage in premarital sex unless she was certain that she was headed to the alter with the person. After her failed engagement, she had struggled to make sense of her own promise. The flesh being weak and marriage no longer a priority of hers, the promise was becoming harder to keep. More than anyone, since she broke up with Richard, Thomas had tried her patience the most.

She often felt this uncontrollable descent to decadence, like a form of self-flagellation, when she allowed herself to recall the young man she was almost with in college, whose name had recently resurfaced after she thought she had finally forgotten him. For years after college, when she thought of him her imagination went to prurient extremes she would never allow herself in person. She had not allowed herself to date him, because of perceived family strictures that would have made a union between them impossible. Her charmed life, she had thought, came at the cost of certain freedoms.

A woman had answered the phone when she finally called the number Melissa gave her, and that woman's voice recurred in Amy's mind. Had she called his home or his office? Melissa never stated which number she got from him. She had nervously said she would call back later, without leaving her number.

Until she embraced Thomas and later gave in to him at the Ritz, she had not known she was on the verge of a cathartic sexual implosion. It was official then, or was it?

After dinner and tea, they retreated to bed. Amy fell silent, as though preparing herself to sleep, her back turned to him, one part shyness and one part guilt in a manner and to an extent she had not expected.

"So, what's going on?" Thomas asked. He had been unusually reticent all evening, speaking through many silences and facial expressions. When Amy did not respond, he ran his hand over her back up to her shoulder and squeezed gently. Amy pulled her shoulders up to her ears and turned around smiling. "What's going on?" he repeated.

Amy still did not say anything. She looked into his eyes, the center of their blue seemed to look past her, searching the inner depths of hers, and she let them.

"You don't want to talk about it?"

"Who said I don't?"

"You're not speaking."

She placed her hand on the middle of his chest. "You're not listening."

"Then help me."

Amy shook her head slowly. Suddenly, she was close to tears and she could not explain why. Thomas reached out to hold her and Amy moved closer into his embrace and buried her face on his chest. They lay that way for a while before she turned around and wiped her eyes and let him spoon her.

"I know you said you didn't want me to visit while you are dealing with this new job. You didn't want to lean on me emotionally."

"So, why did you come?"

"Your mother told me someone at the new office appeared to have hand-picked you for a test."

Amy fell quiet for a while. Thomas also appeared to be done speaking.

"I came into the office to find a really exciting case waiting for me. But then the senior deputy on the case seems to want to do the opposite of everything I think is the right thing to do."

"Can you get off the case?"

"My first assignment, my first week? Besides, I don't want off the case."

"Then call her bullshit on it."

"I don't make any decisions on the case, that means I don't get to call bullshit on anything."

"So, what'll you do?"

"Just what I have been doing. Kate, that's her name, actually instructed me to withhold evidence."

"Did you?"

"Well, not literally," Amy said, and nodded.

"No!"

"Yes."

"What?"

She told Thomas about the general liability insurance policy she had to turn over to the recording company attorney instead of making it available to the defendant's attorney to pay for the defense. Thomas explained that he could get around that problem and instruct the insurance company to pay the defendant, if Amy wanted. His companies included a clearing house for major insurance companies.

"As much as I want to do the right thing, I think this man killed her in cold blood, too, and I'm not getting out of my way to do anything for him."

She turned around and kissed him. "Thanks, though," she said.

"What's Kate's last name?"

Amy shook her head.

"Let's talk about something else."

CHAPTER NINE
Bauchet Street

The unopened letter in the case was both divine intervention and the Devil's handiwork to Paul's family. Sister Ramatu said it was nothing short of a miracle the letter appeared to show that her son did not know Goldie was dead. "Why else would he be writing her after she was already dead?" Mallam Jackson said the Devil planted it to test his faith. In either case, both had God on the job already. Kenneth first learned of what happened at the arraignment from Jo, who drove straight to Norwalk from the hearing. She had asked Nancy which court Kenneth went to and made the drive to find Kenneth at the Norwalk Superior Courthouse during lunch.

"What do you think it could be?" she asked. "Delayed mail?"

"Did you ask Paul?"

"I couldn't see him before they took him away," Jo said, and after a long pause, added, "And, I'm afraid to ask. Ken, this case is growing tentacles by the minute, and we haven't secured the attorney's fees yet. Even if we had the money, Mr. Jones will burn through it before trial."

Jo was emotional as she recounted what happened in court. Kenneth told her that Paul must have told his lawyers what was in the letter, if he wrote it.

"You can't have his attorneys arguing that the letter should not be opened without knowing what's in it," Kenneth said.

"Ken, Paul doesn't write shit down unless he's really angry. That's what his songwriting is about, to calm him down. He never writes a letter to say, 'I love you.' If he wrote that woman, it's not good. It is not something nice he was saying to her. He's impulsive and hotheaded."

"Regardless, he must come clean about the letter to his attorneys."

"Will you ask him?"

"It's better if his attorney asks him, that way it's protected attorney-client information."

"You're an attorney, Ken."

"But I'm not his attorney."

After a while, Jo muttered, "Yet." Kenneth smiled, and forced a smile from Jo. "Please go and see him," she pleaded.

"How about Big?"

"What about him?"

"Could he have sent the letter after Goldie died?"

"I don't think so. He couldn't stand the hold that woman had on Paul."

It took promising to go and see Paul soon for Kenneth to gracefully excuse himself from the meeting with Jo, but he wanted to know what Big knew about the letter before going to see Paul.

Big had driven Sister Ramatu to court but stayed in the parking lot. His blood pressure couldn't handle the hearing, he told her. When Kenneth got to Cool Jo's Café on his way from Norwalk Superior Courthouse, Big seemed excited to see him. He stood astride with his arms wide open and his mouth agape, cheerfully reeking of alcohol.

"Mudderfucker, where you been? You missed some fireworks. Mr. Jones came to the hearing." He gave Kenneth a big hug and almost squeezed the breath out of him. "You were fucking wrong about Mr. Jones. He was representing, big time."

He pulled Kenneth's arm along as he went inside the club. The bar was empty except for a bottle of Courvoisier and a single glass on the counter. Big pointed behind the bar as though he was offering Kenneth a drink, but Kenneth shook his head.

"Paul's happy you's gonna visit him. He's looking forward to it," Big said. When Kenneth said nothing, Big continued, "You still going, right?"

"Of course I'm going. That's why I'm here."

"You want me to come with you?"

"No. What do you know about this letter they say he sent after she died?"

"Them mudderfuckers are crackheads, Kenny. Why Paul gonna write her a letter? She lives down that freeway, right there, and most nights we know which nightclub to find her. It's probably some old mail she ain't opened yet."

"I thought they said the post date on the envelope was recent?"

"It was?"

"Paul didn't say anything?"

"No, they're recording his business and shit in that jailhouse, I wasn't gonna ask him. But I didn't send it, if that's what you're asking."

"No, that's not what I'm asking," Kenneth said and got up to leave. "Does Cool Jo's have a secretary?"

"Yeah…this girl comes in three times a week to put things in order and get us ready for the weekend."

"She still—"

"Oh, nigga wait. You see that shit right there is why you need to be one of Paul's lawyers."

They were walking toward the exit as they talked about the secretary, but Big had stopped to make his last point. Kenneth stopped as well.

"Because I asked you about the secretary?"

"Mr. Jones never asked those questions you asking. Come to think of it, this whole shit turns on whether Paul was right here the night that woman died, like he said he was, and Mr. Jones has never seen the inside of this club. Hasn't even bothered to stop by, and his office is down the street from here. We need you on this case."

"Has Mallam hired Mr. Jones?"

"No, the family is divided. Jo wants you and she thinks Paul does, too."

"And Mallam has the money for Mr. Jones?"

"Shoot, you should have seen the press in the courtroom. You know Mr. Jones wants to be a celebrity."

"He's not gonna do it for the publicity, Big."

"For experience, Kenny, can't you work with him? Just be in it for the family."

"You don't have the money for Mr. Jones, how you gonna have the money for the two of us?"

"We are gonna get the money, Kenny. We are gonna do a concert like 'Live Aid' for Paul, selling 'Free Paul Jackson' T-shirts and pins and shit. We'll come up with the money, I guarantee you," Big said.

•••

KENNETH CLEARED HIS SCHEDULE to visit Paul on Friday because the sheriff might move him away from the central jail. Most defendants whose trials are not imminent are held at the Pitchess Detention Center of the Los Angeles County Jails, about forty miles north of Los Angeles, in the mountains off the freeway to Northern California. Kenneth was afraid that Paul might be moved to Pitchess due to weekend overcrowding, and he did not want to drive that far to see him when he could do so at the jailhouse on Bouchet Street.

Bauchet Street is in the northeasterly end of downtown Los Angeles, around the corner from the train station. It crosses Alameda Street one block north of Cesar E. Chavez Avenue. On one side of Alameda, Bauchet Street crawls around a mini-mart and continues along a filthy back street the city had long since forgotten. In the opposite direction, it dead-ends fifty feet from the jailhouse. Opportunists abound here like maggots, drawn to the misery of those incarcerated and their families.

Kenneth had not been to the central jail on Bauchet Street in a while, but he recalled it well from his first few months in private practice. Most lawyers go through their entire careers in Los Angeles never knowing it exists. Of the few who know it, only the young criminal lawyers starting their careers go there regularly to hone their skills and pay their dues. Until the defendant/accused meets and approves an unknown attorney, most families will not open their wallets for his services. Moreover, the poor young lawyers have state competition from the free services of the public defender's office. Ordinarily, a defendant would not qualify for representation by the public defender if he can afford private counsel, but in most cases, like Paul Jackson's, immediate and extended family members retain the private counsel, not the destitute defendant. Kenneth hurried into the receiving area, where two deputy sheriffs made him empty his pockets, patted him down, and asked him to take off his belt before he went through the metal detector.

"It doesn't ring," he protested, but they just looked at him. Kenneth took his belt off and held his pants up with angry fists.

"Your shoes!" one deputy snapped at him. Kenneth wondered why he bothered giving them his bar card showing that he was an attorney. He obeyed them anyway, taking off his shoes and placing them in a plastic container. He walked through the metal detector, dressed himself again, and proceeded to the visitor's lounge. The visitor's area of the jail was a hall of about sixty square feet where prisoners and their guests met without a partition between them. This meeting place seemed temporarily set up due to ongoing construction at the jailhouse and the décor appeared to have been inspired by a high school cafeteria. Benches lined the lengths of twelve-by-six-foot tables put end to end from one wall to the other with two or three feet of space between them.

Most of the tables were not occupied. After a brief wait, the sheriff led Paul Jackson into the meeting room. Wearing pink jumpers with his hands in handcuffs, he looked toward Kenneth as he waited for final clearance from an approaching guard. His eyes looked like they fell deeper into their sockets for lack of sleep, his six-feet-two inches height looked shorter, perhaps because he was slightly hunched. The guard took off his handcuffs from one hand and cuffed the other hand to one leg of the table where Kenneth sat. Kenneth patted him on the shoulder and squeezed his left hand, the free hand.

"They been treating you well?"

"As good as it gets, I guess."

"Hang in there, they can't break us like this anymore," Kenneth said. Paul smiled.

"Look at you, sounding like your momma's son all of a sudden."

"Ma sends her love, by the way."

"Tell her I appreciate all the support she's been giving my mom."

"I will."

"Can you do my case with your professor friend?"

"Yes. But like I told Jo, I can't do it without the funds to pay the professor and run my office," Kenneth said, watching Paul, whose eyes drifted away from Kenneth to another table and somewhere beyond their visit. "Paul, you know I started at the public defender's office. There are still some senior attorney's there I call for advice on my criminal cases once in a while. They'll do a good job for you."

"Kenny, I have these nightmares where my cell has a death row chair in it, and the public defender always coming around saying 'I'm sorry, man,' 'I'm sorry buddy,' 'I didn't see this coming.' I can't do it, Kenny. I'mma raise the money to pay you to keep your office afloat."

"You sure your pa hasn't signed Mr. Jones yet?"

"He can't do it unless I say so, can he?"

Kenneth shrugged, preferring not to be drawn into a disagreement between Paul and Mallam Jackson.

"Pa brought Omar Jones, and I gotta tell you I am happy with the stuff he's done, if it gets me out of here, but this thing goes to trial, I want you not Omar. He's a businessman, Kenny. He can sell a good yarn. But you the brains. That's why you worried about taking my case. You are giving it some deep thoughts, and he ain't. It's business as usual for him. But you're afraid the system might let me down and you'd be to blame. But you won't. I didn't do this. And I can prove it—with you."

Kenneth leaned back in his chair and considered Paul anew.

"It's okay if you don't believe me, Kenny. But give me the chance to prove it to you."

"When it comes to knowing what happened, in a criminal case, there are some attorneys who want to know if their client did it and there are some who don't. I'm one of those who don't want to know."

"Why not?"

"Because whether you did or not, you're still entitled to the best legal representation you can get if this system is to work for the rest of us. That's what I signed up for when I became a criminal lawyer."

Paul's eyes smiled when Kenneth said this to him.

"Kenny, can you level with me about something?"

"Sure, what?"

"You're not usually about money, Kenney. So, is Big the reason you're hesitating taking this case?"

"Nah, Big has nothing to do with it."

"When you and Big were doing those accident cases, Big hit you, didn't he?"

Kenneth turned away from Paul. Then, he shook his head slowly.

"Nah, he didn't."

"You said you were gonna level with me."

"I am leveling with you."

"So, what'd he do to you? Miguel said he saw you in the parking lot, and you were crying in your car. Just tell me what he did—and I'll drop it. I am not gonna ask him about it."

"Big didn't hit me, Paul. I appreciate what you're trying to do, but I put all that behind me, and I'm not gonna talk to you about Big behind his back."

"I'm sorry, he did whatever he did to you, Kenny."

"I have to go," Kenneth said.

"I understand," Paul said.

Kenneth started to get up, bending over Paul, and as he did, he lowered his voice and spoke before he straightened his back, "You know you have to level with Omar Jones about what's in that letter they said you sent after she died?"

"Kenny, I don't know shit about that letter. I didn't send her nothing like that."

Kenneth stood erect, looking at Paul in disbelief.

Paul gestured to the guard watching them from a distance to indicate that he was ready to go back to his cell, and Kenneth took his leave before the guard got to their table.

CHAPTER TEN

A Past...

THE WEEKEND BROUGHT RESPITE from *People v. Jackson*, and, for the time being at least, Amy's new job felt normal. Thomas had returned to New York but would be headed to Japan a week later through Los Angeles. Thus, Amy had the weekend to herself. She spent it on the phone with Edward, then with Neda, and briefly with Thomas. She spent it watching television and reviewing work files, only leaving the house twice all weekend to go to the gym and to church. A planned outing with Neda during the week and a stopover by Thomas on his way to Japan might leave her less time at the office to do the work she brings home next week.

On Thursday, as she was preparing to meet Neda, Alana called. Amy did not even pick up the phone to know it was her mother calling. Alana always timed her calls to coincide with the most auspicious outings in Amy's life, then offer her opinion on what Amy should wear, do, and say, or how Amy should conduct herself to be consistent with her Wilson upbringing. In the past, Amy did everything her mother said, while protesting that she would not. What could she possibly know about being a lady without Alana? Invariably, though, the nights lost something, like the feeling that the table between you and the person across from you is a well that either falls into an abyss of uncertain excitement or a life-changing mistake and the joy of knowing he is willing to take the leap across just to get to you. On those nights when she checked in with Alana, or Alana checked in with her, Amy felt some of that unknown was lost…sometimes all of it was lost. She never felt the spark her friends often talked about, that when left to their dates' devices their nights could explode. Both the contemplation of that explosion and the excitement of keeping the lid on it was lost. The best nights were those Alana never knew about or the rare occasion that Amy lied to her, perhaps because Alana would not approve. Nights when Amy was "free-falling" with the bad boys, as one of her favorite songs would say. So, when Alana asked what Amy was planning for this evening, Amy said she was going to Cool Jo's Café, just to get a reaction out of Alana.

"With Thomas?"

"No, why would you assume I'm going with him anyway?"

"I thought Thomas flew in to see you on his way to Japan."

"He did, and he is at his hotel."

"What's come over you? Why would you go to a Black nightclub by yourself, when Thomas is there to go with you?"

"Now, how do you know it's a Black nightclub?" Amy asked.

"Cool Jo's? Honey, don't be naive. No self-respecting café goes by such a name."

Amy and Neda had arranged to have drinks at a hotel in downtown Los Angeles and go to a movie afterward. Amy decided to walk. It was windy, for LA, and the night felt cool. The sky was cloudy, though no rain was expected. As was her practice when she went out socially with her girlfriends, she wore the ring from her failed engagement. Traffic was still busy as she walked toward Fourth Street. She had been tempted to drive because she would be coming back late but finding herself alone on the sidewalk while cars filled the one-way boulevard beside her with noise and exhaust fumes, she felt proud of her decision.

At the bar in the hotel, she told Neda about her brother Edward's new girlfriend, Angela, an actress, whom Alana had called to tell Amy about. Edward met her after a performance his hospital staff attended in New Haven.

"Edward now goes to watch plays regularly in the theatre," Amy said. "That should tell you how smitten he must be. He never saw a single play in his life before the one he met her at."

"Then your mother is right. She must be the one. That is how it usually happens. Just when you're not looking, a new world you've never been to or noticed in the past opens up, and the person you've been waiting for all your life just walks in," Neda said.

"What does that say about us? We don't go to new worlds and I've known Thomas all my life," Amy said, raising her glass to her lips.

"A new world opens every day, you just have to sail into it. Unlike you, I'm open for adventure," Neda said. Amy chuckled.

"It could also be the death of you. Goldie, the victim in my new murder case, met the ex-boyfriend who killed her that way. She turned her back on a man she had known all her life for adventure."

"That is really the way you see life, isn't it? Every new day is like one door opening for you, that leads to either adventure or death. And you think, if you don't get up and walk through it, you will never die."

"Oh, I don't mind dying, it's the disappointment of a false adventure that feels like being buried alive. For that, I'd rather stay in bed and order room service."

"How the hell did we become friends?"

"You sought me out for adventure," Amy said. They both laughed.

They were again interrupted by a man offering to buy them drinks, before their glasses were empty. It was the second time someone offered. Amy and Neda looked at each other, then at their half-full glasses and started laughing. They declined.

"Oh, by the way, my mother asked where I was going tonight, and I said Cool Jo's Café just to see her reaction. That's the club the accused in my case said he was in when his ex was killed."

"Then let's go there."

"Are you trying to get me sent back to your office?"

"How would they know?"

"The investigation is still hot, I'm sure there'll be undercover cops at that club tonight. This guy owns the nightclub."

"So…live a little."

"Nah, I'd rather not. I just told my mom that to give her a nightmare."

"Why are you doing that now? Are you back to rebelling from your mom? Come on, think about it. How would you feel if you were her? My mother is the one who tries to get me off the phone when we talk."

"It's different with me and Alana. You were separated from your mother for a while when you left Iran. I can't even imagine that at this age."

"I think that's how your mother feels, like you've moved to Tehran and left her in the Bay Area, at least emotionally."

"No, she gets why...I mean not exactly, but she knows it is about boundaries. She reminded me again today."

"She reminded you that she knows why you're giving her nightmares?"

"...that I take after my grandfather."

"How?"

"Alana says I take after him by running away from my family name."

"I thought your grandfather made the family name?"

"No, my original family name was not Wilson. My great grandfather, John D. Willis, built the family fortune. But he was a rogue character back in Texas. He was a former Texas Ranger who acquired so much land in Texas and later Oklahoma back in the day that even his family was embarrassed to talk about how much he had or how he got it. They said he had to be ruthless to properly protect what was his. Mexicans said his middle initial stood for 'Diablo.' When oil finally hit, people swore he saw it coming. After he died, my grandpa decided to move out west, change his last name to Wilson, and build his own fortune with part of his inheritance. But he mostly turned to things that would give people a better life, like cure diseases, build infrastructure, and invest in key manufacturing products. My mom thinks that's what I'm doing by working here and not in the private industry. She said I run the other way when I see the Wilson name and think I'm out here doing good."

"Do you?"

"Of course not. I'm very proud of my family name...especially when I see my brother rise to it. He carries it well. But I like that my mother thinks that—she can be a bit much."

Neda said nothing and finished her drink.

"I've never told anyone this story; you won't ever repeat it, will you?"

"No, I won't," Neda said and smiled.

"Were you serious about going to that nightclub?"

"We won't stay long, and we can go to the movie from there."

"At least I won't feel too guilty about lying to Alana."

"Don't pretend you are a nice person. It is beneath you."

Amy laughed.

Cool Jo's Café was boxed in a flat-roofed square building on Hope Street, a few blocks south of the hotel where Amy and Neda met. It looked like a warehouse from the street, and there were no signs or lights to suggest it was a nightclub. The neighborhood was fast peeling away from the rest of the city and falling into official neglect. Buildings struggled to reach full occupancy and ladies of the night hugged light poles at corners of the street. Neda first circled the block trying to decide which of the many large parking spaces was safe to park. The lots seemed to have been raised where buildings had been torn down to eradicate their aesthetic nuisance. Behind Cool Jo's Café, Amy noticed another nightclub with a line of predominantly Hispanic Americans waiting in front.

A line of about twenty African Americans stood outside waiting to be let into Cool Jo's Café, too. Alana's perspicacity with no more information than the name of the club seemed uncanny to Amy. She turned to gauge Neda's reaction.

"Did you know that it was an all-Black nightclub?" Neda asked while they briefly sat in the car with the engine running. Amy shrugged.

"It is owned by an African American."

"Do you want to go back?" Neda continued.

"I am not standing in line to go to any nightclub," Amy said.

"Have some faith," Neda said and shut the engine off.

"So, how would two white chicks get past that line?"

"With a State Department ID."

"A what?"

"I have an idea, just come," Neda said, and went to the front of the line.

Amy waited a minute across the street before Neda waved her over. The entrance opened into a hallway leading to a back area from which much of the music emanated. The song "Creep" by TLC was playing. Immediately after the entrance, there were two doors facing each other to the left and right of Amy. Once past the doorman, Neda peeked into the door to the left, and turned quickly to enter the door on the right as though she knew where she was going. Amy also peeked into the door on the left before following Neda. The lighting inside was dim, and the aisles between the booths were beginning to fill with people.

Amy had hoped to steal into a corner of the club with a glass of vodka mixed with grapefruite juice on ice and observe the scene. The only other Caucasian that Amy could see besides herself and Neda was a burly bartender with a baby face and thick brown hair. Neda took off her jacket and approached the bartender. Amy looked around, trying to smile without looking directly at the men. Her eyes met some of the women's gazes and though she could not really make out their expressions, she felt judged as if she had trespassed into one of the few places left for them to be themselves without someone like her being there to judge them.

Many of the woman wore tight dresses, stiletto heels, and black panty hose. The heavier the women, the higher the heels and the tighter the dresses, it seemed. A few wore jeans, loose skirts, and T-shirts, a flower pattern dress, or a white pant suit that must have seemed elegant at the wedding for which it was purchased. Most of the men seemed tall and big boned, in tight fitting T-shirts over broad chests and bulging biceps, but always a jacket. The taller and bigger men seemed to prefer baggy pants with their suits.

"What'll it be?" the bartender asked Neda.

Amy was standing tightly behind Neda as the bartender spoke when she noticed someone's hand come over her shoulder from behind and rest on it. As she tried to turn, expecting the man had mistakenly rested his hand on her, the hand squeezed her shoulder. Amy froze. Her shoulders hunched up to her ears and her spine stiffened to the audacity of a familiarity she could not imagine having with anyone in this club. Then she heard his voice.

"Amy Wilson? What on Earth are you doing here?"

Neda turned before Amy could, with a grin on the verge of laughter. Amy held Neda's shoulders and turned her back around to face the bartender, then Amy turned to see Kenneth in a white shirt and black slacks looking as young as she remembered him six years prior. A smile affixed upon his face, his eyes on hers. His hair was neatly low cut.

"Kenneth," Amy said, but Neda quickly interrupted her.

"What would you like to drink?" Neda asked.

"A greyhound," Kenneth said.

"Not you, her," Neda said, pointing to Amy.

"I'm telling you what she would like."

Amy nodded to Neda and turned her around again before Neda could say another word.

"Excuse me. The ghost of Kenneth Brown, what brings you to life?" Kenneth did not answer, not with words. They gazed at each other briefly, then embraced. The bartender retreated with Neda's order, and Neda turned around to face Kenneth and Amy.

"So, you're really in Los Angeles?" Amy asked.

"So, you got my calls."

"You guys go ahead and find a table, I'll bring the drinks," Neda said.

Amy, still a shade scarlet, said, "Kenneth meet Neda, my dearest friend and colleague. Neda, Kenneth, and I were in college together."

"Together?" Neda asked, as she extended her hand to Kenneth.

"Classmates," Kenneth said. "Please, let me get the drinks."

"You're here alone?" Neda asked.

"I am. I just got here."

"You live in the area?" Amy asked.

"Yes, well, Long Beach."

Neda was looking around the clubhouse for a table as Amy and Kenneth spoke.

"We'll be over there," she said, pointing to the general direction of several booths.

"Sure," Kenneth said. Amy could feel him watching her as she walked away with Neda. She and Neda were seated for some time while Kenneth waited for their drinks.

"So, together in college, ha. How come I never heard of him?" Neda asked.

"It's nothing like that."

"Like what? What is it like?"

"Oh, he's an old friend, and…the nicest guy you ever met."

"Nicest? I'm 'Mommy dearest' and he's nicest?"

"I never called you that…"

"Still, I prefer nicest, he can keep dearest."

Amy waved Neda's teasing away and looked around. She admired the women's many hair styles, cornrow braids that split the rows from the center of the head down to the sides to end at the natural hairline, those with bangs and those with extensions that fell on the shoulders, braids that stood single and separately without cornrows, attached to extensions, thick braids and tiny braids, the short dreadlocks sprouting off the head, not longer than a pinkie, and the long Rastafarian dreadlocks. The blow-dried good old Afro seemed to still hold its own, though it appeared much shorter than it ever was and more common with women than with men.

As Kenneth approached with three glasses of cocktails he barely managed to hold on to, an insouciance filled Amy. The moment she saw him, Cool Jo's felt like a different club than the one owned by the man who'd killed Goldie. She turned to Neda, who was watching her.

"What?" Amy asked.

"I didn't say anything."

Kenneth joined them. Neda accepted her drink from Kenneth and stood up.

"Why don't I take my drink somewhere far, far away from the memory lane you two are jumping on," Neda said. Amy folded her arms across her chest and recrossed her legs. She had wondered how she would engage Kenneth so much without ignoring Neda or rousing her curiosity. She avoided looking into Neda's eyes.

"I'm sorry, I didn't get your last name," Neda said to Kenneth.

"Brown, Kenneth Brown."

"Thanks. I leave my friend in capable hands, I suppose."

"Absolutely, and I didn't mean to break you two up. We can all sit together," Kenneth said.

"Don't worry, you're not breaking us up." Neda cast an encouraging glance at Amy and raised her glass when their eyes met. "Wish me a good adventure," she said and strutted away.

"Cheers," Kenneth replied.

"Don't go too far," Amy said.

"She seems cool," Kenneth added.

"She is."

They looked at each other after Neda left. His boyish small chin, clean shave, and small forehead made him look under the age of twenty-five. Amy placed her hands on the table, looking at them, then looked up at him, blushing.

"It's good to see you, Amy. I was beginning to think I would never see you again, until someone told me that they ran into you at a restaurant."

"You stayed in Texas to go to law school, I heard."

Kenneth nodded.

"I knew you were thinking of law school at first, but you never said anything about applying. You must have been applying in our last year. And we hung out a lot."

"I wasn't sure I could afford it, so I kept it to myself until Texas offered me a scholarship for the first year and in-state tuition for the rest."

"I'm glad they did."

"I sent you an invitation to my law school graduation."

"Where did you send the invitation, Ken?"

"I sent it to Elaine. She told me to send your invitation along with hers together and she would see that you got it. She actually confirmed later that she gave it to you. I thought you would take the opportunity to come see Austin again."

"I didn't get it; I would have come. Not to see Austin, but to see you," Amy said the latter part softly, and slowly, recalling that every time Kenneth's name came up in her conversations with Elaine, she was always the person who brought it up, not Elaine. They were briefly silent, as though each was waiting for the other to speak.

"Which law firm are you with?" Amy asked.

"I was at the Los Angeles Public Defender's Office, but I'm on my own now."

"That's impressive. You didn't think you should have stayed longer at the PD's to get more experience?"

"I was laid off my second year there," Kenneth replied. Amy wished she could take back her earlier comment about his decision, but his smile was amused rather than judgmental, and his gentle demeanor felt endearing.

"Cassandra told me you worked at the DA's, but I didn't believe her."

"Why?"

"I couldn't understand why you would choose the DA's office when you could work anywhere you wanted."

"I always wanted to be in public service, but I moved to LA for someone."

"What does your husband do?" Kenneth asked. Amy was briefly taken aback before she remembered the engagement ring on her finger. She looked at the ring and began fiddling with it.

"Richard and I broke up our engagement about a year ago," Amy said.

"I'm sorry to hear that."

Amy nodded, regretting having to admit it. "Thanks," she said.

"Care to talk about it?"

Amy shifted her attention to the rest of the club and shook her head slowly. The music turned to rhythm and blues.

She saw a very large man descending the stairwell, his legs covered in flowing white pants, then a rotund waist and fat arms under a white jacket. His stomach rose into his chest like the statue of an eastern deity, and his shoulders spread like a padded coat rack. She turned back to Kenneth. He was watching the same man. She looked down at her drink and began to tell him about Richard, a lawyer who graduated from Yale the same year she did and worked as a US attorney in LA.

"How about you?" she asked. "Have you settled down?" He raised his glass and drank his cocktail. A shadow passed over his face trailing a strobe light. "Or did someone break your heart?" she asked.

"Funny, you should ask that," he said.

"Why?"

"What if I said you did?"

"I'd say you're being very unfair." Amy searched him, but he just smiled. "Really?" Amy asked, suddenly curious about his answer.

"No," Kenneth said, resignedly. "You were the kindest person to me," he added.

He turned toward the bar as he set his glass down. It was her turn to follow his gaze, and she saw the big man staring at them from the bar where they had met. There were suddenly two white men standing close to him.

The big man seemed to be staring right at her. She returned her attention to Kenneth. "So, tell me, why haven't you settled down?"

Kenneth told Amy about the law student he dated the last year of law school. They had planned to get jobs in Washington, DC or Atlanta and live together for the first few years of their employment, possibly getting married three years afterward. When she got the job in DC and he did not, her priorities changed. She moved in with a law clerk she had met the summer before graduation. He also told her about the secretary at the public defender's office in Los Angeles, a single mother who saw so much promise in him as a deputy public defender, until the public defender's office terminated his position and he decided to start his own practice. She had moved on. He was tempted to tell her that after that his heart went into hibernation for what he thought would be an eternal winter but decided against it.

As he spoke, he cast occasional glances at the bar where the big man stood but returned quickly to their discussion. Amy felt his sadness, but there was also hope and confidence and energy in his voice.

Soon they were settling back into their old, confiding ways, sharing stories neither of them had shared with anyone in a long time. With Kenneth, Amy felt she had nothing to lose that had not been lost long ago. What embarrassing facts any alcohol-fueled state might reveal paled in comparison to what he knew or must have heard in their younger years.

She recalled inviting him to her twenty-first birthday party at the family estate in Atherton, California. Travel arrangements had been made for him, if he accepted, but he declined. It was after they had decided to become just friends.

"Here's to getting older," Amy toasted.

"That's easy for you to say, you don't look a shade older than when you were twenty-one," he said.

"Oh, stop. Women do own mirrors you know."

"Then you know I'm right."

"Alana respects me more though, now that I'm older," Amy told him. Kenneth had never met Amy's mother, but Amy had often talked about her. He said he thought she had always respected Amy, but Amy insisted it was more recent. "She used to call every day to find out what I wore, where I was going, what I was eating. It drove me insane. Now she only calls every other weekend."

"Maybe she just doesn't like you that much anymore," he said. They both laughed. "I'll be right back," he said, and was quickly on his feet. "Let me get us more drinks?"

"None for me. Thanks. I need to check up on Neda anyway."

"Promise you won't leave without giving me all your numbers."

She took out her pen and scribbled her cell phone, home, and office numbers on a napkin.

"I'll be here when you get back," she said.

In the time that she sat with Kenneth, she had forgotten about Goldie. She recalled the interviews in the police report, of patrons who claimed they did not see Paul Jackson at the club on the night Goldie was murdered. She looked toward the entrance and realized that people inside this section of the club could not have seen Paul exit the club. The room's exit opened into a corridor and one could not see the door to the street. About six feet of space separated the door to the street and the two doors, opposite each other, that opened to the sitting rooms. She got up and walked toward the back of the club where she saw the curved handrails of another set of stairs descending to the back of the club. It was entirely possible for Paul to enter the café from the street, turn into the room where she and Kenneth sat, climb upstairs and come down at the back, take the hallway from the back, and exit the club without being seen to have left by many patrons or those who saw him enter in the first place.

Amy found Neda sitting with three African American women and holding a cocktail of a different color than Kenneth had given her. Neda had once argued that Iranian women were "women of color" and she prided herself on her comfort in multiracial settings.

"Where's Kenneth?"

"He went to speak to someone," Amy explained and introduced herself to Neda's new friends, Shawna, Lynn, and Delores. "Two white guys that look like off-duty cops just walked in here and something tells me they're watching me."

"Is that guy by the door one of them?" one of the women asked. Amy turned around to see that one of the white men had followed her to the back of the club. Her palms began to sweat as the man started to approach their table, and her chest tightened to the thought that this stranger was about to focus attention on her.

"Grab a chair, Amy," the woman named Lynn said to her. Amy reached for the chair nearest her and turned it around as the man approached their table.

"Ma'am, are you Ms. Wilson?" the stranger asked.

"Who wants to know?" Neda asked.

"Mr. Clay."

"Shit," Amy muttered.

"Mmm, I'm guessing that ain't Kenneth," the woman named Shawna said.

"Sister please, ain't no brother named Clay who ain't gay," Delores said, and the African American women all laughed. "You feelin' me?" Lynn said through laughter.

Amy was not amused.

"He had you follow me here?" she asked the man in a raised voice before she realized how loud she had been.

"No, Ma'am. He said to tell you that he is outside."

Amy turned to look at Neda. "Take me to him," Amy said to the man and pointed toward the back exit where, according to Paul Jackson's alibi, he was able to come through without patrons inside the club knowing when he got to the club.

"I'll tell Mr. Clay that you're occupied. You go back to Kenneth and let him know you have to leave," Neda said, standing up.

"I'll take care of it," Amy protested, but Neda's hand was firmly on her shoulder pushing her down. As Neda walked away with the man, Amy excused herself from the African American women to return to Kenneth.

"Amy…Footsie, honey. You be honest with Kenneth about this Mr. Clay waiting outside, you hear?" Lynn said as Amy got up.

"Thanks, I will," Amy said and left them.

•••

"Who's this Farrah Fawcett?" Big asked Kenneth.

"Eh. Oh, just a friend from college."

"You know her well?"

"She's cool."

"I didn't ask you that."

"Yeah," Kenneth said. Big's expression suggested an elaboration was necessary. "I haven't seen her in a long time," Kenneth added, irritated by Big's curiosity.

"Well, you better be sure she's cool, nigger. You see them white boys that just got here? They're your company, and they're packing. You got it?"

"Yeah, thanks," Kenneth said.

"Go tell her a bedtime story. The drinks are on me."

"Sure, Big," Kenneth said, angrily. Big snapped his fingers twice to get the bartender's attention and Kenneth got his drinks immediately.

He joined Amy carrying a pair of cocktail glasses. He had been right behind her as she turned toward their booth in the crowded bar, but she had not noticed him. When their eyes met, he shrugged.

"That guy over there in the white suit bought us drinks. I couldn't say no."

"Why would he buy us drinks? Do you know him?"

"I know him, but he never bought a drink for me before. So, it must be you."

Amy looked toward the bar again and Big was still there but obscured from her view. Kenneth placed her drink in front of her.

"Well, tell him thanks for me, but I have to go Ken. Something came up."

"One last drink then."

"Are you trying to get me drunk, or is he?" Amy asked, bending her head toward the bar.

"I like you just the way you are right now, neither drunk nor sober," he said.

She smiled at him.

"I remember one night in Austin, after we saw that comedy troupe and returned to my apartment. You had had a bit to drink before we went to the theatre and at intermission you drank some more. Elaine later told me you were pretty drunk that night. But to me, you were so much more yourself than I had ever seen you…much sharper than when you let everything get to you. I thought, if anyone was going to take advantage of you, this was the wrong night to try."

Amy considered him for a while, her eyes looking directly into his.

"It crossed your mind?" she asked, smiling.

"No, no, no—" he protested, but she interrupted him.

"I remember thinking just the opposite," she said.

"Really?"

She smiled and shook her head, more in disbelief than disagreement.

"Really," she finally responded, nodding, "I have to go."

He stood up, too, as she collected her purse and her jacket, which was draped over the backrest of her chair. "Let me walk out alone," she said to him. "Someone came to pick me up and he's waiting outside with Neda."

"Those white guys by the bar came with him?" Kenneth asked.

She nodded.

"Yes. It is good to see you again, Ken."

"I'm glad Neda convinced you to come. Tell her she made my day." The sincerity with which he delivered lines like that always endeared him to her. She wanted to hold him, or just touch him, but she resisted the urge.

"So, call me?" she said.

"You can bet on that," he said, and came forward to give her a hug. They held on briefly. She buried her face behind his ear. Then she let go and started walking away without looking at him. Big was watching her when she turned the corner toward the bar and got a clear view of him again. At the door, she looked back toward Kenneth, still standing where she left him, his eyes on her. She pursed her lips playfully at him, and grinned.

CHAPTER ELEVEN
...And The Present

THE AIR OUTSIDE CAME with a gentle breeze of relief from the claustrophobic ambience inside the club. Amy had not noticed how much the crowded space affected her until she stepped outside. Thomas's SUV limousine was parked outside the curb right in front of the club. Beside it, Neda stood with Thomas in conversation, and the chauffeur waited to the side. The other man who had come into the club walked out after Amy and stood across the street, next to another black SUV.

"What the hell is this?" Amy said to Thomas, but he only smiled coolly and looked at Neda as though he had been discussing Amy's reaction with her.

"Amy, get in the car first," Neda said.

"Which car? I didn't come with him," Amy said, her voice rising slightly. Neda turned to look at the line at the entrance to the nightclub. The line of people going into the club appeared longer, and they were looking at Amy, Neda, and Thomas.

"Your mother was worried," Thomas said.

"My mother!"

"Let's talk about this inside the car," Thomas said.

"He's right, Amy," Neda said.

Amy turned from one friend to the other. "Let's go in your car," she said to Neda.

"I want to stay and get you intel," Neda said.

"I don't need your intel. We came together, we're leaving together."

Neda looked at Thomas and indicated he should wait. The two women walked across the road, and Thomas got in the car with his chauffeur.

"Don't shoot the messenger," Neda said. "He said you told him we were going to a movie and you would come to his hotel when we got out, but your mother called with a different story, and he wanted to confirm for her that she was wrong."

"Thomas is no one's messenger. He knows exactly what he's doing and using Alana as the excuse to do it."

"I would come, too, if I were him."

"Well, it wouldn't do either of you any good."

"Are you going to tell him about Kenneth?" Neda asked.

"There's nothing to tell," Amy said. Neda smiled, but Amy deliberately avoided looking directly at her.

"Those men who came inside told him you were with him and he thought you were just going to a movie with me."

"Good, then I don't need to tell him anything."

"Go back with him," Neda said. Amy looked at her and sighed.

At Neda's car, they hugged again.

"I really had fun. We should hang out in places like this more often," Neda said.

"What on Earth did you tell them to get us past that line?" Amy asked.

"I told them we are with the State Department and we were scouting locations to bring some African dignitaries visiting LA," Neda said with a big grin.

"No! You really have a State Department ID?"

Neda grinned and brought out her identity card for the district attorney's office. They both laughed. Amy recalled Neda showing her ID but thought she was just confirming her age, and the man at the gate had waived them through before Amy could bring out her ID.

"Hey, don't make a big deal about Thomas coming here. He'll think there's more to it."

Amy smiled but did not give Neda's suggestion much thought until she got in the car with Thomas. Looking at Thomas's expectant gaze, she sensed a confidence he had that she was going to react a certain way and decided to heed Neda's advice.

CHAPTER TWELVE
20/20

W HEN AMY GOT TO her office on Friday morning, Melissa was sitting in front of her desk with a stack of papers and a pen, apparently doing her work while waiting for Amy.

"Did you know about this listening device that was found at the victim's house in Kate's case?" Melissa asked, standing up.

"What listening device?"

"You didn't review the evidence list you gave the defendant?"

"I did, but I don't recall seeing any listening device."

"There were tiny microphones, the size of almonds, mentioned in one of the police officers' reports, but not anywhere else. I guess they weren't on the evidence list."

Amy opened her mouth to say something but was not sure what to say and took a deep breath instead. "Kate didn't tell you?" Melissa asked.

"We didn't really talk about what was collected at the scene."

Melissa continued to look at her rather distrustfully. "I see...well, the public defender called Gil about hiding evidence and Gil was not happy. They are filing a motion next week."

"What did Gil say?"

"He gave Kate an earful before she left for court this morning. This is unlike her. Usually she takes initiative and runs a tight ship."

"Should I go and see her in Pasadena?"

"No, she called a meeting with the officers in the case this afternoon. Don't make any lunch plans—by the way, the meeting is at noon. Kate will be coming back to the office from Pasadena for it," Melissa said and left, closing the door behind her. Shortly after she walked out, she opened the door abruptly and came back into the office. "Good timing. I was going to write you up if you got here a minute after nine a.m.," Melissa said and closed the door behind her a second time.

"I can be here earlier if you want me to," Amy said to an empty room. Then she sat down dejectedly and wondered how she missed the listening device.

A legal secretary came in to give Amy another message Kate left for her before going to court. It was a phone slip of a call from a radio station that had asked for Kate.

"What do they want?" Amy asked.

"They want to talk about the Jackson case."

"What kind of station is this?" Amy asked.

"Hip-hop, R&B."

Amy wondered whether the hip-hop station would be for Goldie or for Paul. She had never listened to Goldie's sample disc that Helen gave her. After a while, she returned to the secretary.

"Can you call them and make sure they won't put me on the air or record me while I'm talking to them, because I'm not authorized to say anything on the record."

The radio station told the secretary that the morning DJ was trying to get the district attorney's opinion on "why there was always a witness or something left at the scene of the crime when a Black man is accused of killing a white woman, but Lyle and Eric Melendez kill their mother and father with a 12-gauge shotgun and leave blood everywhere, then go to a movie, go to bars and a wine festival afterward, and nobody saw anything." The morning show was over when the secretary called, but they would pass on Amy's message to the DJ the next day.

"I think they were gonna record you or put you on the air no matter what. Even if they said they won't. I've heard this DJ record a lot of pranks like that."

"I am not calling them," Amy said and thanked her.

•••

Shortly before noon, the secretary came to get Amy. Officers Gonzalez and Fritz were in the conference room waiting for her.

"What about Kate?" Amy asked the secretary.

"She couldn't make it."

"Did she say how long she would be?"

"I don't think she's coming."

"But Kate called the meeting."

"I think something important came up in her case," the secretary said.

Amy was glad to see Melissa in the conference room with the officers.

"Kate had a last-minute change of plans and asked me to step in for her," Melissa explained as Amy entered the conference room. Amy nodded to Officer Gonzalez and introduced herself to Officer Fritz, who stood up and shook her hand.

"I figured we should start by laying everything about this case out in the open, so we don't run into another transparency issue like this again," Melissa said as they were all seated.

"How much has Kate told you guys?" Gonzalez asked.

"Besides what's in the record?" Amy asked.

"Besides that," Gonzalez said.

"Nothing," Amy said.

"Can you guys start with telling us if there's a whistleblower in your ranks? I want to know what else they'll be telling the defendant's lawyer, if they haven't told him already," Melissa said.

"There's no whistleblower. But we think someone saw or heard him when he killed her," Gonzalez said.

"Why do you think that?" Melissa asked.

"There's another item in this case that isn't in the complaint we filed," Gonzalez said.

"Besides the listening device that was partially listed?" Melissa asked. Gonzalez nodded, with a tight lip.

"What's the evidence?" Amy asked, convinced that Kate already knew.

"An electronic box that records or transmits the listening device," Gonzalez said, and sat back in his chair, which Fritz took as a cue to lean forward and start speaking.

Fritz brought out ten-by-ten inch pictures from a file and placed them on the table. Amy examined them as he spoke.

"We found this device in her bedroom under the mattress, looks like some computer listening device with a modem," Fritz said and pointed at the device in the picture. "We didn't know what it was and there was no serial number or brand name, just blank. We got some experts looking at it."

"Why was it not listed in the police report?" Melissa asked.

"I was afraid that the defendant's lawyers would start arguing that some professional people were after Goldie. This type of sophisticated device would just put a professional killer at the heart of this case," Gonzalez said.

"You realize that does not help your case right now—what you just said. The last thing this office needs is another big shot Black lawyer saying the LAPD left out a piece of evidence from this case. So, for fuck's sake—please tell me you've got a damn good reason for why you did not include evidence that shows someone might have seen or heard this crime being committed besides what's happening in O. J.'s case?" Melissa said.

"We didn't know who put it there, and we were sure it had nothing to do with the crime," Fritz said.

"And how the fuck were you so sure about that when you didn't know who put it there?" Melissa said.

"He would have taken it out if he knew about it," Fritz said.

"Whoever put that there is afraid to come forward," Gonzalez said.

"What would he be afraid of? Paul?" Amy asked.

"Or Paul's father's organization, or jail," Gonzalez said. "Maybe he was also secretly spying on her."

"Every door in that apartment complex opens into a courtyard where you can see every other door. Someone must have seen something, if not Paul Jackson, then the person who left the device. We think we'll find him before the trial," Fritz said.

"Do you have a lead on that?" Melissa asked.

"Not yet, but we think the girl next door knows something about it. That's why we leaned heavily on her," Fritz said.

"Rachel?" Amy asked.

"Yes, Alvarez thinks Rachel put the device there, not Goldie."

"Why?" Amy asked.

"She was the one looking after the apartment when Goldie went to London."

"She was pretty broken up that day. And she wanted to come in and see the dead woman's body, but we wouldn't let her. She kept begging us to let her come into the apartment anyway," Fritz said.

"Look, if it comes out that there is another thing in this proceeding that we didn't disclose, with the kind of media attention on your department and our office right now, we're looking at an acquittal," Melissa said.

"That's why I brought Fritz here to meet you. He called it from the very beginning. He said we should put everything in the report. I'm taking Alvarez off the case and putting Fritz in charge," Gonzalez said.

"What about the listening device, what do we do about it?" Amy asked.

"I think we go forward the way the record is right now and give them the small microphones but not the electronic box," Fritz said.

"I thought you wanted to disclose it from the beginning," Amy said.

"I did, but we didn't do that; now it's not a good idea," Fritz said.

Amy turned to Melissa, who appeared to force a smile.

"I'm going to discuss this with Kate when she gets back," Melissa said, sounding exhausted. "Thank you, guys."

Gonzalez and Fritz got up to leave. Fritz started to collect the pictures he had laid out on the table.

"Leave those there," Melissa snapped. "Please," she added calmly.

"I can't believe Kate knew this case had serious ethical fuck-ups when she asked me to loan you to her."

"Maybe she didn't know at that time," Amy said.

Melissa considered Amy for a moment.

"Whatever. To be honest with you, I'm pulling you from the case," Melissa said.

"I really want to be on it," Amy said. Melissa looked at Amy like she had no say in the matter. "If something else like this happens, then pull me. But Kate asked for me to be on this case for a reason. I don't know the reason, but I want to have her back…please."

"Suit yourself, but you report everything they ask you to do to me. Whether you tell Kate or not. And if they don't tell you, but you decide it on your own, you report yourself to me as well."

"I will."

Melissa got up to leave, collecting the pictures that Fritz left on the table.

"You said Kate had an emergency, I hope it wasn't anything serious."

"No, old gal friend with issues flew in from New York with some emergency she needed Kate's help on. The woman is a piece of work, I've met her before," Melissa said.

Amy sat in the conference room for a little while after Melissa left. She wondered what Melissa would tell Kate about the meeting and decided to stay out of a fight between the two of them.

•••

THE PUBLIC DEFENDER'S MOTION seeking to examine and inspect the listening device found at Goldie Silberberg's apartment was on Amy's desk when she returned to the office. Judge Pollazo had set the hearing for Monday, upon the request of the public defender to expedite the hearing. Amy went to work, preparing her office's response the rest of the day and the weekend.

CHAPTER THIRTEEN
Truth or Truce

ON THEIR DRIVE BACK from the nightclub, Thomas again explained that he had only come to confirm that Amy told Alana she was going to Cool Jo's Café in jest. He fully expected that his scouts, as he called them, would not see Amy at Cool Jo's Café, and he was just as surprised as they were to see her there. Contrite and remorseful, he was also firm that he had done nothing wrong. The only thing he said that was vaguely accusatory was when he asked Amy when he would meet Kenneth Brown, calling him by his name in full. "It's only fair, if I fly all the way here to watch him spend Thursday night with my gal. I should meet him," he said and chuckled. At that point Amy asked if she could be dropped off at her apartment instead of going to the Ritz, and Thomas did not object. The next day, Alana called and Amy could not quite explain why she was angry that Thomas came to Cool Jo's Café. It was Alana she was angry with but took it out on Thomas. "Did it have anything to do with whomever you were seeing there?" Alana had asked.

"You would think that of your daughter, wouldn't you, mother?" Amy asked.

"Of course not, I'm trying to help you explore your subconscious motivation."

"Please don't," Amy said. She explained that she had not lied to Thomas about going to Cool Jo's Café, not deliberately. The idea to go to Cool Jo's Café occurred to her while she was speaking with Alana after she left Thomas's hotel, and she left it up to Neda to decide if they would go. Had Alana not involved herself unnecessarily, Thomas would not have seen her in such bad light. She would simply have told him that she and Neda had had a change of plans when they met. This was not just something she made up to tell Alana, but something she told herself as well when she realized that what paternalism she had accused Thomas of was misplaced. She decided to make it up to him with dinner at her apartment. Then suddenly Alana said, "Thomas thinks you should ask to be taken off of this case."

Amy was not sure she heard Alana properly.

"Thomas thinks I should be taken off what case?"

"That Jackson case you said that woman assigned to you. He said you can ask to be reassigned and it wouldn't be a big deal."

"How does he know that? How does he know the name of the case?"

"He said your friend told him the man accused in the case you were assigned owns the nightclub."

"But I never told her the name of the case."

"It is not that hard to find out the name of the man who owns the club. What I am trying to say is this case is not worth all the trouble it has brought you in the short time you have been on this new job. Why not get rid of it?"

"And you discussed that with Thomas?"

"Not really; he mused about it, and I listened silently, but I want you to know I agree with him."

"What exactly did he say?"

"He said he found you in an area of Los Angeles where people stood in lines to be searched for weapons before they went into a nightclub. He couldn't imagine mixing with that crowd during the day when they are sober, much less at night and while they are getting drunk."

"That would explain why he's never taken me dancing at least," Amy said.

"There are many decent places to go dancing that are not like that…"

"In LA, mother, they all check you before you go into any nightclub."

Saying this to Alana gave Amy pause. She wondered if Alana rather than Thomas had come up with the angle about mixing with the crowd during the day. It sounded much like what Alana would say. Thomas would know it was routine in any nightclub. Thus, as was common with her, enlisting Amy's friends with or without their consent and employing any artifice she could get her hands on, Alana was back trying to direct Amy's life. Amy decided she would not get into an argument with her about it, but wait to see what Thomas had to say about the matter. She hung up the phone with Alana and sat down to collect herself. Moments when she got into arguments she never could win with Alana, or when she could not tell Alana exactly what she felt for fear of getting into such an argument, consumed her with self-loathing. She must patiently wait out these moments to regain normalcy. Recently, she found strength in dismissing Alana without arguing with her and doing exactly the thing that Alana demanded she not do, but that, too, was not without self-loathing. The condition was just far less than before. She did not have to wait it out too long.

Food as the perfect foil for the evening brought relief. She would use it to show maturity and composure and calmly explain her frustrations about the nightclub, but once Thomas arrived, these considerations no longer mattered. She made a quip about her food not being intended to meet his Michelin-star restaurant tastes, and he showed genuine surprise that it in fact did. It was the first time she had made anything other than snacks for him, which made it their most intimate dining. She cursed herself silently but did not really mind it. Soon she was her usual self with him. She thought of what Alana had said about the Jackson case and decided to set some ground rules around her involvement in the case and this relationship with Thomas. Perhaps, she was testing him as well, but she had not thought of it in that way. He asked what was on her mind, and she told him she would need a break from surprise visits until she could settle into this case. Her new boss was "being an ass she could not afford to slip up on." Rather than tell her to ask to be reassigned, Thomas consoled her.

After dinner, she curled into a yoga pose on one end of the sofa, muted the volume on the television, and turned on the music he liked, Coltrane. He urged her to come into his arms, but she had something urgent to say to him, she said.

"I've been struggling with trying to understand why I was so angry with you at the nightclub. Since Neda already told you how we ended up there instead of the plans we made, I'll skip that part...I'm really sorry I did." She uncurled herself and reached for her wine, then returned facing him directly.

"The reason, I think is...I started off...I don't think of you as someone I am dating, I think of you as someone I would like...someone I want to be the mate I spend the rest of my life with, but I'm not sure I'm ready for marriage at all. Not as sure as I was before I met Richard. I'm not even sure I know what kind of person that life mate I'm looking for is supposed to be. Except that he should be someone I could work things out with as they develop."

"I'd like to think we could work anything out together," Thomas said.

"I thought I could with Richard, too. God knows he wasn't perfect, and neither was I, but I thought we could work things out. Turns out I was wrong. Gosh, was I ever. So right there is the tension. You've emerged as the kind of companion any girl would like to spend the rest of her life with, but I've become entirely shy about marriage. And it all makes me frustrated, especially when people like Alana treat me like I should belong to you already. That part really brought out the beast in me."

"Let me stop you right there. I have never treated you that way."

"Really? If you should fly all the way here to watch an old classmate spend Thursday night with your gal?"

"That was a joke, specifically intended to reflect a different mindset."

"I want to believe you."

"Believe it. And while we're at it, I'll stop listening to your mother. I only acted out of respect for her."

Amy liked that he said that, an honest acknowledgement that he had been wrong and the appreciation of what it meant to her.

"Don't blame Alana for all of it. A part of you really came to confirm the bad news you suspected of me."

"Did I?"

He reached for her hand, but she pulled it away from him.

"Come closer, I want to hold you," he said.

"You come closer," she said.

He untied his shoes and took them off, then laid down with his head on her interlocked feet, and she placed a small cushion to make him comfortable.

"Thomas, I think I was angry with you because I didn't want to lose my freedom, which I feared I had already lost."

"When did you lose your freedom? Is that what they call it these days?"

She slapped him lightly, and he turned on his elbow to look up at her for a moment.

"I am fully aware that I have not completely won your heart over yet. And you've lost nothing if you haven't given your heart to me. Don't worry, I'm up for the fight."

"With whom?"

"College boy."

"Thomas!"

"You just said he was your college classmate."

"He is also a lawyer."

"I know that—"

"Don't call him that again."

"Lighten up, Amy, it's not like he's here to hear it."

"I heard it. Do not refer to him like that again."

They were quiet for a moment. Thomas sat up.

"How did you know he was a lawyer?" she asked.

Thomas hesitated. "Neda might have mentioned it."

"Neda didn't know that."

"Maybe one of the scouts then. Someone mentioned it last night. Why? That's not hard to find out."

"Even with a very common name?"

Thomas shook his head.

"Amy, ever since Keynesian economics surmised that the rich saved and the poor spent, getting personal information on someone like him is as difficult as reciting a nursery rhyme."

"Like him…" Amy repeated slowly as though it were a question.

"Anyone of humble means for that matter. I don't make up the rules. The point is businesses are served the identities and habits of destitute men on a platter all the time. We acquire databases of consumer information from people who think they are getting free stuff or services in return."

"So, you've looked into it?"

"No, but I'm saying that I won't have to invade anyone's privacy or even bend the law to do so. If I call my assistant right now she can get you all the information you need about him."

•••

LATE IN THE EVENING, Neda called assuming Thomas had left.

"He's still here, can I call you back?"

"Oh, you slut; take a break for goodness sake."

"Guess which finger I am holding up, Neda?"

"Your thumb?"

"Guess again."

After Amy hung up, she asked Thomas if he would like to hear Goldie's music and Thomas said he would. She placed Goldie's music disc into her compact disc player, and Goldie's voice filled the living room, singing a ballad titled, "You've Been Cruel Again."

> You've been cruel again
> You've been cruel again
> Without knowing what you do you've been cruel again to me
> With your beauty
> Your humility
>
> …
>
> But I'm with him
> And you're with her
> We both love them, too
> Still it hurts when you smile at me
> You've been cruel again / …

Amy and Thomas kept exchanging silent glances at the beautiful resonance of Goldie's full voice and her seductive rendition of the lyrics.

"I can see why you feel a connection to this case," Thomas said after the song ended.

"Really, why?"

"She sounds beautiful and unapologetic about what her heart wants."

Amy smiled coyly.

Shortly afterward she returned to the Ritz with Thomas to allow him a more comfortable rest before his trip to Asia.

CHAPTER FOURTEEN
Reboot

T HE HEARING ON THE public defender's motion to examine the listening device took less fanfare than the arraignment. The courtroom was largely empty. Mallam Jackson and his men did not make it to court for the 2:00 p.m. schedule. Sister Ramatu and Jo sat in the gallery. Joanna Lark appeared for the public defender, and Mr. Jones continued to appear especially for the family, or so he claimed. Kate appeared for the district attorney's office, with Amy by her side. Four lawyers for the Associated Press, Inc., who had made a special request to be heard by the court that morning, were sitting on the row reserved for lawyers.

Judge Pollazo was again his humorless self. He explained that he saw no harm to the defendant if the office of the district attorney could make the device available as Kate had promised, but he asked the parties to argue the point that the district attorney deliberately concealed the devices to gain an advantage.

"Your Honor, we were as surprised as everyone else to discover the device, and in the abundance of caution decided to send it off for a battery of tests, for prints, other analyses, etc. Not having received the results of those tests back, and as you rightly pointed out, knowing there was sufficient evidence to charge the defendant without the device, we proceeded to file the complaint. There was no deliberate attempt to hide anything. The device is not part of our case," Kate said.

"If the device is not part of their case, your Honor, why did they send it off for further analyses?" Joanna asked.

"In the abundance of caution, like I just said," Kate said.

"Nothing stopped you from notifying the public defender that you were doing so while you ran the tests," Judge Pollazo said.

"You are right, your Honor. But we have not denied the existence of the device and have every intention of handing it over to the defense. It is not like we have had a conviction here and they discovered it. They found out about it before the preliminary hearing, precisely because we made no effort to hide it."

"Your Honor, this device was not even mentioned in the full police report," Joanna said.

"But now it has been brought to light. What is the harm?" Kate asked, seemingly addressing herself to Joanna.

"The harm is in your disregard of the defendant's right to exculpatory evidence that could have prevented his arrest. What else are you guys not showing us?" Joanna asked. Amy cringed at the question, recalling the insurance policies.

"You can save that argument for your trial, counsel. I would think it would be effective to a jury," Judge Pollazo said. This response seemed to quiet the argument of counsel. "I have decided to take the matter under submission and will be issuing my ruling later today. Does counsel wish to add anything?" Judge Pollazo asked.

All the attorneys shook their heads and then in turns said: "No, your Honor."

Big was sitting alone on one of the benches in the hallway when Amy and Kate came out of the courtroom behind Jo and Sister Ramatu.

"Judge Pollazo will rule against us. You know that, right?" Kate said when she got out of the elevator with Amy and there was no one close to hear them.

"Why?" Amy asked.

"He didn't have to take the matter under submission. Joanna did not say anything that wasn't already in their motion, and the judge had all weekend to think about his decision."

"Why didn't he just rule immediately?" Amy asked.

"To buy us time to make sure we are ready to re-arrest him. He'll rule this afternoon," Kate said.

"What would you like me to do?" Amy asked.

"Officer Gonzalez is standing by. I want you there also when they make the arrest. I'll probably be in court when his ruling comes out," Kate said. Amy nodded and thought immediately of Helen Silberberg. Having nothing more to discuss with Kate, she returned to her office.

On her desk was a message slip from the receptionist, stating that one Kenneth Brown had called her three times already. It brought a smile to her face for the first time that morning.

CHAPTER FIFTEEN
The Drag

Amy and Kenneth met in Alhambra for lunch. Kenneth had wanted to stop by downtown, but Amy suggested they meet in Alhambra instead. Downtown Los Angeles was the long route to Long Beach from Rancho Cucamonga, where Kenneth was in court, but Alhambra was on his way.

The city of Alhambra lies a few miles northeast of Los Angeles, where the white neighborhoods of South Pasadena and San Marino towns melt into diverse Asian and Hispanic communities. Commercial structures and residential buildings sprout side by side on Alhambra's major streets. The structures are smaller and the streets are narrower. Mom-and-pop stores and small non-brand, non-franchise retailers thrive on every corner, but mostly along the city's main artery—Valley Boulevard. Tacos, sushi, dim sum, and pho vie for noontime appetites within the same city blocks.

Driving to Alhambra, Amy recalled how she had met Kenneth her first year in college at an open house for students interested in going to the law school. How could she have forgotten that he had an interest in attending law school? She had mentioned meeting him at the event to Elaine, with whom she shared an apartment off Red River Street at the time. Notwithstanding there were over twenty thousand students at the university, Elaine knew him, too, and told Amy that he had been in a history class that she and Amy both dropped their first semester on campus. Amy began to realize the odd affinity between her and Kenneth even then.

Attendees at the event had been asked to indicate by a show of hands how close they were to making a decision about law school when the host called out each class from the seniors to the freshmen. She and Kenneth were the only college freshmen at the open house. They hardly spoke at the event but sat close to each other at different presentations on the law school campus, and toward the end walked together from one event to the other. The following weekend, Elaine asked Amy to meet her at the coffee shop they called their own, off a popular street nicknamed the Drag in Austin, without mentioning that Kenneth was coming, too. Amy was surprised when Elaine showed up with him and introduced them again. They sat in the café until closing, and then stood around Amy's parked car and talked for another hour or so before they all got in the car and dropped him off on their way home.

She knew then she wanted to see him again, and often. At times that night when their eyes met while they chatted, she felt he wanted the same as well, or rather he would be satisfied with nothing more than the pleasure of more of their company. They amused and challenged and encouraged each other without ever judging or arousing each other's insecurities, she recalled. He seemed sometimes oblivious of Elaine, because he would stare right at Amy, and as much as Amy tried to maintain that gaze to let him know she was up to the challenge as well, she could not with Elaine present. When they dropped him at his apartment, he thanked them and asked for her number. His directness in spite of Elaine caught Amy off-guard, and she said the first thing that came to her mind.

"You don't have anything to write it on."

"I do," he said reaching into his pocket. "Besides I'll remember it without writing it down."

She blushed and said, "It's the same as Elaine's; we're housemates." And she drove off without giving it to him.

"Who the hell told you that cat has my number or that I have his?" Elaine asked, amused.

"You invited him to our café. How did you do that without his number?"

"Walked up to him and said hey, want to join me and my housemate for coffee later? Would you believe he actually would not accept until I told him who my housemate was? Like, hello…I should be enough for your sorry ass!"

"Well, you know him better than I do?"

"Why because he's Black? Do I know half the football players, too? And don't even think of answering that!"

"Okay, I'm sorry. I didn't know what to say."

"Really? You, Amy Wilson, in a red Mercedes coupe that makes half the boys in school grab their crutch behind your back, did not know what to say to this poor cat?"

"Eeew! Don't ever associate me with that image again. Yes, I did not know what to say; sue me."

•••

KENNETH GOT TO ALHAMBRA before noon and sat in his old Ford Mustang rewriting his notes from a long list of messages from his office; courts that needed information on documents he had filed, attorneys with questions on their mutual cases, and clients seeking information. What Nancy could not respond to she passed on to him, and in between court appearances or during recesses he used the pay phones to address these issues. A cell phone was still a luxury expense, but one he planned on acquiring soon. Meanwhile, his electronic pager sufficed to keep him connected to his office.

He did not see Amy drive into the parking lot, but he saw her getting out of her car. Her hair was in a ponytail. She turned to open the door to the backseat of her car and appeared to look directly at him seated behind the wheel two rows away. He looked away sheepishly. Out of the backseat of her car, she pulled her jacket with one hand and lifted her handbag with the other, closing the door by kicking it with her heel as she turned away and headed toward the front of the courthouse. She had this way of walking that seemed like her heels were unsteady every time she placed them on the ground to lift them again, and it made her seem to sway ever so delicately from side to side in a manner both sensual and apologetic.

He let her enter the courthouse before he got out of his car and walked around the courthouse to meet her in front as they had agreed. She had chosen the Thai restaurant she knew from her time in West Covina.

"The other night I felt like I was back at the Drag in Austin, like we used to do, except without Elaine. I wanted to make sure that I wasn't dreaming," he told her.

"It was good to see you, too," she said after a long pause.

No sooner than they were seated and had ordered their food did he start to pry into the most intimate conversations they had on Saturday night.

"Are you seeing any one seriously?" he asked

"Excuse me?"

"You mentioned the other night that you didn't marry your fiancé, but you didn't say if you were seeing any one seriously."

"I am…sort of."

"Sort of…?" he asked.

Amy chuckled and turned her attention elsewhere in the restaurant.

"You don't want to talk about it?" he asked.

"No, I figured you haven't bought me lunch yet, so…" Amy said.

"When I first moved to LA, Elaine told me that you were getting married to someone picked for you at your debutant ball."

"Well, they picked the wrong man, didn't they?"

"And now?"

"Is this the new Kenneth Brown? You don't beat around the bush anymore."

"This is all I've thought about since I ran into you this weekend."

"You've thought about who I was seeing with my family's blessing?"

"No, how odd it was that we were running into each other again, after all these years. And what it could mean."

"What else could it mean but a continuation of our friendship?"

"We weren't just friends…in my mind, you know. Friendship with you was probably the hardest thing for me until I finally had the courage to confess it to you…but by then it was too late, or so you wanted me to believe."

She looked at him quizzically.

"I wouldn't want to lose sight of you again," he continued.

"I have a rather jealous boyfriend."

"You're not the type."

"Really?" she asked. "Don't be too sure you know me so well, Ken."

"Was he the one who came to the club with those bodyguards?"

"Yep, that's the one," Amy said.

"I'm not about to give up hope just because someone else is equally interested."

"Equally interested, that's a rather self-important perspective, isn't it?"

"I'm just being honest about how I see it."

"And as far as he's concerned, I'm spoken for."

"How about you?"

"Nice of you to finally factor me into the equation. What about me?"

"As far as you're concerned?"

She laughed as though the question had tickled her. "I agree with him," she said in an amused voice.

"Elaine said I accepted your answer too easily the night I told you how I'd felt about our friendship; she said I gave in too quickly."

"She said that, huh?"

"I won't do that again."

"But we're not in a college anymore, Ken."

"We never closed that chapter, Amy. If we did, you'd be married by now."

This took Amy aback. "Please explain," she said.

"I can't understand why any man in his right mind would break an engagement with you. That tells me it's your cold feet that are keeping you from settling down."

"Again, the new you, even the humility is gone."

Kenneth laughed.

"Well, it may be cold feet, but I can assure you it's not because I'm waiting for some man."

"I'm not saying you are or that I'm the man. I am hoping...actually, I may have dreamt it."

In that moment they sat staring at each other, as if each was trying to understand how seriously the other was taking this conversation. Their lunch was served.

"I like your theory...believe me I do. But I am seeing someone," Amy said after they had sampled their food.

"What does he do?"

"He runs his father's company… He's the CEO of some conglomerate. Why?"

"Just curious. What kind of company?"

"It's a holding company with many subsidiaries. Some insurance related, I think."

"Tell him I won't just let him walk away with you."

"Why don't you tell him yourself, when you meet him."

"Good, so we will meet then."

"I'm hoping we can remain good friends, even if we don't…" She seemed unable or rather unwilling to finish the sentence, putting food in her mouth before she was done speaking.

"So am I," he said. Then, as though to lighten their exchange, he reached into his pocket. "I brought something for you."

Amy looked at him expectantly, as he brought out a picture of Elaine's baby and handed it to her. She immediately brought her hands to her chest as though to control her emotions. Tears appeared to glaze her eyes.

"She's beautiful."

Kenneth smiled, and suddenly wished Elaine was there with them.

Lunch was a much longer affair than either of them had anticipated. They spent most of the time again talking about old friends and college, the practice of law and what they would have done instead if they had not become lawyers. He said he would have continued studying economics and become a teacher. She was not so sure, perhaps a career in politics as an advocate for children or the diplomatic service if she could get in. He told her he was ready to settle down, and it made her blush.

The court's lunch recess was over when they began their stroll back to the courthouse where they parked. He no longer had to go back to court for the rest of the day, and Amy was still waiting for the call from Judge Pollazo and was checking her phone constantly throughout the lunch. Kenneth became aware of the people watching them, or at least observing them, as they strolled back: cop across the street, patrons seated by the windows of the restaurants they passed by, a shopkeeper or two, the boy in baggy jean, but Amy seemed oblivious of them, if not content to be watched under the circumstances.

•••

THE LOS ANGELES DISTRICT Attorney's Office was a short walk from the Los Angeles Police Headquarters, and on returning to the office late from lunch, Amy decided to add another off-site assignment to justify how long she had been out of the office. She went to see Officer Gonzalez without calling ahead. Gonzalez was in a meeting, but when he heard that Amy had come to see him, he left the meeting immediately.

"I took the detectives off standby because of the ruling," Gonzalez said as he approached Amy, who was perplexed by his comment.

"You heard from the judge?" Amy asked.

"No, the sheriff in the courtroom. He said the judge ruled for us."

"The decision must have been faxed to the office, then. I came here from lunch."

She thanked Officer Gonzalez and hurried back to the office. At the office, Judge Pollazo's faxed decision was on her desk. He had directed the district attorney's office to file supplemental charging documents by 10:00 a.m. on Wednesday morning, including all the information about the device, or the case against the defendant would be dismissed with prejudice.

Amy took a deep breath and sank farther into her chair, realizing that this ruling had her working all evening again.

CHAPTER SIXTEEN
Co-Counsel

Professor Cassandra Rayburn's house was one of a few remaining bungalows on the hilly side of Sherman Oaks. A little white cottage on a small green hill at the border of Encino and Sherman Oaks, hedged against erosion with various plants and small trees, on a side street from Sepulveda. It overlooked the exact point where a road split to form two streets, each of which could have provided an appropriate address for the house, but for the fact it had a determined front on one of the streets. On this front side, quite a climb awaited visitors, up twenty or more steep stairs of rugged stone Anthony had put together without a handrail.

"A little old lady owned it before us," Cassandra once explained to her small group of friends while they were having dinner. She bought the house with her brother Anthony shortly after law school. Anthony's future wife, Mary, was their roommate. Anthony and Mary got married and moved out, leaving Cassandra and her English mastiff, Sam, to a fee simple in the little cottage.

Sam, the gentle mastiff, was nearing the end of his life, Cassandra suspected. She no longer took Sam out through the front door, with its steep stairway, and she no longer jogged with Sam, either. Kenneth knocked on the front door, and Sam rose with a grunt from where he sat by Cassandra's ankle. Sam must have sensed it was a familiar visitor because his tail was already wagging before the door was opened, but he stood a fair distance behind Cassandra, waiting for their mutual friend to come to him.

"How's he doing?" Kenneth asked Cassandra, a sensitive subject for the professor.

"He's right there, ask him."

Not well, Kenneth reckoned, and taking a dog biscuit from Cassandra, fed Sam. Cassandra opened the sliding door that led into the garden, and Sam managed to skip happily onto the grass with his biscuit.

"How are you?" Kenneth asked, "…or should I ask Sam, too?"

"I'm sorry. I'm fine. The damn veterinarians won't give me any specifics on his pain, and they won't tell me if it is getting worse or better."

"They probably sensed that you don't really want to know."

"Yeah, well that's not their job. How are you?"

"I got the file in the Jackson case."

"Is that what you have in that box?"

"You don't seem impressed," Kenneth said.

"I thought you brought me a box of flowers."

"Maybe next time, but guess who I ran into a couple of days ago? Amy Wilson," Kenneth said and pushed the box toward Cassandra.

"The woman I met at the restaurant with Melissa?"

Kenneth nodded.

"Melissa never put you in touch with her?" Cassandra asked, opening the box and examining its contents. As Kenneth did not answer, she looked up at him.

"I ran into her at Paul Jackson's club," Kenneth said. Cassandra seemed surprised. "Exactly. I saw her walk right by me and it took me a moment to register. Then I followed her, and, of course, it was her."

"Did this come up?" Cassandra asked, referring to the box between them.

"Why would it come up?"

"What was she doing at the club?"

"Her friend dragged her there on a whim."

"And?"

"We spent the night catching up on the years since college. I can't honestly recall anything we talked about." Cassandra raised her eyebrows. She took two cans of beer out of her refrigerator and offered one to Kenneth, then went to sit on the couch. Kenneth followed her.

"Are you planning on seeing her again anytime soon?"

"We had lunch."

107

"You do realize that Tiffany and the gang are going to roast you for being over the moon for a DA?"

"I'm not over the moon, and she's spoken for."

"Excuse me?"

"She's seeing someone."

"I know…what was that phrase you used?"

"Her words, not mine."

"Ah, I see. Have you accepted this case?"

"I told them I have, but the PD filed a motion about a device that was not disclosed, and the judge ordered supplemental filing. Mr. Jones will withdraw completely this coming week after the filing."

Cassandra appeared to be studying him.

"I need you on this case, now. Casey, you planted this idea in my head. Now, help me grow it."

"I said I was going to help."

"No, I need you fully in it as co-counsel."

"The idea I planted was for you to use this opportunity to showcase your full potential, rather than continue this struggle of a failed businessman trying to run a law practice like it was some radical liberal movement."

"And I will, but I need your commitment that if for any reason I am unable to continue, you will take the reins."

"Whoa!" Cassandra waived her hands in the air. "First of all…no. Second of all, what the hell are you talking about?"

"Casey, I want a situation where we are both in court on every witness examination, every motion, every piece of evidence, even if I am the one presenting or doing the examination."

"What was the part about you being unable to continue, the part where I take the reins."

"Casey, just come into the case with me. I feel we can win it. Let me tell you what I found out."

"The operative word is 'we,' Kenneth. We are either in this together or I am not in it at all."

"Agreed."

"I will sign on as full co-counsel after this Mr. Jones is out."

"Thank you, you won't regret it."

"I don't intend to."

She drank her beer, then began to go through the box of files. Kenneth sat down and drank as well.

"Did you ever wonder why I brought that woman's number to you?"

"I thought she mentioned that she knew me."

"She wondered, I suppose. I wasn't even talking to her about you, but her reaction when I mentioned her name, made me think you were an item in law school, only to find out it was as far back as college."

"When I ran into her, it was like we were back in college and nothing mattered but us."

CHAPTER SEVENTEEN

Flowers

WHEN AMY GOT HOME from the hearing, an Asian woman and her two attendants were in her lobby, and a van full of flowers was in the driveway, waiting for her. Thomas Clay Jr. had ordered them and she had come herself to arrange the flowers in a way that complimented Amy's space, the woman explained.

Asked how many flowers she was delivering, she pleaded with Amy not to send them back. This was the best piece of business the shop had done in two months, and her two attendants were looking forward to their commissions from the delivery already. She beseeched Amy in a voice that wavered between song and speech. Amy agreed, but soon regretted it when she saw the carts of bouquets, boxes, and vases that were being wheeled into her apartment.

"Where are you going to fit all that?"

"It's okay, trust me, it will be very pretty, very pretty, you will feel like a bride every morning." Amy wanted to ask the florist why she thought a bride in the morning felt better than she usually felt in the morning, but the florist was speaking too quickly without stopping and working her hands rapidly, cutting, putting blue hydrangeas with the white Casablanca lilies, pink peonies and purple lisianthus with a scattering of stephanotis, and barking orders to her assistants, who ran out and came back with taller vases and different flower stands.

"Roses can't stand being alone, they are prettier with other flowers. Lilies are like the sun in your living room—they brighten any day. Gardenias in your kitchen will inspire your cooking. Trust me, trust me," the florist kept saying as she worked.

Having planned a wedding, Amy knew something of these flowers and what it took to fill her apartment with them. She found herself admiring the tulips and peonies and lilies of the valley as she watched the florist. On the center table in her living room were two sets of different white flowers mixed with roses in arrangements that were so identical it was difficult to distinguish between the sets without looking closely.

"They will fill your house with the aromas of heaven," the florist said, waiving her hands over the set of arrangements Amy was admiring.

"You don't have to leave them all here, just tell him you delivered them anyway and I saw them," Amy protested, but Thomas's agreement with the florist was that he would pay for as much as they were able to make Amy take, provided they got him proof by photographing the placement. Photographing the pieces did it for Amy. She asked the florist and her assistants to leave immediately. The florist thanked her profusely anyway. If Amy ever needed to send flowers or have them delivered, she would give Amy a huge discount.

Thomas was certainly no Richard, Amy thought. She sat down and wondered what the appropriate response to him should be. The arrangements on the center table recalled the florist's words: lilies are like the sun in your living room. They are beautiful, she thought. In her bedroom, her nightstands on either side of the bed had two large arrangements that included peonies mixed with tulips, at the foot of her bed a pot of mainly gardenias, so green in arrangement that it looked like a vegetable plant rather than a flower. She could not reach Thomas, who was still in Tokyo. He must have known to give her time because he called the following morning, when the first thing Amy saw as she woke up was the beautiful arrangement of peonies on her nightstand. Along with the sun shining into the room, they filled her room with a palpable sense of divine grace and put her in a compassionate mood. Thomas said he hoped Amy liked the flowers.

"I do. Thank you."

"You are welcome."

"Are these flowers still about what happened back at the nightclub?" Amy asked.

"No, when I called on Saturday you were at the office for some important thing you had today. The flowers are just to say you have been on my mind incessantly, and I hope your hearing went well."

"Thank you, it went even better than I expected."

"I'm glad. And I told the florist to keep replacing the flowers until at least the summer."

"I won't see you before the summer?"

"Of course you will, but I'm not there enough and you are not here enough, so the flowers will do for the time being."

"The florists are not allowed in my apartment again."

"They won't come with so many next time."

"They won't come at all. My humble abode is practically a nursery of your making. But I like it. Thanks."

They were silent for a moment. Amy wondered if there was more to the flowers than Thomas was telling her.

"Are you coming this way on your way back from Tokyo?"

"I have to go to Seoul and then Singapore from here. Then New York."

"What else are these flowers about, Thomas?"

Thomas was again quiet for a while before he spoke.

"You know what, I'll scratch Seoul and Singapore and come to LA first."

"Good, but you are not keeping me in suspense until then."

"Sure, but I can't talk more right now. I've stayed away from my dinner guests rather long."

Amy searched for what to say without rushing him.

"You'll call me when you get back from work?" he asked. Amy murmured her acquiescence, then hung up. She had wanted him to say what else the flowers were for because she also wanted to tell him that she saw Kenneth again, but just for lunch. Then the somber weight of his tone as he admitted there was something else caused a mild consternation in her that lunch was a far greater betrayal than she thought. Did he already know? Was he watching her? Thomas kept investigators and security agencies on his phone's speed dial, but he knew better than to invade her privacy. If he was watching anyone, he was watching Kenneth. At moments like these, Amy wished she and Alana were still confidants like when she was in college.

She could tell Alana everything then. Well, almost everything—sometimes she pretended she was asking for a friend who needed the advice but didn't dare to ask her parents. Even then, she knew Alana could tell the friend was a fictional representation of Amy but would still, gracefully, share her thoughts on the matter earnestly and without judgment.

All that ended when Alana tried to reconcile Amy with Richard, her fiancé, without Amy's permission. According to people Richard spoke to on the matter, Alana went so far as to plead with him to save the family the embarrassment of canceling the wedding, and rather break-up afterward. Alana would deny this, of course. Amy only found out when Richard left a message on her answering machine asking her to tell Alana to give him some space. Since then, Amy had not confided in Alana or anyone else on intimate social matters, swearing never again to give anyone the license to think they knew her so well that they could so act on her behalf. She had sentenced her heart to social isolation with time alone as her companion, only emerging because of Thomas's relentless pursuit, therapy, and a sworn agreement with Alana that she would never again interfere in her social affairs. This current state of affairs with a commitment to Thomas and endearment to Kenneth was different and nothing like she had ever experienced. Alone while crowded by men, she needed a confidant of feminine extraction to sift through this developing mess.

•••

PERHAPS NO ONE ELSE at the Los Angeles District Attorney's Office had a better collection of fine wines. Amy's collection was courtesy of her father, who didn't visit without bringing one bottle at least and making a point of replenishing them. Amy got up and poured herself a drink, then called Neda.

"Hey, can you stop by my apartment on your way home from work tomorrow?"

"Do you want to do happy hour?"

"No, I have a filing on Wednesday. Just come by, I have something to show you. It'll be quick."

"Okay, this better be good."

"What do you have to lose?"

"My precious time."

"Or a great bottle of wine."

"I'll be there."

•••

ALL DAY AMY WAS impatient about calling Thomas back. When she was not working on the new charging documents, her mind stressed on all sorts of ideas for what Thomas was going to tell her, but none seemed plausible. Had she misjudged the effect the incident at Cool Jo's Café had on him? He frowned at Neda's suggestion that he join them next time they went to the nightclub, which Amy had taken as his further derision of the incident. Kenneth did not help matters by repeatedly calling her, but she would not take his calls, not while she was anticipating calling Thomas. Taking Kenneth's call would leave her feeling like she was juggling affairs. She cringed at the thought. The fact Thomas's flowers had arrived on the heels of her seeing Kenneth again after the nightclub still troubled her. Perhaps that was why she accepted more flowers from the florist than she ordinarily would. Thomas was competitive. He was up for the fight, he had said. Why would he say such a thing? At the hotel, she had asked him if he really believed she would go out with another man, especially while he was in town.

At about five o'clock, Amy could wait no longer to call Thomas. She called him from the office, and he answered immediately.

"It's about Kate," Thomas said once they dispensed with niceties.

"What about her?"

"I confirmed that she is someone I know."

"Go on," Amy said now seriously concerned.

"It was a blind date…it didn't work out. And I didn't call her again."

"You went on a blind date with Kate? Kate Peck? When?"

"Last year, a few months ago at least."

"And you couldn't recall where she worked to make that connection once I started working here?"

"We met just once. I never saw or called her again."

"Before or after the first time you asked me out?"

"I first asked you out in high school."

"I mean last year," Amy said.

"Have you forgotten what you told me when we first started going out?"

"Of course not, I told you you did not owe me fidelity while I was refusing to sleep with you."

"Can we not fight about this thousands of miles apart?"

"Just once? And you never spoke to her or saw her afterward?" Amy asked, as though she was worried the same thing would happen to her.

"Amy, when you give a man carte blanche to do whatever he wants with other women, while his only desire is to be with you, you may think you're setting him free to live the way men want to live, but in essence, you may be saying that he is not good enough to command your fidelity, or jealousy for that matter. He doesn't measure up. You hurt his self-esteem."

"Are you blaming me for this?"

"Of course not, can I explain?"

"Yes, please, is that why you didn't call her back afterward?"

"Amy, a situation where Kate suddenly becomes your boss was unimaginable to me at the time. And I'm sorry I put you in that situation."

"When did you confirm that this Kate was the same person you had a blind date with?"

"I wanted to discuss it with you the second time I was in Los Angeles, but the thing at the nightclub threw me off."

"You couldn't tell me the following night while we were having dinner or at your hotel, or through the night and the morning we spent together?"

"It felt complicated. I'm sorry."

"Complicated, how? How does it feel less so now?"

"This was why I wanted to fly in and have the discussion in person."

"You told Alana the name of the case, didn't you?"

When Thomas did not answer, Amy continued, rather alarmed.

"Thomas, you told my mom about Kate before you told me?"

"No, why would I do that? I told her the name of the case that you went to the nightclub to investigate."

"And you asked her to tell me to get reassigned?"

"It was entirely her idea, but I told her it wouldn't be a big deal."

"Thomas…after Richard and I broke off our engagement, I realized that what I want the most from any man I'm going to spend the rest of my life with is transparency and honesty, even more than fidelity—if that makes any sense at all. I'm the type of person who would rather get flogged than lied to…so thanks for telling me."

She hung up the phone before he could say another word and picked up her jacket and her purse. As she walked out of the building, she decided she would no longer try to please Kate on *People v. Jackson*, but she would not give Alana satisfaction in seeking a reassignment. Henceforth, the office was on probation for an opportunity to have her work there, rather than she being on probation in a new position.

CHAPTER EIGHTEEN
A Different Woman

Kate came to the office very early on Wednesday to review the supplemental charging documents. Amy watched as she read it. When Kate sternly looked up at her and kept her gaze, Amy expected one of her piercing remarks, but Kate quietly continued reading and did not look up again until she was done.

"You don't think I spoke to Gonzalez about the meeting you had with him and Melissa?" Kate asked.

"I supposed you did, but you weren't there to approve what they were suggesting. I think we should disclose the listening device, I don't see the point of only including the small ones the defendant knows about and not the electronic box found under the bed."

"You know the fingerprints of the only tenant the police didn't get a chance to talk to were on that box?"

"Monsieur Arnot?"

"Yes, and that he moved out before giving notice?"

"Wow…"

"I never asked them to conceal evidence."

"I didn't think you did…that's why I included everything."

Kate looked at Amy skeptically.

"So, you are sticking with me on this case."

"I didn't know my participation was in doubt."

"Melissa said she wanted to pull you, but left it up to you."

"I figured you picked me, so you should decide, not Melissa."

"I picked you because I thought it would be a great opportunity, and you would be more grounded than most of the other attorneys if it should get the kind of publicity we feared because of the similarities with the other circus."

"I appreciate that…"

"You don't know why I wasn't at that meeting?"

"No…I mean, Melissa said a friend of yours came into town."

"That's all you know about it?"

"Yes."

"Okay, you may include everything. Give Gonzalez a head's up."

Amy said she wanted to pay Rachel a visit and sought Kate's permission.

"Sure, go right ahead and while you are at it, plan on handling the preliminary hearing without me," Kate said. "You can thank me later."

"Thanks," Amy said and went to give the support staff instructions to file the documents as Judge Pollazo directed. In her office, she ruminated on the surprise assignment to handle the preliminary hearing. She had done mostly preliminary hearings in her last year at West Covina before this promotion. They were often routine procedural milestones where the judge decided that the case against the defendant could proceed to trial, but on a case this sensitive, given the racial tension in the city, preliminary hearings were never routine. The exposure could bring instant celebrity status, especially if some magazine thought to exploit her family name along with her relationship to Thomas in connection with the case.

Had she made the right decision to remain on the case? She asked herself again and concluded that she had. It was the only professional decision. She did not assign herself cases and knew of no rule in the district attorney's office that allowed deputy district attorneys the freedom to opt out of assignments they did not like or those in which their bosses might have been entangled with their social lives. All the people telling her to request reassignment were doing so on the basis that she was an exception to the rule. Even Melissa said she was worried the publicity that followed the case might further thrust Amy into the limelight because of her pedigree. Hence, that statement Kate made during the meeting: "You are sticking with me on this case." From the look on Kate's face, she was expecting Amy to ask to be reassigned this morning. For that disappointment alone, Amy was happy to stay on the case.

Neda had also told her to get reassigned yesterday when she got to Amy's apartment on her way home from work. There was another look Amy would not forget, when Neda saw all the flowers that adorned Amy's living room.

"What the hell…is it your birthday or something?"

"You know it's not my birthday."

"So, what is it?"

"Thomas."

"He proposed?"

"Nooooo!"

"So…what? I have run out of options."

Amy had deliberately kept Neda wondering until she served the wine. She had asked Neda to check out her bedroom and the guest bedroom and the bathroom, while she uncorked the bottle.

"You got all these because you were mad at him at the nightclub? There's a poor wedding that now has to pay more for flowers because you are so spoiled," Neda said as she sat down to her wine in the kitchen.

"Shut up, Neda. Thomas sent me these flowers to explain that he is the reason why I got my high profile case. Come to think of it, he may be the reason I got this promotion. And here I was thinking it was all on merit." With Neda not responding, Amy continued, "Thomas had a date with Kate and never called her back. When Kate saw that Thomas's girlfriend was transferring to be her junior at the head office, she decided to take the junior under her wing and really measure her up…see what commodity this gal has got that makes TC Holdings want to hang on to her for more than just one night." The expression on Neda's face was now half-amazement and half-amusement. She was silent and drank more wine. Amy told Neda how she found out about Kate and Thomas. Neda at least thought Amy could seek reassignment on the grounds that it was unprofessional of Kate to make the assignment without letting Amy know that she knew Thomas. Amy did not want to have that discussion and changed the subject, telling Neda that was not the reason she had asked her to come over.

"I had lunch with him the Monday afternoon they delivered flowers."

"With Kenneth?"

Amy nodded. "And I couldn't tell Thomas when he called."

"Why?"

"I don't know. I didn't want to. Now the whole thing is driving me nuts because I didn't tell him before he told me about Kate."

Neda and Amy spent the evening discussing both men and what Amy wanted. "I want to take a break from men," Amy told Neda. She did not feel comfortable working for Kate and seeing Thomas at the same time and she did not want to give Kate the satisfaction of reassigning her from the case. Neda had suggested it was not a good idea to break from Thomas because of this incident, but perhaps to take some time to cool off.

"You sound just like them," Amy told her.

"What? Because I said don't do anything drastic?"

"That's exactly what my mother would say. That was what Kate expected when she appointed me to this case, not knowing whether I knew her history with Thomas, or maybe she wanted me to know her history, but she knew I would not do anything drastic. What bothered me the most about all of this...about Alana, about Kate, about Thomas, and even Richard, was that they all make these decisions that get me entangled in their little messes without any consideration for me—because, of course, what would I do should I find out? Nothing drastic, of course. It's like they were working off a manual of my predictable behavior, and the only constant in that manual is that I wouldn't do anything drastic. They know just how a Wilson raised well is expected to act. Now, I want to live, not in their manual but in their consciousness. Every time they make a decision that affects me, I want them to think of the consequences first. I will not suffer for anyone in silence like I did for Richard. Not anymore. I have learned my lesson. Suffering in silence meant not suffering at all."

Neda was left speechless, which was unlike her. Amy, on the other hand had needed someone to unburden her heart on. This morning for the meeting with Kate, she had none of the butterflies or apprehensiveness or contemplation of how it might go wrong. She went in without airs.

The paralegal called her to confirm that the documents were filed as Judge Pollazo directed. Amy thanked her and decided to take a walk away from the office. She walked down Broadway, toward the Time's building to the covered street market near Fourth Street, hands thrust deep in her pockets.

•••

RACHEL WOULD NOT ANSWER her phone, so Amy called Conrad Wetstone, the apartment manager.

"Rachel moved," Conrad told Amy.

"When?" Amy asked.

"This past Sunday," Conrad said.

"To where?"

"She didn't say."

"And her sister, Amber?"

"She returned to Georgia."

"Do you know if Rachel kept using Goldie's apartment after Goldie returned from London?"

"After she came back, she was in Malibu most of the time. I think they were trying to keep her away from that boyfriend after she came back... That's what Rachel said..."

"Why is she running, instead of helping?"

"I don't think she is running. Giving up her apartment was the only way she could make her sister Amber go back to Georgia."

"So, you know where she moved to?"

"I think she's just traveling abroad. And she gave up her apartment so her sister would go home. I'm sorry I don't have a forwarding address, but I know she didn't just move, she traveled."

"How close were Rachel and Monsieur Arnot?"

"I don't know," Conrad said.

Amy thanked Conrad after plying him for more information. She also learned that Mr. Pare was keeping Goldie's apartment exactly the way it was because he wanted to use it for a music video when her record was released. All the people involved in this case were behaving strangely. How could Rachel, Goldie's closest friend, who could help find her killer, leave without a forwarding address? If Amy's close friend was killed in a similar manner, Amy would be calling daily to find out how close the police were to getting a conviction. She would want to know how she could help. Kate had not seemed too concerned about Rachel, Amy thought. Amy, on the other hand, had thought Rachel held the wild card. Every time Amy thought one thing about the case, Kate thought the opposite, or so it seemed, at least until this morning when Kate agreed to disclose all the listening devices. That was a different Kate, Amy thought. Thomas had affected her behavior, leaving Amy to deal with the consequences in that tranquil, well-behaved manner expected of John Wilson's only daughter. The thought infuriated her. The more she thought about it, the more it seemed like she was in a more complicated relationship than she realized.

•••

HER APARTMENT FELT HOLLOW when she got back that evening. Every sound was pronounced in a way that reminded her that she was alone. She turned on the television, something she did almost as a habit every day, but on this night it occurred to her that she probably did it to fill a void left by what was missing in her life, or perhaps to drown out what was uncomfortably present. She kicked off her shoes, took a yogurt from the refrigerator in the kitchen, and came back to the living room, mulling her life. It was probably too early in Singapore or New York or wherever Thomas might be at this time, she thought as she turned her strawberry yogurt with nuts and took a spoonful. *Law and Order* was on, with a storyline she struggled to follow, yet not much different from those she had seen before. The flowers that surrounded her suddenly looked sad. She turned the volume down and contemplated the conversation she wanted to have with him.

"Thomas, I don't think I'm ready for the relationship you want." To which he would say, "Then let's have the relationship you want." She would insist that Thomas listen to her and acknowledge her desires, whether they suited him or not. This would be the conversation to show him she was more flawed than he has ever known, to dispense with his illusion that she is someone for whom flowers can make misogyny seem pretty and she must insist they take time apart to consider the way forward. No longer would she suffer indignities silently for the sake of decorum. This situation must not pass without her asserting exactly what she wanted out of it. Flowers be damned.

CHAPTER NINETEEN
War Chest

BIG REMEMBERED WHERE HE had met the woman who walked out of the courtroom behind Sister Ramatu and Jo after the motion hearing last Monday. He was walking down the stairs at Cool Jo's Café, as he had done the night Kenneth and Amy were at the club. Making an entrance into the crowded bar section, deliberately slow, his gaze had turned toward where Kenneth sat that night with Amy, and he had stopped immediately. "Kenny said they went to school together. It must be her. She's a lawyer, too," Big thought. He abandoned his entrance and hurried back upstairs to his office.

Jo insisted he must not confront Kenneth about it when Big called her after trying unsuccessfully to reach Kenneth. "Why the hell not? You telling me it's okay for this mudderfucker to be sleeping with the enemy?"

"Big, there ain't no enemies here. She's just doing her job, and Kenneth hasn't been to court yet for Paul. Maybe he doesn't know."

"You see, that right there is why you and him are just the same kinda suckers. He better not see that woman after he finds out or she'll be the last woman he ever sees after this case."

Jo got angry. "What the hell are you gonna do, Big? We haven't even paid him and you're already threatening him?"

Big was calm again. Paul was convinced that Kenneth was the lawyer for him, too, which was enough for Big.

"I'mma pay him a visit tomorrow," Big said.

"Let me go and see him first, alone," Jo said.

"You can come, too, if you want. But we're sorting this shit out quick and early. I'm not gonna let this woman mess with Kenny's head on Paul's case."

"You need to calm down. You don't even know if this woman is the same woman."

"Jo, you ain't seen women fuck with Kenny, when the fool's talking about he's in love. Ah, ah, not on this case."

Jo and Big were in Kenneth's office the next morning. Kenneth heard Jo's voice from the inner office and vaguely recalled his mother saying something about Jo coming to see him when he got to the office. Somehow he was pleased that she came. Then he heard Big's voice as well and went into Nancy's office to meet them.

"Hey, Kenneth. I'm sorry to barge in on such short notice," Jo said.

"Oh please, you can barge in anytime," Kenneth said. "Him, on the other hand, I am not so sure," he added with a smile, pointing at Big. He opened the door to his office and ushered them in after hugging Jo.

"You know you ain't even kidding about that, nigger," Big said as he walked toward Kenneth's office.

"John, you don't call anyone by that expression in this office," Nancy said.

"Sorry ma'am," Big said quickly, and hurried into Kenneth's office. Kenneth closed the door behind Big, pausing briefly to exchange a pregnant look with his mother.

Big did not wait for Kenneth to sit down. "The Mallam's got the money to hire you."

"Big, stop!" Jo said, and sat down. Kenneth also sat down, his eyes on Big, who remained standing.

"Kenneth, you can replace the public defender now that the motion is done, right?" Jo asked.

"Yes, as soon as Paul signs the substitution of counsel papers, I'm his attorney. I was going to make time to see him today, but it doesn't look like I can make it."

"Why not? I'll drive your ass there myself." Big had interjected himself just as Jo was about to speak. Kenneth rubbed his hand on his forehead and looked from Jo to Big as if to confirm that Big was serious.

"Big, can I talk to Kenneth alone for a minute?"

"No, we finish talking about whether he's gonna go see Paul, and you two can knock yourselves out."

"Big, it's like I told you before, I can't discuss Paul's case with you. It's attorney-client privilege."

Big pulled the chair in front of him back and lowered his weight into it. He was wearing jean pants, a well-starched white dress shirt flying over his jeans, and high-top sneakers. He leaned forward and placed his fat arms on Kenneth's desk. His voice was calm, slow, and deliberate.

"Kenny, level with me. When did you know that white woman you was with at the club was the bitch trying to throw Paul in the can?" Big asked.

Kenneth looked at him contemplatively, then turned to look at Jo, but Big snapped his fingers, waving the hand back and forth as if to say, "Look this way…at me!"

"Just answer me," Big said. This seemed to pain Jo more than it did Kenneth. She sighed and closed her eyes, leaning back in her chair.

"I have no idea what the hell you're talking about," Kenneth said.

Jo sat upright again, encouraged.

"So, you telling me," Big said, again in a calm but deliberate voice, "you ain't delaying coming into this case because of some white woman?"

Kenneth seemed perplexed by Big's question, and again turned to Jo for some form of enlightenment. The grin on Jo's face vanished as she turned to Big.

"I need to talk to Kenneth privately now, Big," Jo said sternly.

"This ain't over, nigger," Big said and stood up.

Jo waited for him to leave before she told Kenneth how Big had called her last night to say he recalled one of the DA's on Paul's case was a woman Kenneth took to Cool Jo's Café.

"When Big saw her leaving the courthouse on Monday, he thought she looked familiar, but he still couldn't tell she was the person he saw with you at the club until he was at the club last night. He remembered where she was sitting with you, and it all came back to him."

Kenneth took a deep breath as Jo told him about Amy's involvement. He asked if Jo was certain that the deputy DA in the case was Amy Wilson, and Jo said he had just convinced her by saying her name. She recalled the public defender, Joanna Lark, saying Amy's name, and recalled the name Amy called out as she made her appearance in court. Kenneth was eager to call Amy to clarify her involvement. Something about the case had always made him uncomfortable about getting involved, and all the while he thought it was Big, but learning that Amy was on the other side of the case added a surreal dimension to his discomfort.

Kenneth excused himself and called the messenger service to go to court and copy the file in *People v. Jackson* for him.

"I'm sorry about Big always acting like you owe him something. He said you cost him some money on a business you guys did a while back."

"He's out of his mind if he really believes that," Kenneth said.

Jo smiled. "Can I tell you a secret? Big was sent to a foster home in Middletown, Connecticut, like straight from the hospital he was born in, and when he got into school there, white kids liked to make fun of him because he was so much bigger than them, and he liked to pick them up and try to drop them out the window. You can imagine how long that education lasted. Every now and then his mother would try to come and get him, and not succeed. Big was little but he remembers to this day those visits and his mother trying. He ran away, got into trouble, and joined the army. He said what kept him alive sometimes during those tours was the fear that, after searching for him all his life, his mother would finally find him when the US Army sent him home to her in a body bag. You know those guys can find anyone when they want. Anyway, Big ain't so tough like he wants you to think. He loves the relationship you have with your mother. For him, that's the best part of you. He might have hurt you in the past, but now that he knows her, he won't hurt you.

"Thanks Jo, believe me, I'm not worried about him anymore."

Nancy was at Kenneth's door as soon as Jo and Big left. She leaned on the door and stood there looking at him.

"Is it true?" she finally asked after a long pause.

"Is what true?"

"That you were on a date with the young lawyer on Paul's case?"

"That's why Big agreed to leave the room so quickly, so he could have your ears."

CHAPTER TWENTY
The Promise

O N FRIDAY EVENING, AMY sat on the floor of her living room watching the movie *Blue*. Her house phone rang, and she waited long enough to hear Edward leaving a message on the answering machine before she rushed to pick it up.

"Hold the line," she said to Edward and turned off the answering machine.

"Amy, we can't make it to LA as planned, but we're in the Bay Area, can you come up?" Edward said after a brief exchange of pleasantries.

"I would have if you had told me earlier. Why can't you come all of a sudden?"

"There was something I wanted to discuss with you while we were there, and I really want you to meet Angela. But something came up."

"I've been looking forward to it, I'm disappointed."

"Not as much as she is, but she comes to LA a lot, I'm sure you two will meet in the next couple of weeks."

"What was it you wanted to tell me?"

"Have you spoken to Mom?"

"No, are you engaged?"

"Mom and Dad are getting a divorce."

Amy covered her mouth with her palm.

"Why didn't Mom say anything to me?"

"It's still a shock to her."

"Bullshit, Edward," Amy said, her cheeks quickly wetting with tears. "How did you find out?"

"Dad told me…Amy, they've been living separate lives for a long time. He traveled most of the time to avoid that; I think as he gets older, the traveling is getting harder, so…"

"He told you that?"

"Some of it, I deduced the rest."

"Edward, can I call you back?" Amy managed to say, her voice shaking with her last comment.

"Are you going to be alright?" He spoke rapidly, as though he was expecting her to hang up on him.

"No, no, I will be fine. I mean, am I supposed to take this so well? I'll call you back," she said sternly and hung up.

Slowly, she sat down on the floor, unaware of the extent to which she was about to let go. A wail stuck in her throat was about to erupt. She struggled to breathe, then began to cry. When she collected herself, she tried calling Alana, and failing that, carried herself to bed and laid down, clutching a pillow firmly to her breast. At least this explained why her father has been more distant lately. Usually he would have taken the opportunity of Amy's starting of a new position to reach out to her and find out how she had been doing. This time, they barely spoke.

Two hours after she fell asleep, the phone woke her up. She picked up the receiver in her bedroom, expecting Edward, but Kenneth was on the line.

"Are you busy? Can we meet?" he asked.

"Oh gosh, not tonight," Amy said and looked at a clock on her ceiling.

"Amy, please, I wouldn't be calling this late if it wasn't important."

"What is this about?"

"It's about one of your cases. I won't take too long."

"Which of my cases?"

"I'll tell you when I see you."

"Okay," Amy said after a long pause.

"There's a bar in Pasadena called Ménage. It's about five blocks from the end of the Pasadena freeway. You just drive straight from the freeway without turning—"

"No, come to my apartment instead," she said and got up to look at her appearance in the mirror.

"Good, thanks."

"What can I offer you, so I can get it before you arrive."

"Nothing, unless you know how to make great margaritas."

"How long will it take you to get here?" she asked after giving him her address.

"About thirty minutes."

She tidied her living room, showered, and had a few items delivered from the grocery store so she could make Kenneth a margarita. She called Alana's various numbers several times to no avail. While making the margarita, she called Edward and was on the phone with him when Kenneth arrived.

"It's open," Amy shouted out to Kenneth from the threshold of the kitchen. "I have company, Edward, I'll call you another time," she said and waved to Kenneth, who was standing by the door, with his hands behind his back and a puzzled look on his face.

She had not thought through what she was going to tell him about the flowers from Thomas, when he brought his hands forward to reveal six long-stem roses arranged in a plastic wrap from which he had peeled off the grocery store price tag. He looked to her like a child whose lunch box had just been confiscated by the class bully. She hung up the phone and went to him. Still, he did not move, seemingly preoccupied with the scene in her living room. She reached into his hands and collected the flowers from him.

"Thanks," she said and hugged him. She took his jacket and went to hang it in her spare bedroom. She put the flowers in one of the vases that had came with Thomas's flowers, after emptying the vase into the trash.

Kenneth was standing by the mantle, examining a picture he held in his hand. Amy walked up close behind him to see the picture herself and Edward when they were very young. Kenneth smiled at her and put the picture back.

"That was the person on the phone," she said. "My brother."

"Oh, Edward, right?"

"How did you know that?"

"You mentioned him many times in college; you two seemed close."

"Yes, but it's been a while. I didn't expect you to remember."

"I remember everything you ever told me in college, considering how crazy I was about you."

"What can I get you?"

"You're embarrassed to hear me say that," Kenneth said. She stopped and turned to look at him. "There's nothing to be embarrassed about, you were one of the smartest people I knew in college. So, you have a good memory," she said, slightly uncomfortable with the subject and unsure how seriously to take him. "Besides, everyone felt that way about someone back then. We were all prone to extremes," she added and disappeared into the kitchen.

"I have never known you to be prone to any extreme, Amy."

She returned to the kitchen door and looked at him with an amused smile.

"You really should get to know me more, Kenneth," she said. "You still haven't answered my question. What should I get you?" she repeated.

"Do you have my margaritas?"

"I mean besides that."

"A glass of water with ice."

She went back to the kitchen and returned with two tall glasses of margaritas and handed one to Kenneth. Then she sat on the floor and watched Kenneth admire his drink.

"I was kidding about the margaritas, you know."

"Next time be careful what you ask for," Amy replied so softly it was almost a whisper.

"Will you marry me, then?"

Amy laughed.

"How bad is the rain out there?"

"It was worse where I was coming from."

"I had to work all last weekend, so they pretty much encouraged me to leave the office early today," she said. "Where were you coming from?"

"My client's place in Torrance."

"The case you wanted to talk to me about?"

"Yes."

He pushed off from the love seat. Holding his glass carefully, he sat on the floor facing Amy with his legs crossed. He drank again. She admired his tall frame, his dimples and gentle demeanor.

"What's on your mind?"

"I've been retained to represent the defendant in *People v. Jackson*. I heard you're one of the deputy DAs assigned to the case." Before he could finish speaking, Amy was getting up. She turned around to face the mantle, with her back to him, then turned again to look at him.

"I'm assigned to the case for the preliminary hearing and other pretrial matters. But there's a senior attorney on the case. Why?"

"Are you superstitious?"

"When it yields a result that favors me. Why?"

"Isn't it strange that I should meet you the way I did after all these years, only to discover that we're on opposite sides of a murder trial?"

"Well, one of us could put an end to this twist of fate by simply walking away from the case."

"I can't walk away from it now," Kenneth said.

"Okay, so you put up your case as best you can and lose," Amy said.

"My client's father is the leader of the American Congress of Black Muslims."

"So?"

"He was the one African American leader who did not denounce the Rodney King riots. Many of his followers were arrested. Anyway, he thinks this is connected somehow."

"What difference does it make what his father thinks? What else would you expect him to say, that his son did it?"

Kenneth looked at Amy as though he was unsure how to respond to her. "I wouldn't put anything past some officers on the LAPD, Amy."

"Oh, good lord, Kenneth. You don't think he was framed, too?" Flustered, Amy waved him away and quickly went into the kitchen. She set her glass on the countertop and leaned over it, trying to collect her thoughts.

"Well, the trial will tell, right?" Kenneth said loudly, so Amy could hear him in the kitchen.

"Kenneth, seriously, we are not going there," Amy shouted back.

"Okay," Kenneth said.

Amy downed what was left of her margarita, suddenly glad she made them. She poured herself more and drank before walking back into the living room. Kenneth's glass was a third full. She sat down on the couch next to the love seat. Kenneth got up from the floor and sat on the love seat. The affable air of his earlier entrance dissipated into a tense skepticism of self-preservation. Amy felt like she was meeting him for the first time.

"How is it possible that I have known you all these years, and never known your views on race?" she asked, trying unsuccessfully to smile.

"What do you mean?"

"Somehow we have avoided a discussion on race, in all the time that I have known you."

"That is not true."

"So, why do I feel like I can't tell where you stand on racial issues?"

"You know exactly where I stand on all racial issues because it's not different from where you would stand on those issues."

"I would never in a million years buy what your client's father told you, and I could not have guessed that you would either."

"So, we disagree on how to identify racism and when it occurs."

"That is a fundamental disagreement, don't you think?"

"No, people who have more experience with it are better at identifying it than others."

"So, I should buy your theory because you have more experience identifying it?"

"No, and neither should I buy Mallam Jackson's, but I am willing to give it the benefit of the doubt it deserves."

"Is it possible that it's so ridiculous that it doesn't deserve any benefit of the doubt?" Amy asked.

It was important that Kenneth realized she was not going to equivocate on racial or religious issues. She would not accede to any claim that he was the expert on race simply by virtue of being African American.

"Would you believe that five white police officers using wooden clubs would hit a young man fifty times in the middle of a road, just for speeding, for which the law says they should give him a ticket? Would you believe it if you had not watched it on TV?" Kenneth asked, and waited for Amy's response, but she did not say anything. She was not going to argue the merits of the Rodney King case with him.

"Would you believe it if someone told you, that despite that video evidence, those officers will be acquitted by twelve well-meaning people in Los Angeles County, not Alabama, not Mississippi, but the City of Angeles itself? Amy, if it had not been filmed, you would not have believed it. But there are very few African Americans who would say they were surprised."

"If they were not surprised, why did they riot?" Amy asked pointedly.

"Because the system had the audacity not only to let that injustice stand, but…and this is just as important…to expect them to embrace it. That's really what the riots were about—the notion that such racial impunity should be acceptable."

Amy sat watching him, not having touched the second drink since she joined him. In this last exchange between them, his demeanor, the passion with which he spoke, the rage in his eyes, the labor of his breathing, and the logic of his reasoning, she saw a glimpse of what might lie ahead in a trial on *People v. Jackson*, and she did not like it. She could not bear to see him lend believability to the argument that Paul Jackson was as much a victim as Goldie. In their silent interlude, he finished his drink. She went into the kitchen and brought out the jug of margarita and refilled his glass.

"You are not in the Black Muslim organization, are you?" she asked as she poured his drink. He looked up at her to make eye contact as he answered.

"I wouldn't be drinking if I were."

"Please spare me," she said. "Neda was raised a Muslim and still prays. We came to the club right from the bar where we were drinking."

He thanked her and drank from what she had poured for him. She sat down again.

"Kenneth, why did you insist on coming here tonight to tell me you have been retained on this case?"

"I wanted to let you know in person before you found out officially."

"You could have just told me over the phone."

"I don't know. I wanted to convince myself from how you would react to it…"

"Convince yourself of what? What difference would that make? I can't tell you what I really feel about your theory of the case because I'm not supposed to get the racial complexity; I can't tell you what I think of your client because he's African American; I can't ask you anything because a lawyer is not supposed to admit anything to an adversary; but you can sit here and tell me that your client is as much a victim in this case as the woman who lost her life, never mind that I am just like her, about the same age, same race, living in the same city, in the prime of our lives. Never mind that she's six feet under the ground and he's hiring lawyers to play games in court. Is this the reaction you came for?"

"I also wanted to reassure you that we can try a murder case and still care about each other."

"And why do I need reassuring? Isn't representing an accused murderer by definition your job as a criminal defense attorney?"

"Maybe, just maybe I care about you more than you want to know, more than I ever knew."

Amy felt this response of his turn something inside her. "Heaven help us," she thought.

"Kenneth, we are not in a relationship. If you take the case, we will just take a hiatus from seeing each other or maintain appropriate professional distance until it's over. After all, we've both been in LA three years without seeing each other. What's another year or so?"

"Still, the appearance of a relationship may mean that I disclose it to my client."

"No! You will not mention my name to that man. No."

"I care too much about seeing you to want to keep a distance for the duration of the trial."

"And I would be lying if I said I'm not flattered, but what do you expect that to change between us?"

"Maybe nothing, but I am not willing to give up trying."

"For what exactly?"

"To win you over. I don't want this case to put me six months behind the eight ball with him."

She could not help smiling this time.

"You are years behind the eight ball with Thomas. I have known him since we were kids."

"All the more reason not to delay any further." He drank his margarita. She sipped. Since she poured herself a second glass and came back to the living room, she had only sipped it.

"Can I ask you one more question about the case?" Kenneth asked.

"What?" Amy said.

"If you are only attorney for the preliminary hearing and pretrial, and there is another senior attorney on the case for trial, is there really a conflict to worry about? I could have a professor I know take the case for the preliminary hearing and pretrial stage."

This sounded like a plea to Amy. He did not want to give up his client, she thought, and it must be a significant revenue for his office knowing how much private attorneys charge for murder trials. There were obviously aspects of the case she could not discuss with him. "It would be a scandal before it became a scandal," she told him.

After a while when neither said anything else, he slowly got up to leave.

Amy stood up also and took her glass and his into the kitchen. Standing over the kitchen sink, she wanted to tell him that she did not want to stop seeing him for six months to a year either. She unbent herself and went to get his jacket from the room. As she passed the living room, she noticed he was back at the mantle examining the same picture he had picked up when he arrived.

"What is your fascination with that picture?" she asked when she brought his jacket back. He replaced the picture and turned to her.

"You know that cliché, you look like someone I have known all my life?"

"I'm glad you know it's a cliché," she said, grinning.

He put his jacket on and hugged her. She squeezed him for a brief moment and affectionately ran her hands up and down his back and sides, then gently pushed away from him. As Kenneth walked to the door, she stood by the mantle. He was at the door when she spoke.

"Did you pick up your keys?" she asked.

"I never dropped them," Kenneth said, patting his pockets to search for his keys. He glanced at the love seat. There was nothing there; so he turned to Amy, who could not stop grinning. She held up his keys.

"You lifted them from my jacket?"

"They were in your pants' pocket."

"Where did you learn to do that?" he asked.

"From one of your clients," she laughed.

He walked back to her.

"Why would they teach you?" he asked as he drew nearer her. She shrugged and wondered how far he was going to go and if she would let him. Her heart felt full with anticipation as Kenneth reached for her waist with both hands.

"Is this supposed to make me give you back your keys?" she asked through a mild shortness of breath. Kenneth gently pulled her to his body and embraced her, burying his face in her hair. Now he could tell from the softness of their contact that there was nothing between Amy and her designer T-shirt.

"I don't want the keys back," he said.

"Oh, what do you want then?" she asked, leaning back to peer at his face while pressed against his body, his hands on her back and her palms resting lightly against his chest as if she were preparing to push him away.

"Isn't it obvious?" he asked out of breath.

She shook her head slowly, smiling.

He kissed her. Standing on her toes, she pressed herself against him. They remained in that position for a while swaying gently back and forth and sideways, before she pushed him away.

"Stop," she whispered, and he stepped back but still held on to her. "We've both had a bit to drink," she said.

"I'm sorry —" he started to say, but she put her hand over his mouth.

"There's a movie theatre down the street. Why don't you take me to a movie instead, and we'll maybe give the drink some time to wear off before you drive."

He smiled and nodded, letting go of her. Suddenly, he seemed shy to her, which made her step forward and put her arms around his neck, and he embraced her as well.

CHAPTER TWENTY-ONE
Super Bowl XXIX

KENNETH WAS MEETING HIS dinner posse at Cassandra's house for a Super Bowl party, but considering Cassandra's indifference to whether the San Diego Chargers or the San Francisco 49ers won the game, it was just another gathering for the usual couples. He had called Cassandra on leaving the First African Methodist Episcopal Church to say he would like to come early, and arrived carrying beer and bags of ice that Cassandra had asked him to pick up from the store.

"Where's Sam?"

"In the garage. Don't go there and get him unnecessarily excited to play."

Kenneth gestured a surrender. Cassandra had trays arranged on her dining table with unopened bags of different types of chips and covered bowls of several dips. Anthony and Mary would bring the ribs for the barbecue. Pizza and Chinese food were scheduled for delivery shortly before the game started. She opened one of the bags of chips, gave Kenneth a beer, and sat with him by the dining table at the window overlooking the front of the house.

"What happened to you on Friday night? You stood us up."

Kenneth put the can of beer to his mouth, barely concealing the smile the question formed on his lips and looked out the window.

"I had to meet Amy."

"Amy? Am I supposed to know her?"

"The deputy district attorney I went to college with."

"On Friday night? This is serious now."

Kenneth drank more beer.

"And you were right. She's on the Jackson case, but only for pretrial matters."

"You know you've certainly crossed the line where you have to disclose it to your client."

"It's not what it sounds like."

"What does it sound like, Kenneth? You're seeing the deputy district attorney assigned to your client's case, socially."

"I have not filed a substitution of counsel yet."

"Do you still want me on this case with you?"

"Of course."

"Then schedule an appointment to see Paul next week. You are making a full disclosure to him, if there is even a chance of me getting on this case."

"We might not be subbed in by then."

"Still, you've agreed to take the case. Let him know all he needs to make an informed decision on whether to even pay you."

"She's only on the case for the preliminary hearing and pretrial disposition."

"I can understand you falling for this woman. I really can. You seem to have a history that in your idealistic mind think that this is meant to be. But I can't understand you not aggressively pursuing this case, or not realizing that if she cares about you as much as you think she may, she would want this case for you. So, it strikes me that this is neither about the case nor about her. This is your insecurity about not having tried a murder case before giving you cold feet."

"It is not just that…with this case my life won't be the same again. I will spend every minute of the next six months or however long it will take breathing this."

Anthony and Mary arrived next with the barbecue grill in the back of a pick-up truck, which Kenneth helped Anthony unload and set up in the courtyard. Tiffany and Jed, and a neighbor who usually walked his dog when Cassandra walked Sam, and two non-academic staff members from her school completed the party guest list. The all-California Super Bowl affair had a decidedly northern bias that was over as a competitive event three minutes after it started. Thus, most of the men spent their time around the barbecue, where a smaller television had been moved in the unlikely event that the San Diego team performed another miracle like they did the weekend Goldie was killed. No one was talking about the game during the commercial breaks, but those outside went inside to watch the half-time commercial advertisements on the bigger television, to get more snacks, or in search of interesting subjects or gossip for discussion.

"Ken, did you tell a feminist law professor that a woman was spoken for?" Tiffany asked when Kenneth, Anthony, and Jed came to the dining table at half-time.

"Spoken for, by another woman? I hope…" Anthony said.

Others laughed. Cassandra would not let Kenneth answer the question, as she changed the subject immediately.

"Ken took that case of the nightclub owner accused of murder, but now he is not so sure about representing him," Cassandra said.

"Wait! The club where you are not a regular, but everyone knows your name?" Anthony asked.

"Good for you, Ken. So, why are you changing your mind?" Jed asked.

"Are you smitten by some kitten and can't think straight?" Tiffany asked.

"Seriously, Tiff?" Cassandra asked, and Tiffany laughed.

"You should stick that on a T-shirt and sell it like Forrest Gump," Anthony said.

Anthony, Jed, and Kenneth took their drinks and snacks out to the courtyard again, and there Anthony asked Kenneth why he didn't bring the gal Cassandra and Tiffany were talking about to the gathering.

"Is she too good for our humble crowd?" Anthony asked.

"This is a humble crowd like the San Diego Chargers are a Super Bowl team," Jed said.

Shortly after the second half resumed, Kenneth excused himself and left.

CHAPTER TWENTY-TWO
Confessions

O N SATURDAY MORNING, FOLLOWING her evening with Kenneth, a messenger delivered an itinerary to Amy. It was from Alana. An executive jet was waiting in a hangar at Burbank Airport to take her to Oakland, and a car was waiting downstairs to take her to the airport. There was still no number to reach Alana, thus Amy could not protest the itinerary. Besides, it was not unusual for Amy to fly home on a whim, and she desperately wanted to see her mother. Alana knew all this, Amy concluded, and complied.

At Oakland International Airport, Alana was waiting at the hangar. As soon as Amy got in her mother's waiting car, she let Alana know exactly how she felt for having no way to contact her after hearing of the divorce.

"That is not what I heard," Alana said calmly.

"What do you mean, that is not what you heard? I've been calling everywhere for you and no one knew where to find you. No one could tell me how you were doing. I was worried sick."

"I decided to go to the last place I thought your father might possibly look and get off-grid."

"And where's that?"

"Thomas's place in Napa."

"I'm not going there, Mom."

"Of course you're not. He knows you spent last night with some Black guy you knew in college."

Amy fell back in her seat, stirring inside to scream, but trying to regain her composure.

"You are my mother, Alana. How could you believe that?"

141

"I'm asking you if I should believe it."

The limousine was speeding toward the freeway to San Francisco as Amy and Alana sparred.

"You obviously have time for unfounded gossip, so this thing Edward told me about you and Dad must not be true."

"I'm afraid it is."

Amy sat looking at Alana, then out the window and straight ahead through the windshield, unsure what to think or say. Alana also did not speak. They were almost on the Bay Bridge when Amy suddenly started speaking about Kenneth. She explained that he had not spent the night, but he had been at her place where they both had a bit to drink and decided to go to a movie, before he left.

"What was he doing at your house at that hour?"

"I was supposed to meet him somewhere, but I wasn't feeling well after Edward told me about you and Dad. So I invited him over."

"Invitations like that, at that hour on a weekend, change the boundaries of relationships."

"Mom, I spent more weekend nights than I can remember sitting around my living room in college with that man and Elaine, and sometimes just him. Nothing changed."

"And Thomas?"

"What about Thomas?"

"Do you blame him for thinking the man spent the night?"

"What the hell was he doing snooping around my apartment anyway? I am not his property."

"He sent someone to tell you where to find me. And they found him at your apartment."

"Why didn't he call?"

"He didn't want to use the phone in case your father was listening."

"No, I mean why didn't he call to ask me what Kenneth was doing there."

"Because apparently the discussion didn't go so well the last time he ran into the two of you."

"Oh, spare me. What's with this cloak and dagger thing with Dad, anyway? Can you tell me what's going on? I don't want to talk about Thomas. Certainly not with what's going on with my parents."

"You are not going to use this decision by your father as a further justification to delay getting married or live a life of spinsterhood."

"Mom, men are enough excuse for a life of spinsterhood. I don't need to justify it any more than you need a prison to justify that criminals exist."

Looking outside as they approached her hotel, off Mason Street, Alana explained that she had moved to a hotel because Thomas was throwing a Super Bowl party this weekend. She told Amy she would go to see her father this weekend. The news had been a shock to her, and she did not want him to see her fall apart. However, he was telling people it was all a mistake. He had merely asked his lawyers to let him know what the figures would look like if he were to explore the option of a divorce, and they had mistakenly delivered the document to Alana when he asked them to deliver a different document that provided legal advice on the family foundation instead. Amy was quiet through this explanation, knowing Alana was telling her this story because she wanted Amy to support her.

"I would like you to go to Thomas's party."

"Did Thomas tell you that my new boss who was eagerly waiting for my arrival, so she could test my mettle, was his one-night stand?"

"He conceded he might have deserved being pushed away."

Amy rolled her eyes and turned toward her window.

"Amy, dear, you are old enough now where I can tell you this: No man alive is a saint. Exhibit one, your dad."

"Thanks, Mom."

"So, will you call him and tell him you are coming?"

"Oh, I intend to see him on this visit. I guess the Super Bowl is as good a time as any."

They said nothing more on the subject. Amy turned her attention to finding out about Edward and his girlfriend. Edward and Angela would join them, Alana told her, and Amy devised a plan to get them to go to Thomas's party with her.

Before the party, she went to see Thomas to tell him she did not want to attend the party as his girlfriend. They needed a fresh start, she told him, but first she wanted a break. She confessed she crossed a line with Kenneth. He wanted to know what line she crossed, but she would not tell him. It sufficed that she had confessed and she was sorry. She also would appreciate it if Thomas did not share this confession with Alana, given what Alana was going through at this time. Thomas seemed offended by the suggestion, but Amy did not mind.

Edward's girlfriend, Angela, was shy but assertive and much more engaging with Amy than she was with anyone else in the family. Amy took to her as well, which pleased her brother. Edward had never formally introduced Amy to any of his girlfriends, much less flown one across the country to meet her. When they arrived at the hotel, before leaving for Thomas's party, the first person Angela's eyes appeared to settle on in the lobby was Amy. They both smiled. Angela tugged on Edward's sleeve and hurried toward Amy.

They hugged like old friends, Amy and Angela, and Amy pinched Edward on the cheek playfully, seeking to leave him red faced. He was wearing a casual black blazer and a pink shirt with soft leather shoes.

"How has your visit to the Bay Area been so far?" Amy asked Angela after they were all seated.

"She's from here," Edward explained. "Brought up in Berkeley. Her father was a Dutch professor and her mother is American."

"Alright, then," Amy continued. "You went all the way across the country to find the girl from the public school across the street."

"That's an interesting way to put it," Angela said. "We're segregated in our own backyards and have to leave home to find ourselves without the boundaries. I like it."

"She has depth, too. I like her," Amy said.

"She thinks that's what happened to you," Edward said.

"Who said anything happened to me?"

"No one..." Edward said.

Amy turned to Angela, who shrugged. They went to a café, and every opportunity Amy had to steal glances at Angela without seeming obvious, she studied her. Her skin was the hue of Mediterranean tan, her cheekbones rose and her eyes got wider when she smiled, grinned, or laughed, but when she was not amused, they reflected a vulnerability at once sad, hopeful, and apprehensive. This vulnerability led Amy to trust her implicitly. She sent Edward up to see Alana before joining them to leave for the party, and within an hour after meeting, Amy and Angela had discussed everything about Edward, Thomas, and the incidents with Kenneth. She agreed that Amy should take a break from Thomas.

CHAPTER TWENTY-THREE
Professional Responsibility

Kenneth and Cassandra arrived at Bauchet Street on Tuesday evening. Kenneth had gone to UCLA late in the afternoon and waited at Cassandra's office while reading a case she had printed for him. The title of the case was *People v. Jackson*, and boldly across the title page, Cassandra had written, "Karma or Coincidence" and had drawn a smiling face.

They both left the campus after Cassandra's meeting and some time for Cassandra to leave her books in the office and check her messages. Kenneth avoided the freeway because of rush hour traffic and took the inner streets, which were not much quicker.

He weaved the car through traffic on Sunset Boulevard, found Vermont Avenue, and headed south on Vermont.

"What will you tell Paul about her?" Cassandra asked.

"The DA in your case is someone I fell in love with in law school. We hooked up again in Los Angeles before I knew she was going to be assigned to this case," Kenneth replied, glancing at Cassandra before turning his attention back to the road.

"And you call that a disclosure?" Cassandra asked, clearly unimpressed.

"What else would you like me to say?"

"I think you're actually supposed to tell him the nature of the relationship and exactly how long it has been going on. Didn't you read the case I gave you while you were waiting?"

"Hooked up means seeing each other," Kenneth said.

"In Ebonics or some other language?" Cassandra retorted.

"Paul will know what I mean."

"Okay," Cassandra said. "I'll make sure he does."

They were quiet again, but only for a moment, as if to allow what disagreements they had about the issue to dissipate. They came to a traffic jam on Vermont Avenue near the freeway exit, where there was some road construction. Cassandra rubbed her hands together, periodically massaging the palm of one hand with the thumb the other, while looking at him.

"I don't remember the last time you admitted that you were in love with anyone."

"You know the strangest thing was, before college I had never been to Texas, and everyone asked me not to pick Texas. My mother wanted me to go somewhere near home, unless it was Ivy League or a historically Black college, but when Ivy League didn't pan out, I insisted it was Texas for me. I remember my mother saying it was going to be the same experience as with a Black college anyway. You guys are gonna be socializing with the few African American classmates you get, and the white kids will socialize with their white classmates, and so on. But while Mom talked about social apartheid, I thought worse. Then my friends kept trying to talk me out of it. Like, man, you even sneeze on white folks down there, and they'll send those big old police dogs trained to catch brothers for Jim Crow after you."

"I'm guessing this was the nineteen-eighties, not the eighteen-eighties, right?" Cassandra asked.

"Regardless, I was drawn to that school, but I didn't know it then."

"How did you lose her?" Cassandra asked. Kenneth kept his eyes on the road even though the car was fully stopped in traffic closer to downtown Los Angeles. He appeared as though he had not heard the question but after a while began speaking to it.

"She said it would never work between us," he said, then turned to look at Cassandra.

"Why?" Cassandra asked in a gentle tone.

"She never said why."

"And now?"

Traffic was moving again, and Kenneth seemed glad to concentrate on the road.

"I guess I confirmed what she thought," he said. A shy smile formed on his face. Cassandra did not ask any more of him.

After parking the car, they hurried into the receiving area, where the deputy sheriffs watched them like wild cats considered zoo visitors. Kenneth went through his usual routine of emptying his pockets, and Cassandra went through unmolested. They found an unoccupied bench and took up positions on one side of the table. Not a word passed between them after they passed through the metal detectors.

A sheriff's deputy led Paul Jackson into the meeting room again. He looked toward Kenneth and Cassandra as he waited for final clearance from an approaching guard.

"Is this your client? " Cassandra asked.

"Yes."

Paul walked toward them in a pink jumper, with his hands in handcuffs, followed by a guard.

As soon as the guard left them alone, Kenneth patted Paul on the shoulder and squeezed his hand.

"I want you to meet someone. She's the professor at the UCLA Law School I told you about, Cassandra Rayburn."

"Hi," Paul said and shrugged, reaching out with his free left hand.

"I understand," Cassandra said and squeezed it. "How are you?"

"Okay, I guess. Are you gonna be working on my case, too?" Paul asked.

"That's what I'm hoping," Kenneth said before Cassandra could answer. "She's the best young legal mind in California, but eh…there are some things she wants cleared up before she can come in."

"Okay. I thought you got the money all squared up now?"

"Yes, it's not about money."

"What's it about?" Paul asked with a perplexed look, which he turned toward Cassandra.

"First, it is important Paul that you make absolutely certain that your father and Mr. Jones understand that they are not representing you in any capacity while we are your attorneys," Cassandra said.

"I agree, I told Kenneth I'll take care of that already."

"And about this letter they said was sent to the victim after she died…" Cassandra started to say.

"Yeah, I'm gobsmacked about that, too. I'm not even kidding you. I didn't mail anything to Goldie. Don't know what the heck they keep talking about."

Cassandra and Kenneth exchanged glances like they were trying to decipher what language Paul was speaking.

"Paul, you realize that we have an advantage over the DA if we know what's in this mail but they don't. Keeping what's in it from us is giving them the advantage over us," Kenneth said to Paul.

"I did not mail that letter, Kenny," Paul said emphatically.

"Maybe it was mail that was delayed. When was the last time you put something in the mail for her?" Cassandra said.

"If I write her, I usually just send somebody going her way to drop it off for me. I haven't written her in a while. She was in London, and I didn't have her contact address."

"You have no idea what could be in that mail?" Cassandra asked.

"No, I don't."

Kenneth contemplated what Paul had said for a short while and nodded.

"There is something else I need to tell you before Professor Rayburn comes into the case. Not that I wouldn't tell you otherwise."

"What is it?" Paul asked.

"I went to college with the young deputy DA on your case—back in Texas. She and I, together, and before I knew she was gonna be on your case, we hooked up again in LA."

Kenneth and Cassandra waited for Paul to say something, but it was unclear whether he was angry or disappointed.

"You used to go with the DA in my case?" he asked.

"We didn't really date, but we were close in college," Kenneth said.

"Big was right, that's why you didn't want the case."

"No, I didn't even know of it until Big brought it up," Kenneth said.

"Why couldn't you look me in the eye and tell me the truth, Kenny?"

"There was nothing going on. If there was, I would have told you."

"And now?" Paul asked.

"Still nothing."

"Look, Paul, what's important is that we let you know that the deputy DA and your attorney may have been in an affair and may have a mutual social interest in each other. And this has been fully disclosed to you," Cassandra said curtly.

"I get the picture," Paul said. "What can I do about this?" he asked Cassandra.

"You could fire him and get another attorney," Cassandra said. "There is still time for you to find someone who can represent you effectively in this case."

"Will you take the case from him, if I fire him?" Paul asked Cassandra.

"No, I have too much on my plate right now; I wouldn't even consider working on this case if not for him," Cassandra said.

"What else does the law say I can do?" Paul asked.

"The law says I have to tell you the truth about it, so you can do whatever you want," Kenneth said.

"I don't want you seeing her, Kenny, unless it's in court on my case," Paul said.

Kenneth turned to Cassandra impulsively, a rush of adrenalin and blood to his head, and all the while Paul was staring at him.

"You can't stop him from seeing anyone because he is representing you," Cassandra said sternly, as Kenneth began to answer.

"No, Casey. Let me take care of this," Kenneth said.

"That's right, Kenny. Do the right thing," Paul said.

"I can understand why you'd feel that way, Paul. Still, you don't get to dictate whom I see because I'm your attorney."

"She's on the wrong team, Kenny. We go way back and you're gonna choose this thing with her over me? My life? You ever tried a murder case before in your life? And you are gonna let her mess with your head on my case...with my life on the line. I'm saying I believe in you on trust. You think she believes in you like that?"

Cassandra shifted restlessly, as Paul spoke with vehemence.

"I hear you, but I'm not doing anything that would put your case in jeopardy. That's the point. She just works there and happens to be on your case," Kenneth said.

"And if I do come into the case, the relationship will not make any difference," Cassandra added. Paul seemed somewhat reassured by Cassandra's statement, so she continued. "You can replace him now if you want. That's what we came to tell you. We won't have this discussion again after today. So, this is your chance."

"Are you in?" Paul asked.

"As soon as Kenneth says we've got a deal," Cassandra said.

"Good, then it doesn't matter, like you said," Paul said.

Paul yanked at the handcuff attached to the table to get the attention of the sheriff, who started walking toward them to take him away.

Barely outside the meeting room, Kenneth had an urgent question for Cassandra, "Do you believe that?"

"I wouldn't worry about it if I were you."

"What do you think of him?"

"He seems like an intelligent defendant, which is more than you can ask for."

They walked past the cats in the receiving area who watched them silently, blinked, and turned their attention elsewhere. Kenneth considered that their world was different from his for a reason, and the bars separating the two worlds stood like due process, without which the treatment he received from them could have been much worse.

CHAPTER TWENTY-FOUR
A White Lie

Amy's mail and new assignments occupied her morning on a busy Monday. Kenneth's Association of Counsel for Cassandra was among them, as well as a motion to inspect Goldie's apartment with experts. He has been busy, Amy thought. She was happy for him, knowing it gave him a platform to build experience upon, but the idea that he could identify with Paul Jackson, even on the basis of race, still riled her and motivated her to beat him.

He had tried to reach her all weekend, but she had turned her phone off for most of the time she was in San Francisco with Alana and at Thomas's Super Bowl party. Since she returned on Sunday night, she had not called him back. Instead, she had continued to ruminate on whether she had been fair to Thomas. Alana had wondered aloud whether she would have acted so quickly to extricate herself from Thomas, or felt so offended by his affair with Kate, if Kenneth had not suddenly come in to the picture.

"He didn't suddenly come into the picture. I've known him since college. I'm sure I've mentioned him to you before."

"What exactly is he to you?" Alana had asked.

"A friend; someone I was fond of…and I'm still fond of."

"And you are willing to throw away what you have with Thomas for him?"

"I've told you that I'm not doing it for him…What exactly do I have with Thomas?"

"A relationship that is blessed by both families."

"Like you blessed my relationship with Richard."

"You'll never stop throwing Richard in my face, will you?"

"If you insist on sounding like the Mafia, I won't. No."

"Sounding like the Mafia?" Alana repeated quizzically.

"Blessed by the family…" Amy had said.

"What I meant was simply that I know Thomas, I know his last name, I know his father, his mother, his family history. Tell me what do you know of this Kenneth or his background?" When Amy did not respond, Alana continued. "Whether you are looking for a relationship or not, the next man you fall in love with could possibly be the one you marry, given your age; if you marry him, he would be the one at whose disposal you lay the huge fortune of the Wilson Estate; the one whose genes might dictate the roles your children play in life, the nature and times of their death, possibly. So, do not chose him to fit some college ideal or the political sentiments of your time. Those will fade. And love, honey; it starts off as an all-consuming passion, but it is only a language you develop with someone who is there for you or has been there for you. Marriage is more about what sustains prisoners in San Quentin than it is about love."

"What do you know about what sustains prisoners at San Quentin?"

"I don't, but I'm certain it isn't love."

"I'm not planning on marrying anyone right now, Alana. I really do respect what you're saying, and I'm not happy that I'm putting brakes on Thomas. But I am so unsettled right now and I need to find out things for myself."

"Then do me one favor," Alana had said.

"What?" Amy had asked, eager to bring this conversation to an end.

"Promise me that you will give Thomas another chance. Every opportunity that you give Kenneth, you will give Thomas as well. And if afterward you decide it is Kenneth, then so be it." Amy had agreed and said she was keeping an open mind about both men, if they continued to show interest in her.

This was why she had felt some guilt taking Kenneth's call, when she was feeling such relief from being free of Thomas. On returning to the office on Monday morning, she turned quickly to the Jackson case to keep her mind off the weekend's quagmire. The defense's motion to inspect the crime scene convinced her that they were about to focus attention on Conrad Wetstone, and how he discovered Goldie's body in the bathroom. Amy was fairly certain that Kenneth and Cassandra were building a case to

153

discredit Conrad. She brought out the case file and began building a timeline for Conrad and Goldie.

By Tuesday afternoon, the wall opposite her desk was covered with yellow and white Post-it notes with all sorts of notes on them, pages from notepads with arrows and question marks intersected and connected dates on the wall. Amy was sitting back admiring her work on the wall when Kate came to her office.

"What's that?" Kate asked.

"Deconstructing the key defense in the case—the impeachment of apartment manager Conrad Wetstone. I should put that as the title on top of the wall. This was his timeline from the time Goldie returned from London on or about December 28 last year to the day she died."

Kate moved closer to the wall. Amy got up to join her and continue her explanation as Kate examined the wall.

"They start with when Goldie returned from London. The evidence was that she hardly spent time at her apartment, but it does not show what times she was at the apartment—we need that to make sure that Conrad's story doesn't have holes the defense could exploit."

"Each blank page represents a day from December twenty-eighth to January sixth that we don't know of Goldie's whereabouts?" Kate asked.

"Yes," Amy said.

"There are as many blank pages as there are days, except for the day she was discovered," Kate said, perplexed.

"Yes, and the same for Conrad. We don't know what his work schedule was that day, we don't know what his class schedule was, we don't know much about his activities. We know he found the body about eleven a.m. and called the police at two p.m., but we only have his perfunctory explanation in the police report for what he was doing between those times. He said he called the apartment management company and thought that they would call the police, but when the police didn't arrive, he decided to call it in directly."

"Sounds plausible," Kate said.

"I was wondering if we could look at his phone records," Amy said.

"Do all these questions raise doubts in your mind that Paul Jackson killed Goldie?" Kate asked.

"No, but I think they may in the jurors' minds if we don't have answers for them. The idea that Paul's motivation alone was because he was scorned by his white girlfriend just will not sit well with many jurors. They will be looking for holes in it..." Kate had a skeptical expression as she looked at Amy. "I keep looking for holes in it, that's why I think they would, too." Kate continued to look at Amy a little longer after Amy finished speaking, then turned again to the wall.

"What are the arrows?" Kate asked.

"People who could impeach particular times or portions of Conrad's testimony, either because they had contact with him or they would have known that information as well, independent of him," Amy said. Kate observed the wall a little longer, then pulled up a chair and seemed contemplative for a moment. Amy went around her desk and sat down, as though she had been instructed to do so.

"Do you know that he changed attorneys, the defendant in the Jackson case?" Kate asked.

Amy was glad the substitution of counsel papers were sent to both her and Kate's offices.

"Yes," she said, raising her copy.

"Melissa said he's someone you know from college."

Amy felt her heart jump several beats.

"Yes, I went to UT with one of their attorneys but we lost contact after college, and I only learned that he was even a lawyer the day I started this job."

"Are you seeing him socially?"

"I'm sorry?"

"I understand you two were close in college."

"I wouldn't characterize that as seeing him now—"

"You haven't seen him since this case began?"

"We had lunch."

"That's it?"

Amy kept quiet.

"Melissa said he called her incessantly, trying to reach you. So obviously he has designs on you," Kate said.

"I can step down from the case if you feel it will be a problem."

"No, it is not. I would just like to know if this becomes more than an acquaintance."

"I'll let you know," Amy said after a long pause.

"That would be best," Kate said. "Let's keep this discussion between us. I wanted to be sure in case you have to take over the entire litigation," Kate added and walked out.

The conversation left Amy livid. She wanted to go and ask Melissa exactly what she had discussed with Kate concerning Kenneth.

Never before had Amy wanted a drink so much after work, but Neda could never make it to happy hour without planning ahead, and Amy would not go alone. She called Kenneth, against her better judgment—she thought, but Nancy answered the phone. Kenneth was not back in the office and she did not know when to expect him.

•••

Four tall African American men banging loudly on his door and intermittently pressing the doorbell woke Kenneth up at 6:00 a.m. on Wednesday morning. Their banging started gradually, then progressively got louder and more rapid until it sounded like a riot. Kenneth thought it was either a neighbor alerting him to a life-threatening emergency or the authorities coming to question him on an investigation in the neighborhood. He jumped out of bed, irritable and anxious but unsure of what to expect, his face crinkled with marks from the pillowcase and his pajamas twisted. He walked unsteadily to the door. This must be Big, he thought and got angry. He dragged the chain on the door back and yanked on the doorknob to find himself looking at the unfriendly faces of Mallam Jackson's foot soldiers each man wearing a narrow black tie over a white shirt and in a dark suit, their hair cut low and neatly trimmed at the hairlines, smirks on their faces.

Kenneth had first learned that Paul's father wanted to see him when he got home the night before from Cassandra's house. He found Nancy sitting in the living room with the television turned off. She looked like she had been denied sleep for days, and her eyes seemed focused intently on the floor. She said that she was waiting for him to return before she went to sleep, then asked him again if it was true that he was having an affair with the DA in Paul's case. Kenneth could see she had already answered the question herself. He was not having an affair, he told her, but there was some attraction. He explained that he went to college with Amy and they had met before Paul's family retained his services.

"Why didn't you tell me when I was pushing you to take the case?" she had asked. He only found out after Big and Jo came to the office to tell him she was on the case, he told her. Only after this explanation did Nancy tell Kenneth that Mallam Jackson had sent for him at the office. She wanted to go with Kenneth to see the Mallam at lunchtime the following day, but he insisted on going alone.

Mallam Jackson's men introduced themselves with distinctive names Kenneth forgot as soon as he heard them, knowing he could default to calling everyone "Brother" like they did in introducing themselves. One of them said they had come "to give him a ride." Kenneth looked at them again, this time one man at a time, each taller than his six feet one inch height.

"A ride to where?" he asked.

"Torrance," said the Brother who did most of the talking.

"Mallam Jackson?" Kenneth asked, and they all answered with a chorus of "Yes, sir" and several other phrases. "Now you're talking," and "Ain't you the smart one." They were quickly quiet again. Kenneth suggested they should go ahead of him and he would join them after he had showered. They again responded with a chorus, this time "No, sir," each shaking his head. In the way two of them looked at each other, Kenneth could tell these two shook their heads not just to disagree with his suggestion but in astonishment that Kenneth would even think it.

"Look, I've got court this morning. I'm not going anywhere with you all, period; but if I did, I would take my car so I can go to court from there." He opened his door for them. "You're welcome to come in and sit down if you want. But the cops will be here in a minute," he said.

The glare of anger in the men's eyes was unmistakable.

"We'll take you to court and wait," their leader said.

"That won't be necessary," Kenneth said and walked away.

At Nancy's door, which was otherwise his guest room, he knocked lightly, but hearing no response, he put his head around the door and saw her kneeling down with her head and her lips moving faster than the English language required.

The Brothers were gone by the time he got out of the shower and came back into the living room. Nancy was sitting there waiting for him.

"What happened?" she asked him.

"Mallam Jackson's boys came here saying they'd come to take me to Mallam Jackson."

"What did you tell them?"

"I told them I have court this morning, and I'll go and see him later."

"But you don't have court."

"Right, I was trying not to be rude to them. Can you believe they said they would drive me to court, then take me to the Mallam? What the hell am I supposed to be? Their lawyer or their slave? They were completely bent on letting me know they didn't care what I thought or wanted, only to do what Mallam Jackson had asked them to do."

Nancy was quiet, as though trying to control her emotions.

"Mom, please forget them and go on with your day," Kenneth said and started walking back to his room.

"I'll wait for you so we can go to work together," Nancy said, making him turn around and walk back to her. Her right hand was covering her nose and mouth, like she was trying to keep from crying. He put his arm around her shoulders.

"Mom, everything is gonna be alright. Stop worrying about these thugs and this case." Nancy was shaking her head before he finished.

"No, it's not just them," she said, shaking her head more in part to collect herself. "You don't have a car to take you to work. Someone broke into your car and did a lot of damage to it." She grabbed Kenneth's hand as she finished speaking and Kenneth tried to pull away. "Don't...don't... just listen to me," she pleaded. Kenneth pulled away and ran downstairs to the parking lot. All the windows on the car were damaged, the driver's side was bashed in so far that the door jammed. He could only get in through the passenger side of the front seat. The fuel tank was open, and the cover was hanging loose from it. He was sure they had put something in it. As he stood there with his hands akimbo, his mind fantasizing about a thousand different ways to avenge this, Nancy joined him again.

"I am so sorry about this, son," she said. He turned to her and held her.

"It's alright, Ma," he said, "But they have made my decision for me."

"What about?" she asked.

"I am not gonna see him," he said sternly without looking at Nancy, taking his hands away as he spoke, but she held on to him.

"Kenneth, it's not him. He doesn't know they did this to you. These boys make their own rules out of fanatical loyalty that then ties his hands. You're in unstable territory here, son. I know because I have seen this so many times," she pleaded.

"Yes, but he sent them," he said calmly. "Go on to work, I'll take care of this."

"Son, think what they might do next."

"They've done their worst, Ma. I'm getting off this damn case if I have to."

CHAPTER TWENTY-FIVE
Steps

AT A BAR CALLED Steps in the bank building on 330 South Hope Street, Amy nursed a cocktail as she waited for Kenneth. He had returned her call the following day and asked if they could meet on Friday evening, and she had picked the early hours of the evening to meet him near her office. Young professionals, most from Los Angeles's financial district, gather often at Steps for a period of discounted libation between 5:00 p.m. and 7:00 p.m., or for the latest rumors from the law offices that ringed the building. Sometimes they just come to wait out the rush hour traffic before heading home.

Amy's favorite part of the neighborhood was the postmodern-style stairs from which the bar probably got its name. The landmark, Bunker Hill Steps, snaked down five stories from a corner of South Hope Street down to Fifth Street in a concrete undulant design. In the past, she would leave the bar with friends and walk down the Bunker Hill Steps to find a place to eat or pick up taxis on Fifth Street or Flower Street or Grand Avenue. She anticipated Kenneth's entrance. Otherwise, she avoided making eye contact with others and would look out for him. After nine years in which fewer than a handful of men had occupied her thoughts the way he had, she still knew very little about him as Alana had pointed out.

She looked again toward the entrance, and Kenneth was almost upon her, making his way through the crowded bar. Apparently not having seen her, he was looking around.

Amy stood on her tippy toes to wave to Kenneth, who caught sight of her immediately and walked toward her. They embraced.

"It took you long enough," Amy said.

"I have never been to this place" he said. "It's not easy to find."

"I'm buying the drinks tonight, but I have an ulterior motive for that…" Amy said, sitting down again on her stool.

"What's that?" Kenneth asked, squeezing himself into the space between her and the next bar stool.

"You have a one drink maximum for alcoholic drinks, because I can't let you drive drunk."

"I'm afraid I have to tell you something," he said.

"Not about one of your cases," she said.

"Yes, about one of my cases," he said.

"No, we will not discuss that," she said with finality. Their glasses almost empty, he asked her if she would like to get something to eat, but she declined and wanted to turn in early instead. Could they go for a walk then, he suggested, the noise at Steps was distracting. She agreed and placed her glass on the counter next to his. He reached for her hand, and she let him take it.

Outside, she led him toward the Bunker Hill Steps.

"You know, in all the time I've known you, everything I know about your personal life I learned from someone else," he said.

"Who?"

"Mostly Elaine, but she was just filling in the blanks from all the stories that was told about your family."

"Want me to fill in her blanks now?"

"No, I want you to tell me about yourself," he said.

"Hmmm…why don't you start. Tell me about yourself first," she said, putting her hands in her pockets.

"What would you like to know?" he asked.

She thought about it for a while as they walked, and when he looked at her expectantly, she seemed in no hurry and looked back with a smile.

"You said your mother is staying with you, and I can tell you're fond of your mom because you mention her a lot. But I've never heard you mention your dad. Tell me about him," Amy said.

"Sure," Kenneth said, but paused as though to contemplate how to begin. "I don't really know my dad that well. I didn't meet him until I was nine or ten years old. At first, my mom told everyone, including me, that he died during the Vietnam War. She said that to spare me the circumstances of my birth…as she put it. Also, I suppose she was mad at my dad. You see, Reverend Brown was a dashing young deacon at a promising church in Georgia, with a doctorate in theology and philosophy. He was a civil rights scholar as well—notice I didn't say activist, and eventually a war hero. But even before he went to war, all the women wanted a future with him, and my mom was no exception. He, on the other hand, wanted a future with the church, and that meant the chief pastor's or rather the bishop's daughter. When suggestions were made by all camps that my mother consider abortion so she would not ruin her promising potential, my mom took off and got out of there. She landed in Philadelphia. You have to understand, no one thought it was the young reverend's fault. The women were becoming too much for him, and it was impressive that he was only involved in one scandal."

"A few years later, Reverend Brown was conscripted and left for Vietnam. The way my mother learned of it, she thought it was convenient to just let me go on believing he went missing in action in Vietnam."

"How did she learn of it?" Amy asked.

"Apparently Reverend Brown had listed me or acknowledged that I was his son in military papers and listed my mother as the other parent. When he and some members of his company went missing in action, the military felt obliged to inform my mother of it and advise of other rights she may have in the event the status changed. My mom showed everyone who cared the paper to say my dad was missing in action. Well, very soon, with the war ended, MIAs became the big thing in the news, and my mom's little boy was talking of going to find his daddy when he grew up. That's about when my mother sat me down for a heart-to-heart. I met my dad eventually, but by then it was obvious to him I was carrying a very angry chip on my shoulder. My mom was as good as two dads, and there also was my late grandfather."

They were sitting on a concrete bench next to the large fountain at the top of the landmark steps when he finished telling her the story.

"Did you make up with your dad?" she asked.

"Forgiveness is a gift your enemies leave you but hide it deep inside you. It's like a thief broke into your house and stole your most precious items, but before they could make their getaway, you or the police almost walked in on them. So, they found a perfect spot in the house to hide the gems, and walked away without them, hoping to return another day. When you forgive, it's like you discovered where they hid them and put the items back where they belong, but when you don't forgive, it's like you found where they hid them and decided to leave them there and try to forget you ever found them."

"I still don't know which you did. Judging from the chip on your shoulder, I'm guessing the latter," she said.

He laughed.

"I don't have that chip on my shoulder anymore. I think."

She smiled and ran her hand up and down the back of his suit, like she was soothing him.

"Someone really pissed me off recently. Are you saying I must forgive them?" she asked playfully.

"What do you have to lose?"

"Nothing, but you on the other hand…you might regret it."

"Better me regretting something I have no idea about than you carrying that grudge in you."

"I can understand how you felt about your dad, but I would have taken it out on my mother, too. You were probably too young to learn the truth, but I hate lies."

"I took it out on her a bit, too. But I don't think she was lying when she said she conveniently decided not to find out if he ever made it back from Vietnam."

"Talking of lies…I never planned to come to happy hour with Neda today. I wanted her to come, and nine out of ten times she says yes. But I hadn't asked her before I told you she was coming, and when I did, she had other plans."

"So technically, it wasn't a lie," he said.

"Well, just so you know, if you said that to me it would be a lie."

They sat quietly looking down the Bunker Hill Steps without saying anything. Something else she remembered about him—eaningful silences no one felt the urge to fill with words. His story, though, reminded her of the things that were most elusive about him, like the way he made people feel around him.

"Come on," she said, standing up and walking down the steps. He followed her and soon fell into step with her. "I can't see you like this all the time, you know." He nodded, then looked at her as she was looking at him, and they both grinned. "It's true. You seem to still have ideas about me from college."

"I'm agreeing with you," he said.

He sounded resigned in his response, and she was moved that he did. She would have liked him to resist her proposition more, to give them more reason to walk the night before going home. Their night seemed at an end rather quickly, she thought, but she wanted to be around him some more. There was nothing for her to do at home anyway.

"Do you still want to get something to eat?" she asked him, and when he said he would, she told him to go ahead and purchase something to bring to her house.

"What would you like?"

"I'm not hungry" she said, "but I'll have some of whatever you're having."

She took a taxi home while Kenneth returned to his rental car, which was parked at the building opposite Steps.

He arrived carrying a large brown bag.

"You bought Chinese food, didn't you?"

"Why? You wanted something else?"

"No, I figured that when a man says he's bringing takeout in LA, he usually means Chinese food."

"Good, because you are wrong. This is Korean food," he said and opened the brown bag to show her.

She smiled and nodded. "Good job," she said and led the way to the kitchen where she had already set plates on her table.

"Would you mind if I drink some wine while you eat? You've reached your drink maximum and I could use half a glass to relax."

He wouldn't mind he said, and she poured herself half a glass of wine, but brought out an empty glass for him and placed it with the bottom up. He looked curiously at her. "I feel bad," she said, "but I would feel better if you just let the glass sit empty."

"Thanks, anyway."

"Can I ask you something I've been turning over and over in my mind?" she asked, and he said she could.

"You've been out of law school about as long as I have. You said you started at the public defender's office, which means they start you with misdemeanors like me and work you up. And you've been on your own barely one and half years now, maybe two, I guess. Why would the defendant's family search you out for a murder trial and pay you all that money on three years of criminal law experience?"

Kenneth looked at Amy as though he was unsure how to respond to her dissection of his employment history. He turned to his food and ate.

"Thanks for the vote of confidence."

"No offense," Amy added.

"None taken," Kenneth said and continued to eat.

"Why didn't they pick any of the high-profile hot-shot attorneys?"

"They couldn't afford those guys," Kenneth explained.

"They could afford Mr. Jones," Amy said. Kenneth shook his head.

Amy had barely touched her drink, but then she did, wiping her lips with the back of her hand after she was done.

"Paul's father has a racially complex view of everything; Paul doesn't. A woman Paul met in college converted him to Christianity. His father is a faithful Muslim. The old man disowned his only son for marrying somebody of which he didn't approve. They only reunited after that marriage ended in a divorce. Now the old man is the leader of the ACB, which has taken a very hard line on African-American issues, and this case is a permanent blot on his life and his legacy. Obviously, there are aspects of my case that I cannot disclose to you, but an attorney they trust is more important to them than celebrity attorneys. And contrary to your assessment, they also think I'm good."

"What does ACB stand for again?"

"American Congress of Black Muslims... You don't want to mess with them."

"Are you doing this pro-bono?"

"Amy, come on, you don't really expect me to answer that, do you?"

"Why not? We all know the going rate for a murder trial, if they can't afford the hot shots, how can they afford you?"

"Still, all the more reason why I can't disclose that information, let alone to my adversary."

"I didn't know we were talking as adversaries," Amy said and got up to go to the living room, leaving her glass on the table.

"We have an arrangement," Kenneth said as Amy got to the door separating the kitchen from the living room. She stopped briefly to listen. "They don't come up with all the money, but as the case goes on, they'll pay the rest, whatever they can," Kenneth said. She continued to the living room, suddenly wondering what on Earth she was doing revisiting this subject.

He poured some wine into the empty glass but did not drink it, and just ate quietly. The only other reason Kenneth would take the case was for experience, and he did not want to admit it, Amy concluded. She returned to the kitchen and looked disappointed to see wine in the glass she gave him. Kenneth shrugged. She ignored him.

"You are not getting any more money from them. You should have just left them with the public defender's office. They're better funded."

"I know," Kenneth said.

"I don't doubt that you're good, but you could be making a big mistake," Amy said bluntly. Kenneth did not say anything. He did not want her to know he was having doubts about this representation after what happened to his car, and he could not tell her about Mallam Jackson's thugs, except what he had already told her.

"What if they insist that you see the case their way—are you really going to argue that biracial relationships make African American men more susceptible to false murder raps in Los Angeles County?"

"Doesn't it?"

"I was afraid that you'd say something like that."

"And you don't see it that way?"

"Considering you've expressed an interest in a biracial relationship yourself, at least in the past—"

"And in the present—" he interrupted. She managed to keep from smiling.

"It's a fair question then, and you're deflating it?"

"It is fair, but every relationship is different."

"How would our relationship be different from Paul and Goldie's?"

"Race defined their relationship as much as anything else. They were old enough at a time and place, post-LA riots, when race was the elephant in the room they met in."

"And ours—in Texas."

"Austin, we were growing up, discovering ourselves and through that lens our racial differences, those came first—pubescence, innocence, self-awareness before racism."

"You will play the race card in the case, then."

"If it's the only card on the table to save a man from conviction, yes."

"You make it sound like a lawyer is a mercenary for the client," she said.

"With all due respect, your office has the monopoly on mercenaries in the legal profession," Kenneth replied.

"Really? How is that?"

"They apply prosecutorial discretion to suit the prevailing public sentiments of the time, rather than rely on the facts of the case to guide the discretion. Amy, a guilty verdict does not confirm or negate the fact that the accused committed a crime, that's why we have the Fourth Amendment, the Fifth Amendment, the Sixth Amendment, hell, even the First Amendment."

She felt naive for being so honest with him and expecting him to be objective about it. She took another drink of her wine and was surprised at the ease with which it went down. As she lifted her glass to drink again, their eyes met.

"I'm sorry. The last thing I wanted to do was argue with you."

"We aren't arguing," she said.

"Can I ask you a question of my own?"

"Sure. Ask."

"Whatever happens…whether we get to explore a deeper relationship or not, can you promise me that we can still be friends after this case? We will seek out each other, at least on birthdays, and Thanksgiving, and Christmas, and say 'hey'?"

"I can promise you that, but the truth is that I can't keep that promise," she said and finally smiled. "I ran into the person I was engaged to recently. Seeing him again after about a year and half, I could not believe I was going to spend the rest of my life with him. Something in me snaps when I'm disappointed, and goodbyes for me are forever."

"I don't plan on ever disappointing you."

"Except professionally, you mean."

"Are you disappointed that I'm taking the case?"

She considered him for a while before she shook her head and poured herself more wine. As she raised her glass, he raised his as well and drank. She got up and led the way to the living room.

"You know, I can afford a taxi to take you all the way back to Philly and a truck to tow your car along with it."

"Of course, you are a Wilson after all."

"That's right, and don't you forget it. Or get any funny ideas that getting drunk will get you to spend the night here."

"I didn't know that was an option."

"Shut up!"

He laughed, but she tried to hide her amusement.

He raised his glass, and the rest of his drink disappeared.

"Goldie had just signed a contract with the record company. When she agreed to leave Paul for the agent who got her the deal."

Kenneth froze on hearing this, holding his glass mid-air.

"I only told you that because…" Amy paused as if wondering how to proceed. She stood up to put her glass in the sink. "I only told you because there is an insurance policy that may pay your attorney's fees better than they are." Having divulged another piece of crucial information, she became irritated with herself and walked to the living room. Kenneth followed her. She had turned the television on to a country channel and was sitting on the couch with her hands on her knees. On seeing him walk into the living room, she buried her face in her knees.

Kenneth stood at the entrance to the kitchen.

"I'm not sure I heard exactly what you said."

"I'm sure you did, and I won't repeat it."

"Are you mad at me?" he asked. She raised her head to face him.

"You are hopeless," she said, a smile forming in her.

"I know," he replied.

A short bust of laughter escaped her involuntarily. She made a futile attempt to cover her face with her hand as though to stop the laughter.

"Did you give the insurance policy you were talking about to the public defender as part of discovery?" he asked.

She shook her head.

"Why?" Kenneth asked.

"I don't have it. I have the music contract that refers to and mentions it. I just told you as a friend. Frankly, between us, Mr. Jackson isn't entitled to it because I can prove he was already fired as manager before she died. The music company attorney said the policy provides that it will cover the defense of the artist or her manager for any criminal offense."

"But you will still give me the music contract?"

Amy went into her bedroom and came out with the contract she had kept. She handed it to him, and folded her hands across her breast, looking at him. He quickly looked through the pages of the contract in silence.

"You know I could get in trouble for giving you that, right?"

He looked up at her for a moment, not knowing what to say, then he ran his eyes gleefully over more pages of the document and rested them on a page that Amy had folded in for him, stunned.

"You'll let me have this?" Kenneth asked.

"You didn't get that from me. So, you better find a way to get the record company to deliver a copy to you," Amy said.

"I don't know what to say," Kenneth said.

"Say nothing. I don't want to talk about it anymore. Nothing about *People v. Jackson* again, please."

"Okay," he said.

"And make sure you give that back to me if I ever ask for it."

"Understood." He walked over to her and she got up. "Thanks," he said and hugged her. When he stepped away and looked at her, there were tears in her eyes. She tried to wipe them, but he held her hand and leaned over to kiss her cheeks, but she turned her face away. He let go of her hand and hugged her again. This time she held on tightly and appeared to be sobbing softly. When he stepped back again, she was smiling and wiping her face, then she giggled at the expression of either concern or confusion on his face and held his head and kissed him. The music contract fell from his hand as they kept kissing.

He lifted her and straddled her sideways and lowered himself to one knee, placing her carefully on the floor. He rolled around on the floor, and she was on top of him. She pulled away from him and clapped her hands once. Darkness fell upon the living room. She giggled again at his expression just before the lights went out. The only light in the room came from the television. His right hand traced the edge of her T-shirt and went under it, and she kissed him more passionately with each invasive exploration of his fingers over and through places that took her breath away. Their bodies moving rhythmically, his breathing heavy, they panted as though they were sharing a limited supply of air and giving each other the little they had in them. Suddenly, country music filled the room as they rolled on top of the remote control; moments later, she stopped him because it was more than she could take. They did not realize how loud the television was until then and they were lying beside each other. Kenneth picked up the remote control and lowered the volume, but Amy turned the television off, and curled into his embrace. They fell asleep on the living room floor.

Awakened by the cold morning air that seeped through the bottom of the door, she woke Kenneth and ushered him to her bedroom. Then she went and soaked herself in a hot bath. About half an hour afterward she joined him. He was peacefully asleep. Only then did she begin to ponder what she had just done, with him on her bed, in her bedroom, and not even in the guest room. Alana was right. Some invitations change the parameters of otherwise ordinary relationships, permanently, especially at such hours of the night. She could not see a way back to Thomas without disclosing this night to him, and she could not imagine herself ever doing so. Even as she pondered her swift but uncharacteristic descent into actual intimacy rather than mere carnality, she had no regrets.

The clock affixed to the ceiling in her bedroom showed the early hours of Saturday morning. He turned in his sleep and held her, and on feeling her negligee, opened his eyes to see her grinning at him. And for the second time in less than a month, she found herself in breach of her Catholic compromise on premarital sex.

CHAPTER TWENTY-SIX
Love Thy Enemy

K ENNETH FOUND HIMSELF ALONE in Amy's bed when he woke up. The mid-morning sun cast its rays atop the duvet through a slight opening in the drapes, like a painter's allusion to the way he felt.

"Amy," he called out, and listened for her, but heard no one.

He looked around for his clothes. A house coat hung over the foot of the bed. Partially dressed and wearing the house coat, he went into the living room. There sat Amy, watching television on mute and drinking tea from a large cup.

"I was wondering where you were, that's why I called you."

"I know. It would have been too weird if I answered," she said and feigned a shiver. "We are not there, yet. Please!"

Kenneth bent over and reached for her tea cup, and she let him have it.

"Sleep well?" she asked, turning on the volume on the television. He nodded as he drank her tea.

"And you?"

She shook her head, smiling mischievously. They sat down and watched television, discussing their plans for the day like it was something they had done on a thousand Saturday mornings. "I won't see you again like this until after the hearing," she said, referring to the preliminary hearing which was in about ten days.

"We still have the rest of this weekend. Besides, Cassandra will be handling most of the preliminary hearing."

"If you are spending the night here, Kenneth, I'm moving to a hotel," she said. It amused him that she was blushing so much as he looked at her.

Embarrassed, she got up and went into the bedroom. "I'm serious, Ken," she shouted from the bedroom.

"Okay, so we can just have dinner tonight," he said.

"No," she replied and came back to the living room. "No dinner; no more dinners for the foreseeable future. I need to regain my self-control around this…" she said, ending vaguely to avoid saying she lost self-control around him. She took her tea cup back from him.

"How do you think I feel?"

"Your problem," she said.

"Brunch tomorrow?" he asked. Despite her playfulness, he seemed to be asking seriously.

"Brunch tomorrow, then," she conceded.

Nancy was not at home when Kenneth returned. Breakfast was on the dining table. He ate the food, leaving the music contract on the dining table, showered, and fell asleep. The second time he woke up on Saturday, he could hear voices and laughter and the aroma of Nancy's cooking coming from the living room and kitchen area. He hurried into the living room to find Jo and Sister Ramatu visiting. Nancy gave him a look to say she had moved his documents for him, and he heaved a sigh of relief.

They quickly wanted to know if he was really going to withdraw from the case because of what happened to his car. With a sly smile, Nancy again conveyed to him that she had nothing to do with how they came by this information. After the visit by Mallam Jackson's followers, he had called Mallam Jackson on Nancy's urging to say he could not come to see him because his car was vandalized, and he was in court on Thursday. The cleric could not see him on Friday, his day of prayer, and had scheduled a visit for him on Monday. He had planned to see Paul over the weekend to explain the circumstances of his withdrawal over the incident. Cassandra was fully in agreement, then Amy gave him the music contract.

"No, I am not withdrawing," he told them. "I have a meeting with Mallam Jackson on Monday to tell him."

"My dad told us he asked those boys if they had anything to do with what happened to your car that morning. They said they didn't." Kenneth seemed unconvinced. "I know. I don't believe them either. That's why I want you to add the cost of fixing your car to your bill for us," Jo continued.

"Don't be crazy, Jo. I'm not blaming you."

"I know you are not, Ken. I am," Jo persisted.

"And I promise you we will pay every penny," Sister Ramatu said.

"You may not have to pay me a penny at all, Ma. And I might be returning what you gave me to begin with. I think I found the money that will pay all the legal fees for Paul."

Standing over the sink, Nancy dropped what she was doing.

"Are you serious, son?"

"We think the recording company has insurance that covers Goldie and her manager if they are charged with a crime. Paul was her manager. At least that's what we're arguing, and we're going to ask their insurance to pay for his attorneys fees."

"And you think they'll agree to it?" Nancy asked.

"We don't know yet, but usually when their lawyers get involved, they tell them that paying two hundred and fifty thousand is not as much trouble as a bad faith insurance case. So, they may just pay up."

"Two hundred and fifty thousand dollars!" Sister Ramatu said.

"We think that's what they'll cover in attorney's fees for each crime, but that doesn't mean they'll give it all to us."

"When will you find out?" Jo asked.

"I'll send them a request this weekend, and we'll have to see. Usually, they'll say no or stonewall, and we have to file a separate lawsuit. So, we are looking at two months at least if they object."

"In the meantime, we'll make sure you have the funds to fight the case until you get the money from them?" Jo asked.

"I'm afraid so," Kenneth said.

Jo went into her purse and brought out an envelope containing another installment of Kenneth's fees.

"I know I said we wouldn't be able to get this to you until after the preliminary hearings, but when we heard what happened and how you had to go rent a car while they are fixing your car, we had to find what we can to make sure you don't abandon us," Jo said. Before Kenneth could answer, she was stuffing the envelope into his pocket. She patted the pocket after she was done and gave him a hug. Sister Ramatu assured him that he had nothing to fear from Mallam Jackson whatever the outcome of the trial, and Jo confirmed they would tell her father about this piece of good news.

Kenneth left the three women to their meal and went to see Cassandra about the new development. Sister Ramatu assured him that he had nothing to fear from Mallam Jackson whatever the outcome of the trial, and Jo confirmed they would tell her father about this piece of good news.

•••

AFTER KENNETH LEFT THEM, the three women sat looking at each other without saying a word, as though each was hoping the other had the courage to speak what was on their minds. Then Jo spoke in a hushed voice: "you think she gave it to him?"

Nancy and Sister Ramatu nodded confidently.

"It is serious, then." Jo said.

Nancy covered her face with both hands.

"Are you gonna get Rev. Brown to talk to him?" Sister Ramatu asked.

"I don't know what else to do—he won't like it." Nancy said.

"Then don't," Jo said. "It has only helped us, right? Kenny won't sell family out. Don't." Jo continued.

Nancy uncovered her face and looked up at Jo, then as Sister Ramatu, with tears in her eyes.

Mallam Jackson's living room was a large space with no chairs. Oriental carpets that served for sitting lined the walls, with cushions and pillows leaning against the walls. A coffee table in front of Mallam Jackson held a tray with flasks of tea and coffee, and a man in a black suit and bow tie over a white shirt stood like a waiter, a white towel over his left forearm, which he held across his body. Kenneth was standing behind the Brother who announced him, as calm as Nancy had implored him to be. He sat on the floor in front of Mallam Jackson as directed, the coffee table between them. Mallam drank tea and read silently from a book he held open on the carpet without looking up at his guest.

Still without raising his eyes from the book, Mallam Jackson asked if there was no rule barring him from seeing the woman who was trying to put his son in the electric chair. Kenneth explained that the rule required him to disclose the relationship to Paul or withdraw from the case, and he had made the disclosure.

"You sleep with a man's enemy after you take the man's money to defend his family, and all you have to tell him is you can't help it?"

On asking him this question, he looked up at Kenneth for the first time, his eyes frozen in a stare and his body held still. Kenneth did not respond, and Mallam Jackson returned to his book.

"How is it that you did not make the same disclosure to me? I am paying your fees, aren't I?" Mallam Jackson asked.

"I had to tell Paul first because he is the client."

"But you told his mother and his sister before you told him?"

"I did not tell them, sir. I just admitted it when Jo asked me. I'm sorry, but I did not just meet this woman; we were in college together. I didn't know she was involved in this case until I accepted the case."

"Did she tell you about the insurance policy they say you found to pay Paul's attorney's fees?" Mallam Jackson asked, catching Kenneth by surprise.

"No," Kenneth said after a short pause to consider how to answer him. Mallam Jackson looked up at him, and this time Kenneth had his attention.

"How did you find out about it?"

"I was fishing, sir. I wasn't sure there was any policy, but I knew that if I was going to sign a talent in this business with all the problems they could get themselves into, there had to be a policy to protect the company. It's standard industry practice."

"When will you get the money?"

"I sent in a request, but I don't know how long it will take."

"How much did you ask for?"

"One hundred thousand dollars, as a starting position to negotiate…"

"Are you stupid, son? You start your negotiation asking for the moon."

"The policy is for two hundred and fifty thousand. I couldn't justify asking for more at this time, sir."

"She's no good for you, son," Mallam Jackson said after considering Kenneth a while. Kenneth massaged his hands and kept his eyes on them as he did so. "I know you have never been in jail. In there, you can't sleep at night because you are worrying about your family outside or the gangs inside, or because some other jailbird took your bed. Sometimes the heat and stank alone won't let you sleep. And that's before they get a verdict against you, never mind all that talk about being innocent until proven guilty. America uses these jails to shape the future of our people. They put our young men all in there by the truckloads like animals and sooner or later they start behaving like animals." He paused and raised his cup for the attendant to refill with tea, all the while keeping his eyes on Kenneth, who returned his gaze. Receiving his tea, he continued. "Now, a man that gets no sleep is going to be on the edge all the time. He starts to think that if the system's going to treat him like an animal before it finds him guilty, then he hasn't got a prayer in hell of beating his rap. The only thing that keeps him from going crazy in there is hope. He tries to keep hope alive any way he can. Imagine that you are that young man, and while you are in there trying to keep hope alive, your lawyer who is supposed to be looking out for you comes to tell you he is sleeping with the woman they sent to kill you; what's that gonna do to you?"

Kenneth did not answer but looked down at his hands again, eager to be done with this meeting.

"He takes away all the hope you've got left. And that's when your mind really starts to turn on you," Mallam Jackson said, suddenly raising his voice in anger to answer his own question, but quickly stopping to collect himself. "Get him a cup for tea," he said to the man standing there with him.

"No, no, thanks, I don't want any," Kenneth protested lightly. Mallam Jackson nodded to his messenger and the man left the room. He watched the man leave, and as soon as the man closed the door behind him, Mallam Jackson started speaking.

"I tell these young men it is better to die sometimes than to take their judgment on Earth, because they go in there and never come out the same. The charge is trumped up from the start, the sentence is disproportionate to the crime, the prison sells your soul to the Devil, and the damage is permanent. Son, you have upset a lot of people in my family by seeing this woman; but you are like family, so I'll give you another chance to make things right. Don't you ever see that woman again until this case is over, you hear me?" Kenneth thought through what he was going to say and what he should say. As he often advised witnesses before they took the stand to testify, he chose brevity.

"I will see what I can do," he said in a barely audible voice, which was not deliberate, but because his throat and mouth felt dry.

"That's not good enough!" Mallam Jackson said.

"I don't want to lie to you, sir," Kenneth replied.

"Then you better get Mr. Jones back on this case, every minute of every day that woman is in it," he said standing up.

"Paul won't let me do that because my partner would leave the case, too, sir."

"Then you convince both of them," Mallam Jackson said loudly.

Sister Ramatu came into the room.

"Jackson, he is not breaking any laws, and he told Paul already," Sister Ramatu said.

"So, I should let him be?" Mallam Jackson asked.

"Just give him some time. Let's see how things go. Wait until the trial starts. Give him time."

Mallam Jackson stood up, looked at his wife quietly for a while, again with a frozen stare. Then he walked out of the room. Sister Ramatu took a deep breath, then went on her knees as she sat on the ground. She looked up and managed to smile at Kenneth.

"It's alright, son. Why don't you go ahead back to work and leave me with the Mallam, you hear?" Sister Ramatu said to Kenneth.

"Yes, ma'am," Kenneth said. She patted him on the back as he got up.

"I'll come see you later," she said.

When Kenneth was leaving the compound, he saw the four men who had come to bring him to Mallam Jackson the week before.

"Did you buy a new car?" their spokesman asked him, pointing to Kenneth's rental car, and the rest were beside themselves with laughter. One bent over holding his stomach, his face contorted in the joyful grimace of his own laughter, another buried his face on the hood of a car. Only their spokesman, the Brother who appeared to be their leader, seemed more in control of his amusement, barely grinning. But each time the others looked at him, they laughed even louder. Kenneth said it was a rental car he was using temporarily. For a moment no one said a word, as though each was trying to keep from laughing before he had to, until they saw their leader break out a cynical grin, chuckling, and the rest just about fell over with laughter.

Nancy was anxiously waiting for a report from him when he got home. There was not much to report, he told her. Mallam Jackson had just ordered him to stop seeing Amy, he explained.

"Are you going to do it? Stop seeing her?" Nancy asked. Kenneth slowly sat down next to his mother.

"No," Kenneth said. "I don't wanna have to give up my life because I'm handling their case."

"Let me talk to him."

"No!" Kenneth exclaimed.

"Then let me talk to Sister Ramatu."

"No, don't do that either."

"The Lord works in mysterious ways, son. Look how God brought you the fees to fight this case. Can you at least take the time to cool off and seek God's guidance about it?"

"Yeah, Ma..." Kenneth started to say, but he stopped himself because there was nothing his mother considered more offensive than the sarcastic derision of her faith. Instead, he walked away.

CHAPTER TWENTY-SEVEN
Preliminary Hearing

O N THE MORNING OF the preliminary hearing in *People v. Jackson,* Amy woke up with knots in her stomach. She felt her body was making excuses to get out of seeing Kenneth. She had not taken his calls since the Monday after they had brunch together. Every time she thought of him or that weekend, she felt these knots and she felt humbled. They had spent the entire Sunday together.

Returning home from work the following Tuesday, the attendant at her apartment complex pointed out a tall African American man in a black suit and tie over a white shirt who was standing by the doorway.

"He's been standing there for over an hour," the doorman said. "He said he has an envelope he needs to deliver to you personally." When Amy met the man, he would not immediately introduce himself. Rather, he inquired if there was a place he could talk to Amy privately, preferably a coffee shop.

"What about?" Amy had asked.

"Kenneth," the man said. Only then did Amy begin to notice the resemblance the man had to Kenneth and relaxed. "He's not likely to win this case he has with you, and it's putting his life in danger. They'll blame your relationship for him losing and they'll hurt him or, worse still, kill him like a snitch. That is the way of the streets."

The man said he had written everything down in a letter he wanted to deliver for Amy if she was not inclined to sit down with him for a brief chat, but he would rather have coffee with her. Amy took the letter and agreed to have coffee with him anyway. She told him she agreed to coffee to show she was not afraid of them. After the evening with the man, she stopped taking Kenneth's calls.

On Friday, before the preliminary hearing, she had received a motion from Kenneth's office asking the court to continue the hearing for one week to allow him to adequately prepare, as he had just been retained. Her hands literally shook as she held the motion while reading it.

On the morning of the preliminary hearing, she was surprised to find a note from Kate on her door. "My office before the hearing, please, if you can."

She placed her files on her desk, hung her jacket behind her door, and went directly to Kate's office, as suspense would not let her wait to hear what Kate had to say. Her calmness impressed her as she knocked on Kate's door.

"Yes, Amy. Come in," Kate called out from her office, and came around to the front of her desk.

"The defendant filed a motion for continuance of the preliminary hearing."

"Yes," Amy said. "They filed it ex parte on Friday."

"Do you know why?" Kate asked. Amy shook her head. "They know of the insurance policy that pays his fees. Mr. Ross said they sent the recording company a letter asking for the policy."

"Will the recording company comply?" Amy asked.

"I don't know. Did we give the music contract to them?" Kate asked.

"They've never asked for it," Amy said, swallowing streams of her own saliva.

"I would rather we stay out of that battle," Kate said.

"Me, too," Amy said.

"You know that Court TV is planning to put this on the air, right?" Kate said.

"Even the preliminary hearing?" Amy asked.

"I think so…Gil's office approved it," Kate said.

"I didn't know that…"

"Publicity might follow it from around the country, too. Hopefully, it gets overshadowed by the O. J. circus, but chances are it doesn't. Are you ready for something like that?"

"Yes, I am."

Kate paused for a while, and Amy repeated. "I am." Kate nodded.

"Amy, is there anything you would like to tell me about this case...this new attorney you went to school with?"

Amy was visibly perplexed. She adjusted her seating involuntarily as though it would help her listen better. Kate reached behind her desk and picked up a large brown envelope.

"Melissa told me you are seeing someone from New York, is that still the case?"

"I don't understand what you're asking me," Amy said, feeling impatient. Kate offered her the envelope, which she accepted hesitantly. Inside were pictures of her and Kenneth, taken the night they met at Cool Jo's Café, and a copy of a decision. Amy felt tears in her eyes and fought them back. Kate put a box of tissues in front of her and she took a few, dabbed her eyes, and thanked Kate.

"Thank goodness I didn't put on too much makeup."

"It's fine," Kate said.

"We've gone out for drinks a few times, like I said before. We had lunch. I'm sorry, I promised to tell you if it became serious, but I didn't. I promised myself I wouldn't let it get serious as long as I was involved in this case. I think it was already serious even before I got on this case. I just didn't know it."

Kate raised her eyebrows and sighed.

"So, the feelings are mutual?" Kate asked. Amy nodded.

"But I stopped seeing him to avoid further conflicts."

"I'm sorry I upset you. I got this on Friday afternoon, after you'd left the office. I didn't want to discuss it over the phone, and I knew I had to talk to you before the hearing this morning. So, I came in early."

"The pictures caught me off-guard. Who took those pictures?"

"Does it matter?"

"I didn't know I was being watched."

"You weren't."

"I ran into him on a night out with a colleague from West Covina, and someone took these pictures without my knowledge."

"Mr. Jones came to see me at the courthouse on Friday with the defendant's father and his followers...They brought those pictures with them. They promised to make a public spectacle of you if you continue this affair."

"I'm not worried about them. But I stopped seeing him."

"The case I handed you is the California authority that addresses the obligation of counsel representing opposing clients in a case. If you are intimate with him, he has an obligation to inform his client and it appears he told him that he was not intimate with you."

Amy stood up slowly and offered the document back to Kate, barely having looked at it.

"I suppose Mr. Jones has fulfilled that obligation for me," she said curtly.

"That copy's for your files," Kate said declining to take the document back. "...if you still want to be on this case."

"I'll leave it entirely up to you, but I won't be intimidated by Mr. Jones and his client, and I won't let anyone violate my privacy."

"They have a legitimate concern, Amy."

"They should take it up with their attorney, not with me."

"I hope you're not too upset to handle the preliminary hearing."

"No, I'm fine."

"I know I said I wouldn't attend, but my calendar has cleared up, is that okay with you?"

"I'd like you to attend."

"One last thing," Kate said and paused. Then added, "Oppose their motion for continuance. I'll see you in the courtroom."

Amy said thanks and slowly made her way back to her office. There, she sat scribbling unintelligibly on a note pad and holding her forehead in one palm supported by her elbow on the desk. Only then did the title of the case Kate had copied register in her mind, *People v. Jackson*. How ironic, she thought. She was relieved anyway that she had this conversation with Kate before the hearing. It framed her professional relationship with Kenneth in starkly clear terms she had never fully considered and lessened her apprehension of seeing him in court. Still, she felt violated by those pictures and could not wait to give Thomas a call. "Who else could have taken them?"

•••

ALL FREEWAY TRAFFIC TO the City of Angeles jammed within three miles of downtown by 7:30 a.m. Traffic crawled to a stop every thirty seconds as the Roybal building and the Metropolitan Detention Center became visible from the 101 freeway, and the spike on City Hall, the Temple Street Courthouse, and Chinatown were visible from the 110 freeway. Faces behind rolled up windows in cars nearest to the city hub turned to frowns and avoided eye contact with other motorists or nodded contemptuously to each other when unable to do so.

About 8:10 a.m., Kenneth and the frowning faces on the freeway no longer even nodded contemptuously to each other. Most barely looked sideways for fear someone might beg to change lanes and cut ahead of them. Any coffee left was either cold or, worse still, spilled. Everyone looked forward, determined to lunge at every inch of space that opened ahead of them as they crawled toward their various destinations. The delay for traffic toward downtown Los Angeles increased as the cars neared these downtown landmarks, exasperating Kenneth until he exited onto Spring Street and drove to the parking lot behind the Temple Street Courthouse.

•••

BY 8:20 A.M., AMY left for court. The hallways of Los Angeles Central Criminal Courthouse were packed with all manner of despairing families, mostly minorities, and their Panglossian-suited representatives, mostly Caucasian. Along with them, an army of potential jurors marching to courtrooms in numbers not likely seen on other days. Downtown superior courts call their calendars promptly at 8:30 a.m., and most trials start on Mondays. Many in the jury pool come on the first day of trial and are dismissed by the end of the day.

This busy hallway was a welcome sight to Amy as she stepped out of the elevator and meandered around bodies, avoiding eye contact. She had dreaded so much running into Kenneth before the hearing began that she asked Neda to come to court if her schedule allowed, but Neda had a hearing. At risk of being late, she delayed arriving before the court opened, to avoid the awkward gathering of opposing parties at the entrance. The many knots in which her organs had been twisted would be unbearable if she spent even a minute alone with him.

Whilst disappointed that he was representing Paul, she had wondered what kind of performance he might put on for his client. Had this been Neda's case and Kenneth Neda's adversary, Amy would have cleared her calendar to see it, no doubt cheering Neda's cause, but also cheering Kenneth's spirit.

Commissioner Gamilla Barney was presiding over Division 40 of the criminal courts. A short, stout woman with cropped curly hair, she wore her prescription glasses slightly pushed down her nose to peer over them at counsel. Kenneth knew Commissioner Barney from his days at the public defender's office. The bailiff took Kenneth's card and passed it on to the calendar clerk and Kenneth waited for instructions. The bailiff gave Kenneth a form to fill that would allow the commissioner to preside over Paul's case. Kenneth took one look at it and shook his head at the bailiff. At the very moment he was shaking his head, he noticed Commissioner Barney looking in his direction.

"Another attorney checked in for the defense in this case also," the bailiff whispered to Kenneth and pointed into the gallery in the direction of Cassandra who was getting up and walking toward them.

"Thank you," Kenneth said to the bailiff and met Cassandra as she came out of the row of seats. About then, Amy arrived and walked up behind them to give the bailiff her card as well. On seeing Amy as he turned around, he felt the attention of the entire courtroom focused on him. She had looked down as their eyes met, so he looked away as well. For a minute or so afterward, he was deaf to anything Cassandra said to him.

"She denied the continuance in a tentative ruling," Cassandra said.

"I know," Kenneth said.

"We might as well get it over with. It's only a preliminary hearing," Cassandra said, but Kenneth did not respond immediately because he was looking around the room for Sister Ramatu and Jo.

The clerk announced their case. "People of the State of California versus Paul Jackson."

Kenneth, Cassandra, and Amy walked toward the counsel table, all converging single file as they walked through a small gate separating the counsel table from the sitting area. Each wore an expression of calculated restraint. The bailiff exited through a side door and reappeared with Paul Jackson wearing an orange jumper, his hands and feet shackled. He sat against the wall in the jury box, farthest from the proceedings before the court. The calendar was only called to determine the readiness of parties for preliminary hearing, which would likely be after the entire morning calendar was called.

Paul kept his eyes on the counsel table. His physique had become much leaner since Kenneth last saw him; his facial features appeared chiseled with his cheekbones more prominent. His hair had grown longer than he usually wore it, but he was clean-shaven.

Once at the counsel table, all counsel stated their names and whom they represented, one at a time for the court reporter.

"Are we ready for the preliminary hearing?" Commissioner Barney inquired.

"Your Honor, we have a motion for continuance pending because I was only retained after the arraignment and I have not had adequate chance to prepare for the hearing," Kenneth said.

"Have you seen the tentative ruling?" Commissioner Barney asked.

"Yes, your Honor. I was hoping that the court would allow argument to reconsider," Kenneth said.

"Do you have any other information that was not stated in the motion?" Commissioner Barney asked.

"Not at this time, your Honor."

"Does counsel for the People have any response to the motion for continuance?"

"We oppose the motion, your Honor. It is untimely and unnecessary. The record will show that a previous attorney for the defendant brought a similar motion for continuance at the arraignment, and in the end that came to nothing as well. This is becoming a pattern."

"I am aware of the earlier motion. Thanks for reminding me. The motion for continuance is denied."

"So, Ms. Wilson, are you not submitting also to this court for preliminary hearing?"

"I am, your Honor. I signed the consent sheet."

"You are ready for the preliminary hearing?" Commissioner Barney asked.

"Yes, I am," Amy responded.

"You have all the officers you need available?" Commissioner Barney asked.

"They are on call, your Honor," Amy said.

"Well, counsel," Commissioner Barney said, turning to Kenneth. "It seems to me that before you arrived, Professor Rayburn had signed the consent for this court to hold the preliminary hearing, though she may have thought it was a mere formality. She nevertheless submitted the case this morning to this court."

"We will proceed with preliminary hearing at eleven a.m. Ms. Wilson, have your officers ready to go. Professor Rayburn, I am confident that you can adequately represent the defendant. Counsel, you are excused."

Commissioner Barney turned quickly to the calendar clerk without saying a word, indicating she was ready for the next case to be called.

When Kenneth turned around to leave, the first person his eyes settled on was Sister Ramatu, whom he had not seen earlier when he looked for her. A black hijab covered her head, giving emphasis to her stoic stare. Jo was sitting next to her, and she smiled reassuringly at Kenneth.

Kenneth and Cassandra were standing in the hallway with Sister Ramatu and Jo when Amy came out and walked past them with Kate. Kenneth excused himself and followed them. They both stopped and turned around when he called after her.

"May I have a word with you?" he asked.

"Sure," Amy said.

"Alone, please," Kenneth said.

"No, this is my colleague and the senior attorney on the case. She can hear whatever you have to say."

"This is not about the case."

"I can't talk to you about anything else, I'm sorry," Amy said and started to turn around, but Kate put a hand on her arm.

"It's okay, just hear him out," Kate said softly, before walking away. Amy stood quietly for a moment before she spoke.

"I can't speak to you," she said sternly.

"I know you said we won't see each other during the proceeding, but you have not even returned my calls."

"Not here, Kenneth. Not now."

"Then when?"

"I don't know, Kenneth, but that was my boss who just walked away, and she was being polite. Don't do this again, unless it's about the case." She turned and walked away. Kenneth returned to the party of four who were watching them.

"May I have a word privately with you," Cassandra said to Kenneth, and they stepped away from Sister Ramatu and Jo.

"Look, it's a preliminary hearing, Commissioner Barney can find probable cause to charge Cardinal O'Connor with this crime, much less your client, if she wants to, and no appeals court will reverse her decision. Let me do it and you can focus on the trial." Kenneth took a moment to think about what Cassandra had said. His spirits were already low from the conversation with Amy. He agreed.

"But Paul is completely confused right now," Kenneth said.

"Don't worry about that," Cassandra said.

They returned to the others.

"Professor Rayburn will handle the preliminary hearing by herself," Kenneth explained to Sister Ramatu and Jo. "It doesn't really decide anything but that the DA has enough evidence to take Paul to trial." Sister Ramatu put her hand around Kenneth.

"We know, son," Sister Ramatu said, patting Kenneth on the shoulder. Jo gave him a hug.

Kenneth and Cassandra bade them goodbye for now and said they would see them at eleven o'clock. Sister Ramatu and Jo sat on the bench in the hallway and waited.

•••

MALLAM JACKSON AND HIS men were in court when Kenneth returned for the eleven o'clock hearing. Mr. Jones and Big were there as well. There were lights placed at certain corners of the courtroom to illuminate the proceedings. Two cameramen and their large cameras appeared to be recording court already before the proceedings began, and several young people associated with the filming activity were moving hurriedly about, seemingly busy. Sister Ramatu and Jo were seated closer to the proceedings than they were earlier in the morning.

Amy, Kate, and Cassandra were already seated at the counsel table. The view from the back of the courtroom where Kenneth sat was striking. All those who would determine Paul's fate at the preliminary hearing were white women—Commissioner Barney, Amy, Kate, and Cassandra—even the calendar clerk and the court reporter who sat in an inner circle were white women. The bailiff was African American.

The clerk, a soft-spoken tall woman in her early thirties, exchanged glances with the court reporter, an older woman in her forties, before turning to Kenneth.

"Counsel, will you not be sitting with your client at counsel table?" the clerk asked Kenneth.

"No. I'm not participating," Kenneth replied.

"Nonetheless," Cassandra said. "Please come and join us." Kenneth agreed and joined them.

The sheriff walked Paul Jackson into the courtroom.

Commissioner Barney entered the courtroom from a door behind the bench, her black robe saved from dragging on the floor by the high heels of her shoes.

"We are back in the matter of *People v. Jackson*. Let the record reflect counsel are present, defendant is present, and my cough is present as well," said the Commissioner. Only the court reporter seemed amused by this comment.

Commissioner Barney briefly collected herself before she raised her head to look at Kenneth for the first time since she walked into the courtroom.

"I take it Mr. Brown has decided to join this proceeding after all?" Commissioner Barney asked as though she was talking to herself.

"Upon my invitation, your Honor. His presence is a source of encouragement for my client," Cassandra said.

"Very well," Commissioner Barney said, and turned to Amy. "You may call your first witness."

Amy called Officer Fritz to the stand. Fritz described the investigation and what the officers discovered, but this time included a listening device and modem that was found under the bed. He introduced police reports and explained how they were prepared, including, for instance, why there were both handwritten and typed copies of the same police reports. Photographs of the items of evidence collected at the scene of the crime were introduced, but the items themselves were not brought to the hearing, as there were no jurors.

This examination of Officer Fritz took about half an hour as Amy meticulously presented one piece of evidence after the other, showing the manner in which it was collected and the chain of custody, which explained how the items were maintained in the manner they were collected until the hearing. The key facts in the case and the witnesses who provided them also came out of this examination. When she came to Goldie, she made sure the record had the most detail. "Please describe the body as you found it."

"The corpse lay on the floor with one leg twisted under her body like it was broken, her face looking up at the ceiling, her hands spread to her sides."

"Was she dressed?"

"No, not fully, ma'am. She was in her underwear, but no clothes, and she was found by the door of her master bathroom."

For her examination, Cassandra picked the facts apart methodically. Knowing she could not defeat the district attorney on a finding of probable cause, she was only going to focus on the process the police used to collect the evidence, so as not to tip her hand at trial.

Cassandra examined Officer Fritz on the fact that the door was locked when the body was discovered and there was no evidence of a break-in. "What did the officers know of how Mr. Jackson obtained the key to the apartment before they arrested him?" Fritz said they did not have those facts at the time, but they knew he had been in the apartment from the testimony of the witnesses across the street and other evidence found in the apartment. "So, you surmised he must have the key from those facts, was that it?" Cassandra asked, and Fritz again said no. Many questions followed about how long Goldie had been out of the country and who was using her apartment at the time, even after she returned.

Finally, Cassandra examined Fritz on the information obtained from Ms. Ola before she rested.

"The People rest as well," Amy said to Commissioner Barney.

The decision was swift, as if it was written before the hearing was held: "I find probable cause for the crimes alleged against the defendant and bind this matter over to the superior court for trial. I shall issue a more detailed ruling for the record in the coming week," Commissioner Barney said and set the matter for superior court arraignment immediately.

CHAPTER TWENTY-EIGHT
What's In The Name

THE TWENTY-FOURTH OF MARCH became forever etched in Kenneth's memory as the day his life changed for the better. The insurance company delivered the largest single check his office had ever received. He knew it was a check the moment the messenger handed the envelope with the insurance company's return address and asked for his signature. His heart raced, wondering how much they decided to give him, as he signed the receipt. He got the check in Nancy's office and solemnly carried it to his office, expecting a much-reduced amount than what he had requested. They gave him everything. He placed the check on the desk rather slowly, sat down, and looked at it again without touching it to convince himself it was not a replica of some sort or a sample check used to illustrate what the insurance company's check looked like. Then he read the short letter that came with it.

The first person he told was Cassandra, who was of the opinion that the swift payment was "a contradiction of the insurance company's business plan." Kenneth told her to expand their search for experts and consultants to the best available.

Nancy was full of praise to the Lord for getting the check and genuinely oblivious to the irony that she had made the insurance company the handmaiden of the Lord, but Kenneth knew better than to say anything. "The Lord has answered our prayers," he repeated after her. "Yes, ma," he said when she shouted that "no weapon that is formed against thee shall prosper; and every tongue that shall rise against thee in judgment thou shalt condemn" and with many other verses, she exalted the Lord with hands raised up, eyes closed. When Kenneth returned to his desk with his door closed, he could still hear her singing, quoting the book of Isaiah and the Gospels Epistles, and reciting various Psalms. He decided to go to the bank.

Nothing could douse his spirit the rest of the day, but the fact that he could not call Amy to tell her. She had approached him after the preliminary hearing, in full view of Mr. Jones, Mallam Jackson, and his followers, which included two or three of the basketball rejects who had come to his house unannounced. Standing removed from everyone else in the court, she apologized for being so quick with him in the morning but reiterated that she could not talk to him or see him until the trial was over. He asked what had led to her abrupt change in behavior after their weekend together, and she said that perhaps she had come to her senses, and walked away before he could even respond to her. Later, he persisted in using the case as a pretext to call her, but she stopped taking his calls entirely and had them forwarded to Kate.

He went to Neda, and Neda explained that Mr. Jones and Mallam Jackson had gone to see Amy's boss. They threatened to send Mallam Jackson's followers to the courthouse to heckle Amy until she ended the relationship or was removed from the case. Kenneth was surprised that Amy could not give him that explanation, and Neda reminded him that Amy's discussion of anything related to the case with her boss was privileged. Amy should not have disclosed it to any one because the only way Amy knew of the threat was through her boss. Thus, Kenneth's tongue was tied as well. He could not confront either Mr. Jones or Mallam Jackson about the visit because it would mean that Amy had told someone, who told him, Neda reminded him.

Mr. Jones' and Mallam Jackson's threat explained why Amy put on a show for everyone to see that she had walked away from him. His stunned expression was their answer to what had transpired in his brief conference with Amy. Mallam Jackson had got his wish. Kenneth had been shamed in public and angry that he was not given an explanation for his disgrace. Cassandra had intercepted him before Jo could come to him, and brought up their arrangement to inspect Goldie's apartment, which she had been discussing with Kate. This had calmed him and returned him to a professional demeanor.

Nancy was in the bedroom reading the Bible and Kenneth was on the recliner switching channels on the television when loud banging on the living room door startled both of them to their feet. The next round of Big's banging on the door came with his voice calling Kenneth with expletives to open the door. Nancy was in the living room before Kenneth got to the door.

Big pushed Kenneth aside and stepped into the living room as soon as the door was opened. Only then did he see Nancy, who stood by the passageway to the bedroom, looking at him with a bewildered expression.

"I'm sorry, ma'am, I didn't know you was home."

"That's quite alright, Big John."

"Didn't mean to curse," Big said.

"Oh yes, you did," Nancy said and laughed as she turned and went back to the bedroom.

The aroma of the spiced fried chicken and curry rice Nancy had recently cooked still filled the house. Since Kenneth hired a secretary, all Nancy did in her spare time was cook and host people. There was always someone there from her church, for which Kenneth was grateful. The new experienced staff in his office also allowed Kenneth to set himself a time to return home, no later than 7:00 p.m., whatever there was to be done. All the windows were open and the ceiling fan was at full blast, but they were of little help clearing the air.

"What do you want?" Kenneth asked, still standing by the door.

"Is this how you welcome someone to your house?"

"I don't recall you bothering to ask if you were welcome to begin with."

"What the fuck's the matter with you?" Big asked, lowering his voice.

"When you stab a man in the back, Big, you don't come to their house unannounced and expect to be welcomed with open arms."

Big appeared to reflect on Kenneth's comment briefly, seeming unsure what to make of it.

"Who took those pictures at your nightclub?" Kenneth asked, and Big began to laugh.

"Nigga' please —," he laughed. "You trying to blame me for being all alone without your DA gal. Nigga', when was the last time you had any woman that stuck around? Seriously. Your last gal took your permission Kenny, with your permission, spent Valentine's Day with her baby daddy. Because…and nigga', you bought this shit! Because she said it was her son's birthday and she usually met with her baby daddy and her son on that day. And the one before that, where the hell was she from—the islands?" He laughed even louder. "Now that bitch was so smart, she made sure everything anybody knew about you two came from her, while you was promising her that you was gonna be discreet as she makes up her mind whether to date you or go back to her ex. And while you was being discreet and shit, she was going about town telling whoever would listen that you her puppy for now!" Big laughed some more as he sat down. Kenneth was convinced that Big was saying all these things about his past in such a loud voice for Nancy's benefit.

"Nigga', sit your ass down. We family. I don't snitch on family. Mr. Jones cooked that shit up when he found out there might be insurance money to pay him, and Mallam Jackson went with it. Why you think Jo went all out to get rid of him, even threatening to report him to your damn lawyers' association that day you was in court for the hearing?"

Mr. Jones, the conniving devil, had planned everything to ensure no one could speak about it, Kenneth thought, and finally sat down with Big.

"Make this quick, Big. I'm not in the mood."

"So, you gonna be like that all night?"

"The longer you take, the worse I'll get."

Big considered Kenneth briefly.

"I got this visit today about Footsie. I just about ran out of the club to come here, Kenny. Because this shit is too important to wait."

"Visit from whom?"

"Now, get this Kenny. They about to release her album."

"How do you know that?"

"This guy Paul hires sometimes for studio sessions when we got money, he was working on some gig for Goldie's agent, and the agent asked him what 'Footsie' means," Big spread his arms wide with a grin, as though he had just said something Kenneth should be happy to find out.

"What does 'Footsie' mean?"

"The recording company doesn't know, Kenny! And they about to name her record 'Footsie.'"

"Is it a song Paul wrote?"

"That ain't the point, nigga'. Goldie insisted the record company must call her first album 'Footsie.'"

"So, why is that important? Was it a song he wrote?"

"Ain't no song nobody wrote called 'Footsie,' at least ain't none that I ever heard. Kenny, the record company didn't wanna name the album 'Footsie,' but she put her foot down and threatened to sue before they backed off. Now she's dead and they're trying to change the title of the album."

"But first they want to know all they can about why she chose the name."

"Dawg-gone it. You smart, Kenny," Big shouted excitedly, almost jumping up from the couch.

"What's in the name for us?"

Big lowered his voice and leaned forward as though there were a third person in the room with them. "Paul gave her the name," Big said and sat back with a sense of satisfaction. Kenneth looked perplexed. Big leaned forward again. "Kenny, she was making her first album a tribute to Paul. She used to tell Paul that whatever happened between them, she was going to name her first child after him. But one time she also said she didn't see herself having any children. Why she gonna name her first album after the man they say killed her? That doesn't show that she thinks Paul's jealous, it shows she thinks Paul's a good man and he should be proud of what he created." Big lowered his voice for most of the discussion about why Goldie would name her album "Footsie," and it seemed Nancy could not hear him any longer from her bedroom because she returned to the living room.

"Big John. I am gonna make some food for you to take home with you."

"No, ma'am, I'm good."

"I don't care; I'm giving you my home-cooked meal anyway. The only reason I'm not serving it to you here is because I'm afraid you're gonna fall asleep in the car with the food so heavy. Are you sure you are okay to drive?"

"Yes, ma'am," Big left as soon as Nancy had packed some food for him.

Nancy closed the door after Big. Kenneth never stood up to say goodbye, but Big said what Mr. Jones did "was wrong as rain" and said that proved that Kenneth was the right man for Paul, "but Mr. Jones was right about the gal."

Kenneth was lost in thought when Nancy turned to look at him after closing the door.

"Everything okay?"

Kenneth looked up at her.

"Yes. I can't believe I'm saying this, but Big might actually be right about this one."

"Good," Nancy said with a grin and went back to her bedroom.

Sitting alone in the living room, Kenneth thought of Goldie having Paul's interests in mind even while making it clear that their relationship was over. She kept his name in the music contract as manager to enable him to get general liability insurance coverage and kept the promise she made him to name the record after him. Could the same be true of his relationship with Amy, who had severed all communication with him? His thoughts returned to Mr. Jones. He wanted to hate the man, but realizing now how it felt to have a hundred thousand dollars in the bank made him understand the extent the manipulative bastard would go to make money. Besides, the quickest way back to Amy was to please Mallam Jackson and bring Mr. Jones back into the case. At least, he would be our bastard now, Kenneth thought. And we can afford him.

CHAPTER TWENTY-NINE
There Was a Man

O N THE LAST MONDAY in March, Amy woke up with nausea and called the office to say she was sick. Without court appearances, hearings, meetings, or out-of-office visits, she did not want to take the chance she might throw up at the office. Rebecca, the division secretary, called her back. By then she had thrown up, rushing herself to the toilet in a manner she had not done before. There was not much in the retch except a slimy yellow puke with some semblance of what she ate the night before.

"Can you make it to the office briefly?" Rebecca asked.

"I think I'm really sick."

"I believe you, but the woman who lived next to the musician that died, the one you have been trying to find since we filed the charges, is here, in the office," Rebecca said.

"Rachel?" Amy asked.

"Yes, she's here with her sister."

"It's okay, she doesn't have to see me, just let Kate know."

"Kate isn't here, but they met with Melissa and said they will only talk to you. Melissa is not too happy with them. She's ordered me to make sure they don't leave before we slap a subpoena on them."

"I can't. I am really not feeling well."

Amy had felt nauseated a few days last week but never vomited until today. The month of February had passed without her menses. While it was the first time since law school that had happened, she had told herself that it was not entirely a cause for alarm because she had just begun a new job and received the most important assignment of her career, during which she was blackmailed by a militant African American Muslim leader and his followers. She had finally consummated her relationship with the man who had courted her for three months, then met the first man she had been truly fond of in college, and allowed herself the dare of fantasies she had thought impossible with him, only to be paid a visit by his father who convinced her that the American Congress of Black Muslims would hurt him if she continued to see him, especially if he lost this case, which he was more likely to lose given the facts of the case, not to mention the realities of the American judicial system. Kenneth's father had confessed that he had not seen or spoken to Kenneth in a while but had been in constant communication about him with his mother and if Kenneth found out he had paid her this visit, the path back to a relationship with him would be made worse. Even Nancy hadn't wanted him to visit Amy; Nancy only asked him to speak to Kenneth. But he knew that only Amy could stop Kenneth from proving he was "man-enough" to stand up to Mallam Jackson, when he was not. At no time in her career had she been so challenged, and no other eight weeks of her social life had been so complicated. All of which understandably caused enough stress to keep the curse away. It was thus explicable that she might miss a period or two. She did not mind calling herself an old maid if it meant that her worst Catholic school nightmare had not suddenly come true.

"Amy, what's wrong with you?" Melissa asked as she got on the phone after Rebecca went to call her.

"I feel like I am going to faint when I get up. I think I caught a bug."

"I hope you didn't catch anything, but you've not been yourself the past couple of weeks. But we need you here. This woman literally dared me to subpoena her. She said if we do, we'll only find out what she has to say when she takes the stand."

"So, what?" Amy asked, "We can depose her, too."

"We won't want to do that."

"Why not?"

"I think she's hired a lawyer, and he's telling her what to say to us. She said we won't want to depose her unless we want it on the record that one of the officers investigating the murder came back to ask her out that same weekend Goldie died."

"What!"

"My sentiments exactly. But she will only talk to you. She said you're the only one she's going to talk to."

"Why?"

"I don't know. Please come. I'll come get you myself and prop you up for the entire meeting."

Amy dragged herself out of bed, showered, and dressed quickly, wondering how she would keep from throwing up at the office. The nausea aside, Lent began on March 1st, the day it first occurred to her that her fatigue and missed menses were related occurrences. This was also when she last spoke to Thomas. Time away from him was no longer just a wish but a practical necessity. If she were pregnant, she could not imagine talking to him without telling him. Having decided not to talk to Kenneth, it was just as well she did not talk to Thomas. She had wanted to tell Neda, but could not get herself to do so. Neda would worry too much and be in her space as much as Alana would. Both would think her too naïve to carry the pregnancy by herself, and Neda would call her mother for advice for Amy in place of Amy calling Alana. There was no substitute for Alana. So, she did not call Neda. Solitude became the paradox of her condition. She craved the time alone to understand her predicament as much as she craved someone to talk to about it. Alana, though she had been right about warning Amy that this might happen if she got too close, was out of the question precisely because Amy did not want to tell her she was right—again.

She called to confide in Edward, who was safely in the New York tristate area Angela flew in unexpectedly, and had a girls night out with Amy and Neda. The relief she felt from telling Angela and Neda felt like expiation. Neda said very little all night and watched Amy like she was observing a woman in a ritual ceremony, the kind primitive cultures hold. Every time Amy's eyes met Neda's, it seemed to Amy that Neda felt betrayed by all that she had known about Amy until that night. It was as if Neda were meeting her for the first time with a strong sense of déjà vu. Amy would smile and try to put her arms around Neda or squeeze her hand privately or pat her on the thighs, as if to say: It is well. Neda would smile sheepishly, almost nervously, as though she did not comprehend these gestures. To Amy's surprise, she did not feel guilty for Neda's sense that she had been misled by what she thought about her friend. Amy could not be blamed. Moreover, she had begun to worry less about what anyone thought about her the moment she feared she might be pregnant. She may no longer be carrying the Wilson crest alone if she was carrying someone else in her womb, and she didn't care whom she was carrying, just that no one had the mandate on her identity any longer.

On arriving at the office, Amy found Rachel and her sister waiting in a conference room. Rachel had been difficult to locate since she moved without leaving a forwarding address, and while Amy did not think her absence would harm the case, she was afraid that the defense might call her. She was glad to see Rachel had come with her sister Amber.

Amber had the overweight plump of a sweets-filled child, Rachel, the water carved frame of an Olympic swimmer. Both had similar foreheads, evident from the sunglasses perched along their hairlines, which made them seem more alike than if they had not worn the glasses at all. An inch or two shorter than Amy, vulnerable searching eyes, and a disarming smile, Rachel cut an image Amy doubted she could trust. Helen had convinced Rachel to come back to LA and tell her story and Rachel was glad to unburden herself of it.

"There was a man," she began. "The man...he asked me and Goldie to a party in Paris. His friend was throwing a party and all the girls invited would make five thousand dollars just for the week. Goldie was going to perform at the party. We didn't have to do anything we didn't want to if we didn't take the money, but we still get the trip, all expenses paid and one thousand dollars for going." Rachel paused and looked down on her hands.

"You guys went?" Amy asked to encourage her to continue.

"Goldie backed out. I went."

"And took their money?" Amy asked. Rachel nodded.

"I met someone at the party. I knew it was the wrong place to meet someone, but he just seemed different...not seedy at all. After I came back, he started calling me and wanted me to visit him."

"All expenses paid?" Amy asked. Rachel nodded. "And the five thousand dollars still?" Rachel nodded.

"For a week," Rachel said. "After I went to see him, Goldie told me not to go again. She told me to stop taking his calls. So, I stopped. Then this man…who took us to the party—"

"Does the man have a name?" Amy asked.

Rachel appeared hesitant to answer.

"Between us?" Amber said, quietly.

"Sure, between us," Amy repeated.

"Monsieur Arnot," Amber said.

Rachel kept looking at her hands as Amber and Amy had this exchange, then she looked up when Amy asked her a question.

"You said 'us,' I thought Goldie didn't go?" Amy asked.

"Another friend went…but no one was calling her back afterward… Monsieur Arnot insisted that I take the call from the guy I met there."

"Why not?" Amy asked, the anger in her voice surprising her.

"We did not use our names when we went to the party. And he said these people have money and they are connected and they could ruin my career," Rachel said.

What career? Amy wanted to ask, but swallowed streams of her own saliva, feeling a mild choke, and cleared her throat.

"Monsieur Arnot suggested Rachel should take this man's call but tell him that she was married," Amber said.

"Did he buy it?" Amy asked.

"Yes, but he wanted me to still see him secretly," Rachel said. "But he stopped pushing to come to LA and I traveled out to see him."

"A good thing she's an actress," Amber said. "I don't know how you pulled that off."

"Paris again?" Amy asked.

"No, closer. Cancun, Vancouver…but then one day he landed at LAX and called me. My sister was staying with me."

"The man who introduced us…suggested that I ask Goldie if I could use her apartment because she was in London. We already kept each others' spares in case we needed help or lost it and couldn't find the manager."

"How about telling him you couldn't get away from your husband?" Amy asked.

"TI thought about doing that, too, but Monsieur Arnot said I should just get something on him, so if I want to break things off, I just say I will send a tape to his wife."

"You mean blackmail him?" Amy asked, the alarm in her voice rising with each response. Rachel nodded.

"Monsieur Arnot said it would make him back off."

"You sure trusted this man a lot," Amy said, looking at Amber, who nodded. Rachel looked at her hands reflectively.

"That was exactly what Goldie said," Amber said.

"I'm afraid I was beginning to like the guy I met, too, I just didn't want him coming to LA. And when I told him I didn't want anymore, he stopped."

"Did you blackmail him?" Amy asked.

"I don't know, but Monsieur Arnot said he would take care of that. He put the wires and small microphones the police found on Goldie's bed," Rachel said.

"We have to stop here," Amy said.

"Wait, there's a whole lot more," Amber said.

"You have told me too much already. Our office is supposed to give the defendant any information we receive that might point to someone else committing this crime. I'm sure you guys have been following the O. J. case."

"Yes, but Rachel doesn't think the man she was seeing did this. He was nowhere near LA when it happened. She checked."

"Perhaps you're right. But just a friendly piece of advice from me, you'll need a good attorney."

"I've got one. Helen hired a firm to represent me," Rachel said.

"Good—Helen convinced us that you were the right person to protect Rachel if she comes forward," said Amber. "As soon as you walked in, I understood what she meant. If you're not going to be the attorney on the case, we are never talking to the DA again. The lawyer said it was our right, Fifth Amendment and all."

Amy considered Amber for a while. She must have been all of twenty-three years of age, but far older than her elder sister in her wisdom.

"Don't believe everything your lawyer tells you," Amy said and got up. "Please wait here."

Melissa had a paralegal preparing a subpoena for Rachel when Amy got to the office, and Amy had said she would come to Melissa's office to pick up the subpoena after she had a chance to speak to Rachel and her sister. Kate was also in Melissa's office.

"What did she say?" Kate asked before Amy could close the door.

"You were right, she placed the listening devices in the room to blackmail some foreigner, but she's threatening to take the Fifth if I'm not the attorney on the case. She doesn't know what she's talking about, obviously."

"You are trying the case." Melissa agreed.

"Obviously, we need you at least for this woman," Kate said.

All Amy could do was look from one woman to the other, unsure whether she even wanted the case anymore. Her life had become complicated enough, and as Neda had said, there would be other cases.

"I would have to take a lot of your other files from you, because this changes things," Melissa added. Still Amy did not say anything.

"Can I think about this?" Amy asked.

Kate and Melissa looked at each other with slight surprise.

"I thought that this was what you wanted, and why you have been so down recently?" Melissa asked.

"No, believe me this has nothing to do with it."

"When will you get back to us?" Kate asked.

"I just need a couple of days."

"Okay, take a week," Melissa said.

"Did Goldie know about those devices?" Kate asked.

"No, I don't think so. I didn't get that far. I had to stop her, it was everything you feared," Amy said turning to Kate.

"What if the defense gets to her?" Melissa asked.

"I don't see her talking to them. She hired a lawyer like you said," Amy said to Melissa. "And if she does, she'll tell us what she told them and we'll be ready."

"We'll subpoena her just in case," Kate said.

"I think she can help us find Monsieur Arnot," Amy said.

"He's the foreigner she was blackmailing?" Melissa asked.

"No, he put those devices there to blackmail the person and used her as bait," Amy said.

"So, he probably heard Paul Jackson through those devices," Kate said.

"Or he heard the person he blackmailed come back for Rachel, find Goldie, then kill Goldie," Melissa said and shrugged. "There's your trouble," she added to Amy and Kate's quiet stare.

"Son-of-a…" Kate started to say.

"Can I have the subpoena?" Amy asked, interrupting Kate. Melissa took an envelope containing the subpoena from her desk and gave it to Amy.

"There's one in there for her sister, too, just in case," Melissa said.

In Melissa's office, for the first time since she left to meet Rachel and her sister, Amy began to feel queasy as she often did before her nausea and wanted to leave Melissa's office immediately.

"I'll come with you," Kate said, but Amy turned around to stop her.

"No, I have another couple of questions for them. Just give me a few minutes before you join us," Amy said and left the room.

Outside Melissa's door, she stopped and held her midriff to gauge how close she was to vomiting, then returned to the conference room.

"Who used Goldie's bed the day Goldie died?" Amy asked.

"Me," Rachel said.

"And the foreigner?" Amy said.

Rachel shook her head.

"She doesn't want to drag the person into this case." Amber said.

"Monsieur Arnot," Rachel said, before Amber could finish.

"And Goldie was okay with it?" Amy asked.

"She didn't know until afterward. When Goldie got back, she wasn't staying at her place anymore. I told her I needed to use her apartment again, and she just told me to call her when we were done, because she gave her car keys to someone and they were returning them to her apartment. But before I could clean up and call her, she just showed up at the apartment."

"Did you say she gave the keys to Paul?" Amy asked.

"She didn't tell me," Rachel said. "She was playful about it, but she would not say who it was. She might have given the keys to Paul."

"That man, Monsieur Arnot," Amy said, her jaw tightening. "Do you know where we can find him?"

"I don't know..." Rachel said.

"I think you do," Amy said.

"I really don't," Rachel said, and to Amy's continued incredulous expression, added, "Why would I know? He got me into a lot of mess."

"Amy, please, you have to understand, my sister is not a call girl. We were not brought up like that...and I know that deep in her heart she blames herself for everything that happened, but she was just trying to survive," Amber said.

"We're going to need your help locating this Monsieur Arnot, if that's even his real name."

"That's fine," Amber said, but Amy was looking at Rachel and did not acknowledge Amber until Rachel nodded.

Amy put her head around the conference room door and invited Kate and a male colleague, both of whom she introduced to Rachel and Amber. The male staff handed Rachel and Amber the subpoenas and took their contact information. "The trial date is May 8, 1995. You contact our office at least two weeks before that date if you don't hear from us."

Rachel and Amber stood up to leave. As they passed by, Amy held Amber's arm and Amber paused.

"I will do my best for her," Amy said as though it was for only Amber to hear, but everyone in the conference room heard.

After Rachel and Amber left, Amy was left alone with Kate. "Good job," Kate said smiling reassuringly, and extended her hand. Amy shook Kate's hand and slowly sat down as though she could not bear her own weight standing. Kate watched her.

"Melissa said you weren't feeling well. Are you alright?"

Amy looked up at Kate and smiled. She felt a strong urge not only to tell Kate she was convinced that she was pregnant, but to take it further and tell her the truth that she could not be sure it was Thomas's. But for the fact she had not told Thomas, she would have confessed it to Kate.

"I'm fine," she said. "I think I caught a bug. And then there's the stress of this case."

"What stress? You've handled it very well. These women came here asking for you by name because you went out of your way to be nice to the victim's mother, who in turn told them they could trust you."

"It didn't always feel like this, before today."

"What do you mean?"

Amy paused to consider how to begin, or rather whether to begin. Something else she had noticed about her condition was that, aside from the subject of pregnancy, she no longer wanted to leave anything unsaid. She considered what she wanted to say thoroughly.

"You've never really spoken to me like this before..." Kate raised her eyebrow and pointed to a chair as though she was asking for permission to sit. Amy nodded.

"Have I offended you in the way I spoke to you in the past?"

"No," Amy said, contemplating what to say. "Can I ask you a question?"

"Sure, please."

"Why did you pick me for this case?"

"When I got the case, I was just heading home from court. They called me to say LAPD was looking for someone to be assigned to this case. I live off Olympic in the mid-Wilshire area, so I know the place well and decided to drive there and see the officers. When I left that place, I didn't have a good feeling about the case. The woman was killed in her bathroom, her doors were locked—so no break-in. Nothing was taken; it appeared there was no sexual assault either. She was not in any committed relationship, and just got back from London, and there were professional listening devices in her room, and no eyewitnesses."

"I was afraid that was why you assigned me," Amy said grinning. She was truly happy to be finally having this conversation.

"I haven't told you why yet. And it was not because it was a hard case that you would work your butt off on. Later that night, after I left the crime scene, the officers came to my house to tell me they had a suspect, an African American. This shit was like the O. J. case without Ron Goldman. Then that weekend, I did a bit of research and realized this son-of-a-bitch's father was that Muslim Imam somewhere in the South Bay. That's when I thought of you. Publicity was going to follow this case, and I didn't feel I could handle it emotionally…because of things that were going on privately. You were starting that week and I just felt like you have been exposed to publicity all your life so you could handle it better than anyone else I could think of in the office."

"You know that's not true, right?"

"What's not true?"

"That I've been exposed to publicity all my life. If anything, I've been shielded from it far more than most people. My family often finds out that we are going to be in the news before it's published and are able to steer us away from reading it or finding out about it."

"Oops. Sorry. That's not what I was told."

"I wonder what else they might have told you."

"That you are a rather nice person…"

"That's nice of him."

"Her. Not him."

"Melissa?"

"No, Candace."

Amy looked puzzled.

"You don't know who she is, do you?" Amy shook her head. "A college friend of mine. We were both military brats. She went into the intelligence services but left early after being injured and works as a security consultant for uber clients."

"Like Thomas…" Amy said.

"Yes, there…finally, the elephant in the room."

"He was never really in the room between us, as far as I was concerned. I'm sorry to have brought him up."

"How have I spoken to you that was different from today?"

"You have always spoken to me like a subject to be given instructions and sent off on errands, not as someone who was emotionally relatable."

"I get that a lot here, not just with you. Like I told you, I was a military brat. Work is work and then there is a time for everything else. Perhaps I had my defenses especially up for you, but there was never any animosity intended."

"No, I didn't think there was," Amy said.

Kate stood up to leave. "Well, take care of yourself. If either of us were not here, they would replace us in a heartbeat, so don't worry too much about this place when you're not here."

Amy looked up at Kate, this time sizing her up just as Kate had sized Amy up when they first met, and, like Kate, never caring whether it was obvious or not. She could see why someone might think that Thomas would be attracted to Kate. Amy also got up to leave.

•••

THE DAY AFTER THEIR night out with Angela, Neda had called to tell Amy that Kenneth deserved to know it was the threat from Omar Jones and Paul's father that was keeping them apart.

"But it wasn't," Amy had said. She had not told Neda that Kenneth's father had visited her.

"It's a good enough explanation for him. He thinks he did something wrong when he didn't. This would let him off the hook," Neda insisted. Much to her surprise, Amy agreed. Finally, Kenneth also stopped calling. Then her isolation truly began. Cut off from Kenneth and Thomas, distanced from Alana, unable to drink with Neda, and afraid of getting far too close to Angela before Edward made his intentions clear, her circle of confidants, already depleted after her last social disgrace, became nonexistent.

She had resisted doing a pregnancy test, fearing it would be positive and she could not tell anyone until the trial was over. Now she had to do one so she could take care of herself and whomever had taken residence inside her. Fate always throws her a dice of ironies, she thought, and began to cry in her car.

CHAPTER THIRTY
Season of Atonement

A MY TOOK THE TEST that confirmed she was pregnant and called Angela, who got on a plane the following day to be present when Amy told Alana, and she confirmed it also to Neda.

Neda joined Amy and Angela for lunch on Friday after Angela arrived. It was the only time she could see Amy that weekend because Amy had decided to drive home to tell Alana rather than tell her over the phone. Her decision to see Alana in person came out of her conversation with Kate after the visit with Rachel and Amber. It had felt so easy clearing the air with Kate once Amy made known her issues with the way Kate treated her. Going over all her meetings with Kate in her mind, even after Thomas confronted Kate, Amy realized so much of her angst with Kate came from motivations she presumed and ascribed to Kate without ever discussing or verifying them, even with Thomas or Melissa. Once she aired those motivations in that conversation in the conference room, she understood Kate better. This child inside her appeared to be pushing her to clear the paths of her life of any mines that were laid for her so that they would not hurt her child incidentally. It made her bold, if not fearless, to confront nemeses she preferred to ignore in the past, knowing they could not hurt a Wilson anyway, even if they dared. Suddenly, she realized they were hurting her, mentally. And they had been for so long. Every time she had chosen to ignore someone who approached her with a familiarity that presumed she was predictable, they had nonetheless extracted a measure of her brain matter, if only with stress. The Wilson name and resources could protect her from physical harm but not from mental harm. She had never thought of it in those terms and could not wait to confront Alana with it. Alana had taught her that to ignore them was to rise above them.

Neda picked up lunch for three downtown and drove to Amy's apartment.

The three women were sitting over Neda's take-out lunch when Alana called. Amy put Alana on a speaker, because she could not bear a conversation alone with her mother before telling her she was pregnant.

"Did you think about what we talked about last week?" Alana asked.

"Which part, Mom? What are you talking about?"

"What you were giving up for Lent…"

"Oh yes, I gave what you said some thought."

"So, what are you giving up?"

"Guilt, can I give up guilt?" Amy said. Angela quickly covered her mouth with both hands to keep from laughing, and Neda's mouth fell open without words. There was a protracted silence on the other end of the line. "Mother, surely the good Lord can take a joke from someone trying to starve herself for forty days and forty nights."

"I'm more concerned about where the joke is coming from than how it is received," Alana said.

"Seriously, Alana. Lent isn't the time for righteous condemnation. Besides, I have never needed a mother's love more —" Amy said and stopped as she was close to crying, much to everyone's surprise.

"Are you alright?" Alana asked.

"I was going to call to tell you I'm coming to the Bay Area tomorrow."

"Why? Did something happen?"

"No, I just want to spend the weekend with you guys and Nana. I want to see Dad, too. I hope he's not travelling."

"No, he's not."

Alana suggested they both fast together, to seek discernment in their love lives.

"You mean discernment for me, between Thomas and Kenneth."

"And for me with your dad."

"I thought you guys shelved the divorce?"

"Well, he shelved it. But does doing that make him happy, or is he just going along to make your grandmother happy?"

"It doesn't matter. He should find a way to make it what he wants."

"That's what I believe, too. I also believe that if you love someone, you give them a chance to find what makes them happy."

Amy had never heard her mother espouse such an open-minded view, especially of marriage.

"Are you saying that divorce is fine with you now?" Amy asked, her voice appearing to crack again.

"No, of course not, honey. I don't know what I'm saying. Why should I be the one with all the answers?"

"Because I don't, Mommy. I was hoping someone had them," Amy said slowly and began to cry, though she was not sure if she was crying for herself or for her parents.

Angela came from behind, hugged and held her as she shivered through bursts of sobbing.

"Honey, I didn't mean to make you cry. Are you alright?"

"I'm fine," Amy said, collecting herself.

"Are you really coming up tomorrow? Because if you don't, I will have to come down."

"I'm coming," Amy said, and after a while added, "I'll give up dinner and chocolate; I already gave up alcohol, so you should, too."

"Oh, that is cruel!" Alana said. "I was going to do it with you."

"I have a lot to atone for, Mom."

"Don't we all, dear," Alana said before she begrudgingly agreed to the same, and Amy bade her goodbye.

"That was cruel," Angela said. "I can search this apartment right now and not see a single chocolate, but your mother literally has chocolate everywhere, like it's her youth that she's holding on to."

"And I have never seen you even buy one," Neda said.

"You've never seen me miss dinner, have you?" Amy asked.

"Is that safe?" Neda asked, one hand unintentionally over her stomach. Amy shrugged, then buried her head on her lap and wept again.

After they had lunch, Amy returned to the office to see Kate.

"I'm in, if you still want me on the case," she told Kate about *People v. Jackson*. "But there is something I must tell you first."

"What's that?"

"I gave Kenneth the insurance policy that would pay his attorney's fees. After I found out that his clients did not have the money to pay him and were promising to do so over the course of his career."

Kate smiled a more genuine smile than Amy had ever seen on her, with eyes glittering and a palpable energy flowing through her.

"I wanted to hear you say that; I knew already. I will sit in to help you, but all the ethical issues are now yours to deal with. Good luck."

PART TWO

CHAPTER THIRTY-ONE
War Room

O N THE FAR SIDE of town, near the border of the city of Encino, Kenneth and Cassandra pored through boxes of papers and cases in Cassandra's living room alcove. Systematically, they moved from the beginning of the trial to the middle of the trial, throwing up ideas and playing the roles of witnesses.

They first looked at the jury selection process, which Kenneth thought would be a good idea to entrust to Omar Jones, being an early and important visible role in the proceeding, and one where Omar's trial experience surpassed his and Cassandra's. Nancy had pleaded with him to involve Omar in the trial, if he could, to appease Mallam Jackson. Kenneth had already decided to do so, but only on the condition that Omar agreed to whatever rules and conditions Kenneth set for the trial. Omar agreed. A jury consultant had given them a report on the kind of jurors who would likely acquit Paul, and if the pool lacked such jurors, then the next in order of preference, and if the pool lacked those, they had another level of preference. The jury consultant's recommendation ran contrary to what Kenneth would have done otherwise.

They made a point to keep calling Goldie "Footsie" in preparation for doing so at trial and contemplated the order the DA would introduce witnesses.

"They usually start with the police, and proceed chronologically from the discovery of the crime, unless they have something more memorable and dramatic like the 911 call in the O. J. trial. They don't have anything that dramatic in this case."

"Conrad Wetstone would be their most dramatic for discovering the body," Kenneth said.

"But he is also our greatest challenge, so they won't start off with someone so difficult. Plus, they know we obtained a computer simulation of Footsie's apartment and they are sure it is for him. So, they know we are prepared."

Large pictures of Footsie's apartment, every room, every window, the kitchen, and the bathroom where her body was found, were placed against the walls in the alcove. An aerial picture of West Los Angeles hung on Cassandra's living room wall with the location of Paul's club, the ATM he used, and Footsie's apartment complex marked.

Cassandra had three law students helping them on the case. A petite African American girl with dreadlocks; a young man in his early twenties who seemed to always be in dress pants, shirts, and patterned leather shoes; and a red head in her late twenties with a quick smile and brooding eyes. The students prepared a file for every witness and some tenants at the complex where Footsie lived. Each file contained information about each tenant's alibi along with a general dossier, curriculum vitae, and criminal record if any. These preparations would take them into the weekend, sifting through treatises and old cases, anticipating objections, and arguing back and forth the motions they intended for suppressing evidence.

Kenneth reserved a suite for the duration of the trial at the Intercontinental Hotel, a few blocks from the criminal court building, to keep from having to return to Long Beach each day during the trial. He and Nancy checked into the hotel the weekend before the trial.

On the eve of the trial, the three defense lawyers had lunch at the Intercontinental Hotel and agreed on what each was supposed to do, including who would present certain motions, respond to certain objections, voir dire jurors, and even how they would sit at various times during the proceeding. Strangely, it seemed to Kenneth that Mr. Jones was looking forward to his role with enthusiasm.

If there was a moment when the mood of their team captured the weight of their responsibility for Kenneth, it was this time in the restaurant. Less than twelve hours to the beginning of trial, with the man who questioned his ability to represent Paul having just left them, Kenneth contemplated again what losing this case would mean. He noticed Cassandra looking at him intently.

"What's going through that mind of yours?" Cassandra asked.

"I'm thinking it's good we brought Omar in. He'll help in dealing with Paul's family's expectations."

Cassandra nodded.

"And you, what were you thinking?" Kenneth asked her.

"I was thinking how much your mother helped me finally understand you," Cassandra said.

"What did she say?"

"She told me how she discovered a stash of Playboy magazines you had hidden in the basement when you were seventeen years old. Ever since you were eight, you'd buried your head in books, always alone in your room reading. But when you turned fourteen, fifteen, and she still was not noticing any teenage issues from you, she began to worry. Then she found your stash."

"I was reading the articles," Kenneth said.

"Yep, she said you actually said that, and she quizzed you on quite a few of the articles, which you answered correctly. I told her if there was a seventeen-year-old I would believe if he said that, it would have been you."

"Thanks," Kenneth said, avoiding Cassandra's eyes.

"Never mind that. Anyway, she was already beginning to worry about you when she found them. It made her so uncomfortable that she went to see someone about you, find out if she needed to send you to your father. With no steady male role model in the home, she feared that you were emotionally repressed and worried that someone outside might have taken you under their wings."

"It wasn't the only time she worried about those two things. They were basically her constant refrain all my life."

"Well, she really was worried. But the man, I assume he was a shrink… she kept calling him 'the man.'"

"I know, right. God forbid Black people have to see a shrink, never mind all the bullshit they have to deal with on a daily basis in this country, most are more comfortable telling you they went to jail than that they went to a therapist."

"Anyway, the man told her that you were none of those things. You escaped into books as a perfect foil for the harsh reality of losing your father in Vietnam and then finding out it was all a lie that was made up because the man did not have a relationship with you in the first place."

"I remember the man. My mom never told me why she made me see him; I thought it was because she was afraid I would turn into a deviant as they used to say, but before then other kids were already looking at me weird, and calling me queer. The man said they only called me queer because their vocabulary was so limited that the only word they had to describe others who weren't like them was 'queer,'" Kenneth said.

Cassandra laughed. "There was something else the man told her that she never told you," Cassandra said.

"What?"

"He told her it may take another painful event or a harsh reality to bring you out of your world, and into our shared reality. A maturity of sorts. When your mother asked him what kind of incident that might be, he told your mother that she was the only complete good in your life, and her death might well be such an incident. So, she should not worry because when she is not here, you will be fine."

"I don't know about all that," Kenneth said.

"Your mother said this case was that maturity. And she was glad that you did not have to experience a harsh reality or her death to allow her to see it while she was still alive."

Cassandra could not tell it, but Kenneth was close to tears at that moment. He reached for his wine glass, and tried to force a smile, and drank some wine.

"I almost told her that losing Amy again was that harsh reality for you."

He chuckled and seemed to choke a little on his wine, coughing.

CHAPTER THIRTY-TWO
A Familiar Name

MEN CARRYING TELEVISION CAMERAS and microphones milled outside the courthouse, looking for people with any connection to Paul Jackson's trial.

Nancy had arranged for Paul's mother and sister to meet Kenneth and Cassandra at the Intercontinental Hotel instead of the courthouse. Kenneth and Cassandra wanted to tell the women what to expect. Omar Jones was with Mallam Jackson and his followers. They hoped he was doing the same.

"The beginning of a trial is a very technical affair. First, we lawyers bring motions to exclude evidence that we don't want the jurors to see or hear. We do this when the jurors aren't in the courtroom. Then we select jurors," Cassandra explained.

"This might take all week. Expect to be bored," Kenneth said.

"The jurors themselves can hardly stand it. After they're selected, we'll give our opening statements. The DA goes first, then we go. These opening statements will be like a roadmap to the jury for how we will show them what really happened the day the victim was killed. If the trial starts feeling unbearable, just remember that you're not alone. Most people in a murder trial wish the cup would pass from them. Myself included," Cassandra said. Kenneth nodded ruefully. Cassandra asked if Sister Ramatu and Jo had any questions, but they could only shake their heads. Jo looked grief-stricken already, but her mother managed a smile.

Trucks with satellite receptors blocked spaces in the parking lot and on Main, Temple, and Broadway Streets. Most were always there for the O. J. Simpson trial, but their attention that morning was on Paul Jackson's case. As Kenneth and Cassandra got to court with Sister Ramatu and Jo, the crews swung into action. One cameraman rose, pulling a man with a microphone along, the entire group rushed after them with camera shutters clattering. Kenneth and Cassandra declined interviews and pushed through the small crowd while Kenneth held firmly to Sister Ramatu's hand and Cassandra to Jo's. Two of the students from Cassandra's trial advocacy class wheeled boxes of case files after them.

Amy was already in the courtroom.

She wore a conservative black skirt suit, and a wine-red silk blouse. In place of her usual pearl necklace was a thin but intricate looking gold chain with a crucifix. Kate Peck and Officer Gonzalez sat with her. Behind them, a slightly graying white woman in a black dress with brown hair and a stoic gaze, whom Kenneth concluded was Goldie Silberberg's mother. Looking at Helen Silberberg for the first time, bowed and probably aged by grief, Kenneth saw in her demeanor and poise a striking resemblance to Nancy. She made the loss palpable and inescapable, which was exactly the effect that Amy's office wanted her to have on jurors.

Paul's father, Mallam Jackson, sat with Omar Jones, and to Kenneth's surprise, Reverend Brown. Kenneth froze on seeing him. Reverend Brown stood up and waved. Kenneth returned the wave and left everything to go to him. From where she stood by her table, Amy turned around to watch Kenneth meet his father. Father and son embraced, and Amy returned her attention to her table, noticing that many of the eyes in the courtroom were on her. Kenneth felt he was about to cry and held on longer to let the emotion pass. Reverend Brown could not let the emotion pass so easily. His eyes filled with tears. As Kenneth walked away, he could see Amy had her eyes fixed on them and searched for Nancy who was looking as well.

At the counsel table, Cassandra told him Mr. Omar had given a lengthy speech about the DA's persecution of Paul Jackson outside the courthouse, asserting that there was barely enough evidence to justify a search warrant if Paul had been a Caucasian defendant. Mallam Jackson had said it was clear to anyone with half a brain that the prosecutor was racially motivated. At the back of the courtroom, Big sat sweating, and behind the front row Jo and Sister Ramatu.

"We're expecting a lot of people in the courtroom from Mr. Jackson's family," Amy had told Helen. "The man in the back with the colorful skull cap is Paul's father, and the men behind him are from his congregation of Black Muslims. Don't bother with them if they seem to be looking at you." Helen Silberberg, kept her chin up but did not look around the room. On the far side of the same bench, behind the defense team, sat Nancy Brown and Anthony Rayburn as guests of Kenneth and Cassandra. The two law students sat in chairs behind Cassandra and Kenneth, as did Amy's paralegals behind Amy.

•••

JUDGE BARNEY STRODE INTO the courtroom looking bored and irritable but spoke more politely than his wife. Kenneth had not expected the intense disappointment he felt just to see the name "Barney" again on the presiding judge's bench. The selection of judges for criminal trials in Los Angeles County was supposed to be random, but any process that appointed a man to preside over his wife's supposed agitator could not be trusted, he thought.

Judge Barney acknowledged that his wife was the commissioner who presided over a prior proceeding in this case and mentioned that either side had the statutory opportunity to object to his appointment, but that he had not been made aware of any such objection. Kenneth did not make the connection to Commissioner Camila at the time and would not have objected anyway. Judge confirmed that the parties had exchanged exhibits and witness lists, the prosecution witnesses were standing by and could make it on time when called, and both sides were ready to address outstanding evidentiary issues.

"I suppose you have all reviewed this courtroom's standing rules for trials," Judge Barney said. Though Amy and Kenneth confirmed that they had reviewed the memorandum, Judge Barney went over it again: Routines on the presentation of evidence, making speaking objections, when to approach him in hearings, otherwise known as "approaching the bench," when to approach the witnesses, and what times the trial would resume and recess each day.

"Do we have jurors ready?" he asked his clerk.

"They're waiting in the jury room, your Honor," the clerk said.

"Send them up and remind them to wait outside the courtroom until they're called," Judge Barney instructed.

"I have reviewed the transcripts of the request that was made to Judge Pollazo on the letter written by the defendant, or perhaps I should say purportedly written by the defendant, and I intend to rule on those upon conclusion of jury selection, provided both parties agree that the court may open the letter and review it on-camera. Both Amy and Kenneth stated that they agreed.

Judge Barney sifted through the pile of files to the side of his bench and pulled a thick red folder from it. "We will start with the People's motions *in limine*." These were motions Amy filed, seeking to exclude evidence that might be damaging for her case.

Amy stood up and argued for the exclusion of all evidence depicting any kind of sexual activity at the scene of the crime. Each item of evidence was a separate motion to exclude, from the bed sheet to used condoms and other sexual paraphernalia found in the bedroom where Goldie was killed—nine motions in all. Amy first argued that each item was irrelevant because the People did not claim that sex was a motive and the activities obviously took place before the crime. Then she argued that even if the items were relevant, the evidence would show Goldie in such bad light that they amounted to trying the victim, not the accused. As Kenneth listened and watched Amy make the argument, he could see Helen Silberberg wipe her eyes. Sitting directly behind Amy, Helen bent forward, her elbows digging into her knees and her eyes on her feet.

Kenneth was convinced that Amy's motion would not prevail, until he saw Judge Barney nodding his head. When Amy finished, Cassandra stood up and responded that the defense might well wish to explore the notion that the sexual activity had something to do with the crime. Tests of the semen showed that they were not Paul Jackson's. A different person at the scene might have committed the crime. Judge Barney reminded Cassandra again that a victim's prior sexual history was disfavored in the law.

"In the trial of a sex crime, your Honor. But, as the People have just indicated, they do not view this as a sex crime," Cassandra said, in more animated fashion than was common with her.

"I will not have the victim tried in this courtroom," Judge Barney said. Cassandra remained silent and sat down. Judge Barney continued, "I'm inclined to disallow the evidence, but we will have to take up the issue when it arises. Counsel for the defense must advise the court outside of the jury's hearing before any attempt is made to introduce any of this evidence. The motions are denied without prejudice."

"The next motion I have is for the defense," the judge said. "This seeks to exclude a letter apparently sent from the defendant's business to the victim, but was posted after the victim had died. Does counsel wish to be heard?"

"Yes, your Honor," Kenneth said standing up. "This letter constitutes out of court statements obviously intended to mean what they say. Therefore, it is hearsay. Further, as the court noted, it was sent after the victim was already dead, as such it is a post-arrest statement by a defendant who has maintained his Fifth Amendment right not to testify in this proceeding— so far. The letter is hearsay, they are likely prejudicial, the letter is not even relevant to any element of this case because it did not factor into the People's decision to arrest Mr. Jackson."

"How about notice, counsel?" Judge Barney asked. Kenneth looked at the judge as though to ask whether the argument he just made had lost already. Ironically, the judge continued in response to Kenneth's unasked question. "Assuming I disagree with you on Fifth Amendment, which by the way is a testimonial right that should not bar the admission of a document— not coerced into the record, as far as I know. How about motive, notice, and other exceptions to the hearsay rule?" Still Kenneth was slow to respond. Judge Barney continued again. "Or for that matter assume I agree with you, how about motive?"

"Your Honor, to determine those exceptions to the hearsay rule, we would have to open the letter. Our motion is that not having that information without opening the letter, this letter is irrelevant to any issues in this proceeding." Kenneth then looked at a note Cassandra had given him, but it was too complex for his immediate grasp. "We would like consideration of these issues before going further," Kenneth concluded.

"Very well, counsel. Ms. Wilson?" Judge Barney asked.

Amy stood up slowly to deliver her well-rehearsed response.

"First, your Honor, we must concede that the letters are hearsay. They are out of court statements made by the defendant. However, counsel is wrong in his belief that the People wish to use the letters to convince the jury that what is stated in the letters is true. No, far from it; the People wish to use the letters to establish the defendant's state of mind at the time the crime was committed, which by proximity to the date of mailing on the letter cannot be denied. And we do not have to open the letter to make that determination. It is simply a fact that the letter reflects a contemporaneous state of mind."

"But counsel, we don't know when this letter was written. We can't unless we open it," Judge Barney said.

"There is a date stamp on the envelope from which a jury is free to circumstantially infer the possible date it was written. Even if it were written one year before the mailing date, the fact that it was mailed on a date so close to the date of the killing is just as relevant as the date it may have been written. I expect counsel will be able to come right out and argue to the jurors that this document was sent after the victim was dead. The jury is intelligent enough to weigh such facts."

"I think I've heard all I need to make a ruling, counsel," Judge Barney said.

"There is something else," Cassandra said.

"Not hearsay, self-incrimination, or undue prejudice?" Judge Barney asked.

"Not any of those, your Honor."

"Let's hear it then, Professor."

"Your Honor, I believe by keeping the letter and opening it, the People trespass on the personal property of Mr. Jackson without justification. Our motion should equally be construed as an injunction against such trespass."

"Oh, this sounds interesting," Judge Barney quipped. "Please explain."

"Thank you, your Honor. What is written in a private letter is the property of the writer even after the letter has been delivered to the addressee," Cassandra began. "There is no dispute in law about this. In legal parlance, the writing in a letter is intellectual property of the author, just as a play remains the intellectual property of the playwright."

"Can you give me a case to support this theory?" Judge Barney asked.

"Yes, but I did not come with any cases because we prepared this motion with a focus on the rules of evidence; I believe in the early nineteen hundreds the Supreme Court of the Commonwealth of Massachusetts decided the case of Mary Baker Eddy, the founder of Christian Science. In that case, the estate of Mary Baker tried to prevent publication of several private letters she wrote to someone. The Supreme Court of Massachusetts stated clearly that the writer of a letter has the right to restrain, and thus control, any use of the communication in the letter," Cassandra explained.

Judge Barney's countenance remained skeptical though Cassandra's rhetoric sounded compelling.

"Do you have a California case from this century you can refer me to?" Judge Barney asked.

"Not with me here, your Honor. I did not anticipate that I would be making intellectual property arguments in a murder trial. Still, from Lord Chadwick in seventeen seventies England to Justice Story in eighteen hundreds America, the line of authority that says a letter writer owns the very content of the letter and controls its publication is unbroken. I do not believe California or any state with common law origin can rule any differently on this issue."

"How does this then help your client?" Judge Barney asked, seemingly irritated by the lecturing tone of Cassandra's last argument.

"Mr. Jackson has not agreed to open the letter or to its use by the court in this case," Cassandra said.

"Well, let's hear from the People on this subject," the judge said.

"Thank you, your Honor," Cassandra said and sat down. Kenneth was relieved that the issue had not been lost. All the while, Paul Jackson remained stoic and quiet and kept his eyes on the judge, but when Cassandra sat down again, he squeezed Cassandra's hand gently under the table, and Cassandra squeezed his back.

"Clearly," Amy began, "the recipient of a letter has the right to open the sealed envelope containing the letter and inspect the contents as does the estate of that recipient if she becomes deceased. We submit your Honor," Amy sat down. Cassandra quickly stood up again, but Judge Barney was also quick to stop Cassandra.

"I've heard enough, counsel. When you get my ruling, both of you can continue this argument in the court of appeals if you wish."

"We will need this on the record to continue the argument on appeal," Cassandra persisted.

"You have thirty seconds counsel—literally."

"The date stamp on the letter shows that Goldie Silberberg was already dead by the time the post office took delivery of the letter. Dead women can't receive letters and pass them on to their estate."

"Thank you, counsel," Judge Barney said angrily. "That just takes us from intellectual property law to contract law and the mailbox rule, isn't that right, counsel?"

"We will also submit at this time," Cassandra said and sat down.

"I will take the matter under submission. However, in the interim the defense may assume that their motion is denied without prejudice if the matter is not disposed before the conclusion of the People's case in chief. It is so ordered."

Judge Barney went through other motions before he asked both sides if there were other things they would like to discuss before the potential jurors came into the courtroom. Amy and Kenneth confirmed there was nothing further, and Judge Barney directed the clerk to call the jurors into the courtroom. One side of the court's seating area was cleared for the prospective jurors to sit during their selection.

Judge Barney took the jurors oath, read a few instructions to them, and recessed for the morning.

CHAPTER THIRTY-THREE
Full House

JURY SELECTION TOOK THE rest of the day. Omar Jones was in rare form throughout. Judge Barney asked all the potential jurors a few biographical questions and directed the first twelve of them to take the seats in two rows of six against the wall between the witness stand and the defense counsel table. He referred to these special seats as the "jury box or stand."

Amy and Omar took turns questioning the jurors in the stand. After each round of questioning by both sides, each side was offered the chance to eliminate a potential juror for whatever reason the attorneys may wish. Kenneth left the counsel table to Omar and Cassandra during this voir dire but would rejoin them when Omar wanted to huddle. Omar Jones's theatrics seemed to please Paul's family.

Omar struck one juror based simply on where she lived, which was known to be a conservative community. The consultant had identified particular cities and suggested striking jurors on this basis. Amy struck a potential juror for having a brother who worked as a defense attorney in New York City, a possible indication of familial philosophy. These challenges went back and forth between the prosecution and the defense. Every time a potential juror was excused from the jury panel, a new panel member took the place of the excused juror in the jury stand and answered many of the questions the excused juror had been asked all over again.

The district attorney's office had held a mock trial in Orange County, using key evidence in the case and a retired judge whose style most resembled what they expected at trial, and barely got a conviction against the mock defendant. When they asked the mock jurors why they were reluctant to convict the man, their panel cautioned that some of them were resistant because of the evidence that linked Goldie to illicit sexual activity. This was primarily why Amy wrote a motion for each item found in the bedroom, hoping that if she failed to exclude one, she could still succeed in excluding others.

By lunchtime, three jurors were seated, a Mr. Rossiter, Mr. Hooper, and Mr. Gale. Anthony called Mr. Rossiter, a Latin American man from a gang-ridden area of Los Angeles, a disaster, but considered the other two favorably.

"He sounded very well-rehearsed. I think he saw the TV crews outside and said all the right things to get on the television jury. I don't trust him." The student interns agreed with Anthony. "The African American man, Mr. Hooper, on the other hand, I'm surprised the DA kept him. I don't care which branch of the Republican party they got him from, his mind isn't made up and you could win him. But stay away from the African American women among the potential jurors. Those you have to worry about because of your facts."

"How'd you figure that?" Kenneth asked.

"Don't tell me you've never heard a Black woman's opinion of what O. J. got himself into and whether he wins or not?"

Omar smiled. "But they've got a few of them on O. J.'s jury," he said.

"And, like I told Kenneth before, O. J.'s got a Heisman trophy and a few charities to his name—your client doesn't."

"I don't know. They kinda like me and have always been good to me on my cases," Cassandra said.

"Good for you, but Ken has struck out with just about every African American woman he's hit on since I have known him. So, I'd still stay away from them," Anthony said.

"Ha, funny," Kenneth said tersely.

Anthony had more criminal trials than all of Paul's team combined, so they listened. No one told him that some of his recommendations were at odds with the recommendations of their jury consultant.

•••

By the three o'clock break on this first day of the trial, only the faithful remained awake. Only four jurors had been selected. Another African American man, Mr. Tyrrell, joined the selected jurors before the lunch recess. There were still eleven more to complete, twelve jurors and three alternates. The audience shifted restlessly on their chairs.

Alana, who had relocated to Los Angeles for the duration of the trial, arrived after the recess and sat next to Helen Silberberg. Amy had talked to her during the recess and mentioned how the most difficult part of the trial was seeing Ms. Silberberg looking so lonely in the courtroom while Paul's family filled the courtroom and persecuted her with accusatory stares. Without asking Amy, Alana invited herself to the proceeding. It clearly changed Helen Silberberg's countenance. She smiled often as she chatted with Alana and seemed livelier. For once, Amy was glad Alana had interfered in her affairs without asking her permission. Amy and Alana had grown closer since Amy told Alana that she was pregnant. They were perhaps even closer than they had ever been. Amy had taken a limousine to the Bay Area with Angela and called her parents just as they got close to arriving to say she wanted to have the most important conversation of her life with them, and she wanted them together for the conversation. She had chosen her father's office for the conversation rather than the dinner table or the living room, recalling how much weight that space brought to the dynamics of conversations she had with her father growing up, and seeking to turn the tables on him. Alana and John thought she wanted to give them her thoughts about the divorce. Instead, Amy told them she was pregnant. She was not ready to discuss who the father was or whether she would make the decision to marry him. She only wanted to focus on making herself well and ensuring the safety of her baby. Lately, she had had bouts of nausea and fatigue. So concerned was she that she and Angela opted to drive from Los Angeles rather than fly, though her physician had told her she would be fine flying, given her age. What troubled her the most, she told her parents, was her mental health. The sense she disappointed both of them profoundly had kept her up for nights, and for weeks kept her from taking a pregnancy test, wishing the tell-tale signs would just disappear. On saying this to them, she began to cry because as soon as she accepted that she was pregnant after the test came back positive, she had looked forward to being a mother. This was in fact what she was created for, she felt. Alana also began to cry, and Amy could swear her father wiped a tear or two. No one said anything for a while. They just sat silently, wiping their tears with tissues John brought to them.

"How would you like us to support you, honey?" John asked.

"I only came to say I'm sorry, Daddy. I didn't come to ask for anything. But if you could take the weight of this guilt off me, it would really help this baby and me."

Alana came and embraced her and rested her head on Amy's back.

"Consider it done," John said and joined the hug.

Before she left that weekend, she and Alana had seen the family doctors for a battery of tests, prescriptions for the most recent nausea medication that was safe for pregnant women, and supplies of doses of vitamins, B-6 especially. More importantly, it seemed to Amy they had seen these doctors to reassure her that it was safe to fly back to Los Angeles rather than drive. Every night since she got back, she and Alana had spoken, sometimes for hours. When trial preparations began in earnest, Alana took up residence in the Hollywood Hills and got a spare key to Amy's apartment. She would often fly back on weekends and leave Amy and Neda, and sometimes Angela, at her new place. Not once did she broach the subject of Thomas or Kenneth, though Amy was certain she was in touch with her favorite amongst them, and when she began adorning Amy's apartment with flowers, and Amy in jest told her they reminded her of Thomas, she stopped.

•••

KENNETH WONDERED WHAT TO say to Amy when the inevitable moment arrived. Neither of them had been close enough during court recesses to say anything to each other, and after he noticed her watching him with his father, Amy had averted her eyes whenever their glances met. Besides this shyness, it seemed evident to Kenneth that both of them were fully focused on the trial.

At the end of the day, Judge Barney reminded the jurors to remember their parting instructions, especially the instruction not to discuss the facts of the case with anyone or read news materials that might affect their judgment on the case. He recessed the court for the day. Only five jurors had been selected.

Cassandra went to Amy's table as soon as the judge left the courtroom. "Officer Gonzalez, could you give us a moment with your counsel in the conference room?"

"Sure, but I wanted to talk to her for a minute, too. I'm sure I'll be done before you guys get to the conference room and she'll just meet you there."

"That's fine," Cassandra said.

"What is this about?" Kenneth asked Cassandra in the conference room.

"Bury the hatchet. I need your full concentration on this case. You are meeting her alone."

"Are you kidding? I am fully focused."

"Right, still, this is your chance to be alone with her for the only time that will happen in this trial. I've got an early class before court tomorrow. My colleague is covering for me, but I want to catch what I can."

Kenneth looked at Cassandra, but she only shrugged. The door opened and Reverend Brown came into the room.

"Sorry, I should have knocked," he said.

"Oh, no, you are fine," Cassandra said.

"I was going to head to my hotel, but I wanted to tell you that this has been one of the proudest days of my life," Reverend Brown said to Kenneth.

"You are staying for the whole trial, aren't you?" Cassandra asked.

"Yes, I plan to do so, but might have to run back in a day or two," he said.

"Thanks, Dad," Kenneth said. They shook hands this time.

"I better be going," Reverend Brown said to Kenneth.

"I'll come with you," Cassandra said, picking up her bag. Amy knocked and opened the door before they got to it. She offered Reverend Brown her hand with a smile. "Thank you," Reverend Brown mouthed, with his back to Kenneth.

"My co-counsel will hopefully be able to make arrangements to obtain the additional information we need."

After Cassandra and Reverend Brown closed the door behind them, Kenneth and Amy stood, with the conference table between them, looking at each other with longing neither would acknowledge. She was carrying files, which she clutched to her chest with both hands while her handbag hung over her shoulder. They both began to speak, apologized simultaneously, stopped again.

"Go ahead, you first," Kenneth said.

"I was going to ask how you were," Amy said.

"I'm fine, I suppose. And you?"

"I've been better," Amy said. "I really hope I didn't interrupt anything."

"That was my dad, I was not expecting him."

Amy smiled. "I know he is your dad."

"He introduced himself to you?"

"Hmmm, earlier, yes. And I'm not blind."

Amy placed her files on the table, and her handbag on top of the files. "You wanted to talk about something concerning the case?" she asked.

"No, this was Cassandra's idea. I think she feels that we both might want to clear the air before the case fully gets into gear," Kenneth said. Amy nodded. "She didn't give me time to tell her that you won't talk about anything concerning us until after this case."

"Maybe she's right, but this isn't the right place for this conversation," Amy said.

"I just don't understand what happened this time. You know I had nothing to do with Mallam Jackson and Mr. Jones going to your boss. At least level with me. Is this about your family again?"

Amy shook her head.

"I thought we agreed to trust each other with the truth?"

"But you are not trusting me now," Amy said.

"You are not telling me anything," he said.

"I am telling you that I need time," Amy said.

"For what exactly?"

"Keep your voice down," Amy said. She paused and contemplated how to proceed, then appeared to change her mind. "I don't want to take any chances with the case again."

"At least tell me what happened after that weekend to make you suddenly tell Neda to tell me not to even call, because I don't believe it was just about this case."

"I knew you wouldn't believe it was just about the case."

"Is it?" Kenneth asked.

"This isn't helping, Kenneth. I suggest we just drop it for now and walk out of that door as professionals," Amy said.

He picked up his brief case and walked to the door, but she was standing closer to the door and blocking his way. After a few seconds, she stepped aside to let him through.

"Don't leave looking this way. The whole world doesn't have to know what's going on between us," Amy said.

"No, they don't. And I'm not sad or mad, Amy. I just spend so much time thinking about what the hell happened, wondering what I had done this time, wishing I didn't feel this way about you, and just really struggling with everything. I hope that wasn't part of your trial strategy."

"It wasn't…in my plans," Amy said and looked down at her hands to keep from smiling. She wanted to tell him she missed him, too, but feared it would lead to another compulsive embrace and make her emotional in a manner she was powerless to resist.

"Do you want to leave first?" he offered.

"Let's leave together," she said.

"That's fine," he stepped back to let her through, but she did not move.

"I have missed you, too," Amy said, when someone knocked on the door.

Amy picked up her files and handbag and opened the door to find the clerk standing behind it.

"Are you guys almost done?" she asked.

"Yes," Amy said and stepped into the courtroom, leaving Kenneth behind.

"We're closing up," the clerk said to Kenneth, who felt rooted to the spot where Amy had left him, never having heard what the clerk said, but only Amy's words.

"One minute," Kenneth said and closed the door. He put his briefcase down and leaned against the table, unsure why what Amy said had taken him by surprise. Soon afterward, he collected his briefcase and went out of the conference room.

Big was sitting on a bench in the hallway with one hand in a fist gently grinding into the palm of the other hand.

"What did she want?" Big asked, as if to explain his reason for staying behind.

"Nothing, the Prof called the meeting, but she had to go," Kenneth replied.

"Anything new?"

"The thing is, Big, there are things in this trial that I can't discuss with you because of attorney-client privilege. I can't even discuss them with Sister Ramatu, and she's Paul's mother. You gotta cut me some slack."

"I hear you. I just thought she was telling you the record company released Goldie's first single," Big said. Kenneth stopped walking. "It's supposed to drop this week. And guess what the title of her record is?"

"What?"

"Footsie."

"You heard it?" Kenneth asked.

"I heard all her damn songs. Paul wrote half of them, but I ain't heard the album yet. This whole shit started because Paul was giving her the best songs he wrote. I told Paul our first big artist has got to be Black, but he had to give it to his old lady."

"Cool Jo's Café has a recording company?"

Big looked at Kenneth like he was searching for clues of intelligent life.

"What the hell you think we running down there? And I hid the master of all her songs her record company don't have yet."

"So, you've got a CD of the song on her single?"

"I'm sure we've got it somewhere."

"What is the single called?" Kenneth asked.

"A Past That Breathes."

CHAPTER THIRTY-FOUR
The Twelve

WHEN AMY SAW KENNETH the next morning, he seemed more affable and she did not feel antagonized every time he looked at her. In court, the pace of jury selection improved on the previous day's drudgery. By the morning recess, two additional jurors had joined the panel, both women, Ms. Pollock and Mrs. Cole. Kenneth and Omar had gambled on Mrs. Cole because the pool of remaining potential jurors seemed worse for their case.

Anthony, Tiffany, and Jed had come into the courtroom shortly before the recess.

"Your jury seems balanced for both sides," Jed told him, but he was the only one among them who had no experience with criminal defense practice, except for his time on a jury.

"Well, a balanced jury is a complement to the defense, so that's good," Tiffany said.

"Cassandra won't make it before noon," Anthony told Kenneth, "but you don't need her."

"Is she teaching a class?" Tiffany asked.

"She's writing a Writ Application to the court of appeals," Kenneth said.

"For what?" Jed asked.

"To direct Judge Barney to admit evidence of the semen on the bed and other evidence of sexual activity found at the scene of the crime."

"He excluded that?" Jed asked, astounded.

"He left the door open for the DA to try again and exclude it, by which time it would be too late for us to do anything to keep it out," Kenneth explained.

Cassandra arrived during the noon recess with copies of the Writ Application. Judge Barney's ruling, Cassandra argued, was too vague and ambiguous a denial of a valid request and justice delayed until a remedy was moot.

•••

AFTER LUNCH ON WEDNESDAY, the lawyers took their seats as the twelve jurors and three alternates they had selected filed into a hushed courtroom. "Make eye contact," Kenneth told Paul. "Look right into their eyes so they'll see yours, too, and know you are human, and look confident." Paul had simply clasped his hands together and shifted his gaze from juror to court staff as the jurors walked by him.

The clerk had placed note pads with pencils on each juror's chair, and each juror picked up the note pad like it was a sacrament and sat down. They appeared to look at Paul as though they were obliged to do so. Their postures depicted various cultural manifestations of humility and sincerity. Heads bowed or tilted in readiness to listen, backs straightened in preparation for an intellectual exercise. None of the chosen twelve had ever served as a juror in a criminal trial before.

Cassandra sat behind Kenneth and Omar rather than at the table with them, and tried to match each juror's chair with the name and number on the jury list Kenneth had given her. Mr. Hooper, Mr. Rossiter (the one Anthony had called a disaster), Mr. Gale, Ms. Crosbie, Ms. Pollock, Mrs. Cole, Mrs. Tewson, Mr. Tyrrell, Mr. Mellinger (about whom Omar expressed a lot of concern), Mr. Davis, Mr. Lynch, Mr. Birrell, Mr. Kilgariff, and Mr. Phillip (a fireman whom Cassandra argued would be critical of the LAPD's rush to judgment in the investigation, even though he might have law enforcement sympathies for the police as well). Kenneth had not written the name of one attendant. Thus, Cassandra labeled him Alternate No. 3. It was not a typical Downtown Los Angeles jury filled with minorities, but more like a representation of a small-town community. Six of them were white, four Black, and two Hispanic. The three alternates were white. Tiffany and Jed sat with Cassandra behind Kenneth. In the row behind the district attorney's table Helen Silberberg sat next to Alana and a paralegal attendant from Amy's office.

"All rise," the bailiff bellowed, and Judge Barney made his entrance.

Judge Barney went straight to reading the preliminary jury instructions addressing what the jurors were to expect, including the order of proceedings, what was evidence and what was not evidence, objections by counsel and rulings on those objections, side-bar conferences between counsel and the judge, the defendant's presumption of innocence, and the jurors' duty to keep an open mind until all the evidence had been presented.

The full courtroom listened in silence. On concluding his opening jury instructions, Judge Barney sat reviewing the papers in front of him as though he was certifying that he had said everything the law required of him. Kenneth's anxiety level rose with each second of silence. Judge Barney was taking an eternity to arrange his papers. Then came a faint sound of sobbing. Helen Silberberg could not take it any longer.

Judge Barney cast a long hard look at Amy, who turned to the attendant behind her and indicated that Ms. Silberberg be ushered out of the courtroom. Alana took Helen out instead. After their exit, Judge Barney turned to the jurors again.

"You will now please go to the jury room and pick your foreperson."

Everyone sitting at the counsel table stood up as the jurors filed past them to the conference room where Amy and Kenneth had met. Kenneth recalled how some of the jurors earned their living. Except for law enforcement and their wives, the jury consultant had not advised them much on how a juror's occupation would play into their verdict. Ms. Pollock was a waitress, and one of the victims in the O. J. trial had been a waiter, Kenneth thought. Was that good or bad? Mrs. Tewson was a housewife with no law enforcement affiliation, and Mr. Lynch was the proprietor of a café. Once the jurors exited, Kenneth tried to stop thinking about them.

Judge Barney told the court that he would remain on the bench until the jurors returned from selecting their foreperson, but the court would be off the record. After the jurors left the courtroom, Judge Barney summoned the attorneys to the bench.

"I have decided on my ruling on the letter the defense wanted to exclude, which necessitated that I open the letter. I wanted to give both parties the opportunity to see the contents of the letter for themselves before my ruling tomorrow morning."

He handed the letter to Amy, who had approached with Kate, and Amy took a deep breath that sounded like a small gasp. Kate flashed a surprised glance at her. Amy turned the letter over to Kenneth, who read it with Cassandra, neither showing any emotion.

The letter, or rather the note, in the envelope stated:

I'm losing my mind!!!!!!

I always thought I could do anything I set my mind to _____

_____

but I can't eat, can't drink, can't sleep, or get over you no matter what
I try. Don't fucking do this or I'll lose my mind. Over you

There were several crossed out words that were no longer legible. Kenneth and Cassandra returned the letter to the judge.

"You will have my ruling by eight thirty tomorrow morning, which should give you sufficient time to incorporate it into your opening statements if necessary, when we resume by ten a.m."

"Might we get copies after recess today?" Kenneth asked.

"That sounds fair," Judge Barney said. "You can arrange with the clerk."

The attorneys returned to their tables. Amy remained visibly shaken by the words on returning to the counsel table. Kate seemed happy. Neither Cassandra nor Kenneth mentioned anything to Paul when they returned to their table.

About ten minutes after the jurors left, they returned to say that they had selected their foreman.

"And who is your foreman, or woman?" Judge Barney asked.

Juror number 12, Mr. Gale, stood up and said he was the foreman. Kenneth looked back at Anthony, Tiffany, Jed, and Cassandra, all of whom had expected Mr. Rossiter or Mr. Mellinger. No one guessed Mr. Gale would be voted foreman.

Judge Barney congratulated Mr. Gale and thanked the jurors again, admonishing them to take their participation and his instructions seriously, as a man's liberty would depend on it.

CHAPTER THIRTY-FIVE
Opening Statements

J UDGE BARNEY'S RULING ON the letter was in writing and available as he
promised by 8:30 a.m., but he read the ruling to the full court when trial
resumed. The letter would be admissible only if the defendant took the
stand. If the defendant did not take the stand, the DA was invited to make
the case that one of the exceptions to the hearsay rule should apply to allow
admission of the letter but not for the truth of the matter asserted.

A chorus of hushed voices filled the room, perhaps because many in the
audience did not understand what Judge Barney was saying. He banged his
gavel on the bench and looked sternly at the audience; all fell silent again.

"There will be silence in the audience for the entirety of this trial or
I will send people out and never let them back in again."

"May we address the court?" Amy inquired after the courtroom quieted
down.

"Yes, you may."

"We accept the court's ruling on this letter."

Kenneth stood up. "We have concerns about your Honor's ruling,
whether the defendant testifies or not, the prejudice in the letter outweighs
any possible exception the DA may argue to admit the letter in this trial."

"I won't tell you how to try your case, if you don't tell me how to judge
it, counsel," Judge Barney said. "My ruling stands until the People seek to
introduce the evidence."

Judge Barney directed the clerk to call in the jurors. After the jurors
were seated, he thanked them again and informed them that the district
attorney would be making her opening statement.

•••

AMY BEGAN HER OPENING statement and went on to speak for about forty minutes. She thanked and commended the jurors for coming to serve. "There are those who actively come to avoid jury service, but our system of justice would be nothing without the commitment of men and women like you. And because of you, it is the best in the world at guaranteeing that every man or woman gets the opportunity to be heard, when charged with a crime…Regardless of what anyone believes you should do, or what you think the judge wants you to do, our system of justice says you must do what your conscience tells you, based on the facts.

"John Adams said it best a long time ago, 'it is not only a juror's right, but his duty to find the verdict according to his own best understanding, judgment, and conscience, though in direct opposition to the instruction of the court.'

"So, ladies and gentlemen of the jury, your commitment means you must do the right thing in this case, without fear of persecution, condemnation, or judgment from anyone. To listen to the facts and hear the truth and have the courage to find the verdict according to that truth, regardless of what distractions and noise anyone might throw at you.

"Now, let me tell you about the job at hand. On January 6, 1995, the manager of an apartment complex on Armacost Boulevard in West Los Angeles went to the apartment of a young woman living there to take a look at some plumbing problems she had complained about. When he got there, he found the young woman dead on the floor of her bathroom.

"The young woman's name was Goldie Silberberg. Her mother is the lady sitting in the first row directly behind the table where I sat, over there, and her father passed away three years ago. *She was an only child and a free spirit, born to parents who were civil rights activists. Goldie saw no colors she did not like and wore scars few could see for the choices she made at a very early age.* Her grandparents survived the concentration camp in Auschwitz; so her family brought her up to abhor prejudice of any type. *Goldie was pure gold. She did not deserve to die; it is now up to you to see the facts and call it what it is, wickedness.*"

Amy told them that Conrad was in shock after he saw the body, and when he recovered, he called the company that hired him to manage the building and then called the police. "There will be some question about when Mr. Wetstone called the police, but there will not be any question about whether the body he discovered was dead already or if he had anything to do with her death. The point, ladies and gentlemen, is that the defendant's attorneys will try to make a mountain out of every molehill in this trial because they believe that all they have to do for their client to get away with murder is to plant seeds of doubt in your mind."

"Objection," Cassandra said.

"Overruled," Judge Barney said. "But counsel should refrain from trying to characterize what the other side would do," he continued without looking up from his file.

"Thank you, your Honor," Amy said, and continued. "Ladies and gentlemen of the jury, as I was saying, your job is to find the truth and guard it selflessly. When people can't change the truth, they try to bend it or make it seem like half-truths or make you believe there may be another competing truth out there that they just haven't been able to discover yet. There is a Far East saying that 'there are three things that cannot be long hidden: the sun, the moon, and the truth.' All sides in this trial know this, but one side would nonetheless try to hide the truth long enough to sow confusion."

Amy then told them that when Goldie was found dead, she was not staying at her apartment, but had only come to that apartment because she had arranged to meet the defendant there, rather than where she lived, because she did not want him to know where she had moved. She told them the evidence from the apartment manager, the police officers, and her music agent, Mr. Pare, would confirm these facts. What these witnesses had to say about Goldie moving was important to understand because while there may be evidence of some sexual activity at the apartment, none of that evidence had anything to do with Goldie or her death.

In this manner, Amy went through all the evidence she would present to the jury, the statement by Ms. Ola that he was in the apartment earlier in the day, the ATM photographs, and the timeline of the crime juxtaposed against the timeline of Paul's alibi. She did not go through the evidence of sexual activity.

Amy then explained what the evidence would show about Paul. She told the jury that Paul was brought up with racial hatred that never left his blood even as the times passed by. "The son of the leader of a group known as the American Congress of Black Muslims, or ACB for short, which preached so much hatred that even in African American communities their nickname was the Anti-Christ Brothers because they always preached against the 'White Jewish Jesus.' *We already know, and research has shown, that how long you breastfeed a child has implications for his development later in life. Now, you give that child his breast milk with a theory as hateful as the Anti-Christ, and sooner or later he's never going to forgive a white Jewish woman who leaves him for a white man after he has helped make her successful. The evidence will show that this was exactly what happened between the defendant and Ms. Silberberg.*"

Then Amy, standing just three feet from the front row of the jury panel, said, *"You have met the defendant Paul Jackson, ladies and gentlemen; how I wish you also met Goldie Silberberg before she was killed—take a look."* She then walked over to a corner by the calendar clerk and pulled out a cart with a television on it, which she placed in front of the jury. Kate also got up and pulled another television from beside the sheriff. Amy waited for them and turned both televisions on with one button on a remote control. A picture of Goldie smiling emerged on the screen and dissolved into scenes from a Super 8 camera of three-year-old Goldie all bundled up with ten inches of snow on the ground. This was followed by a montage of a skinny little girl in a high school play, then a young woman on campus in college still not as pretty as the woman that emerged in a music video that followed the montage. Helen Silberberg started crying again but tried to muffle the sounds. The paralegal sitting next to her quickly hushed her.

When the short video ended, Amy approached the jury stand again as though she had more to explain to them, but only added, "thank you, ladies and gentlemen, for your time," and sat down. Returning to her desk, Amy could see Alana sitting so humbled and dabbing her eyes to keep from ruining her make-up. Amy smiled reassuringly and kept her eyes on her mother until she got to her table and turned around to sit down.

Kate passed her a note: "Well done. *Where did you get the ACB stuff from?*" Amy panicked slightly and looked over to the defense table. Her eyes met Paul's and strengthened her resolve. She took out her pen and wrote, *"research."*

"Good job," Kate whispered. Officer Gonzalez smiled.

Paul turned to meet Big's icy gaze, full of conviction that someone had betrayed the clan again.

•••

KENNETH ROSE TO GIVE his opening statement. Nancy bowed her head, and perhaps for the first time in a long time felt Reverend Brown's hand reach out and hold hers. They interlocked fingers. Still standing at the defense counsel table, Kenneth deliberately unbuttoned and buttoned his suit before he picked up his notebook and headed to the lectern. Omar, who was still at the counsel table with Kenneth, took a deep breath and looked back at Mallam Jackson with a smile. Paul appeared not to have recovered from Amy's opening statement and perhaps from seeing Goldie so alive.

Kenneth also thanked the jurors and expressed his admiration for this system of justice. Then he went straight to what the evidence will show: "There were no eyewitnesses, no animosity, no criminal history, no motive—only one contrived on breast milk—and no common sense. *Yes, Ms. Silberberg was pure gold, because Paul helped refine her, at least he did for her music. He gave her the stage name 'Footsie' because he loved the way she danced.*

"*Yesterday, as I was walking out of the courtroom, I heard that the record company had released one of her songs from her new record. Guess what the title of her record is? Footsie. Now, why would she want to give her record the name that this man had given her? The evidence will show it was to pay tribute to the man who made her a success. So, allow me if you will, to call her by this name with which she found success, 'Footsie.'*"

Kenneth explained how Paul left his father at fifteen and hitched a ride from Detroit to join his mother in Los Angeles. "*In Los Angeles, the only license Paul Jackson could get to start his business was in a run-down part of the city. Still, he built the most respectable nightclub east of Hollywood. In this case you will hear a lot about 'Cool Jo's Café' but not 'Paul Jackson's Café,' because Paul*

Jackson prefers to give others the limelight. He named his club after his sister Jo, her full name is Josephine, who is sitting right over there with his mother. Industry scouts went to Cool Jo's Café to look for future stars and steal them from him, but he never relented.

"*When Paul met Footsie, she was nearing thirty in an industry where the target age for new artists is eighteen to twenty-five. They fell in love first, then the music happened, but the DA will tell you that when it comes to their kind of love, you can't trust it. The violins you hear don't mean a thing. It is the colors of their skin and the religions they were raised in that matter. If this jury were picked in the 1950s, I would be worried. I'm not worried today because I trust that you all came to your duties as jurors with open minds to judge Paul Jackson, as Dr. Martin Luther King Jr. said, 'not by the color of his skin, but by the content of his character.' I trust that you all have come fortified with 'dykes of courage against the flood of fear.' A great judge in England, Lord Byron, once said that 'love will find a way through paths where wolves fear to prey.' The evidence will show you that the love that these two young people found did just that—one the son of a Muslim clergy who refuses to be silenced about the racial injustice in America, and the other the daughter of a Jewish family who survived the Holocaust. In many places around the world, these two would be stoned for finding each other, but in America they got their chance. Do not let anyone tell you that perhaps they shouldn't have because it ended in tragedy. Their love and her tragedy had nothing to do with each other.*"

Kenneth told the jurors that the evidence would show that while Paul had some past success with a few songs, Footsie was going to be the break of a lifetime with constant royalties as she rose in fame. "*It didn't matter who managed her career to such heights, the royalties would come to Paul, the songwriter who wrote most of her songs. The evidence will show Paul Jackson had every reason to help his muse live, and no motive to kill her.* She was the inspiration of his career and the music of his life."

Kenneth then let the jurors know that the law requires the DA to prove the allegations beyond a reasonable doubt, not just to put evidence in front of them. "When they tell you that evidence of sexual activities has nothing to do with who killed her, they have to show it beyond a reasonable doubt. How? Perhaps bring the people who were there having sex to say they had nothing to do with the crime. When they say they found Mr.

Jackson's fingerprints at the scene of the crime, they have to show beyond a reasonable doubt that the prints were not there long before she was killed. When they tell you she was killed out of hatred, they can't just rely on hearsay. And when they tell you that a woman who had not used her apartment for three months suddenly complained that her kitchen sink was not working, you have to ask yourselves, why would she make such a complaint on a house she was not using?

"Ladies and gentlemen, what the evidence will show is that when life gave Paul Jackson hardship, he gave himself to work, and worked even harder because he believed in the American dream. It was that belief that united him with Footsie, even when their fathers disagreed with their chosen path in music. In the rough, seedy clubs of Los Angeles, when no one else would believe in her, Paul believed in Footsie and she trusted him with her career. Together, they were moving toward great success before a beast cut their dream short."

Kenneth thanked the jurors again and sat down. Omar turned to look at him and caught Paul's eyes instead. "Not bad," he whispered, "but when you had the knife in them, you should have twisted it more, and then thrust it in like Brutus." Paul, who had seemed pleased as Kenneth sat down, nodded to Omar's comment. "You shoulda talked more about Momma…" he said. Looking from one to the other as they spoke, Kenneth nodded, and turned to look at Cassandra.

Cassandra was happy with the opening statement, which came out differently from what she had heard or expected. She had provided Paul with a note pad to write down his comments or anything that occurred to him in the course of the examination of witnesses. Following Cassandra's reassuring smile, Paul passed a note to Kenneth saying the reason he gave her the name had nothing to do with her dancing, but he was grateful, especially for the story, and the fiction of hitching a ride from Detroit to Los Angeles to be with his mother.

"Her dancing was a better story than what Big told me," Kenneth said.

"I like it," Paul said.

Judge Barney directed the jurors to take their morning recess. As the jurors filed out, the attorneys and everyone at the counsel table stood up.

"Who are the gentlemen in the suits and scarves in this weather, the ACDC people?" Judge Barney asked the calendar clerk in a stage whisper.

"I believe so, your Honor, the ACB people," the clerk responded.

Judge Barney scribbled a note and left the courtroom.

"Counsel, Mr. Brown and Mr. Jones, do you have a minute?" the clerk called out. Kenneth and Omar walked up to her, and she gave Kenneth Judge Barney's note. *"No more than three members of the ACB are allowed in the courtroom at any one time during the proceedings, unless they can show they are also blood relatives."* Omar read it over Kenneth's shoulder. Kenneth looked at Omar and, without exchanging words, Omar took the note and went to Mallam Jackson.

During the morning recess Omar walked up to Nancy, shook her hand warmly and said, "Your son is a better lawyer than anyone thought."

Nancy smiled.

"I know, ma'am, except for you," Omar said. Jo raised her hand. "I stand corrected, ladies." He was leaving the courthouse as agreed, not to join them for the rest of the week.

Seeing no likely witnesses other than the officer sitting with Kate and Amy, Kenneth and Cassandra expected the officer would be Amy's first witness. In all, Amy had listed twenty-six witnesses, but only eight of them were key to a verdict: Officer Gonzalez, Officer Fritz, Officer Tse, Dr. Kio, Didi Pare, Conrad Wetstone, Rachel Johnson, and Ms. Ola Mohammed.

•••

WHEN THE TRIAL RESUMED, Officer Gonzalez took the stand and testified that around two o'clock on Friday afternoon, the manager of an apartment complex on Armacost Street in West Los Angeles had called the Los Angeles Police Department about a homicide. Motorcycle patrol officers were dispatched to the scene immediately to secure the area and upon entering the victim's apartment, detectives discovered Goldie Silberberg's body. Gonzalez introduced pictures of Goldie's body on the bathroom floor in her underwear. Her legs were twisted under her, and she was looking up at the ceiling, bent a little to the side. Gonzalez also produced other pictures the police took at Goldie's house on that day.

The police had collected a little skin residue from Goldie's fingernails, but claimed they were unable to match it to Paul Jackson or any other man. They were able to recover impressions of shoes on the tile floor in Goldie's guest bathroom. The tiles had been removed and taken to the lab. Every item collected, however small, had been placed in a separate container and catalogued. As Officer Gonzalez spoke, it was evident that Amy was just using him to identify and mark evidence. Kenneth did not object.

With about twenty minutes left before the afternoon recess, Amy dragged her examination to continue past the recess rather than turn the witness over to Kenneth for cross examination. She introduced what she thought were the most damaging prosecution evidence on either side of the recess.

Like three rapid shots, Amy examined Officer Gonzalez on the beer bottles found in the second bedroom, the impression of the shoe prints taken from a pair of Paul's shoes, and the ATM photographs. Amy had placed a small table in front of the witness stand and opposite the jurors. On this table, she placed the beer bottles, the impressions of the shoe prints and Paul's shoes, and left them exposed to the jury for as long as she examined Officer Gonzalez on them. The veteran officer understood and was in no hurry to give his answers either.

"Is this a good time to recess?" Amy asked Judge Barney when it seemed her delaying tactics were taking away from the impact of the damaging evidence. The clock was still about three minutes from the scheduled recess.

"I suppose it is as good as any," Judge Barney replied.

•••

WHEN THE JURORS RETURNED to their seats after the recess, Judge Barney was already seated and Officer Gonzalez was waiting on the witness stand. Paul had still not said a word since the examination began, even during recess. His note pad was filled with doodles of squares and circles with thick boundaries of repeated drawing. Kenneth tried to reassure him that every murder trial had a measure of damaging evidence against the defendant— otherwise there would be no need for the trial.

Amy asked the judge to admit the evidence she had displayed before the recess and Judge Barney agreed. "This concludes the People's direct of this witness, your Honor," Amy said and sat down.

Kenneth decided to start his questioning on these items of evidence Amy had introduced while they were still fresh on the jurors' minds. He asked Cassandra to keep an eye on his checklist, in case he forgot something.

"When did you first decide that Paul Jackson was a suspect in this case?"

"He was always a person of interest because he was her boyfriend."

"When did you first learn that he was her boyfriend?"

"When the couple across the street told us they saw them arguing, and the lady next door told us they dated."

"And what time during the investigation was that?"

"Early in the investigation, around four p.m. or so; we were still collecting evidence."

"And after that time, when you arrived at her house and were collecting evidence from the scene of the crime, who else did you consider a suspect?"

"Like I said, he was just a person of interest, not a suspect at the time."

"Very well, then. Who else was a person of interest?"

"We were talking to people, but he was the only person of interest at that time."

"Ms. Ola told your investigators that Mr. Jackson was arguing with Footsie earlier that day, and an older man came in, is that correct?"

"Yes, she did."

"And based on that you began to consider Mr. Jackson a person of interest, is that correct?"

"We also had information from her neighbor –"

"I am getting to that, but first focus on my question," Kenneth interrupted him, before continuing. "The first information you had that made him a person of interest based on your testimony here was that Ms. Ola saw them arguing, is that correct?"

"Yes, I suppose."

"But the older man who came in while he was arguing with her was never made a person of interest, is that correct?"

Officer Gonzalez paused a while with apparent displeasure before answering, "No."

"This older man, was he white or Black?"

"Objection," Amy said but was quickly overruled, as she expected.

"He was white."

"What were Mr. Jackson and the victim arguing about?"

"We don't know."

"The older man did not tell you?"

"We did not get the chance to talk to him."

"Wait a minute. LAPD never spoke to the older man?"

"He relocated after the incident."

"Did he move before or after you arrested Mr. Jackson?"

"We are not sure. It could have been before."

"And still he was never a person of interest or a suspect, even though it was clear that the only time anyone saw Mr. Jackson in that apartment, the older gentleman was there as well?"

"All our leads showed that Mr. Jackson committed the crime."

"And the older white man got away?"

"Objection," Amy said.

"Sustained," Judge Barney agreed.

"Do you have any evidence, Officer, that conclusively eliminates the older white man, who was also seen at the apartment at the time Mr. Jackson was there, as the person who committed the crime?"

"I could ask the same question about you or anyone in this room. If we conducted our investigations in that way, we would never solve a crime. There was nothing tying him to this crime."

"He was at the apartment at the same time Mr. Jackson was at the apartment, isn't that something?"

Officer Gonzalez could not hide his displeasure with Kenneth's question. "I've got twenty-five years of my life invested in this job, and it informs every lead in every investigation. That ought to count for something."

"Over and above the United States Constitution?"

"Objection," Amy said. "This is a deliberate mischaracterization of testimony."

Judge Barney sustained the objection.

"We did not charge the defendant for this crime because he was at her apartment earlier in the day."

Kenneth and Officer Gonzalez continued their exchange on what the officers did besides arresting Paul. Kenneth asked about Ms. Olá Mohammed, and what was done to eliminate her as a person of interest, and then he went through the same questions with regards to Rachel Johnson, Conrad Wetstone, and Didi Pare. The longer the examination stayed on the subject, the more it seemed to frustrate Officer Gonzalez, especially when it got to Didi Pare, at which point Kenneth paused and took a deep breath before he continued.

Kenneth walked to a rack holding the defense exhibits and picked up a poster-sized exhibit, which he placed on the easel, but left it covered.

"Your Honor, the defense wishes to mark an exhibit at this time."

"What is it?" Judge Barney asked.

"It's a picture of the building on Armacost across from Ms. Silberberg's building, identifying the apartments with views onto the street and corresponding names of tenants."

"Any objections?" Judge Barney asked, looking at Amy's table.

"None, your Honor," Amy said.

"Your exhibit is marked as the next in order according to our pre-marking discussion. You may proceed."

"Thank you, your Honor. Officer Gonzalez, do you recognize the building in the picture as the building across from Footsie's apartment complex on Armacost Street?"

"I do."

"Do you recognize the names on the exhibit as the names of all the residents of the building as well?"

"I do."

"Which of those apartments in the building across the street was Ms. Ola's boyfriend's?"

Office Gonzalez identified the building directly opposite Goldie's. Kenneth then asked him if the LAPD spoke to the tenants in the next apartment with a similar view to Ms. Ola's and her boyfriend. Gonzalez said they did not speak to any other tenants at that apartment complex.

Kenneth decided to change his line of questioning and brought out the listening device found in the apartment. He asked Officer Gonzalez who placed it there and without hesitation, Gonzalez said Rachel Johnson placed it there. When asked what Rachel was doing with the device, Officer Gonzalez stated that she was an actress and was using it for her work. Kenneth thought the answer absurd and wanted to explore it, but Cassandra felt it was a rabbit hole that would completely diminish the suspicious element of the device. Kenneth decided not to pursue the discussion with this officer.

"Officer, the investigating officers already made up their minds that Mr. Jackson committed this crime before they even left the scene of the crime, isn't that true?"

"No, sir, but we had strong leads pointing to him."

"And you ignored the leads pointing to the older white man, without even talking to him?" Kenneth asked.

"Objection, mischaracterizes the testimony," Amy said, and Judge Barney sustained the objection.

"I have nothing further for this witness," Kenneth said.

"Any redirect?" Judge Barney asked.

"Yes, your Honor," Amy said and was eagerly on her feet.

On Amy's examination, Gonzalez explained that the older white man was not a person of interest because Goldie asked him there, so she would not have to be alone with Paul. Didi Pare and Rachel Johnson could verify this testimony, Gonzalez said. In fact, it appeared Paul waited for a time when he was sure that the older white man would not be at Goldie's to return. Gonzalez stated that the older white man who walked into the apartment when Goldie and Paul were arguing was Monsieur Arnot, an elderly French gentleman of some means who was seeking an anonymous regular life in the quiet West Los Angeles neighborhood.

"Where did he move to?" Amy asked.

"We have information that he went back to France," Gonzalez said.

"In your experience, was it unusual that a person living in such a complex would move immediately after a crime like that was committed in the apartment next to his?"

"No, once something like that happens in a high-end neighborhood like that, people move. He wasn't a suspect or a person of interest, and we don't believe he had the opportunity to commit this crime."

"Nothing further," Amy said and sat down.

CHAPTER THIRTY-SIX
The Manager

Conrad Wetstone's demeanor reminded Kenneth of Jed as he took the stand on Friday morning. Pleasant, quiet, and even-tempered, a studious mind of somber disposition who always seemed occupied with some technical matter, even when he was picking up milk for the family at a grocery store. They were also about the same height, but Conrad was a thin rack of a man in his clothes, with a strong lower body. His cheeks were sunken, his jaw was square, and his eyes deep set, which made his small forehead more pronounced. Jed filled out his clothes more, with a body that, though not fat, made his southern-Italian ancestry proud. Cassandra agreed with Kenneth's observation about Jed and Conrad. She and Kenneth had both met Conrad before without noticing the resemblance.

Conrad testified that he had held the position of apartment manager for three years and knew Goldie well. He had been happy with her as a tenant. Goldie's rent was fully paid for the year, and she never quarreled with anyone, except Mr. Jackson. She had arguments often with him, and one very recently. Asked if he knew what the quarrels were about, he said that in one instance, Mr. Jackson had been parking outside her house and watching her apartment.

"He was stalking her?" Amy asked.

"Mostly he would park outside, across the street until very late at night to see who was in her apartment," Conrad said.

The day before he discovered the body, Goldie had asked Conrad to come by her apartment anytime during the day because her garbage disposal wasn't working properly, and her sink seemed to have a leak underneath. He went into the apartment the following day and found her body twisted in an unnatural position, and naked except for her underwear. At first, he was shocked and sick to his stomach. He called the police when he recovered.

"Did you touch the body?" Amy asked.

"No, I did not," he answered. "I called out her name, but I knew as soon as I saw her that she was dead. I was too shocked to even go near her."

Amy knew that the defense team would go after Conrad for how long it took him to call the police, but she also knew that no one on the defense team had asked Conrad if he called the owners of the apartment complex that day or if they called him. So, she had told him how she would ask the question about how long he waited before calling the police and how he might want to answer it, if he didn't want the defendant's attorney to suggest he had anything to do with the murder.

"Mr. Wetstone, after you saw the body of one of your best tenants, you waited almost three hours to call the police. Why didn't you call them immediately?"

"It was a shock and I was really sick, I felt like throwing up and had to run out of the apartment so I wouldn't throw up in her house. I threw up in my apartment. Then I sat down and called the building owners to tell them."

"Did you call the owners of the building before you called the police?"

"I think so. I didn't even know it took me that long to call the police. Everything happened so quickly. I was sick until the next day. Goldie was one of the nicest people that ever lived there since I became manager. She would travel and say if I knew anybody that needed an apartment while she was away, they could have hers if they'd stay away from her bedroom and bath."

"Thank you, Mr. Wetstone," Amy said and sat down.

As Kenneth stood up, he looked at a man in the gallery. The man left the courtroom and returned pushing a video screen and a laptop on a cart into the area where the counsel sat. He positioned the screen to be seen by the witness, the jury, and the judge. Kenneth and Cassandra had informed Judge Barney that they might need the video accompaniment for this part of their case and the judge had approved it.

Kenneth placed a large blueprint of the floor plan of Goldie's apartment on the easel and stepped back to cross-examine Conrad Wetstone.

"Mr. Wetstone, do you recall what name Ms. Silberberg used when she performed?"

"Footsie."

"You wouldn't mind if I call her Footsie in my exchanges with you, would you?"

"No, of course not."

"Mr. Wetstone, you said you do not recall whether you called the owners of the apartment before or after you called the police, is that correct?"

"Yes, it is."

"Would your telephone records help you recall."

"I thought so, but I looked at them before coming to court today and didn't see their number. I think they may have called me to check in on something and I told them what happened."

Kenneth turned to look at Cassandra over Conrad's explanation and she smiled at him, as though to say she understood. Amy smiled, too, because she thought it would be a good idea to do so for the jury.

"Do you recall what you told the owners of the apartment building had happened and what they said back to you?"

"Yes, I told them one of the tenants had died in her apartment and they wanted to know if she was an elderly tenant."

"Was that all they wanted to know?"

"They also wanted to know which apartment, what happened, and how much the other tenants knew. I told them I didn't think the other tenants knew."

"Do you recall how long you were on the phone with them?"

"Ten minutes or so."

"Did they tell you what they were going to do about it?"

"No, they said they would get back to me."

"They never asked if you had already called the police to inform them about your discovery?"

"I don't recall. I think I told them I was throwing up and I thought they said they would call the police."

"Isn't it true that they did not ask if you had already called the police because you told them you had called the police?"

Conrad sat looking at Kenneth as though the question had been rhetorical. It was not a look of one who did not hear the question, but of one who was waiting attentively for the next question. His hands were on the wooden frame in front of him on the witness box where the jurors could see them, and he was neither fidgeting nor flexing or moving his fingers. If anything, he seemed more confident than he had been throughout Amy's examination.

"Mr. Wetstone," Judge Barney interjected. Conrad Wetstone turned toward the judge as if he were surprised to see the judge sitting there. "You may answer the question."

"No, I don't think I told them that I had already called the police. Maybe they assumed it, maybe they decided they would call to make sure it was done right. I don't recall," Conrad responded. Everything he said came from Amy's suppositions of the possible reasons why he might not have called the police.

Kenneth examined him extensively on telephone records that showed he also called Rachel Johnson and Monsieur Arnot before he called the police, but Conrad insisted he had told the police he spoke to those two, even though he did not mention that he did so on the telephone. He could not remember the details of what he talked about with Rachel and Monsieur Arnot for twenty minutes and responded that he did not recall a lot of questions concerning the conversation.

Kenneth walked over to the exhibit he had placed on the easel and adjusted it as though he were trying to steady it. He also brushed off the edges as though he were cleaning dust from them. Then he took a step away from it and examined it as if it were a work of art.

"Let me draw your attention to the exhibit showing the floor plan for Footsie's apartment."

"Is that an accurate depiction of the apartment where you found Footsie's body?"

Conrad observed the blueprint briefly. "Yes," Conrad said.

"When you got to the apartment that day, how did you get inside?"

"I used my key. The manager has a key to all the apartments and the rental agreement allows us to go in to make necessary repairs."

"Did you notice anything wrong with the lock on the door to enter the apartment?"

"No."

"It wasn't broken or tampered with at all?" Kenneth asked.

"No, as far as I could see, it wasn't tampered with or broken."

"So, it is safe to say that prior to the time you got to her apartment and found her body, no one had broken into her apartment?"

"Objection, calls for speculation," Amy said.

"Counsel, Mr. Wetstone is not testifying as an expert on burglaries, I will sustain the objection..." Judge Barney said.

"Mr. Wetstone, do you have any idea how anyone might have gotten into the apartment without a key or without breaking the lock on the door?" Kenneth asked.

"No, I don't," Conrad said.

"When you open the door to the apartment and step into the apartment looking forward, what's to your left?"

"A wall."

"More accurately, a wall between the coat closet and the passageway, is that correct?" Kenneth inquired.

The video man turned on the screen on the television and showed a wall through a door.

"Looking at the video, does that show the wall you are talking about?"

"Yes."

"And what's to your right?"

"The kitchen." The television screen showed a kitchen as well, and Conrad looked at it and nodded to Kenneth, but Judge Barney instructed him to give a verbal response and he said "yes." The television screen subsequently showed each part of the apartment, but once Conrad confirmed it on the blueprint, it held steady. Kenneth and Cassandra had decided that having the video move around as they spoke to Conrad would distract from his testimony, but to preserve the right to use it in their summation, they decided to introduce it during his examination.

"And separating you from the kitchen will be a low wall on which is the kitchen counter, is that correct?"

"Yes."

Every time, Conrad answered, he looked first at the screen.

"So, once you are at the door, entering, there is nothing shielding you from the person in the kitchen because the wall between the kitchen and the passageway is about four feet high, right?" Kenneth indicated on the easel as he spoke.

"Yes."

"You walk into the apartment about seven feet from the door, still looking forward, you are standing here." Kenneth marked an "X" on the exhibit. "What's to your left?"

"A passageway to the guest bedroom."

"And what's to your right?"

"The counter ends there, and you have about a four-foot space between the counter and the wall in front of you that leads into the living room and the kitchen area."

"Directly in front of the kitchen here is the living room, right?" Kenneth asked as he marked the kitchen area "K" and the living room with an "LV."

"Yes," Conrad agreed.

"You walk across the kitchen and living room area as you are coming in from the entrance to the apartment, and you are standing in front of a door. Where does that door lead to?"

"The master bedroom and the adjourning master bathroom," Conrad said. He looked at the screen to see a shot of the door and the living room from the kitchen area.

"Now, let me stop here for a moment. When you came into the apartment, was the door to the master bedroom open or closed?"

"I don't recall," Conrad said, looking puzzled.

"At some point while you were in the apartment, you went into her bedroom, which was the master bedroom, did you not?"

"Yes, I did."

"So when you went into it. Was it open or closed?"

"I think it was closed."

"You are not sure?"

"It was closed."

"Where is the master bedroom on this exhibit?" Kenneth asked, though it seemed obvious from the exhibit.

"Right inside," Conrad said, pointing. Kenneth marked where Conrad was pointing "MB" and confirmed it with him.

"You walk from the bedroom door to the far wall opposite it, turn right and there is a small passageway to the bathroom, is that correct?" Kenneth indicated on the easel with a pointer as he spoke and placed a "B" mark on the exhibit to indicate a bathroom.

"Objection, your Honor, is there a point to this exercise?" Amy asked.

"There better be," Judge Barney retorted. Some jurors chuckled. "Counsel, still foundation?" Judge Barney asked Kenneth.

"Still foundation, your Honor," Kenneth said.

"Get to your point soon, will you?"

"Mr. Wetstone, what else is in the passageway between the bedroom and the bathroom?"

"A small closet built into the wall on your right, and nothing on the wall to your left."

"You came into the apartment to do some repairs?"

"Yes."

"What was broken?"

"Excuse me?" Conrad asked.

"What did you find was broken and in need of repair?"

"I didn't so much go to repair it as to take a look at it."

"You just admitted right now that you came in to do some repairs."

"Well, she told me to look at it, and if it was something I could repair I would do it, but mostly I just inspect and call someone in."

"What did your inspection reveal?"

"She complained about the garbage disposal. It wasn't working properly and the sink was clogging."

"Where was this garbage disposal?"

"It was under the kitchen sink built into the counter in the kitchen."

"So, you walk into the apartment, go about seven feet toward the wall facing you, turn right toward the living room, pass the counter, and the kitchen is immediately there to your right. Is that correct?" Kenneth indicated the movement on the floor plan exhibit as he spoke.

"Yes."

"You immediately turn into the kitchen by turning to your right, and the counter and the sink are right there?"

"Yes."

"And the master bedroom is behind you?"

"Yes, sir." It was the first time Conrad had addressed Kenneth as "sir."

"So, what were you doing in the bedroom?"

"Pardon?"

"You walk into the apartment to inspect the sink garbage disposal in the kitchen. You don't have to go through the master bedroom to get to the sink. In fact, you have no business whatsoever in the master bedroom. But you go through the master bedroom into the bathroom anyway to see if Ms. Silberberg was dead? Someone told you she was lying dead there and you went to check on her, isn't that true?"

"No!" Conrad exclaimed.

"What were you really doing in the bedroom when you discovered her body?" Kenneth persisted, raising his voice.

There was a short pause before Conrad answered.

"I also wanted to check the water pressure in the shower."

"Footsie complained about that as well?"

"Not specifically, but when I'm calling someone to do something in one apartment, I take any opportunity to see if any other apartment can use the same service, so the contractor doesn't have to come back for the same thing," Conrad explained.

"So, you checked all the showers in the building for water pressure?"

"No."

"Mr. Wetstone, you said earlier that when Footsie would travel, she would tell you that if someone needed to use her apartment, you could let them, provided they stayed away from her bedroom. Isn't that true?"

"Yes, sir."

"But you came to her apartment with only permission to look at her kitchen, and even though her bedroom door was closed, you went in there anyway, knowing she doesn't like anyone else in her bedroom that she has not given permission to."

"I was only doing my job."

"Mr. Wetstone, didn't you say that Footsie had not been staying at this apartment for a while, in fact, she was away in London for about three months, and never stayed there?"

"Yes, sir."

"Why was she worried about a garbage disposal she had not used for over a month and wasn't using because she was staying somewhere else?"

"I don't know, that's what she told me. Maybe Rachel told her about it, I don't know."

"Why didn't Rachel tell you herself?"

"Objection," Amy said standing.

"Overruled."

"Maybe because it wasn't her apartment," Conrad said.

"Okay. How long did you take to inspect the sink garbage disposal?"

"About seven minutes."

"How long did it take you to check the water pressure in the guest bathroom?"

"What?"

"You checked the water pressure in Footsie guest bathroom as well, did you not?"

"No...I didn't."

"You just said that when you go to check a problem, you check all the other facilities. Why didn't you check the shower in her guest bathroom?"

"I found the body before I could."

"Mr. Wetstone, someone told you that Footsie was lying in her bathroom dead, and you went up there to check if it was true, right?" Kenneth said.

"Objection! Objection!" Amy said over the latter part of Kenneth's statement.

"What is your objection counsel?" Judge Barney asked Amy.

"Counsel assumes facts not in evidence. This question has been asked and answered, and counsel is being argumentative," Amy responded.

"It is appropriate impeachment," Judge Barney said to Kenneth's surprise. "You may answer the question," he said to Conrad.

"No," Conrad said.

"You went up to Footsie's apartment at about eleven thirty on Friday morning, perhaps carrying a toolbox, perhaps not. You got into the apartment using your master key to fix a clogged sink garbage disposal that Footsie had complained about, and possibly check the water pressure she never asked you to check. Is that correct so far?"

"Yes, sir."

"You check the sink garbage disposal for five to seven minutes, and what was wrong with it?"

"Nothing, I couldn't find anything wrong with it."

"It was fine?"

"Yes."

"Then you went to the master bedroom and the master bathroom to check the water pressure?"

"Yes."

"Besides the master bathroom, there is another bathroom in this apartment, but you didn't check the water pressure in that bathroom, is that correct?"

"Yes."

"Mr. Wetstone, did you tell the LAPD detectives that you also went to Footsie's to check the water pressure in her bathroom?"

"No."

"Why not?"

"They didn't ask and I was giving them the reason I had permission to go into the apartment in the first place. The water pressure was extra, I was just trying to help."

"Oh, I have no doubt that you were trying to help, Mr. Wetstone. And when you went to check the water pressure in her master bedroom her door was closed. It might even have been locked."

"It wasn't locked."

"But you did not know that until you tried the handle and found out that it wasn't locked, right?"

"Yes."

"So, when you found the door closed at the time, why didn't you just go and check the guest bathroom instead of violating her privacy by attempting to open a door that might be locked?"

"The problem with the water pressure in the other apartments was in the master bathroom, that was why I went to check the master bathroom, but I see what you mean. I didn't think of it then."

"Why did you turn on the air conditioner in Footsie's apartment?" Kenneth asked.

"Pardon?" Conrad said, and Amy objected.

"Rephrase the question counsel," Judge Barney said.

"The air conditioner in Footsie's apartment, was it on when you came into the apartment?" Kenneth asked.

"I believe it was already on, yes," Conrad said.

"Why didn't you tell the police that, when they interrogated you," Kenneth asked.

Conrad said he did, and Kenneth examined him further on what the weather was that morning. If he thought it was odd that the air conditioner was on in January, even for Los Angeles. Conrad said he thought it was odd, and Kenneth suggested again that he never told the police about the air conditioner being on.

"It took two hours to call the police because you and your friends were trying to figure out what to tell the police?"

"Objection!" Amy shouted.

"Sustained," Judge Barney said.

Conrad Wetstone remained on the stand until the end of the day. He explained why he was at home the day he discovered Goldie's body and why he had not gone to Goldie's apartment earlier. Kenneth asked him the condition he found Goldie's bed, whether it has been used for sex, and Amy's objection was sustained. Kenneth tried to suggest that Conrad may have seen items of a sexual nature and the objection to that was sustained as well. Yet, Kenneth felt he had planted enough of a seed in the minds of the jurors with those unanswered questions.

At the end of his testimony, Conrad had scratched and patted his hair into disorder, his shirt was pulled into a bulge at the front, his eyes were red from being rubbed during his examination. He was not alone in his distress. Reverend Brown was developing a headache that appeared to grow in intensity as Amy rose to ask Conrad additional questions to rehabilitate him on areas she felt necessary. Nancy and Reverend Brown stood up to leave the courtroom. Both Kenneth and Amy turned to observe the slight disturbance in the audience and saw them.

"It's time for our afternoon recess," Judge Barney informed the court as Wetstone made his way out of the courtroom. "I would like the attorneys to stay behind for a few minutes after everyone else has left."

Kenneth, Cassandra, and Amy nodded and stood with Paul as the jurors rose to leave. When the parties were alone with Judge Barney, he told them that the court of appeals had ruled on Cassandra's emergency writ. The ruling directed the court to hold a hearing to *show cause why the defendant should not introduce evidence of sexual activity in his defense.*

The court of appeals had agreed with the argument that the failure by the police to identify and eliminate all those who may have been involved in the alleged sexual activity cast doubt on their investigation of Mr. Jackson. Therefore, it was relevant impeachment evidence for the defense. Further, there was no presumption of prejudice when sexual activity is introduced in a trial that is not for a sex crime. However, the court of appeals directed Judge Barney to *show cause* by holding another hearing to let Cassandra make the arguments she made in her writ that were not previously presented to Judge Barney, so the district attorney could rebut them.

"The ruling came this afternoon during the lunch break, so I assumed your copies were waiting for you in your offices. But since today is the last day of the week, I want you to start thinking of what I want you to do on Monday morning because of this ruling," Judge Barney said. "I want all of you to appear on Monday morning prepared to present additional evidence on whether sexual activity should be admitted in the trial. If the police can identify the participants in the sexual activity at Ms. Silberberg's apartment as a means of excluding the evidence by showing that they were not relevant to the crime, I will consider it. If the forensic expert maintains it is irrelevant, I want to know his reasons as well."

Judge Barney seemed unhappy with the court of appeals' ruling, but Kenneth and Cassandra were ecstatic. They managed to maintain their decorum until the judge left the courtroom, then heaved sighs of relief.

•••

ON RETURNING TO COURT after the afternoon recess, Amy tried only briefly to rehabilitate Conrad Wetstone, but he seemed tired and prone to making more mistakes than correct the ones he had made. Afraid that Kenneth and Cassandra would seize upon such rehabilitation to bring him back on Monday, at which time they would have had the weekend to prepare more questions for him, she rounded up her examination on him and handed him over for recross-examination by Kenneth, which was thankfully short.

CHAPTER THIRTY-SEVEN
Show Business

AFTER CONRAD WETSTONE, AMY contemplated calling Officer Tse or Didi Pare, depending on their availability. Officer Tse with Officer Fritz was immediately available and had been waiting in the DA's office since the morning recess. Didi Pare arrived later but went to the courtroom instead of going to the district attorney's office. In the hallway, Paul's father and six of his followers were standing to one side with Paul's mother and sisters. Big sat on a bench by himself, and Helen sat farther away with one of Amy's paralegals. Didi went to sit next to Big.

"Hey, Big," Didi said.

"Mr. Pare," Big replied, shifting away even though Didi had enough room to sit near him.

"Damn, I wish I could smoke in here," Didi said.

"You testifying?" Big asked.

"That's what they tell me."

"You sound like they making you."

"I'm a big boy, too, Big."

"Are you big enough to tell truth to power?"

"You know what they say about taking a donkey to water?" Didi said with a smile.

Their conversation proceeded in hushed tones, and Big stole glances at the bench in the hallway where Helen Silberberg sat with Amy's paralegal. Perhaps because of Big's uncomfortable glances, Amy's paralegal suspected that Didi was the other witness her colleague was waiting for at the office and stood up to approach them. Big saw her coming and spoke hurriedly.

"You guys got all you need to make Footsie another hit?"

"We ain't got much. Nice ditties but no pizzazz."

"Want me to see what I can do for pizzazz?"

"Got something?"

"I always got something," Big smiled.

"Got her other masters, too?"

The paralegal was almost upon them.

"You working or clubbing tonight?" Big asked.

"It's show biz, Big. What's the difference?"

"Excuse me, Mr. Pare?" the paralegal said.

"Yes," Didi answered.

"I'm Ms. Wilson's paralegal. We were waiting for you in our office across the street. May I take you over there?"

"Can I smoke there?"

"Yes, sir."

"When am I up to testify?"

"We're just finishing up the lunch recess right now, but Ms. Wilson will have to tell you whether you go up first after lunch or later."

"I prefer later."

"I'll tell Ms. Wilson."

"I'm working tonight, Big," Didi said, as he pushed himself up from the bench. Big nodded. "Good luck to you," Didi added.

"Much thanks, you conniving piece of sh--," Big muttered, making the last five words largely inaudible.

•••

"SOMETHING'S NOT RIGHT," AMY said to Officer Gonzalez.

Amy was particularly angry that Conrad had neglected to tell her that Goldie had given him permission to use her apartment, as long as he stayed away from the master bedroom, during his preparation. This made his decision to go into Goldie's bedroom suspicious. Amy was also disappointed with herself that she had not covered the question about whether the door to the bedroom was open or closed when she was preparing Conrad for his examination.

If someone left a listening device in the bedroom, it was plausible that they found out that Goldie was dead and called the apartment management and Conrad to tell them. Amy had never asked Conrad that question, and she was furious that neither she nor the police knew the answer. Conrad's difficulty with the defense's cross-examination suggested to Amy that he knew who called the management company. However, she was happy it was Friday afternoon, which gave her two days to go through the entire case file and get back on the right track.

Amy asked Didi into a conference room where Officer Gonzalez and Fritz were waiting for her with two paralegals and asked them to give her the room for a minute.

"Is there a chance I won't be needed?" Didi asked. Amy shook her head slowly. Something in the way Didi smiled at her riled Amy.

"Give me just one minute," Amy said, and stepped outside, closing the door behind her, and then returned a few minutes later. "Mr. Pare, don't take this the wrong way, but we have your DNA information from semen found in Goldie's room."

"DNA evidence?" Didi asked, his face wrinkled as he squinted, trying to focus on Amy. He had seemed carefree and unconcerned by the whole trial. "I did not sleep with her."

Amy folded her arms across her chest and stood staring at Didi, taken aback by what she already knew, yet unsure what to say to him.

"You may not have slept with her, but with someone else…on her bed."

Didi sat down slowly, cursing under his breath.

"I need to speak with my lawyer," Didi said.

"Be my guest," Amy said and turned to leave.

"What else did she tell you?" Didi asked.

"What else did who tell me?" Amy asked. Didi turned to her and grinned. Amy left the room and told the paralegal waiting outside to get rid of him.

Officer Gonzalez, Fritz, Alvarez, and Tse were waiting in the conference room with Kate when Amy returned. Amy had decided that Officer Alvarez would not take the stand on the off chance that the defense knew he asked

Rachel out while investigating the case. Alvarez vehemently denied the accusation, but what else was he supposed to say.

"One of the semen samples taken from the bed belonged to Mr. Pare," Amy said as she walked in and sat down.

"He told you that?" Kate asked.

"No, I suspected that about Rachel and just confirmed it from his reaction."

"You'll still put him on the stand though, right?"

"Yes, but we have to know if the other side has this information."

"I'll take care of it," Alvarez said.

A clearer picture of the entire case had emerged for Amy from the first week of trial. She realized that Rachel Johnson, not Conrad Wetstone, was her most important witness. Rachel was the one witness with a nexus to everyone and the only one who knew anything about what really took place on Goldie's bed. Reviewing the daily transcripts of the trial and making notes of issues for further examination or formulating additional question to strengthen the weak aspects of excused witnesses, Amy drew up a flow chart of the connections to Rachel Johnson.

Amy thought Rachel would have made a good witness, especially because she was an actress, but Kate warned her to be careful with Rachel. Amy said she would use the weekend to prepare for her.

Alana had gone home at the lunch recess and did not return to the courtroom the rest of the day. Kenneth bullying Conrad Wetstone was more than she could take, she said when Amy called her during the recess.

"It wasn't bullying. I thought he was effective."

"You lawyers can call it what you want; it sounded like bullying to me."

"When this is over, I'll tell him you said that –"

"You mean you'll still remain friends after this is over?"

"I may not have a choice…" Amy said smiling to herself.

"Then I think you should tell Thomas."

"Tell him what?"

"The truth…that you may not have a choice…like you say. Tell him whatever you feel. He wants to come and watch the trial. He said he will be out of the way. Let him come."

"You know he is not coming to watch me, right."

"I know," Alana said after a brief silence.

"He probably already has Court TV making a special tape for him."

"They say it won't be ready for a while. I am trying to get tapes for your dad as well. Remain friends with Thomas as well."

"I will. Tell him to make time for me if he does come."

•••

Nancy assembled Mallam Jackson, Sister Ramatu, and the rest of Paul's clan at a suite in the Intercontinental Hotel after the trial on Friday. The suite had a sitting area and a small dining section next to it. Six of the twelve men Mallam Jackson had brought to court stood in the dining section, with Big just at the entrance to it. Two doors opened from the sitting area into adjourning rooms. Mallam Jackson sat in the armchair with two of his men standing behind him. Sister Ramatu and Mr. Jones sat on the couch. Jo sat on a dining chair next to her mother. Nancy had ordered tea from room service for Mallam Jackson, Omar, and Sister Ramatu and bottled water for everyone else as they had requested.

On the drive back to the hotel, Sister Ramatu and Jo had been effusive with praise about Kenneth's performance to Nancy. How could they have missed him, by going to Omar in the first place, they wondered. Even Omar was full of praise for him, they told Nancy, but Nancy tried to warn them as Kenneth had warned her about getting their hopes up too soon. "In every trial, there will be days you want to remember and days you want to forget. Soon enough, the other side will get their days to remember," Nancy told them.

Kenneth and Cassandra joined them at the suite after taking their leave from Anthony, Jed, and Tiffany. They had invited the three to join them, but it was obvious to Kenneth that they did not want anything to do with Mallam Jackson's entourage. Kenneth avoided Mallam Jackson's eyes when he entered the suite and did not go to him or shake his hand, as he was expected to do. Nancy gave him a look of disapproval. He stood in front of Sister Ramatu to place himself more centrally in the room and speak to the gathering.

"Hi, everyone. Thank you, Mr. Jones for joining us. We wanted to get you guys together to tell you of some new developments we have in the case. Also, since the case began, we haven't had a chance to really brief you except for some conversations in the hallway and during recesses. As soon as the day is over, we are rushing to get ready for the next day. So maybe we make this a weekly event for the trial, where we tell you what we think is going on and answer questions you may have for us."

Mallam Jackson raised his hand, much to everyone's surprise. "Yes, sir," Kenneth said.

"No need to make a weekly event, you just call us when you have something to tell us, and we'll come to hear it," Mallam Jackson said.

"Thank you, sir," Kenneth said.

"Hear, hear," Big said.

"Allahu Akbar," the men in the dining section said and repeated after themselves.

"You have earned the Mallam's trust, Kenneth Brown, that is no small feat from where you started," Omar said and let out a laugh.

"You tell him, Mr. Jones. You tell him," the men in the dining section said. Mallam Jackson raised both hands and the room was quiet again.

"Before we go to the new development that Professor Cassandra Rayburn will tell us about, is there any question or concern we can answer?" Kenneth asked.

Jo raised her hand, and Kenneth wanted to tell her that there was no need to raise hands, but having failed to tell Mallam Jackson the same, remained silent and pointed to Jo.

"That letter they said Paul wrote, did Paul write it?" Jo asked.

"I haven't asked Paul yet," Kenneth said. Not everyone knew about the letter. Thus, Kenneth explained the contents of the letter and told everyone that Judge Barney had ruled that it wouldn't be used unless Paul took the stand and at this time, they were not planning to put Paul on the stand. He left out the part of the judge's ruling about the exceptions to the hearsay rules.

"Are you going to ask him?" Jo asked.

"No," Kenneth said and raised a hand to keep Jo from speaking further on the subject.

"If there are no other questions, I would like you to hear what Professor Rayburn did for Paul and won in the court of appeals," Kenneth said.

The suite got quiet. Cassandra stood up to speak. She told them about the sexual items that were found in Goldie's room and that none of the semen matched Paul, and none of the blood samples matched Goldie's blood type, but the blood belonged to a female. She told them that she asked the court of appeals to reverse the judge's decision to reconsider the evidence when they try to introduce it in the case. "The court of appeals directed the judge to allow the evidence or show cause why the evidence should not be allowed." Applause erupted in the room, and those in the dining section came into the sitting area as they clapped standing behind the couch.

"This doesn't prove anything," Cassandra shouted over the applause.

"Like hell it doesn't," Big said, and cast a side glance at Mallam Jackson.

"Really, it doesn't," Cassandra repeated before she turned to Kenneth and then Nancy, who began to laugh. After Mallam Jackson raised both hands again to quiet the room, Cassandra told them there would be a hearing on Monday to determine how the items would be introduced.

Mallam Jackson walked up to Kenneth after the meeting and shook his hand, before heading out. Omar Jones was going to leave with the Mallam but asked to see Kenneth privately.

"I'll have a check in your office by Monday," Kenneth said to Omar, who smiled.

Sister Ramatu left with Jo, who insisted that Kenneth see them out.

"Don't let their attorneys plant an evil seed in you against Omar, you hear?" Sister Ramatu said.

"Oh, no, it's not like that," Kenneth said.

"Oh, yes, it is. This will be a good time to poison the enemy you can't beat," Sister Ramatu said, and to Kenneth's befuddled expression she added. "That's what I'd do."

Jo laughed. They bade Kenneth goodbye and good luck and drove off.

•••

REVEREND BROWN DID NOT return to court after leaving with headaches. Nancy explained that he had not refilled his blood pressure medication before he traveled. He had gone to the pharmacy to pick up his doctor's order and planned to return to Georgia briefly today.

After everyone left the hotel, Nancy told Kenneth to go and thank his father for coming and staying for the trial. She had convinced Reverend Brown to stay at Kenneth's house during the trial since both she and Kenneth were staying at the hotel. The drive from Los Angeles to Long Beach, which Kenneth had done on countless occasions, suddenly felt long as he went to see his father.

When the older man opened the door, the resemblance between the two men appeared to have increased during this visit, and each took a moment to consider the other. Kenneth wondered whether any of the children his father lived with and raised shared such resemblance with him as well. As they shook hands, Kenneth shifted his eyes to the carpet to keep his emotions from getting the better of him. Then Reverend Brown asked for a hug and held on, and it was clear to Kenneth that the older man was not doing any better managing his own emotions either. Reverend Brown seemed uncertain what to say or do. Kenneth commiserated with him about his headache, and he waived it away.

"Make sure you get checked regularly when you go for a physical," he told him. "We have it in the family." Kenneth offered to take him to the airport and he accepted.

Their ride to the airport was silent, interspersed with curious examination.

"Have you been to LA before?" Kenneth asked.

"Conferences," his father said, and the litigator in Kenneth knew to ask no more along those lines because the answer was too precise, as though it had been rehearsed to keep from saying he had visited since Kenneth moved there.

"Do you plan to have kids?" his father asked.

"Eventually," Kenneth answered, "if I can find the right woman."

276

"Follow your heart. Don't let fear or anyone tell you otherwise," Reverend Brown said.

After another long silence, now closer to the airport, Kenneth said, "Thanks for coming." The older man's voice cracked with emotion when he tried to respond. He nodded instead.

CHAPTER THIRTY-EIGHT
Of Jurors And Puritans

EARLY SATURDAY MORNING, BIG waited outside the Intercontinental Hotel. Had Kenneth answered the phone after Big left Didi's office on Friday night, Big would have driven straight to Long Beach to see him. At precisely eight o'clock, Big knocked on the door to the suite. Nancy had insisted on going back to Long Beach and Kenneth was alone. When he opened the door and saw Big, the expression on his face betrayed his displeasure.

"Shoot Big, what time is it?"

"Like eight-thirty," Big said. "I figured you got used to waking up early to go to the trial by now."

"No, man, it's Saturday. I wanna sleep for a change," Kenneth said, and returned to the bedroom to change out of his pajamas.

Big handed an envelope to Kenneth and watched intently as he opened it and took out a sheet of paper and two pictures of Rachel Johnson from it.

"Can you use it?" Big asked.

"Where did you get this?"

"Someone sent it to me."

"Who?"

"I don't know," Big said. "Can you use it?" Big asked again.

"It's a time bomb."

"Just try? Why can't you just use the damn thing?"

"The judge might not even let me use it when I don't know how you got it."

"Just tell him a private investigator came up with it."

"And if they wanna subpoena the investigator as a witness?"

"Then ask her agent, Didi Pare about it."

"You think her agent had something to do with it?"

"Yeah."

"He sent it to you?"

"I done told you I don't know who sent it to me, but it might be him."

"Why?"

"Why don't you just ask him?" Big persisted, louder still.

"It is not that simple, Big. First, I need to get it past the judge, and he's gonna need to know what you're not telling me."

Big said he would keep working on finding out who sent it to him if Kenneth would promise to try and use it in the courtroom.

Kenneth called Cassandra as soon as Big left.

"Casey, you won't believe this."

"I better believe it, Ken. You woke me up from a really good sleep."

"Sorry. But Big just stopped by the hotel with a file for Rachel Johnson. Get this, she's got a madam, and this file tells you how to reach her—at Goldie's address, what she's like on a date, comments from people who've been on a date with her. She prefers out-of-town dates, Vegas is okay—"

"Where did he get it?"

"Exactly, he's not saying. Well, he says he doesn't know. Someone just mailed it to him. He suspects Goldie's manager, Didi Pare. There is a page of an article in a magazine in the file. Listen to this: 'The average age of entertainment industry executives appears to fall every decade as the 18—25-year-old demographic continues to drive the industry's search for that elusive blockbuster. With this growing youth in the ranks of executives, comes power and a tremendous amount of money and few familial responsibilities thus, spurning a new cottage industry in the world's oldest profession—career prostitution or hit-and-run, high-priced escorts. It promises normal, innocent, beautiful young women the chance to make so much money on just one date that they never have to do it again.'"

"When she testifies, we'll use it to impeach her and establish that one of her Johns might be the participant in the sexual activities in Goldie's room." Cassandra said, interrupting him.

"She is not going to show up," Kenneth said.

"Then we use it to impeach Pare, just to get it into the record," Cassandra said.

"We don't know if the information is true yet," Kenneth said.

"We can use any information to impeach the character of a witness regardless of how you obtained that information, even if it's not true. This information is clearly impeachment evidence."

"It could come back to bite us unless we can prove its authenticity."

"Well, get somebody on it right away."

"Sure," Kenneth replied and hung up.

Kenneth surmised that Amy's most important remaining witnesses were Officers Tse and Alvarez, Dr. Kio the forensic expert, Ola Mohammed, Didi Pare, and Rachel Johnson, and he wanted to examine every one of them to some extent on the contents of the file.

Thus far the case remained within grasp of the defense, but a certain madam, if located, could deliver it completely. "Jurors tend to have a puritanical disdain of victims with salacious associations in their past as though it were un-American to convict a man for killing a woman with a vibrant sexual history," Cassandra had explained when she decided to appeal Judge Barney's refusal to rule conclusively on the evidence of sexual activities in the bedroom.

Kenneth was not sure of what he was hearing Cassandra say. Her tone was full of contempt for the very approach she was suggesting they should take in the trial.

CHAPTER THIRTY-NINE
Every Trial Has A Moment

AMY CAME TO WORK on Monday morning as anxious to end the trial as she was to win it, but more prepared than she had been the previous week. She had picked up a cup of coffee and was struggling with all she had to carry as she walked to her office. The police forensic officer, Tse, was scheduled to be her first witness, then the medical examiner, Dr. Kio, but it was Officer Alvarez who stood in the lobby of the district attorney's office waiting for her with an urgent expression and a manila folder.

"Officer Alvarez, are you waiting for me?"

"Can we go somewhere we can talk?"

Amy led the way to the conference room.

"You can't call Didi Pare," Alvarez said as soon as Amy closed the doors to the conference room.

"Why not?" Amy asked.

Alvarez gave Amy the same file that Big had given Kenneth. "He called to give me this."

Amy looked at the folder and raised her head back again, in shock. Alvarez shrugged.

"Son-of-a-...," Amy swore, dropping much of what she was carrying on the table in an effort to keep the coffee from spilling. "Did he say where he got it?" Amy continued, unconcerned about the mess.

Alvarez shook his head.

"We still have to call Mr. Pare. This is about Rachel, not Goldie."

"I think he is trying to tell us that this might smear Goldie, too."

"How?"

"I was vice before I moved to homicide. We did stings on these high and mighty places targeting young students especially. Now, this is LA. The world capital of pretty, for women looking for a job, and sometimes the jobs they come to find don't pan out and they have to pay bills. Any pretty woman could fall for a gig like that: Nurses, secretaries, married women. If there's a fight in Vegas, not all that many women going there care about boxing. So, if Rachel is caught up in it, maybe Goldie was, too."

"If there was a direct connection, we would have found it, wouldn't we?"

"The thing is, they don't keep files like this…" He pointed to the folder in Amy's hand. "There's no number in the phonebook you call to join or to find them. You don't call them, they call you, or they have someone call you. Trying to find those men would have taken far too much time than it is worth when we know they had nothing to do with the crime."

"You don't think Paul knew this all along, before this case?"

"No," Alvarez said.

She examined the folder further. It was a thin brown manila folder with a page of biographical data, and a small 2-by-4-inch picture affixed to the upper right corner. There were three pages of articles on the trade, including the one Kenneth read Cassandra. She wanted Kate to see the file before Kate went to court and asked Alvarez to wait for her in the conference room.

Kate's door was open and Amy walked in without knocking.

"Who gave you this?" Kate asked, getting up from her chair as she read the documents in the file that Amy had placed on her desk.

"Alvarez. Didi Pare gave these to him. He's trying to ruin her and prevent us from calling him because I told him it was his semen on Goldie's bed last Friday."

"How the hell did we not have this information about her before now?"

"Alvarez said they could not have known about it. The business is only successful if it can be kept a secret, otherwise it is illegal."

"Of course, he would say that, wouldn't he?" Kate asked without taking her eyes off the file. After a few minutes, when it seemed like she had read enough, she looked up at Amy. "Can they at least verify if it's true?"

"They can't, not in time for this trial anyway. He thinks there is some truth to it."

Kate walked out of the office and Amy followed her. They met Alvarez in the conference room.

"You're telling me that we basically have Rachel Johnson using Goldie's house for hooking and LAPD couldn't figure it out. Is that what you're telling me?"

"I wouldn't put it that way."

"It doesn't matter how you put it. If I can see it that way, then you can bet there is at least one juror who sees it that way. Do you know what this does to our case?"

"I'm sorry, ma'am," Alvarez said.

"You still want to call this Rachel woman?" Kate asked Amy.

"If they let this document in, I don't think we have a choice."

"Then make sure the document doesn't get admitted."

"Lean on Didi Pare, see if he can tell us anything useful," Kate said to Alvarez.

"I will," Alvarez said.

•••

ON RESUMPTION OF PROCEEDINGS, Judge Barney let only the attorneys, their assistants, Paul Jackson, and Helen Silberberg into the courtroom. Everyone else waited outside while Judge Barney conducted the hearing ordered by the court of appeals. The arguments Kate and Cassandra made during the hearing were not much different from the argument Judge Barney had heard before the appeal. However, his tone was more receptive to Cassandra's argument than it had been before, and he approached every argument Amy made with more skepticism.

He looked from one counsel table to the other and sat back in his chair, appearing undecided. "I want to hear from the witness most knowledgeable about how this evidence is relevant," he said.

"That would be the medical examiner for the People," Amy said, standing up.

"Is he available?"

Amy looked at the paralegal sitting behind her, next to Helen Silberberg. "I think so. In our office," the paralegal whispered.

"I am told he may be waiting in our office, your Honor," Amy said. Judge Barney called a short recess to allow Amy to call the medical examiner to the stand.

Minutes later, Dr. Ebenezer Kio was on the stand. Kenneth was meeting him for the first time, but Cassandra knew him from other trials. He had a very expressive face, perhaps because of his wide eyes. He always seemed about to smile though he never did. His hair seemed deliberately wild and unkempt. His suit was more fashionable than one would have expected from a county medical examiner. There was a welcoming air about him that seemed to suggest that he would not hurt a fly or discriminate against a fellow man. Looking around the courtroom as he walked to the stand, he seemed no more impressed by the judge as he was by the defendant.

Dr. Kio began his examination describing his education and qualifications. Amy took her time going through his training as a physician and fellowships in forensic pathology. When she was done, there could not have been a doubt that Dr. Kio was the most educated person in the courtroom, if not the smartest person. She then examined him on the crime scene, placing significant importance on where the body was found and using the crime scene photos as evidence. The items of a sexual nature found at the scene of the crime could not be conclusively tied to the cause of death, so he formed no opinion as to those items.

"Do you wish to examine this witness now, counsel?" Judge Barney asked Cassandra after Amy was done.

"No, your Honor, it would amount to preparing this witness for my impeachment before the jury takes the stand. I would prefer to introduce another opinion with an expert of my own," Cassandra explained.

"Is that expert here?" Judge Barney asked.

"No, your Honor, I had not scheduled him for this hearing, but I could arrange to have him here by tomorrow."

"Does either side mind if I ask this witness some questions?" Judge Barney asked looking from one counsel to the other. When neither side objected, he turned to Dr. Kio.

"Sir, you say that these items have no bearing on the cause of death, because they could not be conclusively tied to manner the victim died?"

Dr. Kio seemed puzzled for a moment and his expression even more on the verge of laughter than usual. "Yes, your Honor, the items did not have a bearing on my determination of the cause of death, but the manner of death is a completely different determination I do not make. May I explain?"

"Please do," Judge Barney said.

"The cause of death is the medical reason why someone died, and that determination is made by a medical examiner or forensic pathologist like me. The manner of death is the legal determination of how the victim died. There are five different manners of death: Natural, homicide, suicide, accidental, and undetermined."

"So, to my question then, you did not use the items to make a determination of the cause of death but whether the items were used to make a determination on the manner of death is not up to you."

"Exactly, your Honor."

"And what was the cause of death?" Judge Barney asked.

"Strangulation."

"Was the victim on drugs?" Judge Barney asked.

"There were no drugs in her system."

"Any redirect?" Judge Barney asked Amy.

"None, your Honor."

"May I ask a question, your Honor?" Kenneth asked.

"I was just getting to you," Judge Barney said.

"You found semen on the victim, did you not?" Kenneth asked, without standing up as was typical.

"There was donor genetic material in the form of semen on the victim, yes."

"Who was the donor?" Kenneth asked.

"I don't know. That information was not available from the evidence collected." Dr. Kio answered.

"Thank you, your Honor," Kenneth said.

"Did you check the donor semen against Mr. Jackson to try to get a match?" Judge Barney asked.

"It was not Mr. Jackson's, your Honor," Dr. Kio said.

"Thank you," Judge Barney said, and turned to Amy. "Do you wish to start with this witness or some other witness when trial resumes, counsel?" Judge Barney asked.

"I can start with him," Amy said.

Judge Barney directed the bailiff to call the jurors and the rest of the audience into the courtroom. Then he stood up and left.

With everyone seated in the courtroom, including the jurors, Judge Barney returned.

"Thank you, members of the jury. I apologize I had to keep you waiting a little longer this morning. The reason for the delay is that we were trying to sort out what evidence will be allowed in with the next witness, and it is always important to do these things outside the hearing of the jury," Judge Barney turned his attention to the counsel tables. "The defendant may examine this witness on the disputed evidence, and the People may consider their objections reserved, should they choose not to repeat them during the cross-examination. I find that the issues of proximity of the items found and their relationship to the crime are all matters of fact for the jury to weigh and consider."

Kenneth looked at Cassandra with a sigh of relief. Paul jotted a note to say he did not understand, to which Kenneth replied that he would explain it later. Cassandra seemed satisfied.

Judge Barney reminded Dr. Kio that he was still under oath.

Amy asked Dr. Kio the questions she had asked him earlier outside the presence of the jurors and got the same answers, describing the way the body was found and the conclusion that Goldie was killed right where she was found. Dr. Kio also introduced additional photographs of the autopsy and some of the items described, in exactly the manner they were found. She asked Dr. Kio if he could describe how Goldie was strangled, and Dr. Kio said it appeared a hand had been placed over her mouth to smother her that her neck had been grabbed and likely shaken.

"What evidence did you find to support your determination that the victim was strangled by strong hands that were wrapped around her neck?" Amy asked animatedly.

"There was bruising around the neck consistent with fingerprints and semi-lunar abrasions—if I may show my pictures again…" He requested and Amy again introduced the pictures and marked them. "This bruising is consistent with two hands wrapped around the neck during strangulation. I did a dissection of the skin across the breastbone, from which I raised the skin, peeling upward to reveal the neck muscles. This layer of muscles also shows additional bruising consistent with strangulation as described. I then raised the first layer of skin muscle under the skin, which also revealed bruising, as did the next layer of muscle, and the next, showing the amount of force that was used to strangle her."

"When you say there was bruising inside the muscles after you raised the skin, is that the same as bruising one would usually see on the skin?"

"Yes, bruising occurs wherever there are capillaries that burst. On the layers of the skin and beneath them, on the muscles, there are numerous capillaries that burst when one is strangled."

"And how did you determine that she was shaken in the course of this strangulation?"

"The hyoid bone in the victim was broken. This bone is the horseshoe-shaped bone at the top of the neck." Dr. Kio brings out another picture to show Amy, which was again introduced and marked. "This bone could break by the exertion of force from the hands wrapped around the victim's neck, but between two adults, even when the victim is a woman and the perpetrator a man, I conclude it took some shaking to break it as was shown by the evidence."

When Amy completed all this examination she had planned, she asked a series of questions she had not planned.

"Did you find any genetic material on Ms. Silberberg's body?" She was glad to use the medical term for semen because it sounded less prurient.

"Yes, ma'am. We found donor genetic material in the form of semen indicative of recent sexual activity within her genitalia."

"What do you mean by donor genetic material?" Amy asked.

"There are five types of genetic material you can find on a victim— semen, saliva, blood, mucous, and vaginal secretions. To distinguish the genetic material of the victim from any foreign genetic material we find on her body, we refer to the foreign genetic material as donor material."

"Were you able to conduct tests on the donor material you found to determine if it belonged to the defendant?"

"Yes, we did DNA tests, but found it did not belong to the defendant."

"Isn't it fair then, sir, to say that whomever this semen belonged to must have had something to do with her death?"

"That would be completely conjecture ma'am. I only rely on established facts, not conjecture in my work."

"Thank you, sir, no further questions," Amy said and walked back to her seat.

Kenneth and Cassandra had agreed that it would be easier on Helen Silberberg and appeal more to the jurors if Cassandra handled much of the evidence of sexual activity. Cassandra stood up to examine Dr. Kio.

"Do you agree sir, that the evidence shows the sexual activity occurred on the same day the victim was killed?" Cassandra asked.

"Yes," Dr. Kio answered.

"What facts did you use to establish that the sexual activity occurred on the same day as the death of the victim?"

"You identify genetic material because it has spermatozoa. Donor spermatozoa from a healthy adult male will contain two hundred million to four hundred million sperms per milliliter. Upon secretion, over time, it degrades both in quantity and quality, the weakest sperms die, some tails break-off, some dehydrate, and so on. These changes in quantity and quality can be measured against a graph to determine how much time has passed since secretion."

"Can you tell the specific time when the sexual activity took place?"

"No."

"There was more semen on the bed, was there not?"

"Yes."

"Did your tests confirm whether the semen on the victim and the semen on the bed belong to the same person?"

"I did not perform the tests on the semen found on the bed, that's the job of the police criminalist. But I compared the results of the tests on the semen from the body with the results of the tests on the semen on the bed and found that they were different donors."

"Neither of whom was the defendant, Paul Jackson?"

"Yes."

"So, theoretically, there were two donors of genetic material, both of whom were male, but neither of whom was the defendant?"

"Yes."

"And both men, neither of whom was the defendant, were involved in some sort of sexual activity with Ms. Silberberg in her bedroom."

"Objection," Amy shouted.

"State your objection, counsel," Judge Barney said.

"There was no testimony that both semen had anything to do with Ms. Silberberg. Her friend was staying in the apartment, not her."

"Sustained," Judge Barney said, and added: "Rephrase counsel."

"Dr. Kio, as far as we know, there was evidence of sexual activity involving two men at the scene of the crime, none of whom was Mr. Jackson. Is that correct?" Cassandra asked.

"Yes, and likely another woman."

"How did you come to the conclusion that there was another woman, doctor?"

"There was only a trace of one semen in the victim, which suggests that the semen on the bed may have had a different partner."

"Dr. Kio, isn't that speculation?"

"Objection," Amy said calmly, standing up. "Argumentative," she added when she was fully standing.

"Sustained," Judge Barney said.

"There were also condoms in the bin at the scene, is that correct?"

"Yes."

"And did the donor semen in the condoms match the DNA of the donor semen in the victim or that on the bed?"

"The bed."

"That would explain why the semen found on the bed has a different DNA than that found in the victim, would it not? Because it was deposited in a condom, right?"

"Yes. Or suggest the victim was not involved in the activity that took place on the bed."

"But it is also possible that both men shared the same partner, is it not?"

"That is purely speculation, and I don't speculate in my work."

"Even when you can reduce the speculation by a process of elimination?" Cassandra persisted.

"I'm not following you."

"Well, speaking theoretically, you can't be in your office at the same time you are here testifying, so it must be one or the other, right?" Cassandra asked.

"Right," Dr. Kio said.

"So, if we know you are here, even in theory, we can eliminate the other places you could possibly be at this time, is that correct?" Cassandra asked.

"Yes," Dr. Kio answered.

"But we can't eliminate the possibility that the men your tests have placed in Ms. Silberberg's bedroom were involved with Ms. Silberberg on the same occasion, can we?"

"You should be ashamed of yourself, lady!" Helen Silberberg suddenly yelled, jumping up from her chair.

"Order," Judge Barney shouted, his voice resonating. The bailiff was quickly on his feet and hurried toward Ms. Silberberg, whom Amy's paralegal had already started dragging away from the courtroom.

"You are the whore! Not my daughter! Shame on you."

"Order before this court," Judge Barney yelled again. The bailiff had reached Helen Silberberg and the paralegal helping her out of the courtroom. She continued to struggle and was crying hysterically by the time they got her to the door, almost as if from the strain of the manner in which she was being dragged out of the courtroom and her disappointment at her ineffectual struggle.

"I hope someone does the same to you," she shouted before the bailiff managed to close the double doors to the courtroom. All eyes were on Helen as she accused Cassandra of maligning her daughter. Amy was glad Alana had decided not to return to court. If she thought Conrad was bullied, what would she have said of this character assassination?

"Counsel, approach," Judge Barney ordered after Helen Silberberg was taken out of the courtroom. Amy, Cassandra, and Kenneth stood up to approach the judge. All the attorneys huddled next to the judge on the right side of his bench. The witness stand and the jurors were to the judge's left. "Ms. Wilson, I will not have Ms. Silberberg in my courtroom anymore. It is obvious that the strain of this trial is too much for her to bear. And I don't see what benefit comes from it."

"Your Honor, I sincerely apologize for her outburst, I take full responsibility for it as I had failed to warn her of how graphic the examination might turn out to be, given that I took Dr. Kio out of order from what I had planned. I was hoping to prepare her for the nature of this examination during the lunch break because I anticipated that my other witnesses would take at least that long on the stand. We only asked Dr. Kio to be present this morning because of your request."

"I do hold you responsible, but that doesn't change my ruling. She will remain outside this courtroom for the duration of the trial." Judge Barney then turned his attention to Cassandra and Kenneth. "Does the defense have any motions they would like to make concerning this incident?"

"No, your Honor," Cassandra replied. "We accept the circumstances as they are."

"You may return to your seats."

The parties returned to their seats. At this time, Dr. Kio was sitting with his fingers interlaced and placed in front of him on the edge of the stand, his half-smile evidently unperturbed. All the jurors' eyes were on Cassandra as she walked back to the counsel table. Rather than continue standing as she was before the outburst, she sat down, deliberately going over her notes.

"Ladies and gentlemen of the jury, you must disregard the outburst of the woman you have just seen shouting at the defense attorney. If counsel was out of line for even one second in her examination of Dr. Kio, you can bet that I would have called her to order; and that goes for the prosecutor as well." Judge Barney pointed his gavel toward Amy as he said prosecutor. "Now, if such outbursts as you have just heard were allowed to sway the jurors in every trial, then all a party would need to do is plant people in court who would yell and act hysterically every time an attorney elicits emotional testimony, and our system of justice would turn into a farce. So, I urge you. No, I command you, to forget that outburst and concentrate only on the testimony of the witness before you and my ruling as we go forward. I trust and understand that you can do so. Thank you. You may proceed, counsel."

Cassandra stood up again and straightened her dress. She looked directly at the jurors as she picked up her notepad.

"Dr. Kio, I believe my last question to you was whether, as you sit here today, you have established and supported facts that both men whose semen was found on the victim and on her bed, respectively, were not involved with her at the same time on the same bed."

"Not conclusively, no, I cannot."

Cassandra was about to proceed on another line of examination when the judge tried to clarify Dr. Kio's last answer.

"Doctor, when you say not conclusively, is there any evidence at the scene of the crime to suggest there was another woman?"

"Yes, your Honor. There was genetic material in the form of blood we believe belonged to a woman, but we could not conclusively say it was the victim's or another woman's," Dr. Kio answered.

Judge Barney did not follow up on Dr. Kios answer. Cassandra seemed glad to do so.

"When you say 'we,' who are you referring to?"

"The criminalists who worked on the case and me. We shared our tests."

"Why were you unable to conclusively say that the blood on the condom belonged to the victim?"

"This begins to go into the primary area of the criminalist, whom I believe will be testifying as well," Dr. Kio said looking at Amy as he concluded his statement. Amy nodded.

"Did you look at the tests and discuss the conclusions with the criminalist?" Judge Barney asked Dr. Kio.

"Your Honor, I would receive their tests but have no need to discuss my conclusions with them as our jurisdictions are different. I have jurisdiction over the body, and they have jurisdiction over the rest of the scene, that would include the condom in the bin and any traces of blood found on it."

"You may answer the question," Judge Barney said.

"Well, again, we had a very small sample to work with, as usual. We were able to determine it was blood by spraying a chemical on the stain, which makes blood glow in the dark under ultraviolet light. But the amount of genetic material on the condom, coupled with possible contamination from the bin, made DNA sampling inconclusive as to whether it was the victim's or another woman's."

Amy took a deep breath and rubbed her forehead, drawing Gonzalez's attention. Their eyes met, and he mouthed, "don't worry." Amy forced a smile at him. Then she shuffled and reshuffled the papers in front of her.

"Dr. Kio, how long after the body was discovered did you conduct your examination?"

"Three days."

"Would you have determined the cause of death by just looking at the scene of the crime before conducting your examination?"

Dr. Kio was quiet for a what seemed like a long period.

"No, not in this case."

"And in performing that examination, you would have to open up the cranium of the victim, would you not?"

"Yes, to rule out the likelihood that an allergic reaction caused the asphyxia."

"So, you would not jump to the conclusion that physical force was used?"

"Objection," Amy said.

"Rephrase your question, counsel," Judge Barney said.

"Dr. Kio, are you capable of ruling out suffocation due to an allergic reaction without opening up the victim's cranium?"

"No, I am not, but—"

"Thank you, doctor, you have answered my question," Cassandra said.

"Objection, your Honor. The doctor has not finished his answer," Amy said.

"Sustained. You may finish what you were saying, doctor."

"I was going to say that the police operate on a different set of evidence in addition to the evidence I use in my examination and may well be in a better position to conclude that there was nothing present that would cause the victim an allergic reaction in her own bathroom. The police make the manner of death determination and I make the cause of death determination. When the manner of death points to homicide by a particular suspect, the police can make an arrest while awaiting the cause of death determination."

"Thank you doctor. I have nothing further," Cassandra said.

"Any redirect?"

"Yes, your Honor," Amy said and stood up.

"Dr. Kio, let me ask the last question counsel asked you a different way. Are you able to conclude that the cause of death was strangulation without opening up the body?" Amy asked.

"Yes."

"How?"

"There is a thin strip of tissue inside the middle of the upper and lower lips called the frenulum…" He showed Amy pictures from his autopsy, which Amy marked and introduced into evidence before he continued. "When the frenulum is broken, it is often due to smothering or an attempt to smother the victim. One could also examine the eyes for ruptured capillaries, petechiae of the eyes. These are pinpoint hemorrhages in the whites of the eye caused by the pressure in the head building up higher and higher during strangulation until the blood vessels start to rupture, and the weakest blood vessels rupture first. Some of these are in the whites of the eye. In the event of strangulation, blood pressure in the head increases causing those ruptures in the eyes."

"Were those all present in this case on the victim?" Amy asked.

"Yes, they were."

"Thank you, doctor," Amy said. "I have nothing further for this witness."

Judge Barney turned his head toward Cassandra.

"Nothing further from us," Cassandra said.

"The witness is excused," Judge Barney said, and waited for Dr. Kio to leave the courtroom. "We stand in recess."

Cassandra and Amy looked at each other after the judge left the courtroom and looked away at the same time.

•••

AMY NEXT CALLED OFFICER Fritz to the stand. She had wanted to call Officer Tse to elaborate on the evidence collected in Goldie's room but changed her mind after the defense did well with Dr. Kio on those objects. He testified that he was one of the officers who arrested Paul Jackson at his house. He said Paul Jackson spoke freely to them and allowed them to search his house and his car. Paul claimed he was at the club until very late on the night Goldie was murdered, after which he returned to his house and never left again until the officers arrived. An express package had been delivered at his house that morning, but he had not been available to sign for it.

Paul's bank records also showed an automated teller machine withdrawal at 12:04 a.m. the morning of the incident. The location of the ATM was about two miles east from Goldie's apartment, on Wilshire Boulevard, but it would not have been Paul Jackson's route from the club to his house. The officers retrieved surveillance camera photographs from the bank, which showed he made the withdrawal himself.

Officer Fritz then introduced pictures taken from the ATM surveillance camera with the time and date on the pictures. When the officers found the boots Paul wore earlier that day, he started crying and said he wanted to speak to his attorney.

"Up until that time, he spoke freely?" Amy asked.

"Yes, ma'am," Fritz said.

"And he gave you permission to search his house?"

"Yes, ma'am."

"You said you found the boots he wore. Weren't they lying there in his wardrobe with all his other shoes?"

"No, they were hidden in a guest bedroom."

"Objection to the characterization that they were hidden. The officer is speculating about the defendant's intent," Kenneth said.

"Overruled," Judge Barney said.

"Did Mr. Jackson say exactly when he came home the night before?" Amy asked.

"He said twelve midnight, or so."

"Even though you had surveillance camera footage showing him on Wilshire Boulevard at 12:04 a.m.?" Amy asked.

"We didn't have that information when we were talking to him. After we spoke to him, we continued our investigation and found that he was at Wilshire when he said he was in his house," Officer Fritz explained.

This concluded Amy's examination. When Kenneth got up for Fritz's examination, Cassandra had suggested he should not do anything with the ATM record, believing Amy had gone over it too quickly, and any further inquiry by Kenneth's examination would turn a "fleeting anecdote into a moment of history." Kenneth agreed.

"Officer Fritz, when you and other officers left the defendant's house on the night the body was discovered, you placed him under arrest for the crime, did you not?" Kenneth asked.

"Yes, we did."

"Based on the evidence as you described earlier?"

"And the evidence we collected at the victim's house. We were afraid he was already hiding evidence."

"Then, the following day you got a subpoena to search his office, his house, and all his belongings?"

"Yes sir, it was basic investigative procedure. First, he gave us permission to search his house, then when we found the shoe, he demanded we leave, and asked for an attorney."

"What was the connection between the office and the crime?"

"Possible location where evidence might be hidden."

"Was that also the reason why the first police report you prepared did not mention Mr. Jackson's office, which is located in his nightclub, but the typewritten report mentioned that Footsie was going to be at the club?"

"No."

"You did not write the report that way to create a connection between the club and this case that supports your subpoena?" Kenneth asked.

"No, sir. We were just writing the information we received."

"What did you find at the office when you searched it?"

"We did not find anything."

"You mentioned earlier that Mr. Jackson's boots were hidden at the time you found them, right?"

"Yes, sir."

"Hidden where?"

"They were on top of the closet, inside a bag, behind a bunch of old boxes."

"How do you know that isn't usually where he keeps them when he intends not to wear them for a while?"

"Who puts shoes he just wore on top of the closet?"

"How expensive were those shoes, Officer, do you know?" Kenneth asked.

"I don't know."

"Would it surprise you if I told you that they were nine-hundred-and-fifty-dollar shoes?"

"No."

"Have you ever had friends who try to borrow your expensive shoes when they see them lying around your house?"

"No, not personally."

Kenneth and Fritz went back and forth through the next break. Kenneth asked him about the people who claimed they were at the club that night but did not see Paul Jackson. Showing Officer Fritz the layout of the club, Kenneth asked him about the number of people at the club on that Thursday night, the locations of the doors, and where the people he claimed to have talked to were seated. Kenneth wanted to know how Fritz chose his witnesses from the club out of the capacity crowd, and where he got their names. Fritz explained that they talked to the bartender, and the bartender identified some regulars he had noticed at the club that night. Then the police followed up with those regulars. The bartender also said he did not see Paul that night, the doorman did not, and the guard did not.

"These men are not exactly a bus load of nuns, Officer; did you ask them what they had to drink that night?"

"The bartender said he didn't drink at work," Fritz said, then perhaps thinking Kenneth might have potentially contrary, information, quickly added, "the others said they didn't drink much."

Many in the courtroom chuckled, and several jurors smiled.

"But they didn't tell you what they had had to drink?"

"No, sir."

"Did you actually talk to anyone who said they saw Mr. Jackson there?"

Fritz was quiet for a brief moment before he responded.

"Yes."

"Who was that?"

"Mr. Stone."

"Thank you, Officer," Kenneth said. "I have nothing further."

Amy was quickly on her feet.

"Who is Mr. Stone?"

"His full name is John Goldstone. They call him Big."

"Could you describe him?"

"Yes, he is African American, about six feet four, three hundred pounds or more, has a slight mark above his right eye, and sometimes wears a beard," Fritz said. After this description, almost all the jurors glanced over at the empty seat next to Josephine where Big usually sat when he was in court. Kenneth recalled that Big had gone on the quest to get information on Rachel Johnson.

"Why did you think the defendant's alibi did not hold up despite Mr. Stone telling you he saw Mr. Jackson at the club?"

"Mr. Stone. He has a rap sheet that'll go from me to you five times over. He is also the defendant's business partner."

"Were there surveillance cameras at the club?" Amy asked.

"Yes, but Mr. Stone said they weren't working."

"Objection to the hearsay," Kenneth said, standing up. Although the response was favorable to Paul, he had accurately contemplated Amy's next question.

"Notice, your Honor," Amy said citing an exception to the hearsay rule. "The statement was being made to establish how the officer was put on notice of the fact."

"Overruled, you may proceed."

"Did you ask anybody else about the cameras?"

"The bartender said they were working."

"Same objection," Kenneth said, standing up.

"Same ruling, counsel," Judge Barney repeated.

"Earlier, when Mr. Jackson was examining you—" Amy began to say.

"Mr. Brown," Fritz corrected her.

"Excuse me?" Amy asked apparently unsure what Fritz was saying.

"You said Mr. Jackson was examining him when you meant Mr. Brown's examination. He was correcting you," Judge Barney explained.

"Oh, I'm sorry," Amy said, blushing visibly, and turned to look at Kenneth. He was not looking at her, but Paul was, and grinning.

"I'm sorry, again," Amy said.

"It is a common mistake," Judge Barney said without a trace of irony. "Go on, counsel."

"Earlier, when you were being examined by Mr. Brown, defendant's lawyer, you started to say why you felt the shoes were hidden, do you recall that?" Amy asked.

"Yes."

"Could you tell us why you felt the shoes were hidden?"

"Yes, ma'am. It's not my experience that someone keeps shoes that high up above a closet, and even then behind a bunch of stuff when they had just worn the shoes a few hours earlier. There were other expensive shoes on the floor of the closet."

Amy concluded her further examination with this answer from Officer Fritz.

Kenneth stood again to cross-examine Fritz.

"Officer, when you were describing Mr. Stone, you mentioned that he was African American and I realized I had not asked you what race or ethnicity were the other witnesses you spoke to. Was the bartender who told you that Paul was not there African American as well?"

"No, he was white, but the other witnesses we spoke to were African Americans. Mostly."

"Mostly?"

"There was one Caucasian among the people attending the club that I spoke to."

"And they told you he was a regular?"

"No, he was visiting with the bartender that day."

"So, you separated the milk from the chocolate drink just to get the taste you preferred?"

"Objection," Amy said.

"I will withdraw the question," Kenneth said and continued without looking at the judge or giving him an opportunity to rule on the objection. "Officer, did you check the rap sheet of these witnesses you spoke to as well?"

"No."

"So, you don't know if the bartender had a rap sheet longer than Mr. Stone?"

"No."

"And you don't know if his friend, the only other white person in the club that night, had a rap sheet?"

"No, sir, I don't."

"Nothing further, your Honor."

Amy shook her head to indicate she did not have additional questions. The court had barely one hour left before recess for the day. Amy called the doorman on duty at Cool Jo's Café the night Goldie Silberberg died and asked him what his duties were and several questions that confirmed Fritz's conclusions about the club that night, then gradually developed her questioning to where she asked the doorman if he had seen Paul at Cool Jo's Café. The doorman said he hadn't seen Paul Jackson that night.

Kenneth asked the doorman if he was an off-duty policeman from another city. He confirmed that he was a policeman in the city of Inglewood. Kenneth asked if he belonged to an order or fraternity of active and retired police officers, and he said he belonged to such a fraternity. Thus concluded Kenneth's cross-examination of the doorman.

Amy asked to approach the bench, anticipating that Judge Barney was about to recess for the day.

"Do we need the jury for this?" Judge Barney asked and excused the jurors after Amy said they were not needed.

Amy handed Judge Barney the folder on Rachel Johnson and pointed out that she believed the defense was planning on using it to impeach

Didi Pare improperly. Judge Barney reviewed the file calmly, and asked Amy to bring a formal motion if she wanted to exclude the folder from the trial.

•••

ONCE THEY RETURNED TO their tables, Amy walked over to Kenneth, eager to talk to him before the sheriff led Paul away. Gonzalez stood behind and waited.

Paul turned away from his family just behind the defense counsel table where he was talking to them to look at Amy.

"Hi, counsel," Kenneth said.

"I want to apologize again for that slip I made earlier, calling you Mr. Jackson."

"Don't worry about it."

The sheriff's deputy started putting handcuffs on Paul to lead him away, and Amy noticed that Paul was watching her attentively.

"Excuse me," Kenneth said and turned to say some parting words to Paul. The expression on Paul's face suddenly was as unfriendly as Kenneth had ever seen it. Amy and Cassandra, whose glances followed Kenneth, looked at each other. The sheriff led Paul away.

The day in court felt like a disaster to Amy, especially because she had called Kenneth Mr. Jackson. It filled her with shame. How she found the decorum to resume her examination of Fritz as though the mistake had not felt like a sacrilegious slur from a pulpit, surprised her. Judge Barney's comment had not helped, and the satisfaction Paul seemed to get from the mistake when she saw him smiling felt worse than the mistake itself. Everything about the mistake was illuminated in the worst light she could imagine. Of course, it could all be nothing and no one thought anything of it, she thought for a second. Her shame must mean that at least one juror saw it in the same light as she did.

"What was I thinking?" Amy asked herself, and though she searched her intentions earnestly, she could not find any explanation. "What does it mean?" Nothing came of this question either. She sat in her office with her head down on her desk and hoped that this endless recollection that roiled inside her would pass after a while. Her face was buried in her palms when someone knocked on her door.

"Come in," she called to whomever was at the door and heard the person open the door. When she did not hear the person speak, she raised her head and saw Melissa standing at the door.

"I came to see how your trial was going. That well, huh?"

"No, it's okay, I think."

"You are just exhausted?"

"Not really. I made a slip during my examination of the officer and called Kenneth Mr. Jackson."

Melissa stood looking at Amy with a scrunched expression that suggested she was still waiting for the story.

"I didn't even know I did it. The officer had to correct me. I felt so embarrassed."

"It was an honest mistake…right?"

"Of course, but have you forgotten my affair with him?" Amy asked.

"Still?" Melissa asked.

"Can you close my door?" Amy asked. Melissa turned around and closed the door behind her and turned again to Amy.

"I'm pregnant," Amy said. Melissa gasped. "Exactly," Amy added.

"No shit. His?" Melissa asked.

Amy shrugged.

"Does he at least know that you are pregnant?" Melissa asked.

"He doesn't know. I have not talked to him about anything personal since the preliminary hearing…like I promised," Amy said.

"Forget what you promised. You are free now. You have handled this case like a pro and allowed Kate to face another trial. We release you of all the terms of your restrictions."

"Thanks," Amy said.

"Don't forget the fact that they have both been sitting in that courtroom every day of the trial with you and this is the most stressful trial of your career yet."

"I suppose you are right. I guess what was most embarrassing about it was that I did not know I had called him Mr. Jackson until the officer on the stand corrected me, and the judge explained it to me," Amy said.

"Are you a Michael Jackson fan?" Melissa asked.

"Huge fan."

"Then that is what you were thinking," Melissa said. Oddly, Amy thought, it lifted her spirits to see it as Melissa had suggested. Then came a knock on the door.

"Please don't tell anyone about my situation. I just wanted only you to know," Amy whispered. Melissa nodded and opened the door. It was Kate.

"I heard a lot of hushed speaking and whispering, what are you two talking about?"

"She called Kenneth Mr. Jackson," Melissa said.

"In bed?" Kate asked with a concerned look and Melissa started laughing. Amy's face was red all over again.

"No, in court. Eewwww!" Amy protested and Kate started laughing as well. Watching them, Amy began to see the lighter side of the incident.

"Don't be silly," Kate said. "It only means that you miss him and the only thing that stands between the two of you is this son-of-a-bitch you can't wait to get rid of so you can see him again."

Melissa leaned back as if to get a clearer view of Kate, then turned to Amy and pointed both hands at Kate.

"There you go. That makes a whole lot of sense to me," Melissa said.

Amy blushed even more and did not know what to say.

"I've got something better for you to worry about," Kate said. Melissa left waving to Amy.

"What is it?"

"Your hunch was right. Mr. Pare's test came back as a match for the semen on the bed."

Amy picked up the phone and started dialing. Kate came further into the office and closed the door behind her.

CHAPTER FORTY

If They're Not Against Us...

Tuesday, THE EIGHTH DAY of trial, Neda was sitting in the hallway of the courthouse when Amy arrived in court, and she had said nothing about attending the trial when Amy spoke to her over the weekend.

"Is Thomas in the courtroom?" Amy asked Neda.

"He'll come when trial resumes, so you won't have to bother with him."

"Can you tell him to make lunch reservations for us, somewhere close—but not the Intercontinental."

"I will," Neda said. As Amy turned to leave, she added, "You will be nice, right?"

"Of course."

"Seriously, Amy. You screwed up."

"You don't think I know that?" Amy asked, suddenly emotional.

"You shocked me..." Neda said, both women looking right into each other's eyes for a brief moment.

"I know," Amy said and hugged Neda. "I shocked me," she whispered to Neda before she let go and went into the courtroom.

Amy paraded the witnesses Fritz mentioned in his testimony through the proceeding. They were eight in all: the bartender, his friend, the doorman's assistant, an officer from a private security outfit serving Paul's neighborhood, and four bar regulars who were at the bar that Friday night. These witnesses would take the trial to Wednesday afternoon.

Helen Silberberg returned to court, this time with her rabbi, Eli Kollman. Amy was glad to see him, though she could not quite understand why it filled her with such relief, as if she could breathe easier with him present. She let him know that and requested that the judge reconsider letting Helen back into the courtroom. Judge Barney let her back in but directed Amy to make sure she was outside the courtroom whenever testimony that might be too emotional for her was to come up, and to ensure she did not do that in a manner that was suggestive to the jury. Helen thanked the judge and apologized profusely.

Judge Barney also informed the court that he would recess at noon on Wednesday, like he had indicated to counsel last week, to address another matter.

Kenneth's examination of Amy's witnesses was minimal. The bartender confirmed he was introduced to the club by Goldie and that he had a rap sheet also, but only comprising of two crimes. He said two of the regulars Amy had called bought drinks on credit and owed the bar money. The private security officer was easily confused as to which house was Paul's and how he came to that knowledge. Paul gave Kenneth most of the ideas he used to develop these questions. As the information he gave Kenneth proved effective, Paul became more animated in court, wrote more notes and questions, and demanded more explanations when Kenneth wanted to keep the questions short.

Amy avoided looking in the gallery while she was examining witnesses, afraid that seeing Thomas might make her emotional as every little thing seemed to do, especially when she had done something wrong or could have done better. Shortly before lunch recess, Thomas left the courtroom to the restaurant his office had found. They closed it to the public, so Thomas, Amy, and Neda could have it all to themselves for a couple of hours. When Amy walked into the restaurant and Thomas stood to receive her, she hurried toward him, holding back her tears until she embraced him and buried her face on his shoulder. "I'm sorry," she said repeatedly and refused to let go of the embrace. Thomas seemed unsure what to do or say. Neda sat down and picked up the menu, never making eye contact with Thomas or Amy until they both sat down. Throughout lunch, they only talked about the trial and how it was going. Amy could not be sure what Thomas knew of her pregnancy or what he thought her relationship with Kenneth had become, nor was she willing to discuss either. She thanked Thomas for being a bigger man than their mutual friend Richard and asked for his forgiveness as they walked out arm in arm from the restaurant. They would talk more on the phone, they agreed.

•••

Cassandra was not available on Wednesday morning and by lunchtime, Paul was asking Kenneth if they could spend the lunch hour going over questions for Didi Pare, whom Kenneth mentioned might be following these witnesses. Kenneth declined, suspecting that Paul's line of questions might have been informed by the information Big had obtained about Rachel. Pare would not be called on Wednesday because Judge Barney decided to recess early.

•••

On Thursday morning, Judge Barney kept the jury and Helen Silberberg outside the courtroom and held a hearing on the motion to exclude evidence from the file on Rachel Johnson. Authenticity could not be established, so the file and the information in it would be excluded. Kenneth argued that authenticity need not be established, before it could be used to impeach Mr. Pare as to his knowledge of the contents and how he came in possession of it.

"How does it impeach Mr. Pare's credibility? It says nothing of Mr. Pare. It's all about this witness, Rachel Johnson," Judge Barney said.

"I believe this was how Mr. Pare met Ms. Johnson," Kenneth said.

"That is just speculation, your Honor," Amy said.

"I agree," Judge Barney said. "Counsel, I need an offer of proof as to how these documents are connected to this witness before you can introduce them against him."

"Your Honor, we can at least ask the witness if he is familiar with the documents. The scope of what is allowed for foundation, much less impeachment, is broad enough to permit that question," Cassandra said.

"I appreciate your erudition, counselor, but unless you tell me how you got these documents and how they relate to this witness, you are not introducing them against him."

"Our investigator got them from Mr. Pare," Kenneth said.

"Is the investigator going to testify in this trial?"

"We had not planned on it," Kenneth said.

"You may need to rethink that strategy, counsel, but even then, the contents still don't make it in, just the fact that he got it," Judge Barney said.

"At the very least, your Honor, if Ms. Johnson testifies, we should be able to use the documents to impeach her," Cassandra said.

"Go on, make an offer in that regard," Judge Barney said.

"The pictures in the file are clearly authentic pictures of her that she must have been aware of when they were taken, and she can be impeached as to how they found their way into such nefarious hands, if not with her consent, or that the pictures were taken for the very purpose of being used in this manner," Cassandra said.

"What do you say, counsel?" Judge Barney asked, turning to Amy.

"Your Honor, I would rather cross that bridge when we get to it."

"Fair enough," Judge Barney said.

The lawyers returned to their seats.

When the trial resumed, Judge Barney informed the jurors that the prosecution was expected to conclude its case this week. He reminded the jurors of the procedural path he had told them the trial would take. Once the prosecution concludes its case, the defense would present its case.

After these instructions, Amy called Didi Pare to the stand. Pare walked over to the witness box wearing a custom-cut suit with a blue tie and a matching breast pocket handkerchief. Amy was glad to see that he was much better dressed, much cleaner than he had been the week before, just as the paralegals had told him.

"Mr. Pare, what is your occupation?" Amy asked.

"I manage musical artists, and I am an independent artist and repertoire director for several recording companies. I am also CEO of a music publishing company."

"How did you know Goldie Silberberg?"

"A friend of hers contacted me to help her advance her career."

"And did you help her?"

"I tried, but there were obstacles we were both trying to overcome."

"What obstacles were those?"

"Well, Goldie had a great voice but no material, and there's plenty of that type in this town. She was a very attractive woman, too, but the competition with those same qualities is fierce as well."

"So, the lack of materials was her obstacle?"

"No, her ex-boyfriend gave her the material she needed, but he demanded a lot for it."

"By her ex-boyfriend, whom do you mean?"

"Paul Jackson."

"By Paul Jackson, are you referring to the defendant in this case?"

"Yes, ma'am."

"What did Mr. Jackson demand?"

"Goldie signed herself over to him to manage her. All her songs, which were either written or cowritten by him or based on his music, were on his publishing company, and when she sang in the studios, he held on to the masters."

"How did that affect your helping Ms. Silberberg?"

"Well, he insisted he was the only one who could help her and barred her from seeking other help. I think he had actually signed her to his record label, but he didn't have the funds to do anything with it."

"But Goldie came to you anyway. What happened?" Amy was primarily eliciting answers Kenneth would ordinarily inquire about to preempt Kenneth's examination, before going to the heart of Didi's testimony.

"Goldie managed to get her hands on a couple of the masters she made for Paul Jackson after they broke up and got them to me. When I gave them to several of my contacts in the industry, she was an instant hit, and they all wanted to sign her."

"Did the defendant, Mr. Jackson, ever find out the master recordings were missing?"

"Objection, that calls for speculation," Kenneth said, standing up.

"Rephrase your question counsel," Judge Barney directed.

"Mr. Pare, do you know whether Mr. Jackson found out that the masters had been missing?"

"Same objection," Kenneth said knowing he was wrong, but trying to throw Amy off her rhythm with Pare.

"Overruled," Judge Barney growled with an unfriendly glance at Kenneth.

"Well, yes," Didi said.

"How did he find out?"

"It took about one weekend for Goldie to get so many companies in the industry willing to sign her. So, she got angry and confronted Mr. Jackson for not doing everything he had promised her if I could get her three music contracts the first time."

"Objection, hearsay," Kenneth said, standing, but Amy continued with her next question without waiting for the judge's ruling.

"Were you present during this confrontation?"

"Overruled," the judge said anyway.

"She made sure I was present to confirm that those masters hadn't really been sent out before I did it."

"What happened after Goldie confronted Mr. Jackson?"

"He just insisted he had sent the masters out, but afterward…after I had left them, Goldie called me from the hospital, and she was pretty bruised up."

Before Kenneth could object to the suggestion that Goldie was in the hospital, Cassandra placed her hand on him to stop him.

"Did she tell you who beat her?"

"Objection, mischaracterizes the witness's testimony as to being beaten. Counsel is now testifying," Kenneth said.

"Overruled," Judge Barney said as though he was swiping away an irritant fly.

"No, she did not, but she was very afraid—" Didi started to say when Kenneth rose again to object.

"What is your objection, counsel?" Judge Barney asked sternly.

"May we approach, your Honor?" Cassandra inquired.

Amy, Kenneth, and Cassandra approached the side of Judge Barney's bench with the court reporter and spoke in hushed tones.

"Your Honor," Cassandra said, "once the witness conceded that he did not know how the victim was beaten, the rest of his answer becomes irrelevant and speculative to the point of undue prejudice in this proceeding."

"But we haven't even heard the rest of it, counsel. What the witness does know about circumstances surrounding the beating is directly relevant to this proceeding because the People's theory is that the victim was going to leave the defendant, that is why he killed her," Amy said.

"Your Honor, this might be a prior bad act of someone other than the defendant. It's perilous for the witness to speculate about it to any point that may directly or indirectly implicate my client," Kenneth said.

"Your objection is noted for the record, counsel. Will there be anything else?"

"No, your Honor, thank you," Cassandra said, returning to her seat. Kenneth followed her.

"Mr. Pare, you were going to say something about Ms. Silberberg's beating when you were interrupted," Amy continued.

"Yes."

"Please go on."

"Goldie was very afraid to say anything about how she was beaten or who beat her. I gave her assurances of security and protection, but she didn't budge."

"So, did Goldie Silberberg return the masters that got her signed?"

"No, she said they made a contract and Mr. Jackson was going to let her have the songs she needed for the new deal, including the ones she wrote."

"Ms. Silberberg told you this while she was still in the hospital?"

"Yes."

"When you said Mr. Jackson was going to let her keep the songs she wrote, did you mean that he kept her songs as well?"

"Yes, as part of their deal, she had signed over the songs she wrote to his publishing company. So, they weren't just her songs. She was sharing ownership with his publishing company. Most of the music was his also, she wrote mostly the lyrics. He let her have all the songs with her lyrics and agreed to let her find another manager."

"Did she find another manager?"

"She asked me."

"You became her manager. And what happened?"

"Paul backed out of the deal. Goldie already had the songs they agreed on for the deal, so all he could do was hold on to the other masters, and threaten to sue," Didi said.

"And what was Goldie's response to that threat?"

"After she came out of the hospital, I believe, she swore never to see him again."

"To your knowledge, did she keep that oath?" Amy asked.

"No," Didi said. "He also had signed her to play at his club for a long time, and Goldie loved performing, especially to Black audiences. She felt that Black audiences let you know exactly how they feel about your performance, so their endorsement was authentic."

"So, she went back to perform at Cool Jo's Café, but did they date as well?"

"They did not date."

With every passing testimony, Didi Pare appeared to be Amy's strongest witness. Pare said he was helping Goldie find a lawyer to keep Paul away from her. Amy confirmed that Goldie was going to meet Paul the night before she died and ended her examination on this last revelation.

Kenneth wanted to end his examination of Didi Pare on his most convincing note. He wrote his last question down on a sheet of paper and kept it apart from the list of the questions he had written down. From time to time, he glanced at that last question. It was shortly before the lunch recess, and Kenneth knew exactly what his line of questions before lunch recess was going to be.

"Mr. Pare, would you mind if I refer to Ms. Silberberg as Footsie in my exchanges with you?"

"No, of course not. She liked the name."

"Footsie told you she was going to cut off Mr. Jackson for good. Is that right?" Kenneth asked.

"Yes."

"And if that had happened, you would have become her manager as well as her agent and her publisher, is that correct?"

"Yes, I was already her agent, and she had made me manager in every practical respect anyway."

311

"In fact, if Footsie left Paul Jackson, you would be doing exactly what Paul was doing for her as manager and agent."

"I was doing that already."

"And if Paul Jackson goes to jail, you will continue to manage Footsie's music and royalties, including songs cowritten by Paul Jackson, but if Mr. Jackson is acquitted, he remains an obstacle, as you put it, does he not?"

"It makes no difference to me either way. Paul Jackson's contract to manage Goldie personally died with Goldie. My contract was with Goldie and the recording company. It survives her, and Goldie's family has given me authority over Goldie's musical estate."

Kenneth now began exploring the relationship Didi had with Goldie's family, and the managers' rights to royalties, but none of these appeared to damage Amy's case. This testimony took Didi Pare's examination close to the lunch recess. Just before the lunch recess, Kenneth approached the witness stand carrying a large envelope.

"Mr. Pare, at the time Footsie died on January 6, 1995, who exactly was her manager? You or Paul Jackson?"

"For all intents and purposes, I was."

"What does that mean?"

"Objection, argumentative," Amy said.

"I simply want him to explain if all intents and purposes means that Paul Jackson could be manager in any other capacity not included in his qualifying statement."

"Rephrase your question, counsel," Judge Barney said.

"Mr. Pare, was Mr. Jackson Footsie's manager in any capacity at the time she died?"

"No, he was not."

Kenneth opened the large envelope and brought out the music contract Amy had given him, and as he did so, Cassandra requested permission to approach Judge Barney to give him a copy and left a copy on Amy's table as she walked by.

Amy heard herself sigh, and started to bring her hand to her face, but quickly stopped herself and rubbed the back of her neck instead. Her chest felt heavy and her bowels felt like they were knitting knots of her intestine.

She was convinced that Helen Silberberg and Rabbi Kollman were boring holes in her back with the disappointment they felt for her betrayal and struggled not to look at them. She fixed her eyes on Mr. Pare who was reviewing the document he was given.

"Is that the music contract you signed for Ms. Silberberg with the recording company?" Kenneth asked.

"Yes, it is."

"Please tell us who this contract says is her manager."

Didi was quiet for a moment and appeared to be going through the document.

"Mr. Pare, is this the first time you are seeing this document?"

"This particular copy, yes. I'm just making sure it is the same contract I have seen before."

"Take your time," Kenneth said.

"The contract lists Mr. Jackson as her manger," Didi said.

"Thank you," Kenneth said and, turning to the judge, inquired if it was a good time to take the lunch recess. "Good enough," Judge Barney replied.

On their way back to the Intercontinental Hotel, Kenneth told Cassandra that he had been playing for time to get Didi to return after the lunch recess.

"That was pretty obvious, counsel."

Big had waited for Kenneth and Cassandra in the lobby of the hotel. As soon as they were in the elevator at the hotel, Big began to speak about the case.

"You gotta ask Mr. Pare about that Rachel lady," Big said.

"Judge Barney already said we can't use that file you gave us with him," Kenneth said.

"I don't mean use the file, just ask him about her."

"Why?" Kenneth asked.

"He's trying to help us," Big said.

"Are you kidding me, with that testimony he gave this morning?" Kenneth asked.

Big held his explanation until they were all safely in the hotel suite. Nancy was waiting with their lunch. "Didi knew Paul beat Goldie up, but he's not saying that because he don't want to hurt our case. He showed up at Cool Jo's with bodyguards and shit and said he would destroy Cool Jo's Café then call the police if I didn't let him in. So, I did. He drew up the agreement that got Goldie's songs from Paul's publishing catalogue to keep the police out of the shit. And he gave me the information on Rachel."

"We don't want to go back to the beating, especially now that we know who did it," Cassandra explained to Big as though he were one of the defense lawyers.

"Okay. That's cool," Big said. "How about we ask Didi if he's sleeping with Rachel?" Big asked.

"Do you know what he's going to say to that?" Cassandra asked.

"No," Big said. "But I can guess."

"Why do you want us to ask it?" Kenneth asked.

"I think he wants to help," Big said.

"How would it help? If he is going to lie, that is not necessarily a good idea," Cassandra said.

"We're not asking him to lie, though," Big protested. "I thought we just ask him the question, and let him decide how he's gonna answer it," Big said. Cassandra could not fault Big's response and shrugged her shoulders again.

"Big, the reason we gotta know the answer to the question we ask him before we ask it, is that we don't know what the other side has on him. That way we don't walk into the district attorney's trap," Kenneth explained. Much to Kenneth's surprise Big agreed and brought out a compact disk with Goldie's single song release. It was a radio station promotional copy and had the cover of the full record with the title "Footsie" on it.

"At least ask him about this," Big said.

Kenneth could not hide his enthusiasm. "Now you're talking."

"Where did you get that?" Cassandra asked.

"From a friend," Big said and excused himself to leave. It was clear to Kenneth that he had offended Big, but he could not tell what he had done to do so.

"That question might not really hurt, the one about if he slept with Rachel," Cassandra said.

"Of course, I'm going to ask it," Kenneth said.

・・・

KENNETH RESUMED HIS EXAMINATION of Pare after the lunch recess.

"You said a friend of Footsie's introduced you to her?" Kenneth asked Didi Pare.

"Yes, she sent me a demo tape and asked if I could meet with her and I agreed," Didi explained.

"What was her friend's name?" Kenneth asked.

"Rachel Johnson," Didi said, but he had paused before answering.

"Ms. Johnson lives at the same apartment building where Footsie lived, right?"

"Yes."

"In fact, she personally delivered Footsie's tape to you."

"Yes, she did."

"How did you meet Ms. Johnson?"

"I don't recall, probably at a cocktail party."

"Which is it? You don't recall or a cocktail party?"

Didi paused contemplatively again before he said, "It must have been a cocktail party."

"How often have you been to that apartment complex to visit?"

"To visit Goldie?" Didi Pare asked.

"Yes."

"Two or three times," Didi said.

"How about to visit Rachel Johnson?"

"Objection," Amy said, standing up.

"Sustained," Judge Barney ruled.

"So, how often would you say you have been to the apartment building, in general?"

"Asked and answered," Amy objected again.

"I will let that stand, overruled," Judge Barney said.

"About a dozen times, I don't recall," Didi said.

"Mr. Pare, as you walk up to the gates of Armacost Arms, there is a camera above the call box that picks up the person visiting—" Kenneth produced an exhibit and showed Didi. "The day Ms. Silberberg died, I'm not sure this camera picked up everyone visiting the complex. Can you tell us if you were at the complex on that day?" Kenneth asked.

"I may have been, I don't recall."

"You're not sure?" Kenneth asked. Kenneth knew then that Didi had been to the complex. "There is evidence in this case that Ms. Silberberg was in London for about three months. How many times did you visit her apartment complex while she was in London?"

"A couple of times maybe, around that period, I was helping her in any way I could."

"Did she ask you to check her kitchen sink as well?"

Amy objected and Judge Barney sustained the objection.

Kenneth glanced at his note and at the clock and decided it was time for his last set of questions.

"Are you married, Mr. Pare?"

"Yes."

"Did the police tell you that they needed your DNA to compare with semen samples found on Goldie Silberberg's bed and in condoms found in the trash can in her bedroom?" Kenneth asked.

Didi did not respond.

Amy rose again but this time politely. "Objection, your Honor."

"Sustained," Judge Barney said.

"When you visited the apartment building at Armacost Arms, were you going there because Ms. Rachel Johnson was your mistress?"

"Same objection," Amy said.

"Same ruling," Judge Barney replied, and added, "Sustained."

Kenneth picked up a rolled-up poster-sized document and placed it on the easel without showing it.

"Mr. Pare, one of Footsie's songs, 'A Past That Breathes,' was recently released to airplay on the radio, was it not?" Kenneth asked.

"Yes, it was."

"Was that one of the songs that Mr. Jackson wrote and owns all the publishing rights to?"

"I think they wrote it together. Goldie contributed some of the lyrics."

Kenneth placed the large rolled-up poster-sized picture of the compact disc for Goldie's single, and placed it on the easel.

"Mr. Pare, is this a true picture of the compact disc for the song 'A Past That Breathes'?"

"Yes," Didi said examining it more closely.

"And on that compact disc, it has the name of the publishing company that owns the rights to the song now, does it not?"

Didi was again quiet before he answered with an expression that begged where Kenneth was going with the question.

"Yes, it does."

"And that publishing company belongs to you, does it not?"

"Goldie asked me to —"

"Move to strike as non-responsive," Kenneth said.

"Mr. Pare, you are to answer the question, not comment on it. The answer is stricken," Judge Barney said.

"Yes, it is my publishing company."

"And 100% of all the publishing rights of the song that Paul Jackson wrote and used to own as a publisher, goes to your publishing company, none to him?"

"Mr. Jackson and Ms. Silberberg wrote the song and that was the agreement she asked for to get away from his control."

"Mr. Pare, what is the title of the record that Ms. Silberberg made in London?"

Didi was quiet before he answered.

"Footsic."

"Footsie," Kenneth repeated, and paused.

"Is there a song on that record that has that title?"

"No," Didi said.

"What does that mean? Footsie?"

"That was her stage name when she performed around town."

"But what does it mean?"

"It is a name he gave her the first time they met at his club."

"You mean, Paul Jackson gave her the name Footsie?"

"Yes, he did."

"Footsie," Kenneth said. "Would you agree, Mr. Pare, that this record Ms. Silberberg recorded was the most important achievement of her life and the culmination of her dreams?"

"Objection, calls for speculation," Amy said.

"Sustained," Judge Barney said.

"Mr. Pare, of all the titles that Ms. Silberberg could have chosen, if as you claimed she broke up with Mr. Jackson, do you know why she chose the name that Mr. Jackson gave her as the title of her dream, her greatest achievement?"

"So people who have seen her perform could make the connection to the record," Didi said.

"She told you that?"

"Yes."

"Because you tried to dissuade her from using that title, didn't you? That was why she had to give you an explanation. Any explanation."

"Objection, argumentative," Amy said.

"Rephrase the question, counsel."

"Did you try to dissuade her from using 'Footsie' as the title for her record?"

"Some of us thought the record should be called 'A Past That Breathes,'" Didi said.

"But still she called it Footsie—I have nothing further," Kenneth said.

Amy was not sure what she despised more about Kenneth's cross-examination, his use of the contract she had sent to him or Mr. Pare being her witness in this trial. She had not yet accosted him about who sent Rachel Johnson's dossier to him and to the defendants. She wanted him off the stand more than she wanted to rehabilitate him.

She asked him to open the contract Kenneth had given him to the signature page, and when Didi opened it, she asked him who signed it and why.

"Mr. Jackson did not sign it because he was no longer her manager," Didi said.

"If he was no longer her manager, why did Goldie leave his name on the contract?"

"It was the record company's decision, not Goldie's, they didn't think it was a big deal as long as he didn't have to sign it."

"Isn't it true that there is an insurance policy that might also protect Goldie if someone were to sue her for plagiarism on the songs that Mr. Jackson wrote or cowrote?"

Didi was already nodding before Amy finished the question.

"Yes, the insurance policy would provide coverage for Mr. Jackson, only if he is named on the contract as manager, that way Goldie won't be caught holding the bag for his mistakes like she always did," Didi said.

"That concludes my examination of this witness," Amy said and sat down.

"We have nothing more as well," Kenneth said.

•••

AMY CALLED A CUSTODIAN of records from the Bank of America to the stand, and the custodian produced pictures from a security camera on an ATM machine on Wilshire Boulevard. The custodian testified on the bank's practices for collecting records from the camera, how long such records were kept, where they were kept or stored, why the particular records in this case could not have been tampered with, and how the bank came to produce the stills for this proceeding. The custodian also testified on the ATM receipts collected on Paul's account and how they were able to identify the particular machine that issued the receipt.

Cassandra did not want to examine the bank custodian, but she did not want to leave his testimony undisputed for the record either. She asked why the time and date on the photographs did not match the time on the receipt, and the custodian explained that the time on the camera was measuring frame times per second, and the particular frame for the picture that exactly matched the time on the receipt may not be the one showing his face. He said he brought the pictures he thought were best, and the difference in the time on the receipt and the time on the camera was a matter of seconds anyway.

"Would the calibration of the ATM clock result in a completely different date appearing on the picture, if the person in charge of that calibration wanted?"

"I don't know."

"You do know that they are maintained and checked, don't you?"

"Yes, ma'am."

"And calibrated occasionally?"

"Yes, I suppose."

"I have nothing further," Cassandra concluded.

Amy was ready for the questions Cassandra had asked the custodian, and next called the technician charged with maintaining the particular ATM in question. Rather than make the technician the routine witness she had intended, Amy took her time to lay out the technician's credentials, expertise, and background before she began to examine him on the mechanics and maintenance of the ATM.

Cassandra had no cross-examination for the technician. Thus, the conclusion of the technician's testimony took the parties to the end of the day. The technician walked through the double doors and exited into the hallway before Judge Barney called the attorneys to his bench.

"Ms. Wilson, your witness list tells me you have five more witnesses. Is that still right?" Judge Barney asked.

"Actually, your Honor, one witness is not currently available," Amy said.

"Which witness would that be, counsel?"

"Rachel Johnson."

Kenneth turned to look at Big in the stand, and Big slowly shook his head from side to side.

"So, now, we have Officer Tse, the lady who saw them arguing, and a serologist who collected evidence at the scene. We think we can finish those tomorrow, your Honor," Amy said.

"The lady is Ms. Ola?" Judge Barney inquired.

"Yes, your Honor, and of course, we are assuming that the defendant has chosen not to testify, because we would like to call him if he is not exercising the Fifth Amendment right not to testify."

"Counsel, does the defendant intend to testify?" Judge Barney asked.

"No, your Honor," Kenneth said. "He will exercise his Fifth Amendment right under the Constitution."

"Very well. So, we have these witnesses left for the prosecution. Would the defense proceed immediately with its first witness, once the prosecution concludes its case?" Judge Barney asked.

"No, your Honor," Cassandra said. "We'll have a motion for directed verdict for your Honor."

"Will that be a long or a short motion?" Judge Barney asked, as though indicating that such a motion would be purely academic.

"The motion we have will take no more than an hour. I can't speak for the response," Cassandra said.

Judge Barney turned to the jury and informed them that the court would resume at its normal hour on Friday. "The court is in recess for the day," Judge Barney added and exited the courtroom.

"What's a directed verdict?" Paul asked Kenneth as the judge left the courtroom.

"It's a motion to dismiss the case, but we must make it when the DA is done putting up her case, to say she didn't meet her burden to prove her case against you after she has presented all her evidence and her witnesses. If we don't make it, we don't get to appeal that the evidence was insufficient."

Paul nodded.

At the office, Amy explained to Kate that she had to make a rushed decision not to call Rachel Johnson, because she was convinced that the judge would allow the dossier on her if she testified. Kate agreed with her. After their conversation was at an end and Amy was about to leave, Kate said, "thank you."

"For what?" Amy asked.

"Thomas was here earlier in the week to watch part of the trial. He came to my office. I know it was because of you."

Amy shook her head slowly before she spoke. "No, we did not have a conversation about anything personal. We are not really together anymore."

"I understand. But I think your response to what happened made him a better man."

Amy thought about Kate's comment. What happened was that she got pregnant, *which Kate does not know*, Amy thought, and it brought her close to tears. "When you put it that way Kate, then it was well worth it," she said, choking up and walking away.

CHAPTER FORTY-ONE
A Chronic Pain

O N FRIDAY, JUDGE BARNEY's early morning calendar ran slightly over schedule and trial did not resume until 10:30 a.m.

"Anyone looking at Goldie as she lay on the floor would know she was dead," Tse said as he explained the condition he and his team found Goldie's body in. He told the jury he was one of the first officers to arrive at Goldie's apartment after the incident. He repeated much of the same testimony Conrad gave on the stand. Amy wanted to use Tse's examination to support Conrad Wetstone's claim that he had gone to the apartment to check the water pressure. Tse testified that when they talked to him, Conrad had said he was going to check the garbage disposal in the kitchen, and after the police talked to him, they confirmed his claim with the tenant who had complained about the water pressure. Tse then explained how all the evidence was collected.

On Amy's further examination, he admitted the investigation had not progressed much when the police learned of Paul Jackson's involvement, and the first forty-eight hours are the most crucial of any murder investigation and they needed to do something before evidence was destroyed.

"How is that possible," Amy inquired, "when there could have been many leads to other suspects?"

"No, there were only leads to the defendant," Tse testified.

"What were the leads?"

"The imprint of his shoe, the information about the abuse, the prints on the bottles in the guest room, and the fact he was fired as her manager."

"And were there other leads?"

"While we were at the house, Mr. Jackson called."

"When Mr. Jackson called, did you ask him if he was the boyfriend?"

"We did."

"What did Mr. Jackson say when you asked him if he was her boyfriend?"

"He said he was Ms. Silberberg's boyfriend."

Paul frantically scribbled a note for Cassandra after Tse answered: "I didn't say that. I didn't say nothing," it read.

"And what did you do after that?"

"We let the detectives know and we continued the investigation."

"Were there other calls?"

"A few more calls came into the apartment while we were collecting evidence. We talked to the people calling to determine what else they could possibly tell us."

"Were you able to learn anything?"

"Yes, we learned she had changed her mind about playing at the club that night for some reason."

"By the club, you mean Cool Jo's Café, Mr. Jackson's nightclub?"

"Yes, ma'am."

Tse further testified as to the items of evidence that were collected at the scene of the crime, particularly the sexual paraphernalia and their possible uses. He presented more crime scene pictures showing where they were found, leaving nothing out. Amy pretended that she had concluded her examination on this response from Tse, and began to walk back to her table, then stopped as Cassandra began to stand up.

"Just one more thing, Officer. Why would the person who is accused of killing Goldie be calling her apartment when he should have known that she was dead?"

"Classic perpetrator mentality, ma'am. They always return to the scene of the crime, in one form or another to see what's happening, even to see how the investigation is getting along."

"Are you a psychologist?" Amy asked.

"No, ma'am, but I have been investigating crimes for years, and we get training on this kind of crime all the time."

Amy concluded her examination with this response. When she sat down, it seemed to Kenneth like she was relieved to be done with the examination. Their eyes met, but she looked away quickly. Cassandra rose to begin her cross-examination as Amy returned to her table.

"Officer Tse, you said Mr. Jackson called Goldie Silberberg's apartment while officers of the Los Angeles Police Department were at the scene, is that correct?" Cassandra asked.

"Yes, ma'am."

"And he told you he was the deceased's Black boyfriend as well?"

"Yes, ma'am."

"Did he tell you he was 'Black'? Or just the boyfriend?" Cassandra asked.

"He said he was the boyfriend—"

"And you filled in the rest?"

"More or less."

"From the sound of his voice?"

"Objection," Amy said.

"Sustained."

"How did you determine that Mr. Jackson was Black without asking him, Officer?" Cassandra asked.

"Rachel, the lady that lives next to Ms. Silberberg told us. ."

"Do you recall how long Mr. Jackson was on the phone when he called?"

"Just a couple of minutes."

"So, a man calls claiming to be Mr. Jackson, and you ask him what his business with the victim is, and he says that he is her boyfriend? Is that how it happened?"

"No, ma'am."

"Please explain the order of the discussion."

"While we were at the apartment, we received calls and after a couple of hang-ups that we could hear on the answering machine, we decide to start answering the phone. Mr. Jackson called, and at first he was silent, then we asked if he was looking for Ms. Silberberg. He said he was. We say she's not available at the moment and offer to take a message. He didn't want to leave a message and said he would call back later. That's when we asked him his name. He said Paul, and we asked if he was in a relationship with her and he wanted to know why we were asking him that question. So, we told him she was dead. Then he said he was her boyfriend."

"And during this call, Mr. Jackson also told the officers of the LAPD that the victim had been scheduled to play at the nightclub called Cool Jo's Café that night?"

"No, ma'am. I believe we got that from Ms. Johnson."

Cassandra then suggested that the officers were highly suspicious of Mr. Wetstone's decision to go into the apartment on the day he discovered the body. Tse denied the allegation. Cassandra then examined Tse on the listening device, and he said it belonged to Rachel. She had obtained it from a set she worked on and Goldie asked her to put it in her room while Goldie was in London. Cassandra felt this examination was going nowhere fast and abandoned it.

After the examination of Officer Tse, another officer whose specialty was serology took the stand and testified that she had the training and background necessary for collecting and testing crime scene evidence. She repeated much of what Dr. Kio had testified but was more certain than Dr. Kio that the blood found on the condom belonged to a different woman. She also testified as to tests on the traces of drugs found in the bedroom. Cocaine and methamphetamine were found in small quantities on the carpet by the bed, on the bed itself, and in the trash can.

Cassandra elicited exhaustive testimony from the serologist on her background, education, training, and experience with the particular circumstance of this case, which they all admitted was unusual before she let them off the stand, shortly before the lunch recess.

CHAPTER FORTY-TWO
Ms. Ola

IT CAME TIME FOR the last prosecution witnesses. Amy called Ola Mohammed to the stand. *People v. Jackson* had charted a course all its own, not quite the way Amy had expected or imagined it. A grinding work of meticulous attention to detail rather than an intellectual tennis of grand serves and returns between equally matched attorneys. She felt as though each fact, even when it was undisputed, had to be chiseled out of hard stone to an exact measure necessary to represent the guilt of the defendant.

Ms. Ola, a diminutive woman of African descent took her place in the witness box. She spoke softly with a Caribbean accent and seemed honest even to Kenneth. She had a captivating smile. Paul Jackson had never seen her before. She testified that she worked nearby in Beverly Hills and lived farther away in the La Brea area of Wilshire Boulevard. She often went to her boyfriend's apartment when she left work to wait out the traffic. On the day before Goldie died, she had left work early at about 2:00 p.m. and got to Armacost thirty-minutes afterward. Her boyfriend had been at home all day. Ms. Ola testified that she was in the living room at her boyfriend's apartment shortly after she arrived, when she noticed Paul and Goldie arguing. On hearing that Goldie had been murdered, she recalled their argument the previous day and told her boyfriend about it. Ms. Ola testified that she was distraught because she couldn't imagine Goldie dead.

Even before Ms. Ola testified, Cassandra had wondered whether she and Kenneth should ignore her testimony. The thought recurred to Kenneth as Ms. Ola testified. The worst she had done was place Paul at the scene of the crime, which footprints, fingerprints, and DNA had also done. Amy had concluded her examination of Ms. Ola rather quickly, as she had done once or twice before with otherwise important evidence. Kenneth asked Judge Barney to give him a minute and turned to consult with Cassandra. Their new consensus was that Amy should not have the last word on this witness, and Kenneth had prepared some examination for her, anyway. "Keep it short," Cassandra said.

"Ma'am, you said you left work to go to your boyfriend's apartment at midday?" Kenneth began.

"Yes, I was sick and he convinced me to come to his place."

"Did you go back to work that day?"

"No, I did not."

"And you never saw a doctor or went to the hospital for whatever was ailing you?"

"No, I felt better after a while."

"And after you observed the argument between Mr. Jackson and Ms. Silberberg, did you see Mr. Jackson leave?"

"Yes, I saw him walk out of the apartment."

"What about the man you said walked in as Mr. Jackson and Footsie were arguing?"

"No, but I went to lay back down on the couch."

Kenneth rested with this response, but Amy had anticipated it.

"Ms. Ola," Amy began, "did you speak to Goldie after she had argued with the defendant?"

"Yes, she came out to the veranda and I asked her if she was alright."

"She said, 'Yeah…don't worry about him, I made sure my friend would be here when he came.'"

"So, she said the man who walked in on them was a friend of hers protecting her?"

"That was how I understood it."

"Nothing further," Amy said.

•••

"Mr. Jackson, could you please rise?" Judge Barney directed. Paul stood up, and so did Kenneth and Cassandra with him.

"I am informed by your counsel that upon their advice as your representatives in this action, you have decided not to stand witness against yourself according to your Fifth Amendment right?"

"Yes, your Honor," Paul answered.

"You do so voluntarily, without coercion or intimidation, freely and fully understanding your rights and choosing to follow your counsel's advice?"

"Yes, your Honor," Paul said.

"Thank you, Mr. Jackson."

Paul, Kenneth, and Cassandra sat down.

"Will the People call their next witness, please," Judge Barney directed.

"The People rest, your Honor," Amy said.

Judge Barney turned to the jurors and explained that the defense had a motion they would make directly to the judge, as a result of which the trial would resume at eleven o'clock on Monday morning.

"Counsel should be prepared to give me a draft of jury instructions, including special instructions on the People's case, and we will supplement them at the conclusion of the defense's case," Judge Barney directed.

Outside the courtroom, Cassandra and Kenneth spent more than an hour explaining the day's proceedings to Sister Ramatu and Mallam Jackson. They were all happy about the work Kenneth and Cassandra had done.

•••

It had been the longest week of the trial for Amy. When Officer Gonzalez offered her a bet that she had won her first murder trial, she realized that though she had often felt like she was left alone to sink or swim, she had not tried the case alone. Her efforts to keep the affair with Kenneth and her pregnancy from the others at the office had forced her to insulate herself emotionally from Gonzalez, Fritz, the paralegals, secretaries, and messengers, all of whom had worked very hard on the case. Amy stopped just short of crying, she was exhausted and felt her muscles relax. She had often been close to tears since the pregnancy.

CHAPTER FORTY-THREE
An Invigorated Defendant

O N FRIDAY NIGHT, PAUL Jackson had a change of heart. He wanted to testify. Big delivered the news to Kenneth that night, and Kenneth was livid.

"The man has a right to speak up about what they accusing him about. What you mad about?" Big asked.

"He told the court in front of a jury that he was not going to testify. How do you think the jury is gonna see this change of heart?"

"I think they're gonna like him for it."

"Why, Big? We're saying there isn't enough evidence to connect him to this crime, and he wants to hand himself over for them to cross him and try to make the connection?" Kenneth asked with a sneer.

"I may not be a lawyer, but I know I'm good enough to be on that jury. And if I'm on that jury, I'm gonna want to hear what Paul's got to say for himself."

"And you're just going to trust the lawyer trying to put him away for life to ask him real nice and not trip him up?"

"It don't matter what the lawyer's got to ask, as long as he's innocent, right?"

"It does, Big. Innocent people end up in jail all the time. You should know that more than anyone else."

Big looked at Kenneth, then looked up at the ceiling with his arms akimbo before he spoke again.

"You ain't that dumb of a nigger, Kenny," Big said and walked out of the suite.

330

Nancy was in church, and Kenneth was left alone to contemplate what it meant for Paul to testify. He called Cassandra about the new development and was surprised by Cassandra's indifference to the situation.

"I'm sure he understands the consequences. We just have to remind him again and then find a way to help him through it. The key is to get him to let us in on what he's thinking as honestly as he possibly can," Cassandra said.

"Let's hope he really understands the consequences," Kenneth replied and hung up the phone.

•••

On Monday morning, Kenneth went into court early to see Paul regarding his decision to testify, but not to dissuade him. Paul was adamant.

"I would rather go down like a man than hide behind my lawyers, Kenny."

"I just want to understand so we can be ready to back you up. What do you see in the case that you can change with your testimony, or add to it?"

Paul merely shrugged his shoulders. "I don't have anything else to tell them but the same thing I've told you. I didn't do it."

Judge Barney called the case promptly at 9:00 a.m. for the motion on the directed verdict and learned of Paul's change of mind. Inside the courtroom, as Amy arrived and was setting her files down on the prosecution's table, Cassandra walked up to her and told her that Paul had changed his mind and decided to testify. Kenneth was still in holding with Paul at the time, and Gonzalez was standing next to Amy. Amy thanked Cassandra but showed no emotion about the news. Gonzalez pumped his fist, and patted Amy on the back, grinning.

"It means we have to reopen the case for the prosecution, and the defense can't argue its motion this morning. So where does that leave us, besides losing a day of trial?" Judge Barney inquired. Eager to avoid blame for the break in proceedings, Kenneth noted that the judge had asked the parties to work on jury instructions as well.

"Well, that, too, would be a half-baked effort. You could have a completely different set of special instructions than what you come up with today because the defendant testified. So, it's better to leave that as well until we hear his testimony," Judge Barney said.

"Your Honor, perhaps it has all just worked out well, because we gave the defendant the weekend to make up his mind some more, just so we don't have him changing it again on appeal," Amy said.

"I agree with you, counsel. I can see you're not encouraged by this development, though. Technicalities aside, I would think that you would take the offer with both hands," Judge Barney said.

"I am, your Honor, but I'm afraid I may also be a bit under the weather," Amy explained.

"We will adjourn until eleven o'clock then. I hope you feel better," Judge Barney said to Amy. Paul went back to his cell, leaving Kenneth and Cassandra to prepare for his examination. They called in Omar Jones.

•••

AMY HAD WOKEN UP at about 3:00 a.m. vomiting but recovered enough to go back to sleep. Days earlier, she was not only ready to examine Paul Jackson, she was looking forward to it, she told Kate. On this Monday morning she was not as prepared and scrambled between 9:00 a.m. and 11:00 a.m. to refresh her knowledge of what she had prepared before.

Officers Fritz, Alvarez, and Tse stood in the audience at the far back. Kate and Melissa came down with Amy to observe the examination of Paul Jackson. Neda also was in court again as was Alana who had decided to return to court after Amy told her that she was throwing up the previous night. Helen assured Alana that she would not break down again in court, and Rabbi Eli promised to make sure that she didn't. Big gave up his seat to sit on the bench in the hallway outside the courtroom all by himself. The courtroom was full.

Omar joined Kenneth and Cassandra, as he had agreed with Kenneth to represent Paul when he testified. When Big delivered the news that Paul wanted to testify on Sunday, Kenneth reached out to Omar, who was glad to oblige. He visited Paul in the holding cell as well but claimed he did not get much out of it either.

All three lawyers stayed at the counsel table, because space would open up when Paul went to the witness stand.

"Ladies and gentlemen, we had a new development this morning when the attorneys and I met in your absence. The district attorney will be reopening her case because the defendant has changed his mind and decided to testify. Will the People call the next witness?"

Paul Jackson took the stand. He wore a dark blue suit, sky blue shirt, and a yellow tie with tiny black spots all over it. After Paul was sworn in, Amy stood up.

"Good morning, Mr. Jackson."

"Good morning, ma'am," Paul responded with a slightly cracked voice and cleared his throat immediately.

"When did you last see Goldie Silberberg before she died?"

"I saw her the afternoon before they said she died."

"That would be January 5, 1995, a Thursday afternoon?"

"I believe so, yes."

"And where did you see her?"

"I saw her at her apartment."

"You told LAPD officers that you could not recall the last time you saw Ms. Silberberg when they questioned you only two days after you now claim you saw her, did you not?"

"I don't recall what I told them that day."

"Do you recall the officers asking you if you had been anywhere near her apartment at all the day before she died?"

"I don't recall that. They barged into my house asking all kinds of questions and trying to search my house without telling me what they wanted and what it was I did wrong." Officers Tse, Fritz, and Alvarez exchanged glances standing against the back wall of the courtroom, and some jurors saw their reaction because they immediately turned their attention to the officers as Paul spoke.

"So, your testimony today, almost five months after the day Ms. Silberberg died, is a better recollection than what you told the police barely thirty-six hours after she died?"

Omar objected, but Judge Barney overruled the objection.

"Yes, ma'am, I have had some time to think about everything since it happened. I'm sure of my testimony today."

"In fact, you've had a very long time to think about this and other things you will say in your testimony here today, have you not?" Amy asked.

"Objection," Omar interjected again.

"Overruled," Judge Barney said.

"No, ma'am, I've just been wondering why this is happening to me."

Every time Paul opened his mouth to answer one of Amy's questions, Kenneth readied himself for a disaster. When that failed to happen, Kenneth took a deep breath, but he maintained his outward composure. Meanwhile, Amy seemed to gain strength with every passing question.

She divided her examination into time periods that seemed very easy to remember. After examining Paul on his activities between 9:00 a.m. and 11:00 a.m. that Thursday, she examined him on the next block of three hours, and continued until the end of the day, 11:00 a.m. to 2:00 p.m., 2:00 p.m. to 5:00 p.m., and 5:00 p.m. to 8:00 p.m. In each time frame, Amy identified a witness who contradicted Paul's testimony in the courtroom.

In the 5:00 p.m. to 8:00 p.m. time frame, Paul explained that he went to the club early, entered with his own key, and went into the office to work. He left about 11:00 p.m.

"Why was it that nobody saw you leaving that night?"

"I'm sure somebody saw me. I told my partner I was leaving."

"By your partner you mean Mr. Stone?"

"Yes."

"Does he also go by the name Big?"

"Yes, ma'am."

"Was Mr. Stone the only person who saw you that night?"

"No, there were lots of people in the club."

"But none of the people we asked saw you. Can you tell us why?"

"I wish I could tell you, ma'am. Usually people are seeing me in places I haven't been to. People see my lawyer Mr. Brown and call him Mr. Jackson."

Amy paused in her examination to look at Kenneth for a moment, then turned to look at Paul.

"You look nothing like your attorney, Mr. Jackson," Amy said, "but you do look like this guy here." She produced one of the pictures from the Bank of America ATM and unveiled a large copy of the picture on the easel for the jury. "Is this you?" Amy asked.

"Yes, ma'am," Paul said.

"This was taken at the Bank of America branch on Wilshire Boulevard at 12:04 a.m. on Friday morning. On Thursday night, you went to Santa Monica to see Ms. Silberberg again, didn't you?" Amy asked.

"No, ma'am."

"Your testimony is that you left the club in Downtown Los Angeles and went all the way to Santa Monica Boulevard just to get money from an ATM?"

"No, ma'am. I was in the area to eat."

"You told the officers the night you were arrested that you left the club and went home, isn't that true?"

"Yes, ma'am, I left the club when I was done there and went to an all-night food place on the Westside before going home."

"But that's not what you told the officers who came to your house on Friday night—" Amy started to say. Omar objected that Amy was being argumentative, and Judge Barney overruled the objection.

"Mr. Jackson, you told the officers that you left the club at closing, which you expected them to interpret as closing time for the club, but as soon as you realized they had your ATM receipt for the Santa Monica transaction, you decided to say you meant something else, isn't that true?"

"No, ma'am," Paul said.

"The officers misunderstood you? Is that what you're saying? You told Officer Fritz you never went near Ms. Silberberg's apartment, but the bank is near Ms. Silberberg's apartment, isn't it?"

"No, ma'am, the bank is two miles from Ms. Silberberg's apartment. That's not near."

Amy brought out an aerial photo of the West Los Angeles area with large "X" marks indicating the bank and Goldie's apartment.

"Relative to the club, Cool Jo's Café, and your house, Mr. Jackson, this bank is not near Ms. Silberberg's apartment?"

"I didn't tell the officers that I was measuring the distance relative to anything."

There were many inconsistencies between Paul's testimony and what he had told the police when they came to his house, but Paul made the differences seem inconsequential to him. He testified that he took a taxi to the bank close to Goldie's apartment, when he told the police that he had driven his Mercedes. Asked why he lied to the police, he said he was not trying to lie, but just didn't think of what he was saying because of the way they barged into his apartment. He simply told them what he would usually have done, rather than spend time to think back to exactly what he had done. The clothes he wore in the ATM picture were never found, but he testified that they were in his laundry bag, when he told police he did not know where they were if they were not in his wardrobe. He said he was under a lot of stress at the time. Paul seemed completely unperturbed by the inconsistencies Amy was uncovering and did not seem to make any effort to deny that such inconsistencies existed. This attitude of his became Kenneth's most memorable element of his testimony. Yet, Amy seemed at her best with him. At times, it seemed to Kenneth that she was trying something she had not planned at all and it still came out as though it was well rehearsed.

Noon came quickly. Still Amy could not say she had convinced anyone that Paul Jackson was guilty, and the defense could not say that Paul's decision to testify was a good idea. The jurors stretched and turned their heads to relieve their necks, as if they had been sitting all day rather than an hour. Kate told Amy not to get impatient with Paul.

When the court reconvened after lunch, Amy served notice that she might have Paul Jackson for the rest of the day and part of Tuesday. She resumed the afternoon session by playing messages from Paul Jackson's answering machine the night Goldie Silberberg died. Twenty-nine calls went unanswered from one in the morning to seven o'clock the following night. Big made four of the calls.

"Why was Mr. Stone calling you if he just saw you in the office?"

"I don't know, ma'am. You would have to ask him."

"And how about all the other calls? Are you trying to tell us that you were at home and didn't answer the calls?"

"I don't know what it was about that day, I just didn't wanna be bothered."

"Why didn't you want to be bothered, because you killed someone?" Amy asked, as though she were reflecting on the comment.

"Objection," Omar shouted angrily.

"Sustained," Judge Barney said like one awakened from sleep. "Counsel will refrain from such comments."

"Did you count how many calls there were on that answering machine?"

"No, ma'am. This is the first time I'm hearing the messages. The police took the machine."

"There were twenty-nine calls," Amy said. "How old was Goldie Silberberg, Mr. Jackson?" Amy asked. Again, Omar rose to object, and Judge Barney overruled the objection.

"She was twenty-nine," Paul answered.

Amy asked Paul what he had argued with Goldie about when Ms. Ola saw them together, and Paul said they had not argued. He was trying to tell her that Mr. Pare and Rachel were using and exploiting her. He said Monsieur Arnot was a shady Russian not French and he actually financed Goldie's record before a record company agreed to pick her up. Didi was lying. That man would own everything, and Goldie would have to tour like crazy to make any money for herself.

Amy uncovered the letter sent after Goldie died, which stated that the writer could not get over Goldie.

"This note was found in Ms. Silberberg's unopened mail after she died. Did you write this note?" Amy asked.

"Yes, ma'am."

"To Ms. Silberberg?"

"Yes."

"Was this a warning to her?"

Omar rose again to make another objection and seemed surprised when Judge Barney sustained the objection.

"I want to answer it, your Honor," Paul volunteered. Omar, who was still standing, looked at Kenneth and Cassandra. Judge Barney appeared to be considering Paul's request.

"We will withdraw the objection," Omar said, as he slowly sat down.

"No," Judge Barney said finally. "Counsel, you may rephrase the question."

"Why did you write this letter, Mr. Jackson?"

"It's not a letter. It's a song."

"It's a song?" Amy asked, slightly taken aback. "Like 'Kill the police'?" Amy added, as if to recover from her surprise.

Omar objected successfully again.

"This was a rap song?" Amy asked looking genuinely puzzled at the absurdity of the position.

"No, ma'am, a ballad. Would you like to hear it?" Paul added quickly.

"Move to strike the defendant's question as non-responsive, your Honor," Amy said.

"Motion granted. The court reporter will strike the second part of the witness's answer. Mr. Jackson you must restrict yourself to answering the questions asked, and not ask any questions of your own," Judge Barney instructed Paul.

"Yes, your Honor," Paul said.

"When did you write this letter, Mr. Jackson?" Amy continued.

"I wrote it two days before Goldie died."

"That would be on Wednesday?"

"Yes, ma'am, Wednesday night to be exact."

"Then you saw her on Thursday afternoon, why didn't you give it to her then?"

"I told her about it, but—I didn't want her manager to steal it."

"When did you actually put it in the mail?"

"I didn't," Paul said. "I forgot all about it until it came up in this trial."

"You don't know how it got in the mail?" Amy asked.

"I do. I found out later," Paul said.

"You wrote this letter or song as you put it, because you were angry, didn't you?" Amy asked.

"I wasn't happy with the situation, but I wouldn't say I was angry," Paul answered.

"You were angry that Goldie was not returning your calls?"

"No, ma'am. I was sad because she was not telling me what was going on with my songs," Paul answered, showing the first sign of irritation.

"By not returning your calls?" Amy insisted.

"Yes, ma'am," Paul said, more quietly.

"In fact, between your house, your office, and a cell phone you carried, you called Goldie a total of fifty-six times in the week before she died," Amy said.

"I don't recall calling her that much," Paul said.

Amy produced phone record exhibits and placed them on the easel as she went through the phone calls and counted them.

"You couldn't get over her, no matter what you tried to do, right?" Amy taunted Paul.

The last question lingered without an answer for a short moment as Paul collected his thoughts. He seemed to be losing his nonchalance.

"Mr. Jackson," Amy said.

"No," Paul said.

"No, you couldn't get over her no matter what you tried to do?" Amy asked.

"No, I was just beginning to get over her. The truth about the way I write songs is that when I can write a song at all about anything or someone, it means I've come to terms with the situation, whether it's someone dying or leaving me or cheating on me," Paul said. "The song sets me free."

"You think the song meant you were coming to terms with losing Goldie, even though you meant what you wrote at the time?"

"Yes, ma'am, but not losing Goldie. Letting Mr. Pare have her. I never lost her," Paul said touching his heart.

"What happened between the time you wrote the song on Wednesday night and the following Friday, when Goldie died, to make you snap?"

Omar jumped up angrily to object and Judge Barney sustained the objection.

"When was the last time you saw Ms. Silberberg before you wrote that message?"

"Two or three months before she died."

"That was after she left you?"

"We agreed to go our separate ways."

"But she managed to do that while you spent Wednesday night scribbling notes about how you couldn't get over her no matter how you tried?"

Judge Barney asked Amy to rephrase the question even before Omar could object.

"When you met Goldie on Thursday morning, did she call you or you called her?"

"She called me."

"What time did she call you?"

"I don't recall exactly, but I think it was about ten a.m."

"And what time did you get to her house?"

"About two p.m., ma'am."

Amy walked over to her desk and looked at her notes and wrote on a piece of paper.

"That was when you borrowed her car to return it that night?"

"No, ma'am," Paul seemed to frown on this question.

"And what did she call you to tell you?"

"She said she'd been in London, that's why she couldn't call me back. She said her record was due out in a couple of months, and she was calling it 'Footsie' as a tribute to us—what we started."

"Did you ask her why she didn't just pick up the phone in London to return one of your numerous calls to tell you what she just told you in person?"

Paul appeared unprepared to respond for the first time since Amy started examining him. He tilted his head as though the question Amy asked had just occurred to him, but before he could respond, Amy spoke again.

"I'm through with this witness for now, your Honor," Amy said and returned to her table to sit down.

•••

THE TIME WAS 3:35 p.m. Kenneth and Cassandra wanted to take Paul off the witness stand as quickly as possible. Kenneth wrote a note to Omar saying they should not keep him on the stand too long. Omar replied, "I know now why he wanted to testify."

"Good afternoon, Mr. Jackson."

"Good afternoon, Mr. Jones."

"Why did you write that song?"

"Because I wanted to get Goldie's attention."

"You believed she would call you if she knew of the song in the mail?"

"Yes, sir. I left messages, sent people, but she didn't get back to me. Mr. Pare was brainwashing her against me, then I found out she'd gone to London," Paul said.

"Now, I believe earlier in the DA's examination, you wanted to explain how the song got in the mail. Could you explain that to us, please?" Omar asked.

"Yes, sir. You see, we run a nightclub and a recording studio, sometimes. So, we don't receive a lot of people in our office for business. You want to talk business with me, I could say why don't you stop by the nightclub on Thursday night or Friday night or come by the recording studio? We don't have regular secretary or receptionist type people. We don't need them regularly. So, we hire this girl to come three days a week, nine a.m. to three p.m. Monday, Wednesday, and Friday. I wrote the song on Wednesday night. Then Goldie called on Thursday to say she went to London, that's why she couldn't call, so it was no big deal. But I just didn't take the envelope with the notes off my table, so the part-time girl thought it was there for her to mail out. That's how it happened," Paul said.

Omar placed the note back on the easel.

"You said the letter was a song, Mr. Jackson?"

"Yes, sir."

"But People will say it doesn't look like a song."

"If Goldie was here, she would tell you it's a song."

"Why is that?"

"Because I always hid the lyrics of new songs in letters I wrote her. And because if she were here, I'd sing it for her."

341

"Why don't you sing it anyway?"

Amy objected, but Judge Barney overruled the objection. There was relief on Paul's face when Omar asked him to sing the song. It appeared to be the moment Paul had bet upon. When he cleared his voice, the look on Amy's face was of derision, but as he began to sing, she turned to look at the jurors, all but one of whom was looking at Paul. Only one man was looking at Amy, the foreman, and the expression on his face struck Amy as saying, "How could you?" She looked at Officer Gonzalez who was simultaneously looking at her at the same time. Amy looked up the name of the juror by his position in jury box and scribbled a note for herself, "Mr. Gale!"

Paul focused his attention upward, as though he were singing to a higher being, and he closed his eyes a lot, and his voice filled the room, rising with edge and descending with light gentle vibrato. When he was done, tears rolled down his cheeks.

I always thought
That I could do
Anything, I put my mind to

But I can't get
Over you
No matter what, I try to do

I can't lie
It's not right
I'm losing my mind over you. [Don't make me lose my mind over you]

"Thank you," Omar said, offering Paul a box of tissues from the defense's table. "We have nothing further, your Honor," Omar said.

Amy quickly stood up to follow up on Omar Jones's examination. It was evident that she wanted to finish off Paul Jackson.

"Counsel, we don't have enough time for your further examination before we adjourn for the day," Judge Barney told Amy.

"I have just one question, your Honor," Amy pleaded.

"I stand corrected, we have more than enough time," Judge Barney said. "I hope…" he added. A juror chuckled.

"Mr. Jackson, can you write down the song you just sang right now? The exact lyrics just as you sang it."

"Yes, ma'am."

"Can we have some foundation as to why counsel is making my client take her notes for her?" Omar said.

"Counsel," Judge Barney said looking at Amy as she approached Paul carrying a notepad and pen. "The court reporter has accurately transcribed his testimony."

"I will provide foundation in a moment, your Honor, but can we have the defendant finish transcribing first?"

Judge Barney agreed. Then Paul looked up to say he was done writing.

"The lyrics are obviously very different from the note he claimed was the same as the song, and they may yet be different from what the court reporter has transcribed, when he writes them down."

"Very well," Judge Barney said.

Amy requested that the lyrics Paul wrote on the stand be marked and admitted into evidence. Omar did not object, and Judge Barney granted the request. The court recessed for the day. One or two jurors smiled as their eyes swept past the defense table.

"Thanks," Paul said to Kenneth when he returned to the defense table. Cassandra paused to look at him as though he had just managed a rare human connection with her.

•••

HELEN SILBERBERG AND RABBI Eli joined Amy at her office after adjournment to tell her that they had had enough of the trial. They were leaving that evening on the last plane to Seattle. The news felt like it punctured a pressure chamber in Amy's veins and heart that forced all the anger, anxiety, and frustration that Amy had while examining Paul Jackson to slip out through a tiny hole that both relieved and weakened her. She sat down like she could not bear to stand and felt the tears pour down her cheeks.

"Oh, Amy dear, you have done everything you could for me. None of this was going to bring my Goldie back, and win or lose, he will rot alive. I won't get any kind of satisfaction from the outcome. I'm just glad we made him answer for what he did. Whatever happens to him, I'm still alone, and I have to go back and start putting myself together." She put an arm around Amy's shoulder.

"You fought from the heart," Rabbi Eli said. "Thank you."

Amy wiped her eyes and blew her nose.

"I'm sorry for…This was not how I saw this trial happening."

"Don't worry about it; we should go back home now," Rabbi Eli said.

Amy stood up and hugged Helen tightly and held on. When they finally let go, Helen, too, was wiping her eyes.

Driving home with Alana, Amy told Alana what Helen said about having had enough of the trial. Alana could not agree more. If Amy's recent bout of nausea checked out as nothing for Alana to worry about, Alana would return to the Bay Area in a couple of days.

CHAPTER FORTY-FOUR
An Unfinished Conversation

CASSANDRA HAD LITTLE HOPE for the motion she had prepared for the close of the prosecution's case in chief, but she made it anyway. She argued that the state had failed to show any evidence that Paul Jackson killed Goldie Silberberg. Judge Barney acknowledged her presentation and denied the motion.

The defense witnesses went very fast but for Dr. Ike Ogan, the defense's forensic pathologist. Kenneth spent even more time than Amy did with Dr. Kio listing his training and education until it appeared that Dr. Ogan had replaced Dr. Kio as the most educated, experienced, or smartest witness to take the stand. Dr. Ogan insisted the police conclusion that someone suffocated Goldie Silberberg was premature at the time they reached that conclusion. He insisted the police could not have ruled out an allergic reaction or such as a cause of Goldie's suffocation until they removed the throat organs and examined the interior of the cranium. When Amy pointed out that a subsequent examination of the removed throat and the interior of the cranium was consistent with the earlier conclusion, Dr. Ogan was not impressed. He stated that the problem with premature conclusions is that the initial conclusion might have colored the subsequent determination. He acknowledged Dr. Kio was respected in the field of pathology and did a good job, but deplored his lack of control over the pathology investigation.

Aside from Dr. Ogan, the rest of the witnesses seemed like a mop up exercise to Amy. They added nothing new to the evidence. Yet, Cassandra saw each of them as planting seeds of doubt, one witness at a time.

•••

AFTER LUNCH ON WEDNESDAY afternoon, Kenneth and Cassandra were sitting together in the hallway, away from their clients. Amy walked over to them.

"Hey," Amy said to both of them.

"Hi," Cassandra said to Amy with a smile and quickly added, "I'll give you two some time alone, no hurry. We'll hold the proceeding if we have to," Cassandra said and walked away. She took the Jackson women into the courtroom.

"Kate said you were sick and Cassandra knows I have been trying to find a private moment with you."

"Oh, does she?"

"I realize that you don't want to talk about personal matters, but are you well?"

"I'm fine. Just exhaustion and lack of sleep, I guess."

"I'm sorry…This is almost over."

"Thanks, I'm glad to know you still care after everything. Neda told me I've been mean to you."

"I liked her the moment I met her. The way she ceded her evening with you to me."

"Oh, that wasn't for you. She's convinced Iranian women are women of color, so every opportunity she gets, she tries to prove it."

Kenneth grinned, and so did Amy.

"I hope I never draw you in another case my whole career."

Amy waited a moment before answering him.

"Me, too," Amy said with smile, and brushed his arm, running her palm up and down it. "But let's finish this trial before we finish this conversation."

•••

JUDGE BARNEY INFORMED THE jury that the trial was closed to taking evidence and the parties were ready to make their closing arguments. He explained that the deputy district attorney Amy Wilson would make her arguments first, and Paul Jackson's attorney would then follow. After that, the deputy district attorney might choose to speak again.

He read some of the jury instructions regarding closing arguments and burden of proof and then turned the floor over to Amy. Kenneth tried not to look at her as she stood to address the jurors.

Amy moved the television in the courtroom closer to the jurors but did not turn it on immediately. She thanked them for their participation and their patience. "Your timeliness and the absence of even a shred of misconduct is a testament to your commitment," Amy told them.

Having lauded the jurors only briefly, Amy plunged into her argument. "No one had the motive, the opportunity, and the means to commit this crime as Paul Jackson did. He was unhappy with Goldie, not because she left him," Amy explained, then paused. Winning had suddenly taken on a different perspective. Kate was sitting behind the prosecution table watching her.

"Paul Jackson's anger was most palpable because he thought Goldie left him for Mr. Pare. For Paul Jackson, it was a measure of his worth in a sense, and to him it meant that he could not measure up to someone who couldn't write the songs for Goldie, as he had, after all that he had sacrificed. Paul Jackson's arrogance wanted to own Goldie. He saw her right to choose whom she wanted to be with as exploiting him. But the facts will show, and the records prove, that no one exploited Paul Jackson, least of all Goldie Silberberg. Rather, it was Paul who exploited Goldie. He felt incapable of winning her unless he also made her promises he could not keep. He invited her to sing his songs in his studios, perform in his nightclub. He built up false hopes for her and sought to destroy her when she realized what he was doing to her. Goldie Silberberg became successful the moment her songs reached the industry Paul Jackson had been claiming he sent the songs to. And Paul Jackson snapped." Amy snapped her fingers simultaneously with the last word and paused.

Amy then went through the evidence, explaining them and discarding Paul's explanation on the stand. Amy listed all the evidence presented in the trial in bullet form on a large board. The last item on the list was Paul Jackson's testimony. When she got to Paul Jackson's testimony, she began to sing the first two lines of Bob Marley's song, "War."

"Ladies and gentlemen, that was a song Bob Marley wrote from a speech Emperor Haile Selassie of Ethiopia gave to the United Nations in 1963. Bob Marley simply saw that speech, liked it, and set it to music. Musicians have been doing this for ages, from the Psalms of the Bible to the speeches of heads of state, but not to save a murderous soul. Paul Jackson may be a good musician and a talented songwriter, and when he is caught in a clear lie, he tries to use that age-old practice of converting words to music to his advantage and turn his angry, hateful letter into song. He did that in his cell, where he's had a lot of time to make up his story. He probably came up with the idea after his attorneys told him not to testify as you all were told last Friday. He needs to be sent back to the pen to think some more about what he has done."

Amy stopped talking, walked over to her table and picked up a transcript of Paul Jackson's testimony. She walked over to the television and video player and turned them on.

"What was Paul Jackson's testimony about?" Amy asked rhetorically before Goldie Silberberg's video appeared on the screen. She stepped away from the television to stand by the defense table. When Goldie's image appeared on the screen, Amy pressed the mute button on the remote control, and left the television without sound. "Paul Jackson would say just about anything to save his neck because Goldie Silberberg cannot speak here to tell you the truth. So, the defendant tells you that Goldie Silberberg called him, and he says that she told him she had just returned from London. But who will speak for Goldie on all these claims?" Amy asked. "You should. Let your verdict be the voice a society gives this talented daughter, taken too soon from the brink of success by the wickedness of jealous rage now pretending to be an oppressed Black man."

Amy stopped after speaking these words and watched Goldie's video without the volume. "Ladies and gentlemen, you've heard this wicked man sing, now hear the angel he took away," Amy said and turned up the volume as Goldie began to sing "A Past that Breathes."

If you could reach into the past
And mend a broken heart
Changing the path
Of a life
Why don't you?

And if all that you'd have to say
To ease someone's pain
Is that you're sorry
Honey,

What stops you?
You may have a past that breathes
And it is still hurting
Why don't you do something
To ease its pain."

"Goldie Silberberg, ladies and gentlemen," Amy said, "she would have been a star, but for the heinous act of the defendant."

She turned off the television and sat down.

•••

"Don't rush," Cassandra whispered in Kenneth's ear as he stood up to make his own closing argument. Kenneth also thanked the jury and acknowledged it had not been an easy trial to follow, suggesting the evidence could have been clearer. He immediately started to attack inconsistencies in the police record.

"When you think of who had the best opportunity to commit this crime, you must start your list with identifying those persons whose semen were found on Goldie's bed. The police did not identify any of these people, and they have not explained how these people could not have been involved in the crime."

"Motive for committing this crime is anyone's guess. Paul had a stronger motive for keeping Goldie alive. She was going to be a star with Paul's music. Why would he kill her with such a motive? Paul Jackson's songs were going to climb the charts, a vehicle he could use to get other successful acts as well. It didn't matter who managed Goldie or whom she slept with, she was always going to be a gem to Paul. Think about it. Think about the title she gave her record, this record that was the culmination of her life's dream—what did she call it? She called it 'Footsie.' You heard Mr. Pare's testimony that there was no song on her record with that title. And you also heard Mr. Pare say that the record company tried to make her pick a different title. But she refused. She wanted to name that record like it was a child she had with Paul; in a sense, it was their offspring. So, she gave it the name that Paul gave her. What bound Goldie and Paul was far more than these officers could understand. Their relationship was far deeper than you and I could sit here and speculate about. Yes, they had disagreements, show me a relationship that doesn't. Yes, they fought, show me passionate lovers who don't and I will show you a passion that is false. Dredge up all you want from their past, but you will never dredge up facts that amount to Paul killing Goldie."

Kenneth caught the first full sight of the gallery when he turned around to place an exhibit on the easel. Nancy was sitting with Paul's mother and Jo. Tiffany, Jed, and Anthony had also walked into the courtroom sometime during Amy's closing. Kenneth placed the police report on the easel and highlighted the time of the report.

"By 11:54 p.m. on the night the body was found," Kenneth explained, "Paul Jackson was already charged, convicted, and sentenced in the minds of Officers Fritz, Gonzalez, and Tse and their colleagues. All that remained was how to sell his conviction to you. This trial for them was a formality, an inconvenience brought about by the United States Constitution. It is up to you to make it abundantly clear that the protections of the US Constitution is neither a formality nor an inconvenience, but the very foundation on which we all either stand or fall together regardless of race, creed, or class." Kenneth noted that the medical examiner, Dr. Ebenezer Kio, had not examined the body of the deceased by the time the police concluded that Paul Jackson had killed Goldie Silberberg. Dr. Ogan, the forensic pathologist for the defense, had made it clear that the police should not have ruled out other causes of asphyxiation until they opened the skull and the throat of the Ms. Silberberg.

"They want you to rubber stamp their rush to judgment, their reaffirmation of the worst stereotype in our society, the same old lies about Black and white in America. But they forgot one thing: due process. Today it is Paul Jackson's due process that they arbitrarily deny, tomorrow it could be anyone, maybe yours or mine." He began to recount to the jury his experience with a woman he fell in love with in college. "We were both kids really, but we were fully aware of the stigma our culture placed on the affection we so clearly felt. One day, in November of our last year in college, we came back from a comedy concert and, for the first time I mustered the courage to tell her how I felt about her. And she just said it wasn't going to work. No whys...no ifs...no buts...just 'it won't work.' That was how she ended it. Afterward, everything they said Paul Jackson did, I also did. I wrote letters and did not have the courage to mail them to her. I called several times, and when her answering machine came on, I hung up. I drove out to her house and parked in front of her house for a long time because I was too afraid to come in uninvited, and I just wanted to ask why or to catch a glimpse of her. Little did I know that one day everything I did would be enough evidence to charge me with murder. Was it smart of me? No, but is that alone enough for murder? Again, the answer is 'no.' Paul Jackson and Goldie Silberberg gave love a chance. Unlike my college friend and I, they had maturity on their side, they knew what to expect, and they knew love was worth every bit of that stigma they were going to face. What happened to Goldie was tragic, but what Goldie and Paul had was very true and special. The two events are not related. Don't let anyone convince you that they are, or that Goldie made a mistake when she fell in love with Paul Jackson because it just does not work."

Next, Kenneth addressed the absence of Rachel Johnson. He told the jurors that the prosecution had the burden of proof, which included the burden of coming forward with the evidence and Rachel Johnson was clearly someone out there who could shed light on who really killed Goldie Silberberg, but the prosecutor had failed to call her. "You must ask yourselves why she is not a witness in this case," Kenneth said and then proceeded to examine how Rachel Johnson figured into the testimonies of key witnesses Fritz, Conrad Wetstone, Ola Mohammed, and Didi Pare. He again examined the evidence of sexual activities at the scene of the crime and the fact that the police could not identify the participants. "If anyone was close enough to Goldie to identify those participants, Rachel Johnson was; in fact, Rachel Johnson got Goldie her big break because she sent Goldie's music to Didi Pare." Kenneth then put a diagram on the easel showing the timeline of Paul's alleged movements on the night that Goldie died, based on the testimony of the police and various witnesses. He particularly noted that the medical examiner placed Goldie's murder at about 3:00 a.m., but the last time Paul was seen in Santa Monica was midnight.

"Look at the evidence. The police don't know the person or persons who undressed Goldie Silberberg, but they have someone's semen in her. They don't know when Paul Jackson supposedly went to her apartment that night. They don't know who killed Goldie Silberberg, they only want her Black boyfriend to pay for it. If you convict Paul Jackson on this evidence, you convict us all for believing in this system of justice with all the attendant protections of the United States Constitution."

•••

AMY WAS CERTAIN KENNETH had not waited outside her apartment after the incident in Austin when she told him a relationship between them would not work. Kenneth did not even have a car in college. Perhaps he substituted coming to her house in Los Angeles for what happened in Texas. But Amy knew he had called her several times without leaving messages.

She had not thought of what happened that November night in Austin in a long time. She was touched by the recollection. Yet the argument that Paul Jackson and Kenneth Brown could be the same people was appalling to her. She wanted to destroy it.

On rebuttal, Amy told the jury to look again at the evidence. "There was only one person with the motive, the opportunity, and the angry propensity to kill Goldie Silberberg, and that was Paul Jackson. His footprints where all over her house, his ATM was withdrawing money around the corner from her about the time of her death, at midnight—she died at three in the morning. He had clearly had enough to drink. You heard the defendant confirm what Ms. Ola said, that he went to Goldie's house at two p.m. When he said that, I could not believe he confirmed it and I had to go back to my table and look at my notes, because Ms. Ola also said that he left immediately after an older gentleman walked in as they were arguing. So the defendant never had the opportunity to go to the guest bedroom and drink two bottles of beer that he never put in the trash. In fact, he forgot he left that evidence there that night because he was running for dear life after killing an innocent woman. Now, his attorneys could have cleared up the fact that he came to the house when Ms. Ola said he was there, but also left when Ms. Ola said he left. His attorneys never asked him when he got the chance to drink that beer in the guest bedroom. As you sit in that jury room, you must accept that there is no dispute in this case that it was the defendant's fingerprints and DNA on those bottles. If he drank that beer in the afternoon when he was there, don't you think Goldie would have at least put them in the trash? This man, Paul Jackson, lives about twenty miles away in the Valley and works another twenty miles away in Downtown, and he was in West LA, pulling money. Obviously, he was planning to stay a while.

"And who is making this case about race? Them!" Amy said pointing at the defense table. "No one said Paul Jackson's relationship with Goldie was wrong, but the evidence shows he could not deal with it when she moved on. His own letter to her said so. He thought he could but realized he couldn't. Even if you buy his story that the letter was not written in a blind rage. His lackey finds the letter after he has been arrested and decides to confuse things by putting it in the mail?

"Do not believe for one second that anyone is coming after Paul Jackson because he is Black. There is just too much of that going around this town that when we abuse the claim, we take it away from those who legitimately have a case to make for it. There's a big difference between the woman Mr. Brown knew in college and Goldie Silberberg. There is a Grand Canyon-sized difference between the two women, and that is this: Goldie Silberberg is dead, and the woman in Mr. Brown's story still breathes. She might one day meet Mr. Brown again and say I wish I told you why I said it wouldn't work or if there was anything we could have done about it, but I'm here now. Paul Jackson took away any chance Goldie had to love again, even to love him in the future. That was how possessive his rage was."

Amy gave the jury statistics on domestic violence, murders of spouses and lovers, and crimes between family members to explain why people in the inner circles of a victim's relationships are usually looked at first in most investigations as persons of interest.

"In Paul Jackson's case, he went from being a person of interest to being a prime suspect for one reason, and one reason only: He was so guilty it took him four months—from January to May—to come up with an alibi!" Amy said. About Rachel Johnson, Amy said the defense wanted the jury to go off on a wild-goose chase rather than focus on their client. "If the defense thought Rachel Johnson could shed light on their case, the defense should have called her themselves. They knew where she lived, they have her name, the police report gave them all they needed to make her a witness. They want to turn this case into sexual perversity in Los Angeles, we don't. None of that evidence that was found on the bed had anything to do with Goldie."

Amy then went through some of the jury instructions the jurors would need to guide their decision. She explained the burden of proof instruction, the circumstantial evidence definition, the admission against interest, the absence of evidence, and availability of a party, among other instructions.

When she sat down, the two closing arguments had taken the proceeding past the lunch recess. Judge Barney read out a few more jury instructions and recessed for lunch.

Paul Jackson sat frozen in his seat. In the audience his sister and mother could barely hold their tears. Anthony, Jed, and Tiffany weaved a path through the audience in the opposite direction of traffic to join Kenneth and Cassandra at counsel table. Melissa joined Kate, Gonzalez, and Amy. As Kenneth, Cassandra, Anthony, Jed, and Tiffany began to leave the courtroom, Kenneth excused himself and went over to Amy.

"I wish your college friend were here to hear your closing argument. She might have given you a second chance," Kate said smiling at him. They were speaking for the first time.

"I will take that as a compliment," Kenneth replied.

"You should. She never beats around the bush," Amy said to Kenneth, and Kate looked at Amy curiously. Amy introduced Melissa to Kenneth, and Kate and Melissa left them alone.

CHAPTER FORTY-FIVE
A Long Embrace

A FTER RETURNING FROM LUNCH, Judge Barney gave the case to the jury, and the jurors marched into their private room to deliberate. This was the conference room where Amy, Cassandra, and Kenneth had met the first week of trial. Usually, the lawyers made themselves available during jury deliberations to be called if the jurors had questions or the verdict was returned. Lawyers waited in the hallways with their clients' families or gave the court's clerk a number where they could be reached when needed, provided they could be in court within thirty minutes. Kenneth and Cassandra chose the latter option. Nancy and Paul's family sat in the hallway and waited. Amy returned to her office, across the street from the courthouse.

At 5:30 p.m. Nancy returned to the hotel in a more somber mood than Kenneth had seen her in since the trial began. "The jurors did not look like they were close to a verdict," she said. "They came out of the courtroom looking like they just walked out of a morgue, when at trial they would come and go in groups of two or three chatting. Now, everyone is on their own, walking out separately, like they had a fight."

"That isn't necessarily a bad sign," Kenneth told her. He had worried that they might return a verdict quickly, which might mean they agreed on guilt. With Nancy's explanation, he felt that there had at least been a disagreement in the deliberation and his first wave of panic subsided. He began to look forward to seeing Amy again and told Nancy he would be keeping the hotel suite until the end of the week.

He waited an hour before calling Amy to give her time to get back from work. Amy said she had been expecting his call when he asked if she could meet with him. Something in her voice told him she looked forward to seeing him as well.

"Give me an hour to jump in the shower and get dressed, then come over," she said. Kenneth decided to take a shower as well.

In exactly an hour, he met her in the lobby of her building. She was wearing a long black skirt, ankle length boots, and a turtleneck top with a silk scarf. She carried her jacket and a flat black purse. Her hair was neatly pulled back in a bun.

"Where are we going?" she asked.

"Are you worried about being seen together because of the case?"

"No, I'm done with that case. Don't even mention it again."

He could not agree more. They drove silently until they got on the Santa Monica freeway from Downtown Los Angeles, then started talking to fill their awkward silence. He asked about her visit to the hospital again, what the doctors had told her. "Nothing new," she told him and in turn asked about his dad. He could not return after the first week like he promised, Kenneth explained.

"Were you disappointed?" she asked.

He paused. It was the first time he had thought of his dad's absence in that manner. A part of him had avoided the disappointment of even thinking of whether he was disappointed. "I don't know but I told him it will soon be on Court TV anyway," he said.

"Don't be disappointed. My mom couldn't stand it either. She said it's like watching a great thriller with your child in it, not knowing if she is going to make it out okay."

"Makes sense," Kenneth said. "My dad had issues with hypertension during his visit, that was partly why he had to leave. He wanted to see his regular physician." He recalled they could not stop talking when they had met at Cool Jo's Café. Suddenly they were like strangers, and it did not bode well for the evening he wanted with her. He drove to Santa Monica beach and found parking along the street. Taking a small bag out of the trunk of his rented car, he led the way across a sandy path toward the water. There were park benches along a running track that formed a sort of boundary around the beach. Couples were lying on towels and blankets they'd spread out on the sand, and in the distance, young people were walking barefoot at the edge of the water and playing with the waves that came crashing in.

"Why did you pick this place?" she asked.

"I wanted a quiet place to talk," he said.

She smiled. As soon as they got on the beach, her boots came off and she carried them in her hands. She walked ahead of him, her bare feet treading lightly. There was a seductive lightness about her when she began to relax, and he missed that more than anything when they were apart. The sound of waves coming onto the shore and pulling away got louder until she stopped at a fairly isolated part of the beach and turned to him.

"How's this place?" she asked, dropping her shoes on the ground.

"It's quite a large beach, are you sure?" he replied, breathing harder than she.

"I'm positive," she said.

"Good."

She spread her coat and dropped her purse on it.

"No, I brought something to sit on," he said and brought out hotel swimming pool towels from the bag he was carrying, spreading out one for her and one for himself. He also brought out a bottle of red wine and wine glasses. "I don't know if drinking here is legal. So, I hope we don't get in trouble."

"That's okay. I know people," she said.

"Let's hope the City of Santa Monica gives a damn about the people you know. In the meantime, we'll stick to the plan."

"Which is?" she asked.

"Run like hell when the authorities show up."

She laughed. He poured a glass of wine for her and one for himself, and toasted the end of the trial. They were at a slightly elevated part of the beach, but only about twenty yards from the water. The moon was not luminous enough to reflect the color of the sea, just a dark bed stretched out into the horizon. Constant as though it was measured, the sound of the waves added a hypnotic mood to a gaze into the darkness. They sat quietly, starring out to sea.

"You're a pretty good lawyer," she said without looking at him. He laughed because the comment was so unexpected, and she turned her body to face him.

"You are not so bad yourself," he told her. They began to kiss. When they stopped kissing it was out of sheer exhaustion. The towels could not keep the sand from her hair or even her body. He tried to dust the sand off her shoulders.

"Wasn't there something you wanted to talk about?" she asked.

"It's okay if you don't want to talk about it. Let's wipe the slate clean," he said.

"I'd rather not. I grew up a lot these past few weeks," Amy said.

"How do you mean?"

"I don't know that I can tell you how…After that incident where your client's father went to see my boss, I started retching in the toilet. At first, I thought it was just rage. Then I found myself throwing up in the morning."

"Are you pregnant?" he asked.

"That was the question on my mind. Usually, I would panic. Gosh, I'm not ready. I'm not married. I'm Catholic. What am I going to tell Alana? And all these thoughts would go through my mind, but there was none of that. I just sat there on the bathroom floor thinking about me. How to take care of myself first instead of worrying about whether I would have to go this alone. Not 'oh God, please forgive me,' but 'oh God, please bless me'; not 'what would my mother think,' but 'what would my child need.' It sounds like really simple common sense, but it was a massive paradigm shift in my thought process. I was so much, so much more calm and deliberate. And I…"

Her voice began to break up as she came near tears, and looked away from him, out to sea again. She wiped her eyes and appeared to force a smile, then turned to look at him.

"What did the doctors say?" he asked after she seemed to have collected herself.

"You see…you have looked right past me to find out if the doctors said I was pregnant. Never mind my sob story, tell me what I really want to hear. Who knocked you up?"

"No, no," he protested.

"Yes, yes, admit it."

"Okay, but that's because you're here and I can see you are well now. And you have not touched your glass of wine."

"The doctor said I was fine, thank you."

"Did he confirm that you are pregnant?"

"Yes," Amy said looking right into his eyes. They were quiet for a moment. "Why don't you ask me what you really want to ask me, Ken?"

"There were three inseparable friends whose destinies seemed inextricably intertwined. Now you and Elaine are having babies, it is only fair that I should think I am having one, too," he said, rather sorrowfully. Amy chuckled.

"When you put it that way, it is hard not to forgive you for asking. But you'd have to find that out for yourself, like Elaine and I did for ourselves."

She considered him for a while and looked away into the distance.

"About the way I treated you after the weekend we spent together, I'm sorry, but you cannot see me through the prism of anything that happened in this case or with anyone else in your community. You must see me only through your experiences with me and me alone. I'm sorry I hurt you."

"I understand," he said.

"No, you don't. Your father came to see me after that incident. He told me how they vandalized your car. How your mother had called him to come to you finally, and how he knew that he could not convince you to do what your mother wanted, but that if you loved me, then I could."

"That's how you knew that the ACB was also known as the Anti-Christ Brotherhood?"

Amy grinned.

"Big thought I told you that, but I didn't even know that about them."

He finished his wine and lay down again on the sand, pulling her on top of himself and they started kissing again. Minutes later, their lips sore from kissing, and their derrières aching from sitting, they dusted each other's bodies and headed back to the car. She would not go back to the hotel with him and he didn't want to go to her place until the verdict was returned. This was why he waited for her in the lobby when he went to pick her up.

•••

ON THURSDAY AFTERNOON, THE jurors had an interesting request for the judge. They wanted Conrad Wetstone's testimony read back. Judge Barney called the lawyers to the courtroom to explain the request and hear any objections.

Cassandra and Kenneth both appeared with Paul Jackson, but Amy was not in court. Kate appeared for her. All counsel acquiesced and the court reporter read the testimony to the jurors.

Several jurors took notes. Kenneth continually looked over his shoulder, expecting Amy to walk in on the proceeding. As soon as the jurors returned to their deliberations after the reading, Kenneth and Cassandra explained the situation to Paul and his family.

"In this case, the jurors have asked for a reading of the most crucial witness' testimony and that, in my opinion, means they understood the facts presented in the case very well," Cassandra said to Paul. Outside the courtroom, Kenneth explained the same factors to Sister Ramatu and her daughters.

"Conrad Wetstone could be an advantage to either side. We thought he was pivotal to the DA's theory of the case because it seemed logical that he knew there was a dead body in Goldie's bathroom before he went to the apartment," Kenneth explained.

"I'm convinced it's good for Paul," Sister Ramatu said.

"Keep your head up, Kenny. You've got this jury thinking, and that's good. They didn't just bite what the cops were feeding them, hook, line, and sinker," Jo said.

Kenneth nodded. She hugged him like she would Paul and continued her vigil with her mother, sitting on the bench in the hallway outside the courtroom. Kenneth excused himself from them.

When the jurors came out of their deliberations for the afternoon recess, Sister Ramatu and Jo were sitting in the hallway, and as the jurors left for the day, they were still there, sitting in silent prayer. The second day of jury deliberation passed without a verdict.

Kenneth pondered the outcome of the trial after the jurors left on Thursday without a verdict. Ten hours of jury deliberations seemed both encouraging and disturbing in equal parts. What were they talking about in that conference room? Which particular items of evidence were they stuck upon? Had some not paid attention during the trial? How were they divided? Are women against women? Were whites against Blacks? Minorities on the same side or either side? He sat in his hotel suite, another wave of panic swirling inside him. As much as Kenneth feared a conviction, he also feared a hung jury, which would clearly mean a new trial. He would not represent Paul Jackson again in a new trial, and he would try to dissuade Amy from serving as the prosecuting attorney.

CHAPTER FORTY-SIX
To Everything...A Time

ON FRIDAY, THE COURT directed all counsel in the case to appear after lunch. Kenneth believed the jurors had reached a verdict. He and Cassandra arrived early. Nancy and Paul's family were in the hallway waiting for them, as were a group of newsmen and camera men with press badges. Paul's father was with his entourage, and the cameras seemed particularly interested in him. Omar stopped by to say he was in a courtroom on another floor and would be joining them as soon as he could. Alvarez, Tse, Fritz, and Gonzalez were with Amy, Kate, and Melissa. Many of Amy's colleagues were in the courtroom as well sitting in the gallery. Melissa had alerted Andre, Amy's former boss, before lunch and he joined them while the court was in session. The news vans also returned.

The clerk of the court asked the jurors to wait in their deliberation room. This signaled to the lawyers that the jurors had not reached a verdict. Kenneth informed Paul's family immediately. With everyone seated in the courtroom, the judge explained his purpose for calling the parties back.

"It looks like we are headed for a hung jury," Judge Barney explained. "Before the jurors went to lunch, they informed the clerk that they were seriously deadlocked, and it didn't look like they could do any better. They said their division has held along the same lines for about a day now. We've heard loud arguments at times through the walls. So, it certainly isn't that they haven't tried. I wanted to see what you as counsel want to do."

"Do we know how many are on either side of this deadlock?" Amy asked. "Without knowing which side they're leaning toward, of course," she added quickly.

"No," Judge Barney said with a smile.

"What does the court recommend?" Cassandra asked.

"I would like to call them in, and just as Ms. Wilson here has suggested, ask them to tell us how they are divided in terms of numbers, without disclosing how they're inclined to vote on the verdict. If they are fairly evenly split along the middle, I'll tell them I have no desire to let them go until well into next week and send them back. If their division is rather lopsided, where only two or three jurors are holding up a verdict, then we'll send them back for the day, and come back here to declare a mistrial at the end of the court day."

Cassandra was inclined to accept this arrangement, when Kenneth started to argue a contrary position.

"Your Honor, it would seem to me that if the jurors have only one or two people in one position, then we are closer to a verdict than we are to a mistrial and should give them more time for that position," Kenneth argued.

"Perhaps you're right, counsel. My experience, though, is that one or two holdouts after more than a dozen hours of deliberation starts to create a mob atmosphere in the jury room. And if the two holdouts change their minds, they do not do so entirely of their own volition," Judge Barney explained.

"Still," Kenneth persisted, "it has been a grueling process. These jurors have been sitting here for the better part of three weeks and we have barely given them two days to deliberate. Can we give them until the middle of next week?"

"Why don't we ask them what they feel they can achieve with more time. And if their response is encouraging, we'll give them until the middle of next week," Judge Barney said.

"That will be agreeable to the People," Amy joined quickly. Kenneth looked at Cassandra, who shrugged her shoulders.

"We will go along with that as well," Kenneth informed the court.

"Let's get the jurors in here, then," Judge Barney directed the clerk. As the jurors walked to their box, their foreman stood aside as each took a seat in the chair assigned on the first day of trial.

After the jurors were seated, Judge Barney asked their foreman to stand again. "Without telling us how each side is inclined to vote on the verdict, Mr. Foreman, can you tell us how many jurors you have on each side of your deadlock?"

"Yes, your Honor," the foreman said. "We are eleven and one."

Several people in the gallery gasped. Judge Barney locked his eyes on Kenneth.

"Very well," said Judge Barney. "I have discussed the situation with counsel and we would like you to go back and see what you can do further. This was not an easy trial. There was a lot of evidence and maybe more time would do you good. And perhaps, if you have this weekend to rest, you may come back refreshed with a different perspective on your prior positions."

"Your Honor," the jury foreman began, "I don't see how that's possible. We've looked at all the evidence in this case, twice. We've gone over the testimony. Everyone took really good notes. Everyone remembers what they were doing when anything was said in the trial. We know the issues. We were born with them. This jury is permanently deadlocked."

As he spoke, some jurors nodded their heads.

"Nevertheless, I will send you back to continue your deliberations, and we will see where you are at the end of the day," Judge Barney said.

"Thank you, your Honor," the foreman said, and led the jurors back to the room to continue their deliberation.

"Let's reconvene at four p.m.," Judge Barney said to the rest of the courtroom.

Almost immediately, Paul's family crowded Kenneth and Cassandra in the courtroom. Paul was speechless as the sheriff led him away.

"How did you know the jury was lopsided, Ken," Jo asked.

"When the judge started to sound like he was doing us a favor by calling a quick mistrial if the deadlock was lopsided, I thought he suspected that most of the jurors were leaning toward us."

Paul's mother began to cry. That was when Kenneth noticed that Nancy was not standing with them. He looked outside the huddle surrounding him and noticed Nancy just leaving Amy a little further down the hallway.

"So, you think the eleven are for Paul?" Sister Ramatu asked through her tears.

"We could be wrong," Cassandra said. Jo also began to cry. Cassandra and Kenneth tried to comfort them, but Nancy returned and told them it was perfectly all right to cry, to let it all out. She cried with them.

•••

AT 4:45 P.M., JUDGE Barney's courtroom in the criminal courts building was as full as it was on the first day of trial. The jurors were seated, Amy and Kate were at their table with Gonzalez. Kenneth and Cassandra sat at defense table waiting for Paul to arrive. Paul's family, including his father, sat together in the gallery behind the lawyers. Big sat at the far back. Everyone from the district attorney's office who was in court after lunch had returned.

The room was silent and cold. The court staff spoke in hushed tones. Jurors did their best to avoid making eye contact with anyone.

The sheriff led Paul Jackson into the courtroom and sat him between Kenneth and Cassandra. Then Judge Barney entered, indicating that everyone should remain seated. He directed the foreman to stand again.

"Have you reached a verdict?" Judge Barney asked.

"No, your Honor," the foreman answered.

"Are you unable to reach a verdict?" Judge Barney asked.

"Yes, your Honor," the foreman answered.

"Now, given that this trial was fairly involved, and the evidence large for the short time in which it was tried, do you find that additional time would help some amongst you in reaching a verdict?"

"No, your Honor."

"How are you divided?"

"Eleven to one," the foreman said.

There were several sighs in the courtroom. Judge Barney turned to the court to make the announcement everyone expected.

"I hereby declare a mistrial in the case of *The People of California v. Paul Jackson*. I find the jury has worked hard and carried this responsibility entrusted upon them with utmost dignity. Does either counsel wish the jury polled?" Judge Barney asked.

"Yes, your Honor," Kenneth said.

"Yes, your Honor," Amy said.

Judge Barney turned again to the jury and asked that each of them indicate his or her verdict by stating guilty or not guilty.

Juror number one said "not guilty," juror number two said "not guilty," juror number three said "not guilty," and a series of "not guilty" verdicts was joined by each juror until the foreman, who happened to be juror number twelve. The foreman said "guilty."

A gasp emanated from the courtroom as though the entire audience had done so in one voice. The followers of Paul's father cursed and swore under their breaths. Amy scrambled quickly through her notes to find the name of the only juror she had scribbled during the trial. Mr. Gale! When she looked up at the jurors, he was the only one looking at her again, this time he appeared to smile. She managed to smile back.

"Order," Judge Barney shouted, banging his gavel. "Order." He was visibly angry. It was the first time throughout the trial he showed so much emotion. "Bailiff, walk the gentlemen with the ACB out of the courtroom immediately," he directed. Paul's father was not one of them.

"Bullshit," one of the men shouted, but Paul's father raised one hand and the men were instantly silent. They also rose to leave the courtroom before the bailiff got to them.

"Bailiff, you do understand they are to leave the courthouse entirely, not just the courtroom," Judge Barney said.

"Yes, your Honor," the bailiff said.

Judge Barney thanked the jurors and told them they were free to go, but asked them to wait again in the jury room while the clerk arranged security for them. The jurors filed back into the jury room.

"I will release the defendant on ten-thousand-dollars bail subject also to him submitting his passport to the police before he is released," Judge Barney said.

"Your Honor," Amy began, standing up. "The People expect to refile their case against Mr. Jackson as early as next week. Thus, he remains as much a flight risk now as he was before the verdict, even with the submission of his passport."

Kenneth got up slowly with his counter argument, but Judge Barney raised his hand indicating Kenneth should not bother.

"Be that as it may, counsel, the People have not yet refiled. When you do so, we will address it," Judge Barney said.

Kenneth requested that the judge permit the police to release Paul over the weekend provided the conditions are met. Judge Barney agreed.

Paul sat still as though he had not understood the proceeding. Then he began to cry. Kenneth put an arm around him, and he hugged Kenneth and buried his face on Kenneth's shoulder. Omar walked into the courtroom and walked straight to the defense table. Cassandra told Omar the jurors could not reach a verdict, and he patted Paul on the back. Paul started to thank Cassandra as the sheriff came to lead him away and hugged Omar.

Kenneth could see Amy was shaken by the outcome as she made her way out of the courtroom. Leaving Cassandra with the Jacksons and Omar, he left the courtroom for a short while and when he returned about fifteen minutes later, they were all still in the courtroom and looking at him curiously. He thanked Cassandra.

"You made this happen, Casey," Kenneth said.

•••

AMY COULD NOT HAVE imagined how disappointed the result of the trial would make her, even knowing in the end that the jury would not reach a verdict. All but one not-guilty vote felt like a complete loss to her. Yet, it fell on her to call Helen Silberberg with the news. Kate, Melissa, and the police officers all gathered in the conference room for the call. Amy knew it would be no consolation to Helen that Paul Jackson would be tried again. At times, during the trial it seemed Helen wished that he was not in fact guilty despite all the evidence to the contrary. Amy told her that the jury could not reach a verdict and apologized for letting her down. When Helen told Amy she was proud of her and how she handled the case, Amy fell apart for the first time in front of everyone and could not stop sobbing. She got up and left the conference room and Kate followed her. Melissa finished the call.

"Do you know why this trial is taking place in Downtown instead of the West LA Courthouse, when the murder was in west LA?" Kate asked when they got to Amy's office and closed the door.

"No, I just assumed it was the right venue," Amy said.

"It isn't. It is here because the 1994 Northridge earthquake damaged the West LA Courthouse and it is undergoing repairs. The repairs should be done this year. All you needed was a hung jury and we get to retry the case in West LA with a more intelligent pool of minds, and the chance to fix the rough ends in the investigation. It will still be your case to win," Kate said.

"Thanks, Kate," Amy said.

Melissa and Neda joined Kate in Amy's office after the call to Helen Silberberg.

At times the mood felt like Amy had lost a loved one rather than obtained a mistrial in a case. Officers Gonzalez, Alvarez, and Fritz waited in the conference room, discussing the deterioration of the jury system. Several times over, all around the office, even among support staff who never heard the evidence, the same question was repeated: What evidence was the damn jury listening to? None of the jurors would speak to either Amy or Paul's defense team, the officers, or anyone from Paul's family, but they spoke privately to reporters and seemed to agree to appear on certain television shows.

•••

COOL JO'S CAFÉ WAS full again and Big was back in his element, walking the floor with the slow swagger of an African elephant. He was dressed in a flowing white suit and blue cotton shirt, he even waltzed every time he passed the dance floor. There was a news van outside, which was perhaps part of the attraction for the capacity crowd on this night. They were filming the lines of people trying to get into the club. "Tomorrow we really celebrate with half-price drinks and free admission, baby," Big told the newsmen. "Come back tomorrow. The boss will be here."

•••

AT CASSANDRA'S HOUSE IN Sherman Oaks, Kenneth excused himself from his usual group of friends and the law students that had gathered. He called Amy and left her another message, then rejoined the crowd. It was the third message he had left her since the judge declared a mistrial. He only wanted to know that she was fine, he told her. "I understand you need some time alone now, but please give me a call. I'd like to hear your voice."

Cassandra and the rest of Kenneth's dinner posse had found themselves in Japantown after the verdict, drinking warm sake when Cassandra's trial tactics students began calling to say they were gathering at her house. So, they all drove to Cassandra's house in Sherman Oaks and continued their celebration. They were not so much celebrating the mistrial as they were the district attorney's loss, Tiffany explained to one of the students. "Yeah, baby," Tiffany said. "I love it when the system works." Anthony tried to sing Bob Marley's song "War," but he only knew the first three lines and the chorus. He hummed away, nonetheless. Cassandra and her students joined him and provided the rest of the lyrics.

Kenneth left Sherman Oaks and drove to Cool Jo's Café on his way back to the hotel. Cool Jo's Café was about a mile south of the hotel. The lines were still long, but the doorman stepped aside to wave him through and some in the line clapped. He smiled and waved. Big complained that he had been looking all over the town for him.

"What's up?" Kenneth asked.

"We planning a big party tomorrow, and you better be here," Big said.

"I don't know, Big. I can't promise you I'll be here but I'll try."

"What the hell are you talking about? You da main man of the occasion. You gotta be here."

"Yeah, I've got a lot to do, Big."

He took Big aside and gave him all the papers establishing that Paul's bail had been met. He had managed to get to the court administrator's office before it closed for the week and filled out the forms necessary to establish that bail had been paid and arranged the security for the bail. There was still further processing that Big would need to do at the sheriff's office when he delivered Paul's passport, but Paul could be out by Saturday evening at the latest.

"Shoot, nigga', you done grown up with this case and shit!" Big said.

"That's why you were looking for me, right?"

"Yeah, I wanted to find out when we were going to take care of the bail this morning. You didn't have to use your money, dog. We had it covered."

"I know. You can pay me later. I just noticed the court was still open for business when we got the mistrial and I could still get across the street and get a cashier's check from the bank."

Kenneth left Big watching him as he walked away.

"Better not be with that bitch when you telling me you can't make the party. Real men finish what they start."

CHAPTER FORTY-SEVEN
...*Conversation Continues*

THE NIGHT KENNETH SPENT at the hotel alone was the loneliest he could remember. Without the case, there was a void he could not yet define much less begin to fill. He could no longer go back to the struggles of his old practice and mundane caseload, but he did not yet have anything else on the level of *People v. Jackson* that would continue the intensity of the last few weeks. Perhaps he could seek employment elsewhere.

He still could not reach Amy on Saturday afternoon. The more he waited for her call, the more he wondered how he could survive a relationship with her that sent him to such lows of disappointment when he didn't hear from her. It was still as excruciating as it had been in college when he waited to hear from her, and as suffocating as it had been a few weeks earlier when Neda told him Amy did not want to speak to him. At these times he felt like the outsider looking in on her and wondering who was there instead of him. He couldn't bear it any longer.

He had been in bed all morning and afternoon until Nancy came in from her Saturday choir meeting. She said she had come to take as much of the things she brought to the hotel from Long Beach back with her, but then she asked Kenneth who the woman in his closing argument was, and Kenneth knew she had come to see if he was there with anyone. He told her everything about Amy.

•••

AMY DROVE BACK FROM the grocery store with Neda at 5:30 p.m. to find Kenneth standing by his rented car in the driveway to her apartment building. She smiled as she parked her car behind his and got out to meet him while

Neda busied herself getting their things out of the trunk. He had worried that Amy wouldn't receive him well because he had come unannounced, so he was relieved to see her smile.

"Why are you driving a rented car, anyway?" Amy asked

"It's more reliable than mine. I didn't want a car that would break down on my way to court."

"Do you always do that when you're in trial?"

"Not always. Half my trials couldn't handle the added expense," Kenneth said.

"You remember Neda, don't you?" Amy said as they rejoined her.

"Of course." Kenneth and Neda acknowledged each other and shook hands. Kenneth took some of the bags of groceries that Neda had taken out of the car.

"I've been calling you since yesterday," Kenneth said.

"I know," Amy said.

"To gloat?" Neda asked.

Amy laughed.

"That's not even funny," Kenneth said.

"Blame Neda. I've been with her since yesterday, and she wouldn't let me take your call."

"And you call yourself a woman-of-color," Kenneth said to Neda as they got into the elevator.

"I can't believe you told him about that," Neda shouted.

"Who? Me? I didn't know it was a secret," Amy protested.

"You know what? Here," Neda said, passing the rest of the groceries she was carrying to Amy. "He can drive you to the airport."

"Oh, come on. Why wouldn't you want me to know that?"

"It's not just that, you're both hopeless and I don't want to be caught in the middle of it," Neda said, standing to the side of the elevator and holding the doors open for them.

"Are you sure you don't want to come in for just a minute?" Amy asked Neda, as she walked out.

"No, this is better," Neda said in French. "Are you gonna be okay?" she asked, still speaking French. Amy nodded with a smile. They kissed each other on both cheeks. "No discussion of the case," Neda said to Kenneth, "and make sure you drive her to the airport," she added as the elevator closed.

Amy told Kenneth that Neda wouldn't let her answer any calls that had anything to do with the case, including his. When they got into the apartment, she told him that she had to leave immediately for the airport because she was expecting guests.

"Your client must be happy with you," Amy said to Kenneth as they drove to the airport.

"I haven't seen him," Kenneth said. "I was so relieved that I laid in bed all morning like I was worn down from literally carrying him on my shoulders and now I'm not."

At a private airstrip by the airport, Thomas came out of the lounge with Edward and Angela. Kenneth pulled up to the curb and Amy got out to hug Angela. As Edward introduced himself to Kenneth, Amy went to Thomas and hugged him as well.

"You remember Kenneth," Amy said, holding Thomas's arm.

"Of course," Thomas said, "I watched you in court. Well done, counselor."

"Nice to meet you," Kenneth said and shook hands with Thomas before Amy led Thomas away. Kenneth turned to Angela, who told him that Thomas offered them his own jet, and they thought it was too nice a gesture to refuse. Kenneth and Edward loaded the vehicle with bags. Amy returned from seeing Thomas off and got in the back of the car to sit with Angela.

Kenneth took the wheel and Edward sat in front. They started out toward Alana's place in Hollywood. Suddenly driving was stressful for Kenneth. His fingers griped the wheel so tightly. He wondered if he was driving too fast, too cautiously, or annoying, but gradually relaxed as they included him in their conversation.

"I heard you two were breaking the law by seeing each other while you were trying a murder case," Edward told him after Kenneth had inquired about their flight.

"Not quite breaking the law, but we were required to disclose it to our clients."

"And you won, I heard," Edward said.

"Edward!" Amy and Angela shouted simultaneously, and Edward laughed.

"We'll talk later, I guess."

"Okay, let's change the subject," Angela said.

"You guys hungry?" Amy asked.

"Yes," Angela said.

Kenneth got on the freeway. Their discussion proceeded in such a light-hearted manner until they were waiting to be served at the restaurant later that night.

"Tell us about yourself, Ken," Angela said to Kenneth.

"What do you want to know?" Kenneth inquired.

"Tell us something that Amy doesn't know," Angela said.

"Amy doesn't know a lot about my background," Kenneth explained.

"Yes, I do. I mean, I put it together from our discussions over the past ten years or so, but I know a lot."

"Did you say ten years?" Edward asked.

"Yes, this is the same guy from college," Angela explained.

"So, what part don't you know?" Kenneth asked Amy. Amy averted her eyes and shrugged. "No, really, I want to tell you." Amy gestured dismissively that it was not important.

Dinner was served and everyone was quiet as the waiter placed the food. Kenneth and Amy kept looking at each other.

"Well, here it is," Kenneth said as soon as the waiter left. "I hope you don't mind me asking in front of your brother and his fiancée."

"Asking me what?"

Kenneth stood up and reached into his pocket. Angela brought her hands up to her chest as if to hold her heart still. Amy began to smile reflexively. Kenneth got down on one knee and opened his hand to reveal a small black box, which he opened for Amy. Amy covered her eyes with her right hand, the left hand pinned to her breast with her right elbow.

"Amy Wilson, will you marry me?" he asked. Amy slowly stretched out her left hand for him and he slid the diamond engagement ring onto her ring finger. People sitting at tables next to them began to clap and so did

Angela and Edward. Amy took her hand away from her eyes to reveal her tears. She held on to his hands and pretended to pull him up, but she never actually answered him.

"Are you sure about this?" Amy said through her tears, such that it came out almost as a whisper.

"I have never been more sure of anything in my life."

Amy turned to Angela, as though she was looking for her help. Angela in turn looked at Kenneth like she had discussed this previously with Amy.

"You know she's pregnant, right?" Angela asked.

"Yes, I do."

Edward slowly put his drink down, his eyes briefly locked on to Amy's.

"What if the child is not yours?" Angela asked.

"If she would let me, any child of hers is a child of mine."

There was a prolonged silence amongst them, none of them yet eating. Edward poured himself more wine.

"Then ask me again," Amy said, and Kenneth started to get up. "Don't get up, just ask me."

"Amy Wilson, will you let me, Kenneth Brown, be the father of your child?"

"I will," Amy said in a barely audible voice and got up. Kenneth got up to meet her. They embraced to the applause of everyone in the restaurant, again.

CHAPTER FORTY-EIGHT

The Future is Pregnant

EARLY THE FOLLOWING MORNING, between the hours of one and two, Kenneth came out of the bedroom in the suite at the hotel. The concierge had given him a message from Big when he arrived last night with Amy, asking him to call anytime he got back to the hotel. The number on the message was Cool Jo's Café, and Kenneth knew they would still be at the nightclub, probably until the break of dawn.

Kenneth went out to the hallway to make the call. As soon as the phone rang, Paul answered. He had been released on bail that evening and wanted to know why Kenneth was not at his celebratory party. Kenneth apologized. Paul wanted to see Kenneth immediately, but Kenneth told him that wasn't possible and promised to see him later in the day.

Cool Jo's Café was down the street from the hotel, about a mile to the south. Kenneth hung up the phone believing he had convinced Paul to wait and meet later in the day, but less than thirty minutes after he hung up the phone, there was a knock on the door of the hotel suite. Amy had just entered the bathroom. Kenneth felt sufficiently alone to answer the door. He hurriedly put away Amy's purse and shoes, which were in the antechamber and opened the door to find Paul standing in the hallway reeking of alcohol.

Kenneth could hardly hide his frustration with Paul. He tried to keep Paul by the door, but Paul pushed him aside and walked into the suite.

"Let me see what the money from my defense is paying for, Kenny? My money!" Paul said in a very loud voice.

Kenneth continued to restrain himself, and even managed a smile.

"It's good to see you out Paul, but this isn't a good time," Kenneth said.

"Why not Kenny? Is she here?" Paul asked.

"Go home, Paul. You're drunk," Kenneth said because it was the only thing he thought he could say.

"As you should be, Kenny. We are celebrating my success."

"Paul, I will come and celebrate with you, just go, and give me time to change."

Paul considered Kenneth for some time, then appeared to relax. He hugged Kenneth coldly and sat down.

"You're right, Kenny. But I gotta get this off my chest. I couldn't sleep without talking to you."

Kenneth remained standing. He was convinced Amy had heard Paul, but he wasn't sure Amy could hear them when Paul spoke in a normal voice like he had begun to do.

"It's almost three in the morning."

"Kenny, I've been in jail the past few months and you won't give me some freedom at three a.m. You know what that feels like?" Paul asked.

"No, I'm not saying you shouldn't be here. I'm just saying we don't have to talk about nothing right now," Kenneth pleaded.

"No, Kenny. This experience has taught me to seize every moment of freedom and leave no business undone. Now, you my number one business, Kenny. I wasn't even out of jail and you're back on a date with Ms. DA. You are letting this woman change your priorities, man. This is serious," Paul said with indignation.

"I told you we were together before your case started. I brought in Professor Rayburn and we got the job done—" Kenneth said.

"But the job ain't done, Kenny. The job ain't done at all. I'm facing another trial for murder, harder than the first one," Paul said.

"They haven't charged you yet, Paul. When they charge you then we know you've got another case."

"Bull, Kenny. You heard her say she was gonna refile. I'm as good as back in court with a new trial. Now, I'm grateful for the one you done, but the work ain't done, Kenny. The work ain't done yet."

At this point, Amy had been in the bathroom a very long time. Kenneth became convinced that the only reason she remained in the bathroom was because she did not want to come out with Paul in the suite. He wanted to tell Paul that the two of them should take the conversation outside, but he knew it would convince Paul that Amy was in the suite. If he had told Paul there was a completely different woman in the suit, Paul was certain to open all doors to see who it was, anyway. Kenneth felt trapped, not because he didn't want Paul to know Amy was in the suite with him, but because he knew Amy wouldn't want that. He sat rubbing his sweaty palms.

"What do you want me to do?" he asked Paul.

"Nothing," Paul said, "Don't make the same fucking mistake I made. The way you win my case has got the whole country reading about you like you won the O. J. trial. Hell, I bet Jonny is gonna be reading about you by Monday morning. Don't let this woman take it all away, Kenny. This woman ain't some starving artist looking to do you because you can help her make it. She's John Wilson's daughter. These guys own third world countries. She ain't gonna take you more serious than people they exploit over there. Give it up, because when you realize she's played you like a plantation banjo, you just might strangle her," Paul said.

"We're engaged, Paul," Kenneth said. Paul muttered something unintelligible and got up as though he was about to walk away then quickly picked up one of the side tables and sent it flying against the wall away from Kenneth. Then he forced a laugh. "You are fucking kidding me because you don't wanna represent me, ha?"

"I'm serious, Paul. You can call my mother and ask her," Kenneth said.

"Your mother is in on this?" Paul asked.

"I proposed to her yesterday, and we called my mother to tell her. She's given me her blessing," Kenneth said.

"How about my trial?" Paul asked.

"You've got Omar Jones, Paul. Your dad always wanted him anyway."

"Fuck Omar!" Paul yelled. "I don't need another lawyer, man. You can't leave me hanging like this, Kenny."

"Paul, you gave me this case because you couldn't afford the big shots and they wouldn't take the mortgage arrangements. Now you've got the money to hire them," Kenneth said. "I got you the money for a big law firm. The insurance company will pay for your defense again."

"But nobody knows the case like you."

"They will have the transcript of the trial."

"When were you gonna tell me?"

"Soon," Kenneth responded. "Paul, I've never felt this way my whole life and I'm not about to give it up for anything or anyone. I'm sorry."

Paul was quiet for a long time. He covered his face with his palm. Kenneth took the opportunity to look toward the bathroom. He could see, the door was slightly ajar, and the lights were off. He wondered if Amy was looking back at him. Without raising his head, Paul began to speak.

"That's exactly how Goldie made me feel. Then she met Didi and broke it off because he told her to do it. Just like that, and I almost went insane—I never begged—"

"We don't have to talk about this now, Paul," Kenneth pleaded.

"I never begged a woman in my life, Kenny, but after a few months without her, and she called that week she died, I begged. And she was real nice again. We had this thing we used to do when we fought; the person that wants to make up will ask to borrow the other's car and then they would return it really late, like one in the morning, then sneak into bed and say they brought the keys back, if you know what I mean. When I called Goldie, she was being so nice, I thought maybe I'd take the chance and ask her if I could borrow her car—"

"Stop, Paul, stop please." Kenneth shouted. "I don't wanna hear this, not now!"

"Well, you should," Paul shouted back at him. "You're about to make the same damn mistake." His next words were very slow and in a low voice. "I killed her, Kenny. I never committed a crime in my life before, not even stealing candy from a store, but this woman made me kill her. I went back to return her keys like we used to do when we made up after a fight. I got into the apartment and she was going at it with some son-of-a-bitch. I couldn't believe it. She set me up to hear it—she knew she had me over the barrel for leaving me, she wanted to finish me off. At first, I was so ashamed of myself I didn't know what to do. I went into the guest bedroom to wait them out with beer and I don't even recall when I fell asleep. She saw me there early in the morning and called me a pervert. She said I should have left when

I noticed someone else was in her apartment. I couldn't believe it. She took her keys and told me to show myself out. Then she went into the bathroom to clean up her filth—"

"It wasn't Goldie having sex in her bedroom," Amy said from behind Paul. Paul turned to look at her.

"It wasn't Goldie in the room that morning. She wouldn't do that to you." For a moment Kenneth was not sure whether Paul would go after Amy or come at him. He readied himself for either fight, knowing he was too tired for even a walk in the park. Paul turned and ran out of the suite.

"I'm sorry, honey," Amy said, but Kenneth was still mortified. "It didn't matter that he confessed, Ken, we already had everything we needed to nail him. When the jury asked for Conrad Wetstone's testimony again, we contacted Conrad and told him his testimony was about to let a guilty man go free. That's when he told us you were right. Someone told him Goldie was dead and he went to her apartment to see for himself. It was Mr. Arnot, the French man, except he was not French, he was Russian. He put those devices in Goldie's room for Rachel because her sister was staying at her apartment. Goldie wasn't comfortable with it, but she was no longer using her apartment anyway. Well, the listening device Mr. Arnot placed in Goldie's room picked up Paul's argument and possibly Goldie dying. For some reason, he did not want to get involved and skipped the country altogether. But we'll get him back," Amy said.

"You will never use anything Paul said here?" Kenneth asked.

"We know the truth already."

"Promise me, you won't repeat a word he said," Kenneth insisted. "Amy, promise me."

"It is probably still privileged anyway, since I eavesdropped on it."

"Promise me anyway."

"I promise," Amy said. "Where are you going?" Amy asked as Kenneth started to walk toward the door.

"I have to talk to him," Kenneth said.

"No, you don't, Ken. He knew I was here. He is deranged. To him, that was a performance he wanted me to watch. He's not stupid. He knew what he was doing," Amy said.

"He's drunk," Kenneth protested.

"No, he isn't. Ever since the judge declared a mistrial, it was like he was dying to tell me he did it," Amy said. "Please don't go."

"I feel terrible just leaving him like that," Kenneth explained.

"How about leaving me like this, Ken? Please don't go," Amy pleaded.

"I won't be long, I promise," Kenneth kissed her hurriedly before running out.

"I'll be right here waiting," Amy shouted after him. "Naked," she added, but Kenneth was too far down the hall to hear her.

By the time he ran out to the street, Paul was nowhere in sight. He looked down Olive Street in the northerly direction and back down south, but there was no sign of him. Opposite the hotel was an elderly retirement condominium and between the elderly retirement home and the civil courthouse was a large space that served as one of the parking lots for the civil courthouse.

Kenneth asked the valet attendant if he saw which direction Paul went, and the attendant pointed Kenneth in the direction of the courthouse. Kenneth ran that way, and as he turned eastward, he saw Big walking toward him.

"What happened?" Big asked.

"Where's Paul?" Kenneth asked.

"He just ran past me like a mad man and I'm supposed to drive him back. What'd you do now?" Big asked Kenneth.

"Nothing," Kenneth said.

"What'd you mean, nothing?"

"Can we please find him first, I need to explain something to him," Kenneth pleaded.

"We'll go in my car and you can tell me what happened in the car," Big said.

"Yeah," Kenneth agreed.

Big led him to his car in a dark parking lot against the north walls of the retirement home condominiums.

"Start talking," Big said as they walked toward his car.

"Paul confessed how he killed Goldie," Kenneth explained. Big stopped but seemed unable to say anything to Kenneth.

"To you?"

"Yeah."

Big stood looking at him in disbelief.

"So what? You his attorney. Whatever he tells you is privileged anyway," Big said and started walking again.

"I think Amy heard him. That's why I'm trying to tell him that it is still privileged regardless of who heard it."

"Amy the DA, Amy? She's with you tonight?" Big asked.

"Yes," Kenneth said.

They entered the parking lot and Kenneth went to the passenger side of the car. Big opened the driver's door and reached over the passenger seat to open the passenger-side front door. Big then unbuckled his belt and pulled it out in one swift pull as Kenneth was getting in the car. He got in the car and threw the belt over Kenneth's neck as Kenneth sat in the front seat of the car. Kenneth struggled and kicked, trying to get a hold of the belt around his neck, with what felt like his last breath, he muttered, "Think of ma, Big, think of my ma, please," and almost immediately the belt slackened. Kenneth pushed away and ducked underneath and out of the chokehold. Coughing, he hurriedly tried to open the door. Big landed a punch on his head knocking him against the door, which Kenneth had managed to unlock but not open. He was dazed. Leaning over him, Big opened the passenger-side door and shoved him off the passenger seat out of the car, but Kenneth's legs were still in the car. Big started to back the car out with the passenger door still open. Kenneth's leg slowly fell onto the lot. Big reached over and closed the passenger door but did not drive away. In the darkness, Kenneth could only hear the rustling of his car, idling on the road. Kenneth laid still, convinced that Big was looking at him. He muffled the choking coughs he could not contain.

Then, Big drove away.

ACKNOWLEDGEMENTS

This novel would not have been possible without the relationships that shaped my study and practice of law and the individuals who encouraged me to write. From Texas to California, there were too many to mention, but a few, I must: Lon Otto, who saw a great story when others suggested I give it up; Jay Schaefer for his straight talk and honest assessment; the Community of Writers I met at Squaw Valley—especially Susan Moke (d. 2013), who in just one week left indelible prints on everyone she met, as if it was her sole purpose in coming to the workshops; Vlada (Teper) and Maddy (Meg Rae Murphy), here's to you and that cabin we filled with four accents, from three continents, each uniquely American.

I would like to thank friends like Steven Basileo, Tiffany Keating, Cassandra Shivers, Anthony Rayburn, Cynthia Morales, Pouneh Ghaffarian, Sophia Park, Jimmy Yamasaki, Cindy Philapil, Joan Lark, Margie Lezcano, Mavis Sanders, Zandra Bailes, and Ed Russey, Jr. – any resemblance between you and characters in this book is purely coincident. I am indebted to Dr. Ikechi Ogan who let me cross-examine him numerous times for this book; to Dr. Laura Dansky for her insights; and to Dr. Maureen Mbadike — my madness and sanity, indivisible — for her unwavering believe in me and for our two wonderful children, Odiso and Chukwuemeka.

Finally, to the team at Rare Bird who made this book a reality, thank you.